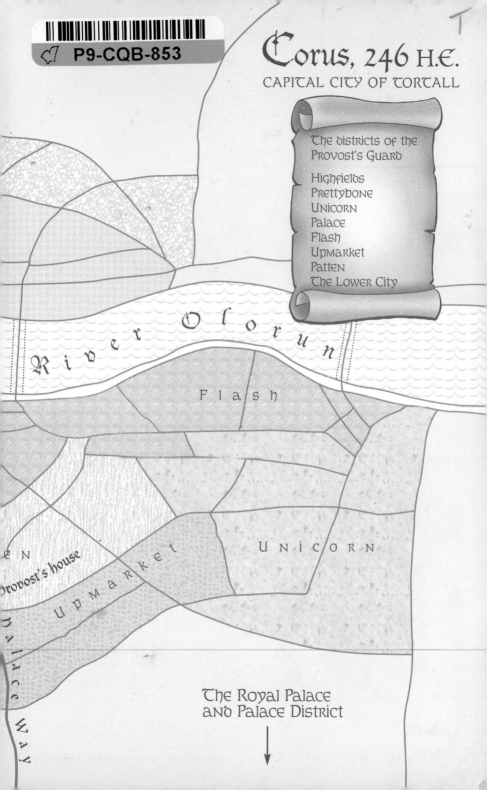

TERRIER

BEKA COOPER

BOOK ONE

TERRIER

TAMORA PIERCE

RANDOM HOUSE  NEW YORK

Copyright © 2006 by Tamora Pierce
Jacket art copyright © 2006 by Jonathan Barkat

All rights reserved.
Published in the United States by Random House Children's Books, a division of Random House, Inc., New York.

RANDOM HOUSE and colophon are registered trademarks of Random House, Inc.

www.randomhouse.com/teens

Educators and librarians, for a variety of teaching tools, visit us at www.randomhouse.com/teachers

Library of Congress Cataloging-in-Publication Data
Pierce, Tamora.
Terrier / Tamora Pierce. — 1st ed.
p. cm. — (Beka Cooper; bk. 1)
SUMMARY: When sixteen-year-old Beka becomes "Puppy" to a pair of "Dogs," as the Provost's Guards are called, she uses her police training, natural abilities, and a touch of magic to help them solve the case of a murdered baby in Tortall's Lower City.
ISBN-13: 978-0-375-81468-6 (trade)
ISBN-13: 978-0-375-91468-3 (lib. bdg.)
ISBN-10: 0-375-81468-X (trade)
ISBN-10: 0-375-91468-4 (lib. bdg.)
[1. Police—Fiction. 2. Magic—Fiction. 3. Fantasy.]
I. Title. II. Series: Pierce, Tamora. Beka Cooper; bk. 1.
PZ7.P61464Ter 2006 [Fic]—dc22 2006014834

Printed in the United States of America 10 9 8 7 6 5 4 3 2 1

First Edition

To Tim

This one's all yours.
It's time.
And you deserve this and more,
for putting all that effort into us.

Corus, 246 H.E.
The Lower City

The Cesspool runs south of Koskynen Street and west of Westberk and Charry Orchard

N
W — E
S

River Olorun

Northbridge
Market of Sorrows
Market Bridge
Kingsbridge
North Gate
Rovers St.
Nightmarket
Jane St.
Koskynen St.
Stuvek St.
Jane Street kennel
Daymarket
Stormwing St.
Mutt Piddle Lane
Mistress Noll's Home
Nipcopper Close
Westberk St.
Beka's lodgings
the Mantel and Pullet
Festive Lane
Holderman St.
Magistrate's Court
Mulberry Way
Charry Orchard St.
Palace Way
The Court of the Rogue
Gold St.
Provost's House

The Common

Temple District
(has its own guards)

The Royal Palace and Palace District

1 mile = 1/2 inch

Prologue

From the journal of
Eleni Cooper,
resident, with her six-year-old son,
George Cooper,
of Spindle Lane, the Lower City,
Corus, the Realm of Tortall

March 18, 406 [H.E.: the Human Era]

In all those lessons for which I was made to memorize chants and prayers I never used, couldn't our temple priestesses have taught one—just one!—lesson on what to do with a boy who is too smart for his own good?

I am at my wit's end! My George was taken up for stealing and I had to go to the Jane Street Guard station.

I thought I might die of the shame. I know it is this place and the friends he makes here. Even the families who do not teach their children the secrets of theft look the other way because it puts food on the table. And I am too newly come. I cannot tell them, "Keep your children away from my son, Do not let them teach him to steal."

I want him to rise in the world. We are poor now, but I pray we will not always be so. And I cannot afford a better place to live. My family will not have me back, not after our last meeting. So I am left here, trying to raise a lad who sees and hears and thinks too much, in the city's worst slum.

At the station there my scapegrace was, seated on a bench with the Guard who'd caught him. "It was but a handful of coins left on a counter, Mistress Cooper," the Guard said. "And I recovered them all. It's his first time, and I owe you for makin' my wife's labor so easy." He looked at George. "Next time it's the cages for you, and maybe a work farm," he warned. "Don't go makin' your good mother weep."

I grabbed George's arm and towed him out of there. We'd no sooner passed through the gate into the street when he tells me, "Up till a hundred year ago they was called Dogs, Ma." He was talking broad Lower City slang, knowing it made me furious. "Ye know why they changed it? They thought folk mightn't respect 'em if they went about callin' them after curs like they done for three hundred—"

I boxed his ear. "I'll have no history lessons from you, Master Scamp!" I cried, tried beyond my sense of dignity. "You'll keep your tongue between your teeth!" Everyone we passed was smirking at us. They knew our tale, knew I'd been dismissed from the temple. They believed I thought myself better than they were, because I kept my home and my child as clean as may be and taught him his letters. Let them think it. We will not always live in the Cesspool. My George is meant for better things.

Thieving is not among them, I swear it.

When I got him to our rooms, I let him go. He stared at me with his hazel eyes, so like mine. The beaky nose and square chin were his father's, a temple worshiper I saw but for one night. George would be the kind of man women would think was so homely he was handsome, if he lived. I had to make certain he would live.

"The shame of it!" I told him. "George Cooper, how am I to face folk? Stealing! *My* son, stealing!"

He looked me boldly in the face. "We're gettin' no

richer from your healin' and magickin', Ma. I hate bein' hungry all the time."

That cut me. I knew he was hungry. Did I not divide my share so he had more, and it still wasn't enough? So he would not see me in tears, and because he needed it, I sat on our chair and turned my rascal over my knee. I gave him the spanking of his young life.

I stood him on his feet again. His chin trembled, but he refused to cry. The problem is, my lad and I are too much alike.

"There's more important things than wealth," I said, trying to make him *listen.* "There's our family name. Us above all, George, we don't take to thieving." I had thought to wait until he was old enough to understand to tell him about Rebakah Cooper, but I believe the Goddess's voice in me was saying it was time. He *needed* to hear this. I took down the shrine from the wardrobe top, where I kept it safe from small boys. I opened the front to show him the tiny figures of the ancestors.

"See how many of your great-grandfathers wore the uniform of the Provost's Guard? What would our famous ancestress say if she knew one of her descendants was a common thief?"

"We've got a famous ancestress?" George asked, rubbing his behind.

I picked up Rebakah's small, worn statue. I took it out often when I was a girl, because *she* was a woman, of all the ancestors who wore the black tunic and breeches of the Guard. There was the cat at her feet, the purple dots of paint that were its eyes worn away just as the pale blue paint for her eyes was worn away. The shrine was old, given to me by my great-aunt when I was dedicated to Temple Service.

I showed him the figure. "Rebakah Cooper," I said. "Your six-times-great-grandmother. Famed in her day for her service as a Provost's Guard. She was fierce and law-abiding and loyal, my son. All that I want for you. And she was doom on lawbreakers, particularly thieves. Steal, and you shame her."

"Yes, Ma," George said quietly.

"Remember her," I told him, giving his shoulder a little shake. "*Respect* her. Respect *me*."

He put his arms around my waist. "I love you, Mother," he said. Now he talked perfectly, as he'd been taught. He helped me to clean up from the medicine making and to make supper.

It is only in writing about this day that I realize he never said anything about thieving.

No, he will obey me. He is a good boy. And I will make an offering to my Goddess to guide him on Rebakah Cooper's path.

FROM THE JOURNAL OF
MISTRESS ILONY COOPER,
MOTHER OF REBAKAH COOPER,
RESIDENT OF PROVOST'S HOUSE,
PALACE WAY AND GOLDEN WAY,
CORUS, THE REALM OF TORTALL

Novembur 13, 240

My hart is the betur for this day. When my Beka told me the pijins talked to her I feerd she was mad. I feerd my lady wood lok her up as my lady dos not lyk Beka. Beka mayks my lord lyk being a komun Dog to much.

I thot to take Beka to my husbands mother. Granny Fern wood no if ther was madnes in his blud. So I tuk Beka ther today and left the littel ones with Mya.

Beka had bred in her pokets and fed pijins all the way to Klover Lane. She says the birds say wher they was killd. I feerd somwon ov Provosts Hows wood see the bred and say she stole it.

Wen I told Granny Fern why we come Granny laffd.

She is no mor mad than me, she says. Beka has the magikal Gift. Tho som say its not the Gift exakly. Its not biddebel. You hav it or you dont. Bekas father had it and his sister and unkl befor him.

I sayd a prayr to the Godess. My girl is not mad. Gifted is not good but its beter than mad.

Granny Fern mayd Beka churn her buttr. Beka thumpd the churn so hard! Granny Fern told her, You can tickl the magik a bit. You need to, girl. Elswys the ghosts that ryd the birds will dryv you mad with tawk you onli heer part way. Pijins cary the dead. Them as died suden, them as had biznis to do.

Them as got merderd, Beka says.

Pijins ar the Blak Gods mesingers, Granny says. They gathr souls to tayk to the Peesful Relms, but som wont go. They hold to the bird until they see whats becom ov them. And they talk. Som ov what they say is useful, Beka. Thats why you must lern how to heer theyr voyses. Hav you herd othr voyses, Beka? On street corners mayhap?

I dont no, says Beka.

Lets go see, says Granny.

We finishd the buttr ferst bekaus it dont wait. Then Granny took us to a street corner but to bloks frum her house. A dust spyner was ther, spyning leevs and dirt arond and abowt lyk a smal wirlwind.

Yore fathr namd it Hasfush, Granny says. Or told us his name is Hasfush. Hes one ov the dust spynrs that nevur goes away. Step in and lissen, Beka.

Beka nevr argus with Granny Fern. Onli with me. Into the spynr she wakd.

What if she choaks? I askd.

She wont, says Granny. She haz the Ayr Gift.

The dust spynr got smal. Beka cam owt a mess.

I hav to wash her, I says. My ladee will hav a fit.

Beka lookd at Granny. Hasfush is alive. He told me evrything he hurd. Then he got happi.

Next tyme bring him dirt frum othr parts ov the citee, Granny says. Yer fathr sayd he lyked that. Ilony, send her to me in the afturnoon. I wil teech Beka how to heer the ghoasts and the dust spynrs. Its writ down in a book ov the famlee.

She can taym it. The listning. She isnt mad.

I was so afeerd for my Beka. I no I wil dy frum this rot in my chest. My childrun must mayk theyr own way then. Beka wil hav the hardist tyme. She was in the Lowur Cytee for to long. Magik wil help. Evun frends that ar birds and street wind and durt wil help.

From the journal of
Matthias Tunstall,
Provost's Guardsman,
resident of Rowan's Lodgings,
Bott Street, Patten District,
Corus, the Realm of Tortall

November 13, 244

Tonight my lord Gershom took Clary and me to supper at Naxen's Fancy. It was his way of thanking us for
bringing down Bloody Jock. (I would have done more than
hobble him and bring him for a court to sentence. The
scummer would rob a couple, killing the man and kissing the
woman while her man was lying there.)

It was our third supper at Naxen's Fancy. Me and
Clary could never afford the place on our own, but when
we wind up big cases, we get a fine dinner there with my
lord. So the wine was flowing well, and there was brandy
after supper. We were all feeling good, and Clary asks the
thing we both always wanted to know: how did my lord
manage to hobble the Bold Brass gang six years back?
Seemed for a year they roamed Prettybone, Highfields,
and Unicorn Districts, helping themselves to the treasures
of folk who pay the Rogue not to be burgled. There was
even talk that His Majesty was looking for a new Lord
Provost. Then suddenly there was the whole gang in
chains, my lord with new estates awarded by the King,
and the Vice Provost transferred to a command on the
Scanran border.

"What stories did you hear?" my lord asks with that little smile, like he knows a very good joke.

We tell the ones we heard most. One of Bold Brass's
women caught her man with someone else. A palace mage
lowered himself to Dog work to get revenge on the gang for

robbing him. The gang had killed a horse some duke loved and he paid for the mages himself.

My lord starts a-laughing. "None of those are right," he says. "It was a little girl, only eight years old."

I look at my glass of brandy. "This stuff is better than the swill I'm used to," I say. "I could've swore you said the Bold Brass gang got took down by an eight-year-old."

My lord nodded and says, "She took against one of them. He was living with her mama. When he found out her mama had lung rot, he beat her up and took all she had of value. The girl Dogged him. Dogged him like you two would do it, kept out of his sight. If she lost him, she just found him later at his favorite places."

"How'd she know he'd be worth all that work?" Clary wants to know. "Why not just stick a knife in him?"

My lord says, "The piece of pig turd gave her mama jewelry he couldn't have come by honest, then took it back when he left."

"Yeah," Clary says, "she's got to be from the Cesspool. Those Cesspool little ones know what kind of baubles belong down there and what don't."

My lord goes on. "So Beka—that's her name, Rebakah Cooper—finally Dogs him all the way back to where he met up with his mates. She spies on them and knows she has the den of the Bold Brass gang. Then she goes to her nearest Dog, only this Dog don't believe her."

Clary mutters, "Probably Day Watch." My partner

thinks the only Dogs worth bothering with work the Evening Watch like us.

My lord says, "So Beka goes to her kennel, but they laugh at her. She even tries to tell my Vice Provost. He has her tossed in the street. He thought she was trying to witch him. Beka's no mage, but she has these light blue-gray eyes. When she's angry, it's like looking into a well of ice. She was angry by then. It's unnerving in a little girl, but she can't help her eyes. So one day I'm riding through the Daymarket and this mite of a child grabs my Oso by the bridle. You know Oso—he doesn't like surprises. I almost drew steel on her before I saw she was a child and how Oso calmed down when she talked to him. She was telling me if I wanted the Bold Brass gang, I'd best listen to her. My Vice Provost's ready to take a whip to the girl. Meantime, I feel like I'm looking into the eyes of a thousand-year-old ghost. Unlike my Vice Provost, I'm not spooked. I listen to her. And she does it. She gives me the Bold Brass gang. Then she thinks she can disappear, but I know a trick or two of my own. I find her home and her family. The Coopers are living in my household now."

"Meaning no disrespect, my lord, but why?" I ask. "A handful of gold shows you're grateful."

He shakes his head. "A mother with lung rot, and my healers say she can't be helped. It's too far along. Five bright, promising little ones—Beka is the oldest. All in some Mutt Piddle Lane midden. The mother's an herbalist

on her good days, but those are going to run out. I'd an idea
Beka was already learning to steal. His Majesty was about
to find a new Provost. I owed that ice-eyed mite. Beka
Cooper saved me from disgrace. I think she'll make a good
Dog when she's old enough. Her brothers and sisters will
do well in the world, given a chance. And her mother will
die in comfort. I believe in thanking the gods for saving my
position." My lord raises his glass. "I love being Lord
Provost."

We raise ours. "We're glad to have you," Clary says.
"Who else takes notice of the Dogs who do the work?"

Now I can't get that story out of my head. Dogging a
cove like that when she was only eight. I hope if she does
go for the Provost's Guard that she doesn't think she
knows all there is to what we do. She'll quit soon enough if
she does. I hope my lord doesn't build her up that way.
She'll die of boredom and wash out before she's been in
the work for a month. Or she'll think because she did it
once, and did it young, that she knows it all. Then she'll
just get herself killed, and maybe any other Dogs who are
with her, too.

The Journal of
Rebakah Cooper

Wednesday, April 1, 246

Written on the morning of my first day of duty.

I have this journal that I mean to use as a record of my days in the Provost's Guard. Should I survive my first year as a Puppy, it will give me good practice for writing reports when I am a proper Dog. By setting down as much as I can remember word by word, especially in talk with folk about the city, I will keep my memory exercises sharp. Our trainers told us we must always try to memorize as much as we can exactly as we can. *Your memory is your record when your hands are too busy.* That is one of our training sayings.

For my own details, to make a proper start, I own to five feet and eight inches in height. I have good shoulders, though I am a bit on the slender side. My build is muscled for a mot. I have worked curst hard to make it so, in the training yard and on my own. My peaches are well enough. Doubtless they would be larger if I put on more pounds, but as I have no sweetheart and am not wishful of one for now, my peaches are fine as they are.

I am told I am pretty in my face, though my sister Diona says when my fine nose and cheekbones have been broken flat several times that will no longer be so. (My sisters do not want me to be a Dog.) My eyes are light blue-gray in color. Some like them. Others hold them to be unsettling. I like them, because they work for me. My teeth are good. My hair is a dark blond. Folk can see my brows and lashes without my troubling to darken them, not that I would. I wear my hair long as my one vanity. I know it offers an opponent a grip, but I have learned to tight-braid it from the crown of my head. I also have a spiked strap to braid into it, so that any who seize my braid will regret it.

I am so eager for five o'clock and my first watch to begin that my writing on this page is shaky, not neat as I have been taught. It is hard to think quietly. I must be sure to write every bit of this first week of my first year above all. For eight long year I have waited for this time to come. Now it has. I want a record of my first seeking, my training Dogs, my every bit of work. I will be made a Dog sooner than any Puppy has ever been. I will prove I know more than any Puppy my very first week.

It is not vanity. I lived in the Cesspool for eight year. I stole. I studied with the Lord Provost for eight more year. Three year of that eight I ran messages for the Provost's Dogs, before I went into training. I know the Lower City better than I know the faces of my sisters and brothers, better than I knew my mother's face. I will learn the rest quicker than any other Puppy. I even *live* in the Lower City again, on Nipcopper Close. None of the others assigned to the Jane Street kennel do. (They will regret it when they must walk all the way home at the end of their watch!)

Pounce says I count my fish before they're hooked. I tell Pounce that if I must be saddled with a purple-eyed talking cat, why must it be a sour one? He is to *stay home* this week. I will not be distracted by this strange creature who has been my friend these last four years. And I will not have my Dogs distracted by him. They will ask all manner of questions about him, for one—questions I cannot answer and he will not.

My greatest fear is my shyness. It has grown so much worse since I began to put up my hair and let down my skirts. I was the best of all our training class in combat, yet earned a weekly switching because I could not declaim in rhetoric. Somehow I must find the courage to tell a stranger he is under arrest for crimes against the King's peace, and detail those crimes. Or I must get a partner who likes to talk.

I am assigned to the Jane Street kennel. The Watch Commander in this year of 246 is Acton of Fenrigh. I doubt I will ever have anything to do with him. Most Dogs don't. Our Watch Sergeant is Kebibi Ahuda, my training master in combat and the fiercest mot I have ever met. We have six Corporals on our watch and twenty-five Senior Guards. That's not counting the cage Dogs and the Dogs who handle the scent hounds. We also have a mage on duty, Fulk. Fulk the Nosepicker, we mots call him. I plan to have nothing to do with him, either. The next time he puts a hand on me I will break it, mage or not.

There is the sum of it. All that remains is my training Dogs. I will write of them, and describe them properly, when I know who they are.

Written at day's end.
As the sun touched the rim of the city wall, I walked into the Jane Street kennel. For our first day, we had no training before duty. I could enter in a fresh, clean uniform. I had gotten mine from the old clothes room at my Lord Provost's house. I wore the summer black tunic with short sleeves, black breeches, and black boots. I had a leather belt with purse, whistle, paired daggers, a proper baton, water flask, and rawhide cords for prisoner taking. I was kitted up like a proper Dog and ready to bag me some Rats.

Some of the other Lower City trainees were already there. Like me, they wore a Puppy's white trim at the hems of sleeves and tunic. None of us know if the white is to mark us out so Rats will spare us or so they will kill us first. None of our teachers will say, either.

I sat with the other Puppies. They greeted me with gloom. None of them wanted to be here, but each district gets its allotment of the year's trainees. My companions felt they drew the short straw. There is curst little glory here. Unless you are a veteran Dog or a friend of the Rogue, the pickings are coppers at best. And the Lower City is rough. Everyone knows that of the Puppies who start their training year in the Lower

City, half give up or are killed in the first four months.

I tried to look as glum as the others to keep them company. They are cross that I wanted to come to Jane Street.

Ahuda took her place at the tall Sergeants' desk. We all sat up. We'd feared her in training. She is a stocky black woman with some freckles and hair she has straightened and cut just below her ears. Her family is from Carthak, far in the south. They say she treats trainees the way she does in vengeance for how the Carthakis treated her family as slaves. All I know is that she made fast fighters of us.

She nodded to the Evening Watch Dogs as they came on duty, already in pairs or meeting up in the waiting room. Some looked at our bench and grinned. Some nudged each other and laughed. My classmates hunkered down and looked miserable.

"They'll eat us alive," my friend Ersken whispered in my ear. He was the kindest of us, not the best trait for a Dog-to-be. "I think they sharpen their teeth."

"Going to sea wouldn'ta been so bad." Verene had come in after me and sat on my other side. "Go on, Beka—give 'em one of them ice-eye glares of yours."

I looked down. Though I am comfortable with my fellow Puppies, I wasn't easy with the Dogs or the folk who came in with business in the kennel. "You get seasick," I told Verene. "That's why you went for a Dog. And leave my glares out of it."

Since Ahuda was at her desk, the Watch Commander was already in his office. He'd be going over the assignments, choosing the Dog partners who would get a Puppy or just agreeing to Ahuda's choices. I asked the Goddess to give Ersken someone who'd understand his kindness never meant he was weak. Verene needed Dogs that would talk to her straight. And me?

Goddess, Mithros, let them be good at their work, I begged.

Who would I get? I know who I *wanted*. There were three sets of partners who were famous for their work. I kissed the half moon at the base of my thumbnail for luck.

Outside, the market bells chimed the fifth hour of the afternoon—the end of the Day Watch and the beginning of the Evening Watch. Dogs going off duty lined up before Ahuda's desk, their Puppies at their backs, to muster out. When Ahuda dismissed them, they were done for the day. Their Puppies, six of our classmates, sighed with relief and headed out the door. Before they left, they told us what we were in for, each in their own fashion. Some gave us a thumbs-up. A couple mimed a hanging with a weary grin. I just looked away. What was so hard for them? They'd had Day Watch. Everyone knew that Evening Watch got the worst of it in the Lower City.

With the Day Watch gone, Ahuda called out the names of a pair of Dogs. They'd been lounging on one of the benches. When they looked at her, she jerked her thumb at the Commander's door. They settled their shoulders, checked each other's uniforms, then went inside. I knew them. My lord Gershom had commended them twice.

Once the door closed behind them, Ahuda looked at us. "Puppy Ersken Westover. You're assigned to those two Dogs for training. Step up here."

Ersken gulped, then stood to whistles and applause from the veteran Dogs. I straightened his clothes. Verene kissed him, and our fellow trainees clapped him on the back or shook his hand. Then Ersken tried to walk across that room like he was confident he could do the job, in front of about twenty ordinary folk and the Dogs of the Evening Watch.

Hilyard elbowed me. "*You* coulda given him a kiss, Beka, to brighten his last hours."

I elbowed him some harder. Hilyard was always trying to cook up mischief.

"My kisses ain't good enough?" Verene demanded of him. She punched his shoulder. "See what sweetenin' you get when they call *you*."

Ersken came to attention before Ahuda's desk. She looked down her short nose at him. "Stop that. Relax. The Commander's giving them the speech, about how they're not to break you or dent you or toss you down the sewer without getting permission from me first."

The Dogs laughed. One of them called, "Don't

sweat it, lad. We're all just workin' Dogs down here."

"They keep the honor and glory and pretty girls for Unicorn District." That Dog was a woman whose face was marked crossways by a scar.

One of them said, "Up there, the fountains run rose water. Here they run—"

"—piss!" cried the Dogs. It was an old joke in the Lower City.

The Commander's door opened. Out came the two Dogs. They looked resigned. The heavyset one beckoned to Ersken. "Heel, Puppy. Let's get our glorious partnership rolling. You don't say nothin', see? We talk, you listen." He clamped a thick hand on Ersken's shoulder and steered him to the door.

Ahuda called, "Remember, tomorrow you Puppies report an hour early for combat training before your watch. No more easy starts like today!" Ersken's Dogs let the door close. Ahuda then called for a new Dog pair to see the Commander and for the next of us to wait for his training Dogs. It was Hilyard's turn. Just as she'd threatened, Verene gave him no kiss.

While we waited for the Dogs to collect Hilyard, a citywoman called, "Sarge? Be there word of who left old Crookshank's great-grandbaby dead in the gutter?" We looked at her. She was here to visit a man in the Rat cages out back, mayhap. She had five little ones with her. She must have feared there was some killer out there and refused to leave them at home.

Ahuda shook her head. "There is no news, mistress. If you're scared for your own, I'd counsel you to let go your fear. Crookshank is the evilest pinchpenny scale and landlord in the Lower City. He buys for coppers what's valued in gold. If one of his firetraps burns with a mother in it, he sells the orphans for slaves. He's got more'n enough enemies. Any of them could have strangled that poor little one."

"Aye, but no one kills women and children," muttered a Dog. "They're no part of business."

Ahuda glared at him. "We'll catch the Rat and flay him living, but I'll bet anyone here Crookshank drove some poor looby to Cracknob Row. Your little ones are safe, mistress."

It's true, Crookshank is the most hated man in Corus. It's true also that family is off-limits if they aren't in your enemy's line of work. To kill a rival's child kin is to become outlaw.

"I'll wager the ol' scale got the best to seek the lad's killer," a cove said. "Come on, Sergeant. Who'd Crookshank buy special t' get put on the murder? I heard he got teams on each watch out seeking."

"He did, not that it's your business," Ahuda said, not looking up from her writing.

"Who's it on *this* watch?" someone else called.

Ahuda looked up with a scowl, ready to tell these folk to hold their tongues. It was old Nyler Jewel who said, "Why, me and Yoav, good cityfolk."

They all stared. Doubtless they knew that Yoav's sister hung herself but three months back. Her husband had sold her to pay a debt to Crookshank, then she had killed herself in the slave pens. Jewel and Yoav would never sweat to seek Rolond Lofts's killer, no matter how much his great-grandda paid in bribes. The Dogs picked from the Night and Day Watches were also Dogs with a grudge. Crookshank had so many enemies he didn't even know them all.

While Ahuda read out the names of the fourth pair to see the Commander, Matthias Tunstall and Clara Goodwin came in. I put my head down so my bangs hid my eyes and watched as they found themselves a patch of wall to lean on. Of the three good pairs here on Jane Street, they were the *best,* Goodwin a Corporal, Tunstall a Senior Dog. They could have had any posting in Corus, but they'd kept to the Lower City.

One night, my lord had invited them to supper for a task they'd done very well. I hid in the drapes of the little supper room at Provost's House to hear the legends talk. Lord Gershom offered them a place in Highfields, but they'd refused. Tunstall said, "Clary and me, we know the Lower City. The worst ones know our little ways. The people of the Court of the Rogue have memorized our bootprints, bless their silly cracked heads. It suits us, don't it, Clary?"

And Goodwin, she'd chuckled.

"The pickin's are richer elsewhere." My lord Gershom was amused, I could hear it. "The Happy Bags of bribes for the kennels are fatter in other districts."

"We're humble folk," Goodwin said. She had a voice like dark honey. "We like humble pickings. And the bones that come from the Rogue's Happy Bags are rich enough."

I'd never be assigned to them, I knew. They didn't get Puppies.

Goodwin and Tunstall gossiped with their friends among the Dogs as other pairs came out with a Puppy. The Lower City veterans are a hard crew, wearing metal throat protectors and metal-ribbed arm guards as well as the regular uniform. Even other Dogs are wary of these folk, respectful of their ability to stay alive.

I *would* be the last one called. I looked around as my last yearmate left with his Dogs. I wiped my sweating hands on my breeches. Then I nearly swallowed my own tongue, because Ahuda called, "Tunstall and Goodwin."

"No!" Goodwin looked at me, her brown eyes sharp. "No. *No.* We don't get Puppies. We don't *like* Puppies. No offense, whoever you are. We have *never* had a Puppy."

"You're past due, then." Ahuda had no sympathy in her eyes. "Your luck just ran out."

Goodwin headed into the Commander's office like a hawk that had sighted prey. Tunstall ambled after.

They are a mismatched pair. Corporal Goodwin is

two inches shorter than me. She is built strong, wears her dark brown hair cut short. She has a small beak of a nose, full lips. They said she'd put down a Scanran berserker when he'd killed three men in a fight, her alone with her baton. She is fast and all muscle. She's been a Dog seventeen years.

Senior Dog Tunstall has partnered with her for thirteen. He's been a Dog for twenty in all. He is about six foot three, long-armed, long-legged, with deep-set brown eyes and a long, curved nose. I think he looks like an owl, though he's popular enough with mots. He wears his hair cropped short all over his head. There is gray in it and in his short beard and mustache. He is funny and easygoing. He could be a Watch Commander, even a Captain. So could she. Neither of them want it. Kennel rumor says he is some kind of hillman, mayhap even a renegade from one of the eastern tribes. Whatever he'd been before coming to the Provost's Guard, he is one of us now.

"Rebakah Cooper."

From the laughter in the room, it wasn't the first time Ahuda had called my name. I went to stand before the desk. She looked down at me. "Don't let them rattle you," she advised. "You've got the best. That's the *only* extra chance I wangled for you. And if you're smart, you won't depend on your *other* connections high up to grease your way."

I looked down. As if I'd ask for help from my lord!

"Better not be cooing *our* tales in his ear, neither." I didn't know the voice and I didn't turn to look.

"She never did when she was a runner. I knowed she saw plenty. She had three *years'* worth of chances." *That* was a voice I knew, Nyler Jewel's. "Never you worry about lil' Beka."

I just watched the floor. I hate being talked about. All the same, turning to talk back like Hilyard or Verene would do made my tripes wring out. Besides, I could hear shouting behind the Commander's closed door. Since the Commander is a man, I knew it was Goodwin who wasn't happy.

She walked out of the Commander's office, slamming the door. I added another prayer to my string of them. I wanted to survive my Dog partners. She came up to me and looked me over. "I have two rules for you, Puppy."

I looked down. I always do, I can't help it. Meeting people is the hardest for me. It never gets any easier. She grabbed my chin with her hand and forced me to meet her eyes. "Look me in the face when I'm talking to you, Puppy Cooper. Two rules. Speak when you're spoken to. And keep out of my way." She let go of my chin and glared up at Tunstall, who had joined us. "All right? Time to start the babysitting detail."

He smiled, looking even more like a tall, gangly owl. "Come on, Puppy Cooper." His voice is deep, with a little bit of accent.

I followed them outside. I wasn't going to tell Goodwin that I well knew the rules to follow with our training Dogs: *Speak when you're spoken to. Keep out of the way. Obey all orders. Get killed on your own time.*

"Practice tomorrow at four!" Ahuda called after me. "Every day you have street duty, Cooper!"

Between the kennel door and the Jane Street gate is the courtyard where message runners and people with kennel business wait. The crowd was bigger than usual. They knew Puppies were being assigned and wanted to see who got what. The noise they made when they saw Tunstall and Goodwin with a trainee was deafening: whistles, laughter, plenty of comments about what Tunstall might do with me.

I tried not to listen. I didn't *think* the body could bend in those directions. Not that I'd know. Most of the other girl Puppies had been with a lad or two—and some mots, like my old friend Tansy, are already married by sixteen. I tried it once. It seemed well enough, but my mama's life was reason enough not to let myself get hobbled by a lad. And there was my dream. Since Lord Gershom brought my family into his house, I have only wanted to be a Dog. Falling in love would just ruin things.

Passing through the gate, I saw movement in the shadows. One cat-shaped shadow came over to walk with me.

"Pounce," I muttered, "scat! Go away!" Pox and

murrain, he never listened! I told him I didn't want him about this week! The curst animal *always* finds me. I'd locked him in, folly though it was. I had shuttered the windows, and barred them, and locked my door. I had made sure he was inside—I'd heard his yowling as I ran down the stairs. Eventually he always gets out, but I'd hoped he'd take the hint and leave me be! "I'm on duty!"

"I'd best not be hearing noise from you, Puppy," Goodwin called over her shoulder.

I shut up and flapped my hands at Pounce. He ignored me, dratted creature that he is. Stupid cats stay home when they're locked in. I wouldn't have this problem if he were normal.

"Tunstall, why is there a cat following us?" Goodwin asked. "I don't want to be falling over some stray black cat."

"It's not a stray, Goodwin. He wears a collar." Tunstall bent down and scooped up Pounce. I glared at my cat, silently daring him to scratch or bite. Instead my contrary animal turned his whiskers forward in a cat's smile, and let Tunstall scratch him under his chin. Pounce didn't even struggle when Tunstall halted in a patch of fading sunlight to inspect him.

Then he saw Pounce's eyes. "Mithros. Goodwin, look."

Goodwin looked. She swore. It's about half and half, who swears and who talks religion, when they see

Pounce's face. I can't blame them. I nearly fell out of
the stable loft when I found a kitten with purple eyes.

"Are you a god?" Tunstall asked Pounce.

"Manh!" my idiot cat said. He added a few sounds
like *mrt,* as if to prove his catness. For once they even
sounded like cat to me. So many of his cat noises seem
like speech.

"If he is a god, he chooses not to say," Goodwin
said.

"He wears Cooper's collar." Tunstall looked at me.
"Do you have a magical kitty cat, Puppy Cooper?" he
asked me, raising an eyebrow. "You may answer."

The words stuck in my throat. I shook my head,
wishing I could fall through the slops and garbage of
Jane Street. He's just Pounce, I wanted to say. He's odd,
but you get used to his ways. But of course I couldn't
say a word.

"*Her* cat?" Goodwin looked at Pounce's collar.
"And with those eyes, he's not magic?" My soon to be
sold for dumpling-meat cat reached out and patted
Goodwin's nose. "Stop that, you." But she smiled when
she said it, and she scratched him behind the ears.
Pounce rubbed his head against her hand like *she* was
the one who spent precious coppers on meat that she
chopped for him herself. "You brought your *cat*? Speak
up, trainee."

I tried. I did. And I remembered her warning to
look her in the eye. So I managed that, but the speech

just wouldn't come out of my throat.

Goodwin lifted Pounce from Tunstall's hold. "Did you bring him to the kennel?"

That was easy. I shook my head and got out, "N-no, Guardswoman." I didn't think I could call her "Dog" without permission, or even "Goodwin."

"He followed you here." Goodwin's fingers were brisk but affectionate behind Pounce's ears. The little traitor wrapped his forelegs around her neck.

"Yes, Guardswoman." I would have given anything not to have to meet her clear brown eyes.

"Clever cat," said Tunstall.

Goodwin put him down. "You, scat. She has work to do. Hard work, staying out of my hair."

I glared at Pounce—*Wait till I get you home, you ungrateful furball!*—and pointed in the direction of our lodgings. He trotted across the street. I couldn't watch him further, because Tunstall and Goodwin were on their way.

People greeted them from doorways and stalls, wanting to know who the Puppy was. I hung my head as they laughed and shouted their offers to buy me or play with me. And for the hundredth time I cursed my shyness that made it so hard to talk to my Dog partners, even when I was bidden to, or to answer the street folk back, the way Tunstall did. "But she's *our* Puppy, Inknose. If we let her fetch you, she'd just hurt you." "Leave the lass alone, Wildberry, you saucy wench.

She'll never be as beautiful as you and your sisters."
"Shut up, Paistoi. You ain't paid the Dogs for the last batch of Puppies you sold in Siraj."

In between his remarks to them, Tunstall explained things to me. "Since we're a senior pair, Cooper, we have no fixed route. Three nights a week, starting tonight, we roam the Nightmarket and the Lower City between Rovers Street and Koskynen, Northgate and Stormwing. That's Wednesday, Friday, and Sunday. We go where there's likely to be trouble. Thursday and Saturday we're in the Cesspool, Stormwing Street to Mulberry and Charry Orchard. We do our own seekings unless assigned one by Ahuda, we get papers when we need help on a seeking, and we have our flocks of Birdies who give us what we need in order to seek. And if we have aught that's good, we wander off our wanderings. Clary? Aught to add?"

She looked at him. "I'm bored."

Tunstall scratched the back of her head. "And you say *I'm* a barbarian. At least I know how to train a new warrior. Halt right there, Cooper. Look about you. What do you see?"

It was too easy. Not ten feet away, a pickpocket moved in on a pickle woman. I put my hand on my baton, but Tunstall slid over like ink in water. He laid his baton gentle-like on the boy's hand just as the lad touched the mot's purse. Tunstall shook his head. The pickle woman started to shriek at the thief. Tunstall gave her a smile and a copper. "How about one of your pickles, sweetheart?" Like anyone in the Lower City, she got distracted by business. When she started to fish for a pickle in the barrel, Tunstall raised his baton from the lad's hand. The pickpocket ran.

Tunstall traded copper for pickle with a bow and took a big bite of his snack.

"Oh, get on. No wonder they call you lads Dogs, thinkin' you can charm an old hag like me with a wag of your tail!" The pickle seller bridled and blushed, then tucked her coin away and headed on down the street. There was a twitch to her hips. I'd wager she'd give her husband an extra-warm night, thinking of the tall Dog who had flirted with her.

"If her husband comes looking for you, I won't be your second, not after the last time." Goodwin nudged him with her elbow. "I stood there like an idiot while you made the cove laugh so hard at your jokes he ended up buying all of us breakfast. Some duel *that* was."

"Well, I didn't kill him, and he didn't want to kill me. Everyone was satisfied, except maybe for the seconds." Tunstall looked at me and beckoned for me to come up level with him. "Now, Puppy, you saw him. That's good. You'd've made a fuss—maybe not so good. What grade pickpocket was he?"

Great Mithros, a training question. My brain scrambled. Then I remembered and met Tunstall's eyes. "He'd no knife, so he was a true pickpocket. Slow as he is, he prob'ly won't live to be a master pickpocket."

Tunstall prodded me. "And what's the street word for 'master pickpocket'?"

"'Foist,' sir," I replied.

"So she knows the words," Goodwin muttered. "So what?"

Tunstall patted her shoulder, then turned to me. "Well, we don't go around raising a fuss for minnows, Puppy. I don't like standing before the Magistrate any more than I must. It's less time spent out here looking for truly dangerous folk."

That made sense. I nodded and saw that Pounce had returned to sit at my feet. I tried to nudge him away with my boot.

"Come on," said Goodwin. "The evening's young, and I was thinking we might pay Crookshank a visit. I'd like a word with him about that load of pink pearls that went missing off of Gemstone Mews. If he's half as cracked by grief as they say, mayhap he'll get careless in his talk."

I *did* look up then. She was grinning, with all her teeth on show. They were strong and white, like the wolves' in the royal menagerie.

"Now, Clary, that's not nice," Tunstall told her. "He's in deep mourning for little Rolond." Quick as a snake, he looked back at me. "Puppy, who's Crook-shank?"

He startled me, so that I answered without thinking. "Biggest of the Nightmarket scales. Owns a piece of most of what's lifted, half of the luxury goods, minimum. A quarter of the loaner trade. He's got about twenty buildings in the Cesspool. Twenty more in the greater Lower City." I swallowed and remembered where I was and who I spoke to. "Sir."

"What do you expect, Mattes?" demanded Goodwin. "She's lived in my lord Gershom's pocket for eight years. She had to pick up *something* if she wasn't completely stupid. Knowing isn't the same as doing." She walked out into the crossing of Gibbet Corner and Feasting Street, where stalls filled the huge square before us. We had come to the Nightmarket.

I nearly fell over my like-new boots with surprise. She knew who I was! I was fair certain it wasn't covered in what the Commander said when I was assigned to them. She'd known of me before.

Does she know I'm friends with Crookshank's granddaughter-in-law Tansy, and my mama with his daughter-in-law Annis? I wondered sudden-like. How? No one from their old Cesspool district was ever allowed at the house. So I should tell the Dogs. . . .

Trotting to catch up with them, I changed my mind. It wasn't needful. Tansy wouldn't come out to say hello to visitors, if Dogs could rightly be called visitors. She hadn't left the house since Rolond was found dead. If Annis came to see us, she'd never give me away. She was a hard one, as fit a woman who made herself her father-in-law's right hand. I could tell Goodwin and Tunstall I had friends in the household later, when we were off the street.

The Nightmarket was stirring up for business. The torches were just lit, the sun being behind the wall in the Lower City. Plenty of folk were still at their daily work. This was quiet time. Buyers and sellers were talking among the stalls, collecting gossip, beginning to cook, adjusting weapons. It's my favorite time in the Nightmarket.

We walked along. Stall vendors and market regulars called greetings to Goodwin and Tunstall. Two other pairs of Dogs worked the Nightmarket, but we didn't see them.

I was trying to wave Pounce off again when Tunstall halted. I could see that big beak of his twitching. "I smell apple-raisin patties," he announced.

Goodwin turned to him and rolled her eyes. "Glutton," she said, her smile a mocking hook at one corner.

Tunstall led us down the bakers' and spicers' row of the market until he stopped at the stall that spread those good smells. I don't know anyone who won't swear before all the gods that Mistress Deirdry Noll is the best baker in all Corus. And Tunstall's luck was in, because Mistress Noll herself was minding the trays of baked goods. "Mattes, I should have known that you would sniff out my patties!" she said with a laugh. She even reached up and tweaked his nose. "Give me your handkerchief, you great lummox. Mistress Clary, how do you fare this good evening?"

"As ever, Mistress Deirdry," Goodwin said. "None of your daughters could take the stall tonight?"

"Not tonight." Mistress Noll placed six fat patties, heavy with cinnamon, on Tunstall's handkerchief. She looked as she always had to me: plump, her gray hair braided, pinned, and coiled at the back of her head, brown eyes, a small nose and straight mouth. She wore a brown cloth gown under her white cook's apron. Seeing her like a Dog must, I guessed her age to be about fifty now.

She tied Tunstall's handkerchief to make a bundle of patties and handed them over. He reached for his purse. She put fists on hips and drew herself up as tall as she could go, which was no more than my shoulder.

"As if any Dog in the Lower City paid me for something to get him through to his supper!" she said, all huffy. "I'd smack your face if I could, Mattes Tunstall!" She looked at Goodwin. "Men! No notion of what's a gift!" She flicked out a slip of cloth that had been washed so often it was almost sheer and settled three patties on it. "That's for you, Clary, since I know you're nicer about your handkerchief than he is, the big barbarian."

Tunstall mumbled something through hot filling and crumbs.

Goodwin leaned in and kissed Mistress Noll's

cheek. "Thank you," Goodwin said, her deep voice amused. "Don't mind him. He wasn't housebroke when I bought him."

Mistress Noll looked down. "Pounce, you little beggar, what are you doing here? Don't tell me you've run away from Beka. The two of you are melted together."

My friend cried, *Look in front of you!* in cat talk. It amazes me that he can decide who will understand him and who will not. He's done so since he bade me to find him four years ago, when he was a noisy kitten.

This time I was the only one who understood. Mistress Noll only chuckled and offered him some fish paste she'd been using for dumplings she fried at the brazier in the stall. When she straightened, she saw me. "Goddess bless me, it *is* Beka! All grown up and—partnered with you two?" She looked at Goodwin and Tunstall.

"She's a trainee, not a partner." Goodwin smiled, barely. "How'd *you* get to know her, Mistress Deirdry?"

Out came another worn bit of clean cloth. Mistress Noll popped three apple fritters onto it—she knew well they were my favorites.

"Hey," said Tunstall, "hers are bigger."

I grinned at him. Then I ducked my head.

"Well, you'd best take care of her. I've known her all my life, and you couldn't ask for a better-hearted gixie," said Mistress Noll. "I told her she ought to have let me make dumplings of *you* years ago," she told Pounce, scratching his ears.

Pounce mewed sad enough to pull her heartstrings. He might have been thanking her for the scratch with his last, starving breath. I glared at him, telling him with my eyes, *You're disgusting. Tell me you didn't have a beef supper before I left.* He licked his chops as Mistress Noll gave him an even bigger ball of fish paste.

Goodwin asked, "Mistress Deirdry, did you hear about old Crookshank's great-grandson?"

Mistress Noll looked at Goodwin sidelong. She knew she was being played for information. Tunstall gave her a big shrug, as if to say, She's my partner. What can I do?

Mistress Noll busied herself with pressing dough on a small table by the cook pot. "As if anyone didn't know, poor little mite. It's a disgrace, it is, taking a quarrel with the old man into his family. Barbaric. Mayhap they carry on so in Scanra, or Barzun, but not here. Whoever did it won't last long, breaking the Rogue's law like that."

Tunstall grimaced. Goodwin sniffed. The Rogue is old and should make way for someone young and strong who could keep order among the city's thieves. Instead he's fixed the Court of the Rogue to keep himself alive. He doesn't look out for the people of the Lower City anymore, only his chiefs and the folk who add to his treasure chests.

Pigeons started landing on the stall's canopy. "Scat, you nasty things!" cried Mistress Noll, grabbing a broom and jabbing at the canvas. "Don't you go leaving your mess on my goods! Beka, stand somewhere else!"

"Mistress Deirdry, she's our trainee, she must stand with us," Tunstall reminded her. "And what's she got to do with pigeons?"

I swallowed and thanked the Goddess I hadn't done just as Mistress Noll had bid me. I'd have been in trouble if I'd moved at someone else's order. Above us I heard the whispers of voices as the birds whirled and spun over the thumping canopy. Bits of human talk were coming through pigeon calls, as always. "Rest at . . ." "Spend it . . ." "Mama!"

Pounce's loud and imperious meow cut through the noise. As if he'd given them an order, the pigeons flew over to Moneychangers' Hall and settled on the carvings that decorated the front of the place.

"Beka always has some tailing her," Mistress Noll told my partners. "A bit of strange magic, I wouldn't doubt. It's in her father's family." She smiled at me. "Maybe one of the birds got reborn into your cat, girl."

"You'd think they'd be roosting, this hour of the night." Goodwin brushed her sleeves as if she thought to find droppings on her.

"There's so much light here they carry on like it's day," Tunstall said. He plunked down a copper noble. "One of your beef pies, Mistress Deirdry, as a grieving gift." He leaned closer and said quietly, "Any little whispers about anyone who might have been around the Crookshank child who shouldn't have been?"

Mistress Noll carefully settled the pie into a cheap basket. "Mattes Tunstall, you know very well anything useful doesn't come to someone like me. No one shares anything with old folk. We're finished, we just haven't died."

"But *you're* not finished," Tunstall told her with a flirty smile. "You sharp old folk are everywhere, aren't you? You're everywhere, and you see and hear everything."

"And if you *did* hear something . . . ," Goodwin hinted.

"It would be a wondrous thing. Still, I'd pass it on to the two of you, respectful as you are. Would that others were like you." Mistress Noll gave Tunstall his change and the basket. "Fare you well. If you return the basket, you'll get five coppers for it."

"No problem," Tunstall said with a grin. "I'll just have my Puppy fetch it back to you."

Crookshank's house was to the rear of the Night-market, the biggest house on Stuvek Street. Pounce wandered off into the market whilst a manservant let us in. We waited in a sitting room as he fetched Annis Lofts. I wondered yet again if I ought to tell my Dogs that my mama had been friends with Mistress Annis.

She came before I could fish the words from where

they were stuck in my chest. She wore black for Rolond, a long black tunic over a black underdress. She'd been crying.

"You can see Father Ammon, for the good it will do you," she said. It took me a moment to know who Mistress Annis meant by "Father Ammon." He'd been Crookshank for so long, I'd forgotten the old scale's real name was Ammon Lofts. "He's done little but sit in the dark. He hates you two enough, mayhap he'll move for you. This way."

Goodwin looked at me. "Puppy, sit," she ordered as she and Tunstall followed Annis.

Instead I walked around the room, pricing the little pretty things and hangings. Crookshank had probably bought furniture and all with one day's taking of stolen goods, and he'd've paid them that stole it only a part of its worth. That was what scales did.

In a moment Mistress Annis returned. "Well, he didn't throw them out." She tried a smile on me, but it didn't work that well. She offered me no embrace, for all her sorrowing. "Look at you, all kitted out like a Dog. Will you start tattling on old friends, then?"

"All Dogs walk that line," I told her.

"So you do." Her face shook. "Oh, Beka, I wish your mother was still with us. I miss her so much."

"I miss her, too." Only two years Mama has been gone. It still hurts. "I know she would comfort you if she could."

She wiped her eyes. "You'd think I'd be done with tears by now. But Rolond was only three! Who would kill a baby only three, who went up to everyone just as friendly as you could ask for?" She blew her nose. "Will you see Tansy? It will do her good."

I wanted to see her. It's hard nowadays. Crookshank don't like his granddaughter-in-law mingling with old friends from the Cesspool. Old friends from the Cesspool who live in Provost's House are even worse. And with a child and husband, Tansy finds it even harder to get away. "I was ordered to stay here," I said, trying not to whine.

Annis gave me the oddest smile. "Do you think they'll complain to know you're friends with Tansy? Dogs are always looking for a back door to a house. Up till now, they've never had one here. They'll be delighted."

I didn't know about "delighted," but I used my wits for a moment. Annis was right. They would be glad I had friends in Crookshank's very own family. I hope they won't be vexed if I don't go bearing tales. From the little I have heard from Tansy, Crookshank is a cruel father-in-law and grandfather. I won't bring his anger down on Tansy and Annis by taking tales to my Dogs if I can help it.

I nodded.

"I'll tell your Dogs where you are, if they're done with Father in any hurry," Annis said. "He was growling and snapping when I brought them to him, though. They'll want to see what they can wheedle out of the old coin cutter. Come. See if you can get Tansy to eat sommat." She led me through the house, past servants who nodded at her and gawped at me. I wish I could say it was the uniform that drew respect, but I glimpsed smirks and pointed fingers as they remarked on my Puppy trim. Only my first day of wearing it, and I can't wait to get that part of the uniform off.

"She's got another babe coming," Annis told me as we climbed a narrow servants' stair. "She can't starve herself like this." Two stories up, we came out of the stair and walked down a hall. Annis showed me into a fine bedchamber.

There Tansy lay on a large bed, staring at the ceiling. I could see the swell of her belly. She has may-hap four months to go yet. The room wasn't a good place to think of such things, with a bed draped in black muslin. The small mirror was draped in black, too. Tansy wore a black gown and a rumpled head cloth. Annis whispered to her, begging her to sit up and greet me.

"Go away!" Tansy cried, flinging herself across the big bed. "I don't want to live!"

There was a water pitcher nearby. I picked it up and said, "Excuse me, Mistress Annis." I judged my throw carefully and tossed the water all over Tansy.

She shrieked and came off that bed like a scalded cat. She hurled her sopping head cloth at me. I dodged it. Then she came at me, ready to claw my eyes out. I grabbed her wrists, just liked they'd taught us.

"Shame on you, wailing like a cracknob, not thinking about your poor mama-in-law or that babe you've got coming," I told her. "Shame! You hold Rolond's ghost here. Let him go on to the Black God's realm peaceful-like." I knew it was a lie. It was being murdered that kept that baby's ghost about, but Tansy will fret herself to death if you don't speak stern to her.

She crumpled up and began to cry. I sat her on the bed and took the drying cloth Annis gave me. "Are you going to eat something now, like a sensible girl?" Annis asked her. "Or do I refill the water jug?"

Tansy nodded. "Soup, please." Her voice was hoarse. "Mayhap some rolls. And . . . and milk." She smoothed her hands over her belly. When Annis went to get those things, Tansy looked at me. She gave me a quivery smile, though she was still crying. "You never had patience with me. Even when you was five and me eight, you was still lecturing like a granny."

"Especially when you was making an ass of yourself," I reminded her. "If you're going to mourn, do it proper, in a temple. Give Rolond toys for an offering, or his favorite sweets. But this does you nor him no good at all."

Tears rolled down her face. "Who would kill Rolond, Beka? A little boy who laughed whenever he saw a new face?"

Like as not, that's how whoever doused Rolond caught him, I thought. "The Dogs will find out, Tansy. They'll catch whoever done it and make them pay." Except that I knew better. Jewel and Yoav had the hunt on Evening Watch. They didn't see the sweet little lad I had known. Rolond had never grinned for them to show off his new teeth, or played pat-a-cake. When they thought of Rolond, they thought only that someone had made Crookshank suffer by killing him. I am near positive the Dogs that have this hunt on the Day and Night Watches feel the same.

It's the way things are always done. That doesn't make it right. Rolond was innocent of Crookshank's wickedness. He deserves a Dog seeking justice for his murder, even if the Dog is only a Puppy. At least I know him as himself.

Tansy wiped her eyes on her sleeve. "Goddess bless us, you're dressed up like a Dog. A Puppy. You'll get yourself killed, Beka. Knifed in an alley somewhere, strangled, dumped in the river—"

I glared at her. "And you weeping in a chamber is better than me doing honest work?"

Tansy held her head up. "Leastways I'm not poor and scraping burnt porridge from a pot to feed . . ." Her mouth trembled. "I wanted out of Mutt Piddle

Lane, Beka. Herun wanted to take me out of there. I've a good man and a fine house."

I couldn't argue. It's thanks to my lord Gershom that *I* am out. That Mama had a decent bed to die in, and that my sisters and brothers are learning proper trades.

Since talking was discomforting, I did what the training masters said and looked Tansy's room over. The Lofts family lived well. The clothes presses were fine cedar, ornamented with mother-of-pearl and polished brass. A table supported pots for perfumes and lotions. Tansy had shell combs and brushes, ribbons in a carved wooden bowl, and a figure of the Goddess as Mother to bless her room. Shelves on the walls held pretty things with no real use to them. I wandered over to look at a row of stone figures. Among them was a piece of uncarved rock. In the candlelight it sparked bits of colored fire from a light pink bed, rough to my fingers like sandstone. I turned it every which way, fascinated. The fires came from smooth pieces in the stone, strips, dots, and even one tiny shelf that shimmered pale red, blue, and green in a creamy setting. The stone was really no bigger than the first joint of my thumb, including the nail, but it invited me to stare at each piece of it.

"What's this?" I asked, turning to show it to her.

"Goddess, take it! I don't ever want to see the curst thing again!" Tansy cried. "Herun brought it to me.

Gave it to me like a jewel, said it's going to see us all move to Unicorn District. The next day they stole my Rolond. It's ill luck, is what it is!"

"I don't see magic signs." I held the stone to my nose and sniffed. "I don't smell oils or suchlike."

"I don't care." Tansy was weeping again. "You know what they say. If sommat new comes in your life and bad luck follows, then it followed the new thing. If bad luck follows you, Beka, my advice? Throw the rock in the Olorun with a curse to whoever sent it."

I put the stone in my pocket. "Tansy, can you think of anyone fool enough to try this way to attack Crookshank? Or why?"

Her eyes flashed. "Go away, Beka. You talk like a Dog. Just take that bad luck rock with you."

I hesitated, but I knew I'd made a mistake. I went to put my arms around her. When she drew away, I gave her a glare of my own. "It's not the Dog as wants to hug you, pox rot it." She hesitated, then let me hug her. "Gods bless. The Black God will keep Rolond's spirit safe until you come to him again," I whispered. I hope so, anyway. He *was* murdered. The Black God may not have him yet.

The door opened. Annis came in with a maid, who held a tray of food. "The Dogs are asking for you, Beka," Annis told me. "I told them I'd hoped you'd do Tansy good, and I was right. Get along with you." She hugged me, too, and kissed my cheek. "Do you burn the incense for Ilony's ghost?" I nodded. Annis pressed a copper into my hand. "Buy that lily-of-the-valley scent she loved, and tell her I miss her."

"I'll do that, Mistress Annis. Goddess bless you and yours." I ran off, remembering the way downstairs. I didn't want Goodwin and Tunstall waiting for me a moment longer than needful, particularly not if they were vexed that I'd left my post.

Goodwin scowled when I came up. Tunstall was munching a pastry. He swung the empty pie basket on his finger. "Trot this back to Mistress Noll, Puppy, then meet us right here," he said as we walked outside. He flipped the basket into the air.

I caught it and did as I was bid, shouldering my way through the small crowd of customers. I looked around for Pounce, but he was nowhere in view.

"You were longer than I expected," Mistress Noll said. She passed me the coppers she would have kept if Tunstall hadn't returned the basket. "Don't tell me they actually talked to the old bootlicker."

I shrugged and smiled, then returned to my Dogs. That's one of the big rules: *Dog business stays with the Dogs.* Of course she wanted to know if Crookshank had said anything. *I* wanted to know if he'd said aught of interest. Not that I dared ask.

My Dogs waited still before Crookshank's house. Though the Nightmarket was filling up and those that passed greeted them, I noticed that folk took care to give the two Dogs some room. Goodwin stood with her feet apart, balanced, hands hooked in her belt, her dark eyes not missing a face. Tunstall juggled his dagger, flipping it from hand to hand, always catching it by the hilt, though it spun end over end in the air.

"Puppy," Goodwin said, pointing to the spot right in front of her. "Mistress Lofts informed us *she* was a friend to your mother, and *you* are a friend to the young Mistress Lofts, the mother of the dead child. How is it you neglected to mention it to Mattes or me? Look at me when I'm talking to you, Puppy Cooper."

"You didn't ask, Guardswoman Goodwin," I said real fast.

"She's got a point, Clary." Tunstall gave his dagger a last flip and tucked it into its sheath with the same move he'd taken to catch it. "When you have connections someplace where we're poking our noses, Cooper, speak up. We're good, but we're no mind readers."

"Did Tansy say anything?" Goodwin asked. "No, don't tell us here. Save it till we're secure. You'd better not have depths, Puppy Cooper. People with depths are usually more trouble than they're worth."

"She says so because *she's* deep," Tunstall explained to me as Goodwin walked on.

"I heard that," she called over one shoulder.

I fell in behind them, turning the rough stone over in my hand. I wanted to keep it to myself, seek on my own to see if it was important or not. Herun Lofts thought it was valuable, and he'd been raised at Crookshank Lofts's elbow.

Still, the training masters were strict about that kind of thinking. No going behind a partner's back. *Definitely* no going behind your training partners' backs. But how could a sparkly little piece of stone change Crookshank's fortunes and so Herun's? I knew rubies, emeralds, and sapphires didn't look too promising when they were dug from the ground, but at least they were single, solid rocks.

The clocks were chiming the eighth hour when we heard an uproar. We followed shouts into the Nightmarket. A crowd was by the square's fountain. From the way folk yelled and traded coin, there was a fight at the heart of the crowd.

Tunstall rose on his toes to get a look. "The Parks brothers. Some poor scut must have looked at them wrong. They're taking it out of his hide."

Goodwin poked one cheering man with her baton. "What are the odds?"

"Three to two against the new fish," he told her without looking away from the fight. "He's supposed to be wrestlin' champion in his sheep scummer village. He says his brothers are *bull* throwers—Mithros, if those two are the brothers . . . I'm offerin' five to three *against* the Parks lads!"

I heard wood splinter. Someone screeched for the Guard. Goodwin sighed. "I was about to make some money. Tunstall, Puppy, come on. Puppy, just stand by with your baton out and watch. If someone tries to brain me or Tunstall, *then* you can move. Otherwise keep out of our way."

I got out my baton and followed as they pushed through the crowd. They used their batons when their voices didn't make folk move fast enough. We shoved into the fighting ring. The breaking wood must have been the nearest ale seller's stall. The poles that supported its canvas sides had been broken. Its roof hung down. Leather jacks and wooden cups were scattered over the cobbles in puddles, at least until the quick fingers who haunted the Nightmarket ducked in to steal them.

What held the crowd's attention was the five brawling coves at the center of the mess. I knew the two Parks brothers. The other three were country lads who were country big and country built. One of them proved it when he picked up the older Parks brother and lifted him over his head. He aimed for the five-leveled fountain, dedicated to the memory of King Jonathan the First.

Goodwin stepped in. Gently, for a Dog, she thumped the country fellow across the belly with her baton. The air went out of him. He dropped his man.

Another country cove, with eyes as blue as the sky and a face as open as a field, stepped in to save the first one from the small woman. He didn't know Tunstall had come up between him and the remaining cove. My male partner didn't even take out his baton. Tunstall just grabbed the second cove's head and the third country man's and banged them together like eggs. Then he let them sit down.

The Parks who'd been fighting with that third country man was too stupid to be glad his battle was over. He roared and charged Tunstall, head down. Tunstall turned to the side and swung up his bent knee. He caught the charging Parks brother on the chin. The cove decided to lay down.

I looked at the Parks brother who'd been dropped. Plainly he'd struck his head hard. He lay unmoving. Goodwin bent down to check his heartbeat. Then she peeled back his eyelid. "Well, if he's got a brain, it's still working. He—"

"Hey!" someone yelled behind me. "Boys, cityfolk done attacked the Weatherskill lads! To me! To me!" I turned. Three more country men were running straight at me. The one in the lead, who did the squalling, had a chopping knife out. It was fully two feet of blade on a hilt. Evidently no other Dogs had seen it and made him stow it before he walked the streets.

I did as Ahuda had taught. This cove watched Tunstall and Goodwin. He never saw me smack his wrist with my baton. When he dropped the weapon, he bent to grab it. I hit him on the spine, praying I hadn't done it too hard. I didn't want to cripple him, just stop him.

One of his friends grabbed my arm. I got hold of his little finger with my free hand and bent it back hard. I'd had it done to me. I know that's too much pain to bear for long. Sure enough, he let go with a yell.

Then Goodwin and Tunstall were there, taking care of the two louts still standing. When they were all down, Tunstall got his whistle. He blew three short blasts and two long, the signal for the cage Dogs on duty outside the Nightmarket.

"Take all these scuts," Goodwin said when they came. "Let them argue about what happened while they enjoy the cages." She looked at Tunstall and me. "I don't know about you, but I worked up an appetite."

Someone yelled, "I had bets on that fight!"

"Nobody won, cracknob!" someone else called. "Ye don't win an' ye don't lose. Get yer coin back or maul them as stole it!"

"You with the bets!" Tunstall's bellow could shake the palace. "Pay back every copper you hold. If I hear that anyone cheated a bettor, that cheater sees me on his doorstep—or hers—on the morrow!"

"He means it, too," someone whispered. "Give the money back, y' looby. Tha's Tunstall talkin'."

As we passed through the crowd, I heard folk murmur. "Nice work, Puppy." "Neat job." "Cool head, this one." "Ilony Cooper's oldest girl. You know the one." "Mother woulda been proud."

Goodwin moved back to walk next to me. "You think you're their gold girl now, Cooper?" she asked, speaking for my ears alone. "Wait till you have to take in someone they love, someone popular. One of the ones with the easy smile and the charming way about them. You'll learn fast enough whose side they're on. Now, I thought I told you to stand fast and do nothing." I opened my mouth. She raised a finger. "You did right. That harvesting knife would have been a real problem, and you were closest. Just don't make a habit of it, understand me?"

"Yes, Guardswoman Goodwin." I met her eyes for a moment, because I had to, before I looked away, cursing my shyness.

She and Tunstall led me down Pottage Lane, to a small eating house called the Mantel and Pullet. Everyone there knows my Dogs. They even have their own table.

Tunstall gave me a copper noble and jerked his head toward the bar. "Ale for us two, and whatever you're drinking," he said. "We'll order you the baked rat special."

I had his measure enough to dare a small smile before I hurried to the barkeep. He'd already drawn ale for Goodwin and Tunstall in leather jacks with their names burned into the sides. "What of you, pretty Puppy?" he asked, leering at me. "A nice strong ale to loosen your belt? Wine for your first day?"

I didn't *have* to look at *him*. "Barley water, sir, if you please."

"You're joking." His voice was flat as he said it.

"No, Master Barkeep. Barley water, please."

"You've something against my good brown ale? Strong enough to stick a spoon in! 'Tis good enough for any Dog or soldier as walks through that door, good enough that the King himself, gods save him, has drunk it, whilst *you* turn up that dainty nose—"

A man leaned past me and knocked on the plank bar. "Listen, keg tapper. Rather than waste time yapping at a pretty girl who's not interested, why not occupy yourself pouring out for me and *my* ladies, and let her be about her business?"

I glanced at him and stepped to the side. He was lean and deadly-looking, with blade-scarred hands and sharp bones. He was also white-skinned and dark-eyed, with hair so fair it was nearly white. He winked at me as he leaned in for the barman's attention. I figured him to be in his early twenties. I was first in my class at guessing men's ages, so I felt sure of that.

A barmaid passed me a mug of water. "If you wants a jack, bring yer own," she told me, eyeing the newcomer with wicked intentions. "With your name on't, so's you won't be tasting anyone else's mouth leavings." She skipped away from the barman's slap. I went back to my Dogs with our drinks.

"Took you long enough," Goodwin said. She grabbed her jack and downed half the ale. I placed Tunstall's before him. Like everyone else, he watched the newcomer. The cove took his drinks over to a pair of women who had grabbed an empty table. One was plainly Scanran, a tall blond mot two or three years older than me, wearing men's clothes and a sword. The smaller one was brunette, of mixed blood, my height. She wore a sleek blue dress. I could not tell her eye color in the murky light.

"What do you think, Cooper?" Tunstall asked. "Guard from some other city? Off-duty army?"

"The blond mot could be a mercenary of some kind." It was easier to speak if I looked at her, not him. "The cove's never been near military discipline." I remembered a Y-shaped scar in his eyebrow and the scars on his hands and muttered, "Or if he was, it didn't go well."

Goodwin emptied her jack and shoved it at Tunstall. "I'll have a second. Tell that bar scut if he gives our Puppy a hard time again, I'll make him eat a keg after I empty it."

As Tunstall left us, Goodwin said, "Read me out the man. Don't look at the man. Look at me."

I opened my mouth and croaked. My throat had gone dry. I cleared it. No sound at all came out.

Goodwin snorted. "Drink some water, and *don't* look at me, then, if that helps. Mother save us, you'd think I was a monster. The man, Puppy, the man. He might be escaping with the crown and scepter this very moment. Tell the kennel Dogs who they're sniffing for."

I drank and read out the man's looks as I was taught in training. "Early twenties, five feet, ten inches, slim, muscled. Sideways forked scar, left eyebrow. Hair very fair, eyes black, skin pale. He's never worked hard labor, not with that skin. Long nose, full lower lip, thin upper. High cheekbones, thin cheeks. Very striking. Blade scars on the hands. Carries a purse and his belt knife in sight. Knife at the back collar, one inside both forearms, knives over each kidney, boot knives. I'm not sure if there's a buckle knife. If there is, it's a design I don't know. Earring, left ear, silver skull."

Goodwin leaned back, whistling softly. "Very well, then. You've earned your supper. I won't throw you in the river, either." She looked at the ivory man, rubbing a scar on her cheek as she did. "That's a very danger-ous new cove who's come to town, and what for? Trou-ble, no doubt." She seemed to be talking to herself.

Tunstall came back with more ale for both of them. He was followed by a cookmaid with a tray of supper. My Dogs hadn't stinted. There was eel tart, roast hare, split-pea soup, and cheese fritters, along with a loaf of country bread and butter to spread on it.

"Eat up," Tunstall ordered as he cut into the hare. "It gets busier as the evening gets older." He and Goodwin served out the food. "So what do you think of our pale cove?"

Goodwin was ladling soup. "All the city knows that Kayfer Deerborn is a joke as a Rogue. The carrion crows and the hopefuls are coming to town. It's to be expected."

I knew what she meant. Our thief king rules because he lets his district chiefs keep the biggest part of their profits. In return they guard his life. Now word is out. The chiefs aren't as vigilant, or they're lazy. More and more young folk are restless under a Rogue who lets no one move up in the way of things. It's time for a new ruler, they're saying.

Goodwin reached across the table and tugged my hair. "Puppy! Tell us how you came to be talking all friendly-like with the dead baby's mother while me and Tunstall traded lies with Crookshank. Don't look at us or we'll be here all night. Just report."

I drew on my plate with my dagger and told them how Mama was friends with Crookshank's daughter-in-law. How Annis was a customer when Mama sold perfumes, soaps, and herbs. When my lord Gershom took us in, Annis stayed friends with us. She and Mama often shopped the Daymarket on Mama's good days. How one time, I went to see *my* friends and Tansy got the notion that we should go to the Daymarket. There we found Mama, and Annis, and Annis's son. Herun looked at Tansy's curls and dimples and bright eyes. . . .

"Young love," Tunstall said with a wistful sigh. "It's so simple. Remember when it was simple?" he asked Goodwin.

"Simple for *you*. You're a simple creature," Goodwin told him. She made a beckoning gesture to me. I have a feeling I will get very familiar with this gesture, a come-on twitch of just two of her fingers. "What did Annis and Tansy say tonight at Crookshank's?"

I repeated all of it, as exactly as I could remember. Then I handed over Tansy's rock. Tunstall pushed aside the plates and set it between them. He reached into a pocket and fetched out a small thing like a white pearl. He blew on it and set it on the table next to the stone.

Light spread from the globe. While the room's lamps flickered, this light was steady. As it touched the stone, it brought glints of fire from its surface in colors like cherry red, sapphire blue, grass green. The shiny step-like bit changed, now red, now green, now mixes of both colors with flecks of blue.

"Pretty toy." Some of the other Dogs had come over. It was Jewel's partner who spoke. "Where'd y' get it?"

"Tansy Lofts, Crookshank's granddaughter-in-law that married young Herun Lofts, she gave it to our Puppy," Goodwin told him. "Ever seen anything like it?" I was trying not to slide under the table. I did make myself as small as I could. I *have* to get better at being around folk.

More Dogs and a few off-duty soldiers came to see. Seemingly the customers not on the side of the law knew to mind their own business in this place. Of them Goodwin asked, all either shook their heads or said no.

Otterkin, one of the Dogs with the magic Gift, touched the stone. It sparked, throwing off lights in the colors of its glassy bits, then turned back to normal.

"It's no spellstone," Otterkin said. "I suppose it could be used for one, but it's like none I was ever schooled with." She shrugged. "You could always take it to Master Fulk."

Everyone groaned or rolled their eyes. I clenched my fists and watched my Dogs. I'll take the stone to Master Fulk if they order me to, but he'd best play nice.

"We should, though I trust *your* expertise over Fulk's," Goodwin told Otterkin. "I saw him turn a boil into a case of them once, all over the poor Dog who went to him for help." The other Dogs muttered agreement.

Tunstall's globe faded. He picked it up, then the sparkly stone. "It'll make a nice toy for your cat," he told me, handing the stone to me. "Young Herun Lofts isn't the sharpest arrow in the quiver. No doubt he thought he'd discovered rubies, or some such. Anything else to report, Puppy?"

"Nothing more to report, Guardsman," I mumbled, wishing the others would go away.

And they did wander back to their tables to finish

their suppers. Goodwin ordered me to do the same.

One more big thing happened after supper, but I am too weary to write of it now. And too miserable. On the morrow, mayhap, I will hurt less in my pride. I will write of it then.

I will not be the Puppy who is made a Dog in the shortest space of time.

Thursday, April 2, 246

Written before baton practice.

Some details of my work I do not want to write out. It is bad enough that they happened. I will record them in a general way, but it is more than I can bear to write each word of it.

Last night, after supper, we went back to the Nightmarket. There was a cutpurse. Tunstall lunged for him and saved the purse, but missed the thief.

Goodwin pointed at the runaway Rat and said, "Puppy, fetch."

I was gleeful. I could prove how good I was. I was after the cutpurse in a leap. I chased him down Stuvek Street. My training forgot, I never saw his lookout. The cove stuck out a foot and I went flying.

There'd been a seller of fried food. On one side of his frying cart was the crate of fresh fish he cooked up for passersby. On the other side was the pile of heads, guts, and tails left as he cut those fish up for the cooking. I made my acquaintance with the pile, full out. The cutpurse escaped.

Now it is day and my pride *still* hurts. I do not want the world to see me again. I do not want any *Dogs* to see me again. My sisters, my brothers, Lord Gershom, all will have the tale by now. My lord will be wondering how he could have been so mistaken in me. Diona, Lorine, Willes, and Nilo will do as brothers and sisters always do. They will never, *ever* let me forget this.

Can a mot die of shame? If I report back to the kennel tonight (if I don't just pack my things and head for the nearest ship away from Tortall) I will find out.

Everyone who saw me clapped. Vendors, shoppers, street Players, and Rats whistled, stomped, and cheered. Except my Dogs. Tunstall was busy hobbling the lout who had tossed me into that mound of fish garbage. Goodwin just stood there, arms crossed over her chest, one eyebrow raised.

It was near the end of our watch. Goodwin sent me to the docks to rinse off under the big barrels they kept for the fishermen. She ordered me just to go on home and care for my uniform. I fetched a change of clothes, then took myself to the bathhouse around the corner from my lodgings. There I scrubbed me *and* my uniform. The attendants were more used to waiting on street women and Players than Puppies. They swore by the Goddess they couldn't smell fish by the time I was done, but they smirked as they swore. I couldn't tell. I think the stench was burned into my poor nose. I passed over a five-copper piece for a special jasmine and lavender bath and soaked until I couldn't smell a thing. Then I went home and threw myself into my bed.

I will be known forever as the Puppy who chased a cutpurse and caught fish garbage instead. My descendants will pretend I'm not in their bloodline. No—no one will want to make descendants with me.

I might have hid until I'd worked up the courage to run off to sea, but Pounce is determined. He washed my nose. He meowed and clawed at my bedclothes. He dug all around me until he found a way in. His yowls were deafening inside the covers.

"Pesky beast," I growled, winding him up in sheets and throwing them off the bed. "*You* don't have to face the world."

Will you waste all your free time sulking? he asked. *Get up!*

When I stood, there he was, on top of the blankets. I wish I knew how he did that. "I told you to stay home last night, and not go a-playing off your tricks on me." I checked the bolts on my shutters. They were still fastened. "What do you do, magic them open?"

He just sat on the bed, looking at me, head cocked sideways, his whiskers shoved forward in his small cat smile. "I hate it when you charm me," I told him. I draped him over my shoulder. He purred and climbed around the back of my head, then washed my temple. He stayed there, balanced, while I poured water in the basin and cleaned my teeth and face. Combing my hair was more activity than he wanted, though, so he sat on my lone table for that. I was probably smiling like a looby the whole time. I don't know why I am so fortunate as to have this magical creature for my friend, but he makes things better, the little and the big. When Mama died, Pounce comforted all of us, not just me. Today he eased my sore heart.

I pulled on breeches, shirt, and boots and gathered a string bag and my belt purse. I had time to shop, feed my pigeons, eat, and still run away to sea if I didn't laze about anymore. I was putting what I'd need for the day in my pockets when I saw the stone that Tansy had given me among my bits of things. I carried it to the window and opened the shutters. The mid-morning sun poured in as a couple of pigeons landed on the sill. While they made simple pigeon noises, I found the bag of cracked corn I kept inside the window and spread some on the sill to quiet them.

Then I held up the stone. The sparkling pieces were even brighter in the daylight. I turned it here and there, fascinated by the colors. The little red bits were the best. The only time I'd ever seen red so bright was in the paintings in the great temple of the Mother Goddess the day Mama took me for blessings on my first monthlies. I kept turning it, finding new spots that cast off light, until Pounce leaped to my shoulder and yowled *Wake up!* in my ear.

"Pounce!" I yelped. He'd shattered some glass bubble around me. I looked down. The pigeons were gone, their corn all eaten. The sun had moved enough that a shadow lay on the edge of the sill. "How long was I standing here, gawping at the rock?" I asked my cat.

Pounce said, *Long enough,* and jumped to the floor.

"Someday I'm selling you to a dumpling maker," I told him. I shoved the rock into my breeches pocket. Then I closed and locked my shutters once more.

Pounce and I rattled downstairs. As we passed through the door to the street, my landlady leaned out her window and called, "Would ye bring me some fish, then, Beka, there's a good gixie."

I heard folk laughing as we went down the lane. It's going to be a long time before I stop hearing *that* little joke. I heard three different types of it before I got to Bis's bakery. The one I liked despite myself was how Pounce had done well for himself, making his home with a Fishpuppy.

Old man Bis grinned when he saw me and took my three coppers. The four-day-old bread bin had more than enough to fill my bag. It feels good to know that I no longer get bread there for my family and that I can afford more than a lone copper's worth.

I was about to go when Bis offered me a small loaf of bread in the shape of a fish. He'd glazed its scales with egg to bake up shiny. He cackled when I bit the thing's head off and gave Pounce the tail.

"You'll show 'em, Beka Cooper!" Bis told me. "I seen it when you was naught but a peck o' rawhide an' eyes like ice. I see it now! Fish guts and all!"

I shook my head at him and fled. I don't know where the old man came by such belief in me. How did he even tell me apart from the mumper children that waited around the shop in hope of a stale roll? But he'd known me right off when I moved back to the Lower City. He'd offered me a fruit bun in welcome. It was why I'd chosen his shop for getting my precious stale bread.

Pounce and I wandered on down through the Lower City. I do love it there during the day. Mothers sit on their doorsteps, gossiping with friends as they sew, feed their babes, and buy from passing vendors. The pigs are everywhere, snuffling in garbage when the dogs and cats aren't vexing them. The pigeons are everywhere, too, hunting out food. Children run around the muddy streets and in the dooryards of places big enough to have them, playing games and chasing animals. Mostly folk here walk or ride horses or mules. No one comes down here in a carriage. The streets are too narrow. The mud tracks twist and take quick turns. Now and then a wagoner might get lost hereabouts. He'll be stuck, and before he knows it, his cargo is gone. So, too, are his clothes, purse, and whatever poor beast pulled the wagon.

There is always something going on: a deal, a birth, a wedding, a fight, lessons in sommat or other. Folk are alive in the Lower City, not bottled up like the merchants and the nobles. They laugh at what they find funny, and they weep if they are sad. If they have a little, they help their kin and friends. And they want better lives, however they can manage to get them. I am just the same. I knew plenty of mots and children who'd been like Mama, at the mercy of a Rat, who'd thought no one would help them. I'd made sure that Rat paid for his thieving. Who would do that for other families like mine had been?

Most of the folk who lived here knew me by sight and to nod to, though I'd learned being a Dog, even a Puppy, made a difference. The little ones would run up to me, laughing and holding out their hands, yelling, "Put the cords on me! I been bad!" And their parents would chuckle, but the laugh never reached their eyes. Everyone in the Lower City knew of goings-on that cracked the law, even if they never took part. Any Dog wanting to curry favor or make a mark could drag someone in for questioning and come away with a tidbit of tasty information.

I'll not be doing that. I suppose it's easy enough to bully strangers, but the folk of the Lower City are my neighbors. Besides, I have sources most Dogs don't. My Birdies aren't human, but real, winged birds and creatures of the air.

I walked down Messinger Lane to the corner of Holderman Street. There was Glassman Square. Mots sat on the rim of the big pool at the center, visiting and filling their buckets. Other mots and gixies did laundry in stone tubs fed by pipes from the pool. I bought two Scanran pasties with mutton, onion, and currants, sharing the gristly meat with Pounce. Then I wiped my fingers on my handkerchief and sat on one of the raised stone blocks around the square.

As soon as I began to rip the first stale loaf of bread into small pieces, the pigeons came in hordes. They are the most common birds in all Corus. Folk kick at them, dogs chase them, cats and children kill them, hawks eat them, and still they thrive, the silly things. They go everywhere, see everything, and serve the Black God of Death, carrying those who are not ready to enter his Peaceful Realms. Their colors are mixed. I have seen ones who are wondrous shades of copper and pink and others who are almost as black as Pounce, with a blue-green tinge to them.

My old friend Slapper, who landed on my knee, is one of the blue-black ones. He'd come to me first in my Lord Provost's stable yard, yet somehow he had tracked me here. I'd named him Slapper for his bad habit of hitting me with his wings. He was also dirty and had a clubbed foot, a hunched back, and wide yellow eyes with the tiniest of pupils. He looked as if he'd accuse you of plotting to murder him in his sleep.

I offered him bread. He grabbed for it (I've been feeding him for three years and he still doesn't trust me) and in the grab, he fell off my knee. I put down my hand and let a heap of bread crumbs fall next to my leg. Slapper balanced himself on his bad foot and went to work on them.

In came Pinky, a bird I'd met just a week ago, a silver and dark pink pigeon whose wings are tipped in snowy white. She is a bold wench, shoving her way right up to me. Fog is more of a pale blue-gray, with a blue-green collar and dark wing tips. White Spice is clean and white, perhaps someone's pet, with copper-colored spots from the back of his neck down to the middle of his wings. He is a handsome fellow and knows it, always strutting before the ladies.

I have not named them all, of course. Like the pigeons who live around the Lord Provost's house, they are quick to learn a source of food. It took these fifty-odd birds but three days of my coming here at this time, with my basket, to know me and to gather when I began to rip up my bread. I wished I could say I did it for my love of birds.

But they are not pets. They are informants. Seated at the heart of this flock, I listened for the ghost voices. The pigeons cooed and *chrr*ed deep in their throats, vying for food. Slowly, out of their sounds, the words of ghosts rose.

"Didn't know he'd come home so early," a mot's voice said. "Why'd he come home so early?"

"These dolts never tie doon the loads right." The cove spoke with the burr that comes from the mountain folk of the north. "Sloppy work, sloppy."

"I don't like this, Gary. That looks like a slave ship. I'm right, aren't I? You've been trading in slaves!" The voice was a mot's, and frightened. Seemingly her folk belonged to the growing faction that hated slavery.

"Mama, I'm cold. Naught looks right. Mama, they took me away. I didn't want to go, but there was a parrot, and then I was sleepy. I want to come home!"

A dog ran through the pigeons, scattering the flock. I cursed as Pounce took off after the dog with a yowl, swinging his claws. The dog yelped as Pounce leaped to his back and dug in. Shrieking, the dog fled the square, Pounce still attached to him.

I broke up more rolls, waiting for the birds to return. Unless a hawk was near, they would come back. They never forgot meals. Even the city's beggars could learn from them.

And here they came, recovered from their fright. I tossed out small pieces as they dropped to the stones, talking to each other. As they settled, once more the dead began to speak. I looked for the pigeon who carried that small child's soul on his back.

"There was a little girl and a little boy with me. They was scared." That was him. Lucky for me that after they're dead, even the smallest baby can tell its tale with a clear voice. Perhaps, as the priests say, the soul is ageless.

"Why did the hooded men take us, Mama? There wasn't a parrot. They lied, and then they made me sleep. They gave me porridge with bugs in it. And—"

The entire flock took flight. I looked up. High

78

overhead glided a red-tailed hawk. I sighed. It would be long before the birds came back if a hawk was nearby. My gathering here was done, for today at least. But now I knew something. A very young boy had been kidnapped and held with other children. It could have been slavers. Slave taking is disliked in Corus, but it isn't illegal. Kidnapping children without their parents' leave is illegal, though.

He could have been Tansy's Rolond.

It was near half past one by the time I'd visited all my little flocks. I had time to see Granny Fern before my watch. I helped around her house, meaning I did work and she went around after me fixing what I'd done, explaining how I did it wrong.

We talked about Diona, Lorine, and the boys as she made us a lunch of green pancakes with sorrel and ginger, then noodles with cheese. There was even cheese for Pounce. She finished with a winter apple tart for me. "And this," she said, handing me a parcel wrapped in reeds as I was kissing her goodbye.

I took it unthinking before the smell reached my nose. Fish.

"For the furball," she said wickedly, and closed her door in my face.

"For my furball indeed," I muttered to Pounce as we returned to my rooms. The city's bells were ringing three of the clock. "Today was the first day she's *given* you food. Just did it to score a bit of fur off of *me*."

Pounce said, *She's a wicked old woman. I like her.*

"You would," I said as we climbed our stairs. "You're wicked yourself." I let us into my two little rooms.

Pounce only looked smug and began to wash. I got ready for practice and watch.

Night, after duty.

As soon as I walked into the training yard behind the kennel for baton practice, the others began to jeer. I dumped my uniform bag on the side of the yard and picked up my training baton, wishing I could sink into the beaten dirt. It would have been bad enough only to have Puppies to comment on my shame, but life isn't that simple. Three years' worth of Dogs were also there to talk about my smelly fate of the night before. Baton practice is demanded of Puppies and Dogs for four years of service—three for the Goddess and one extra for Great Mithros. The higher-ups figure if you survive that long, you are getting plenty of practice on the streets.

A group of my fellows circled me, sniffing loudly, saying the fish smell lingered yet. I thought about breaking the rule about no stick work without the training mistress in the yard, but Ahuda settled that for me. She arrived unnoticed. She knocked the feet from under two of them and raised dust from the quilted jackets of two more with her split bamboo stick. Even with padding and her armed only with bamboo they would show ugly bruises—she was that good.

"You think you wouldn't've been taken last night?" she asked them. "Not even when they hit you like this?" Her baton went sideways into Hilyard's ribs. He collided with Verene, tumbling down on top of her. "Or this?" She got a second-year Dog named Phelan in her next blow, thwacking him over the shoulders. She swept the baton so fast I never saw it move, slamming Phelan behind the knees. He yelped. We had no padding there. I winced as Phelan pitched forward.

Quick as that she jumped over him, her baton headed straight for my gut. I blocked it, holding my baton vertical and two-handed. I jammed my knee up into her side. She wasn't there, of course. She never is. Her baton slammed the side of my left knee. She was nice about it, though. I stumbled, but I didn't drop.

On she went to Ersken. She showed everyone in the yard that it wasn't wise to laugh at someone who got taken by surprise. That afternoon I would have sold an eye to be as good as she was. I loved her. She left them with no breath to laugh.

After, when we had washed and climbed into our uniforms, Ersken walked over and hugged me one-armed about the shoulders. I looked into his blue eyes and smiled. Ersken handled my shyness from our first day by ignoring it. He liked to hug and stand with an arm about a mot. We mots got used to it. We even treated him the same. I used to wonder how Ersken, with his soft brown curls and gentle eyes, would fare as a Dog. Then when we were called in on a riot at Outwalls Prison, he worked as hard and as tough as any of us, putting new-learned fighting skills to use. He could be strong at need.

He didn't need it just now. "Fishpuppy's going to wear off, Beka," he told me. "The first time you startle them, they'll forget it entire. Besides, if it hadn't been you, it would've been me. I went full-front in the gutter last night. I'd've been Slimepuppy for certain, if not for you."

I giggled and gave him a quick hug back, then slid free of his kind arm. I wouldn't want anyone thinking I could not stand on my own.

My welcome inside the kennel was as cheerful as at training. The Dogs hooted and laughed when they saw me. "Hello, Fishpuppy," called Jewel. "Guess you'll remember that Rats have lookouts now, eh?"

Someone yelled, "Fish for supper, everyone?" Even Ahuda grinned as the others laughed and whistled.

I ground my teeth and saw my Dogs. Tunstall beckoned me over. When I fell in next to him, I heard Goodwin sniff the air. I looked at the floor.

Then she said, "A kennel is no place for a cat, Fishpuppy."

I asked him to stay home! Yet here he was, seated

right in front of Goodwin, looking up at her with his whiskers forward in his cat smile.

"Guardswoman, I *swear* I didn't bring him." I felt sweat trickle down my back. "I *swear* by the shield of Mithros—"

Tunstall put a hand on my shoulder. "Don't call Mithros into a small matter with a cat, even a purple-eyed one, Cooper. I believe you."

You would *not* believe me if I told you the truth, I thought. You would not believe if I said a Great God might be the only one who could tell you anything about Pounce!

Goodwin crouched and tickled my traitor cat under the chin. "You know you're a handsome fellow, don't you?"

Tunstall leaned down slightly to whisper to me, "She likes cats."

"I heard that," she said. Pounce leaned into her scratching hand. "What's not to like, small lord?" she asked him. "Discreet, clean, following your own course in life. You take commands from no one, not even Fish-puppies."

I winced. Pounce, the nasty thing, leaped onto Goodwin's shoulder.

"Well!" she said, and actually laughed. She straightened, Pounce riding her shoulder as he did mine. "It seems he's determined to go with us."

He knows who to grease to get his way. This time he chose Goodwin as the one to convince that he had the right to trot along with us like the four-legged dogs some pairs took with them. I could see those dogs from the corners of my eyes. They sat and watched my cat with mild interest. None of them showed any signs that they might chase him.

"Muster up!" bellowed Ahuda. She looked as crisp as if she hadn't just spent the last hour thrashing us. Everyone formed ranks. "First item. No word on Crookshank's great-grandchild from the assigned pairs on the three watches. Goodwin and Tunstall got some conversation there, including words with the grandmother and the mother. Nothing useful, but there may be more where that came from.

"Second item. Tonight's collection night. Birch and Vinehall, check each coin as it goes in your Happy Bag. No more counterfeits. Hobble anyone who slips fakes into your Bag. The rest of you, keep an eye on your coins, too."

I could see the two Dogs she had mentioned turn deep red with shame. Not only had they brought useless coin to the kennel, but counterfeiters were worse than murderers. They could turn a kingdom's money to trash in weeks if they weren't caught.

"Well, you curs aren't filling Happy Bags sitting on your rumps," Ahuda snapped. "Muster out. Not you, Goodwin, Tunstall. Master Fulk has time for you now."

I didn't miss the trade of sour faces between my partners. I didn't blame them, either. "I had to ask for him," Goodwin said. She sounded almost ashamed. "If only so no one thinks we're holding back what rightfully ought to go in the Happy Bag for the split. You still have the sparkly, Fishpuppy?"

I dug it out of my pocket and offered it to her. She waved it off. "Give it to Fulk. Come on."

The three of us (and Pounce) went into the small office that served the mage on duty. There was Fulk, perched at his desk on a chair that guaranteed he would be head and shoulders above any working Dog. Mage Fulk was a nasty, grubby little man even on duty. He'd not shaved his gray and brown whiskers; his curling brown and gray hair looked like it hadn't been washed in a week or ten. It was his eyes I liked the least: green and full, too moist, with brown stains under them, like he never slept.

No, I disliked his eyes secondmost. It was his roaming hands, with their pinching and stroking fingers, I disliked even more. Every girl runner and trainee did. I'd heard more than one junior Dog complain of him, too.

I kept to the back, letting Tunstall stand between me and the desk.

"Well? Where is it?" Fulk demanded. "I haven't got all night."

I offered the stone to Goodwin again, but she

jerked her head toward the mage. The look in her eyes said I'd best not vex her by hesitating.

"You let a *trainee* hold this thing?" Fulk made the word sound dirty. Then he smirked. "Trainee Fish-puppy, at that."

"We do when it's *our* trainee." Tunstall had such a warm voice, it was strange to hear it go cold. "And whatever we Dogs might call each other, you're not a Dog, Fulk. Give him the stone, Cooper."

I stepped up (I couldn't make my Dogs look bad, not when Tunstall had spoken for me) and put the stone on the desk. Quick as a snake, Fulk grabbed my wrist. He smiled into my eyes, his fingers rubbing my arm. I went still, thinking of the punishment I might get if I pinched his wrist until he bled.

"Let her go, Fulk." Goodwin's voice was iron. The mage and I both looked at her. "Touch her again and I'll start an investigation on you for continued breaches of the Goddess's Law protecting women. I've heard whispers. Mayhap it's time I looked to see if there's anything behind them."

Fulk let me go. I looked at Tunstall, entirely confused.

He gave me a smile. "At the last eclipse, the Mother of Starlight temple chose Magistrates. Goodwin's now the Goddess's Magistrate for the Lower City. She signs a writ, and the warrior mots with the sickles come for him."

Fulk grabbed the sparkly stone with fingers that shook. He released some bit of crimson light that sank into it. "I am a mage with power of my own, and the protection of the King," he muttered, but he was sweating. Tiny sparks of light leaped from the stone, then dropped back into it. He held it up. From the look in his eyes, we were forgotten.

He produced more red fire. It slithered over the stone and dripped to his desk. He muttered and passed his hand over the rock, his palm trailing red light. The stone shimmered, then went dark. "Valueless in terms of coin. A curiosity. I will test it further, then report to my Lord Provost. You Dogs are dismissed." He looked at us and frowned. "I'm keeping it. Aren't you supposed to be making collections?"

Pounce leaped onto his back from behind his chair. Fulk yelled and thrashed, dropping the stone and breaking a couple of the jars on his desk. He scrambled after the stone. So did I, fearing that it might be fouled by the oil that spilled from the jars. The stone skipped from Fulk's reaching fingers, spun onto the ancient floor, and dropped through an empty knothole in a plank. There was no telling where it had gone.

Fulk *screamed.* "That cat! Who let it in here? I loathe cats!" He sneezed. "Get out! I must make a summoning spell. . . . Take that disgusting animal with you!"

Despite the jumping and shouting and the leak of

magical things, I had to duck my head to hide a smirk. All Corus knew Fulk couldn't Summon. If he could, he might have his own work as a mage, not kennel work.

Then I thought on the lost stone. I liked it. It was the best of the Lower City, ordinary enough, with tiny specks of real beauty where you would never seek it. It was gone. Like as not, some four-legged rat was carrying it off to impress his lady rat.

We left Fulk's office, Pounce leading the way.

"What was going on in there?" Sergeant Ahuda wanted to know. "If you killed him, you get to find us a new one."

"He's alive and whining," Goodwin said. "We're tired of playing with the mage. We're off to the Court of the Rogue."

Goodwin and Tunstall were silent as we walked into the street. Pounce left us. Seeing my Dogs slip their batons from their belts to carry them two-handed, I did the same. As they settled into the walk that must be in their bones, I calmed down and began to think. With my brain working, I scarce noticed the calls of "Fish-puppy" from some of the folk we passed. The thought that had been waiting for my attention bobbed to the surface. Did my Dogs notice the thing that I had seen? The light was very bad in Fulk's lair. I was the only one standing close to him.

Surely they had seen it.

Still, my duty was plain. I cleared my throat.

"Speak up, Puppy," Goodwin said. She never took her eyes from the faces around us. Tunstall kept his on the windows above.

"Um—he lied," I said. "Fulk did. He knew something big about that stone."

"You're good at observing," Lord Gershom had told me often enough. "Tell people what you see. A good Dog trusts what she observes."

I had to believe my lord knew what he was talking about. I swallowed the lump in my throat. "Fulk came all over greedy. He wanted the stone, and he didn't want us to know it was worth sommat." I could feel my face turn red and blessed the shadows. I finished with a mumble. "At least, that's how I think it."

Goodwin and Tunstall halted, so I halted as well. Then they did an odd thing. Goodwin dug in her belt purse, and Tunstall put out his hand. Goodwin put a coin into it. Tunstall flipped it in the air, caught it, tucked it into his pocket, and turned to look at me. "I bet her a five-copper piece you'd picked that up."

Goodwin turned, too, her arms folded over her chest. "He's being nice. I also bet you wouldn't have the guts to tell us. So I was twice wrong. Yes, we saw."

I took a tiny breath of relief. It would have been very bad for me, then, if I'd kept quiet. They'd have thought me either too stupid to watch Fulk's expression or too shy to do as I was told and report to my Dogs.

Tunstall ran his fingers over his short-trimmed

beard. "Otterkin said there was nothing to the stone."

"She's the same as Fulk," Goodwin answered. "If she could do more than charm mice from her flour, she wouldn't be a Dog. Fulk nearly wet himself when that sparkler lit up." She shook her head. "Curse it the stone was lost. Gods know what's under the kennel. Snakes, maybe. Mud that slithers clean to the river. The place has been here since the first King's reign—"

I heard a familiar yowl, blocked by something. My cat made that sound when he was truly pleased with himself. I looked for him. Pounce trotted between my feet and dropped something on my left boot.

Slowly Tunstall bent and picked it up. I didn't dare move as he used his water bottle to rinse cellar slime and who knew what else from the sparkly rock. I knew the look that Goodwin and Tunstall gave first me, then my cat. It was the same look I often felt on my face when Pounce did something uncanny.

"He's *just* a cat? You're no mage, or anything?" Goodwin asked me after she'd been quiet for too long. "Don't look at me, just answer, Cooper."

"I found him in my Lord Provost's stable loft, Guardswoman," I said, being as polite as I could. "He was a purple-eyed kitten. And you'd have heard if I was a mage."

"He does strange things often, does he?" Tunstall asked.

"Often enough, sir," I replied. I picked my cat up.

"Were there portents when you were born?" Tunstall sounded as if he asked a normal question. "Eclipses, eagles in the birth chamber, things like that?"

I was so startled I looked up at him. He seemed more like an owl than ever, though I never heard of an owl whose eyes twinkled with a joke. "My papa lost a copper noble piece, betting I'd be a boy. Mama says it was the last big coin Papa ever had."

Goodwin took the stone from Tunstall and dried it on her tunic. "Why don't you and—"

"Pounce," I said.

"Pounce," she replied. "Why don't you two guard this for a while? Whilst Tunstall and me see if someone trustworthy can tell us about it. Because now we know a thing. If Fulk wants this bad enough to lie and keep it to himself, then mayhap Crookshank's grandson Herun was right. Mayhap there is money in these things, and Crookshank is up to something."

"And maybe got his grandson killed," Tunstall said with a nod.

"Step closer and put the cat down," Goodwin ordered. As I obeyed, she bent to adjust her boot and slipped the stone to me. I tucked it into my breeches pocket as I straightened whilst Goodwin told Pounce what a good fellow he was. No one on the street would know I had the stone.

"Now. Let's get to work, girls," Tunstall said. "Time to shake the tree."

Other Dogs collect Happy Bags from each business that wants to know otherwise ill-paid Dogs will watch over them with diligence. Tunstall and Goodwin gathered none of those. They called only on the Rogue, at the Court of the Rogue. We walked on west of the waking Nightmarket and the Market of Sorrows, where the slaves were sold. I hate it. The smell makes my tripes cramp. Too many families around Mutt Piddle Lane come here to sell extra children to make a little money, if they don't try illegal sales for more.

Up Koskynen Street my Dogs and I turned away from Sorrows, headed deeper into the part of the Lower City called the Cesspool, where Mutt Piddle is. There are no street torches here, except those provided by drinking houses, outdoor gambling, and brothels. Houses are kept together with rope and magic charms. The pigs that root in street garbage are rail-thin. Hard and hungry folk with nowhere else to go hold the Cesspool's streets after dark.

Children swarmed us, begging for a copper. Once, I'd been among them. Now they surrounded me, thinking I was new meat. I twirled my baton from the thong around my wrist and swept it around me in two half circles, moving them back. "You crew don' go flappin' your ticklers my way," I told them softly in Cesspool cant. "I'm no more an eye for you than the Ladymoon."

They wasn't used to hearing their own gab from a Dog. They scampered.

My Dogs turned to watch me, their faces a study. "You do that very well," Goodwin said.

I looked down.

"Fishpuppy, I'm talking to you." There was a warning in her voice.

I met her eyes. "Eight year we lived on Mutt Piddle Lane, Guardswo—"

"Goodwin," she corrected me. "I suppose you have family around here still?"

"Yes, Guar—Goodwin. My Granny, a few blocks from here."

"I was told something of the kind," she said finally. "But it's one thing to hear the gossip and another to hear your own Puppy talk like a Cesspool Rat. How many more secrets have you got, Cooper?"

I thought of the corner dust spinners. Mistress Noll had already hinted to them about the pigeons. "Very few, Goodwin."

"Good. I hate secrets. Don't talk Cesspool cant anymore. You're a Dog, not a Rat." She set out again, Tunstall beside her, Pounce and me behind.

Half a block west on Festive Lane was a big black stone house. It had been a noble's place once, when the city was new. As the nobles moved to other places, merchants had taken it. When they moved on, it had served as a courthouse for a time, then a kennel. For a long while it was home to dozens of poor families. Now guards in leather armor stood watch around the ten-foot-high wall, crossbows trained on the open ground in front of them. Torches blazed in iron holders all around the wall and on the building inside. Guards on the gate opened it to let us through without so much as a challenge.

The Rogue expected us.

Inside the house, we walked down a hall filled with petitioners, armsmen on the watch for trouble, thieves, rushers, them that sell their bodies—mots and coves—and the children of the folk who share the building with the Rogue Kayfer. Under the dirt and smoke stains, I could see the place must have been beautiful once. Someone went to trouble carving out the stone columns and wooden moldings. Now both were chipped, scratched, and smoke-stained.

A lean spintry in a loincloth and not much else decided to amuse himself by teasing the Puppy. Surely he knew I was too busy, and too poor, for his services, but he beckoned to me, flexing hard chest muscles. I looked away. It was a *very* tight loincloth.

"She's on duty, my buck," Goodwin said. Did she ever miss *anything*? "Find yourself another playmate."

"I'll settle for you, flower," he said, giving her a going-over with his eyes. "I love full-blown roses, who know what a man is for."

"I have a man—a *real* man. One who doesn't break when I play with him." When she grinned, all her teeth flashed. The spintry shrugged and moved off.

I couldn't imagine Goodwin having a man.

Then I saw a familiar face, one I never thought to see in the Court. I cleared my throat.

Tunstall glanced at me and saw where I looked. He poked Goodwin before he strolled over to Mistress Noll. "Grandmother, I'm shocked!" he said, bending down to kiss her cheek. "What brings you to so nasty a place?"

"Maggots in my flour. My merchant says the Rogue buys his best now," she said, her face sour. "Taking advantage of an old woman making her way in the world, I say. I left Gemma with my stall and come to make my plea to the Rogue to send some of the good flour my way. I'm sure he'll want something for his trouble. He always does."

"Alone?" Goodwin asked with a frown.

"Goddess, never!" Mistress Noll pointed to just inside the hall. One of her sons and another cove were talking with one of the guards in quiet voices. "Yates and his friend came with me. It's good to have one son who still lives in Corus." She lowered her voice. "How did your visit with Crookshank go?"

"As well as you'd expect," Tunstall replied.

"I heard Beka here got to see her old friend Tansy." Mistress Noll's eyes twinkled as she looked up at Tunstall.

"You knew Beka and Tansy Lofts were friends?" Goodwin asked.

"They used to play on my street," Mistress Noll said. "That Tansy was a pert gixie, wasn't she, Beka? But pretty as a flower even then. We all knew she'd catch some lucky cove's eye. Ah. I think Yates finally got the right lad to bribe."

To be sure, Yates was beckoning to her. She went to him. I looked at the floor. Didn't Mistress Noll have words with Tansy once or twice? And what if she had? Mistress Noll's a mother. She'd speak kindly of a mot who'd lost her first child. Anyone would.

"Let's go, Puppy. Time to show off that uniform," Goodwin told me. "Chin up. We're here in the name of the Lord Provost."

She must have guessed that would be the spell to put iron in my spine and bring my head high. I could walk bold for the man who had taken my family out of the Cesspool.

Pounce kept well back as we entered what must have been the great hall in the days when nobles had lived here. Now it was the Rogue's throne room. The chiefs sat at tables near one end of the room, their doxies and rushers around them. On a platform inches above the floor, at a level with the broad hearth, was a fellow I guessed to be the Rogue himself—Kayfer Deerborn. He sat on a throne made of cobbled-together crates, wooden barrels, and pieces of furniture. There he talked with a brown-skinned Carthaki woman in breeches and a shirt. There were tattoos around her eyes and ruby studs on the rim of one ear. She had the look of a slave trader to me. Two more Carthakis waited just off the platform at her back. The one in a slave's collar held the leashes of two big mastiffs. He was even more muscled than the mastiffs.

Waiting there for Kayfer to notice us, I took the chance to fix him in my memory. All the Cesspool's older women said how broad his shoulders were at one time, how blue his eyes, how quick his smile. I saw a flabby cove in his early forties with a smooth arch of nose who was losing his short brown hair. The eyes were very blue, with plenty of lines around them. He wore a black pearl drop as big as my thumb in one ear, a silver hoop in the other, and a gold ring with a sapphire the size of a pigeon's egg on his right index finger. There were tales about how he got that gem.

The smile was well enough.

Kayfer clapped the slave trader on the shoulder. She unhooked a purse from her belt, but she wasn't so rude as to hand it to him. Instead one of Kayfer's mots guided her to a small room on the other side of the hearth. The trader's guard, slave, and dogs followed. The Rogue beckoned to one of his chiefs who was standing.

"We get to wait," Tunstall said, his lips barely moving. "It's how he proves he's still the Rogue."

"Some Rogue," a familiar voice drawled. We looked to our right. The bone-pale cove from last night and his two ladies sat against the wall with the rushers who served the Rogue and his chiefs. "Sits on his arse like a sarden king and bribes others to stand for him. I'd hope for someone livelier in charge here."

Goodwin glanced at Kayfer. He was whispering with the chief who had gone up to him. Tunstall ambled over to one of the female chiefs, Ulsa. Her district was Prettybone, across the river. Ulsa grinned and nudged out a chair for him with her foot. He took it.

Goodwin sat on her hunkerbones in front of the pale cove. His right-hand mot, the small one who was as sleek as a cat, sat at his side with her ankles crossed, fingering her gown. I saw her hand could reach her knife or a curious series of coins knotted in crimson thread that hung from her belt. These looked like magic. The big blond mot at the man's left only leaned back against the wall, one hand dangling from her propped-up knee.

"Now, laddybuck," Goodwin said, friendly as a rat about to eat her young, "why don't you tell me what kind of lively you're looking for? I'll direct you where to find it, away from Corus." She smiled, but it wasn't a nice smile.

He gave her the same kind of smile. Then he looked at Tunstall, who had made the Prettybone chief laugh. Lastly he looked at me. I turned my eyes away.

The cat mot nudged him with her shoulder. "Stop it, Rosto," she said. "Fidget someone who fidgets you back." She nodded to Goodwin. "He's Rosto the Piper. I'm Kora, and that's Aniki." The blond who looked to be a swordswoman raised a lazy hand in greeting. "We heard life was more . . . interesting . . . in Corus, so here we are." She gave Goodwin a friendlier smile by far than the one Goodwin gave her.

"Scavengers always come looking when they hear of a feast. So far it's been long put off," Goodwin told them. "Kayfer—his chiefs—have done away with any challengers."

"Oh, we're not looking to challenge," Rosto said. "We hope to be entertained. Scanra was that bare of entertainment."

"Here's a fine-looking cat," Aniki said. Pounce had arrived. He sauntered up to her. "A very handsome, elegant—" She gulped.

"Purple eyes," Kora said quietly. "Odd-colored eyes in a creature mean it's god-marked." She leaned forward and stroked my cat, who butted his head against her palm. He is soft on mages.

"He's the Puppy's," Goodwin said, watching them. "He's a clever beast."

Pounce gave the ripple of *mrt*s that was his laugh, though I was the only one who knew it.

Rosto looked past us and raised his eyebrows. "Hello. What's this?"

In walked Crookshank, gaunt, unshaven, hollow-eyed. His narrow leggings were wrinkled, as if he'd slept in them. His knee-length tunic was little better. There were stains on it, too. His black hair was snarled. Two of his manservants followed him, empty sword and dagger scabbards at their belts. The guards had taken their weapons.

Tunstall left off talking to Ulsa and came to stand by us. Goodwin rose, too. I placed myself at Goodwin's elbow, making sure I did not block anyone's view. Aniki, who was nearest to me, winked.

"Kayfer, you two-faced scummer, we was *partners!*" screeched Crookshank. "Even a sucking leech like you shoulda been content wi' your share, you greedy-gutted spintry!"

The Rogue stood on his platform, rubbing the top of his head. "I beg you, Ammon, calm down," he said, his voice soothing. "Whatever your grievance wi' me, we can surely sort it out."

"Grievance? You call my great-grandson's murder a grievance?" Crookshank yelled, pointing at Kayfer, his bony finger quivering. "What kind of monster takes a wee child from his family and murders 'im for profit? Did you think you could hide behind notes smuggled into my house and I would not suspect you?"

Kayfer stepped down off his platform, both hands out, his face as sorrowful as a professional mourner's. "Ammon, I know it is your grief which makes you say these things."

"Butter just melts on 'is tongue, doesn't it," Rosto murmured.

"Bad laddie," Aniki told him. "Hush. Listen to a master work."

I glanced at Goodwin and saw the corners of her mouth twitch. I began to think mayhap she liked these three impudent rascals from the north.

"Of course it's my grief, Stormwings take your eyes!" screamed Crookshank. "Your Shadow Snake murdered my Rolond, when he was not in our business!" Tears rolled down his face. I almost felt bad for him. Then I remembered that he'd kicked my cousin Lilac's family from their lodgings when she was having a bad time, and Lilac lost her baby.

"Ammon, the Shadow Snake is a bogey to frighten children." The Rogue's voice was as smooth as warm oil. "You must be cracked spun with grievin', to say I'd deal with a monster out of tales. And as for me of all folk sendin' anyone t' harm a *child* . . ." His voice cracked when he said "child." "Ammon, I swear on the names of my own grandbabies, I did not do it." Kayfer's blue eyes were steady on Crookshank's brown ones. They did not waver. Not a muscle of his mouth twitched to give away a lie. I supposed the Rogue would have to be the realm's best liar, but I believed him even so. Kayfer went on, "In the name of Bright Mithros and the Goddess herself, I swear it. I would never bring such harm to any family of yours. We depend on each other, old friend. I never conjured up a nightmare like the Snake. I never gave the task of murderin' your little cove t' any of my chiefs. My chiefs would never do such a thing at my biddin'."

"Curst right we would not!" cried Dawull, the huge, redheaded chief who had the Waterfront District on both sides of the river. Kayfer shot him a glare, but Dawull only smiled. I wondered when Dawull might decide that a Rogue's take from all the chiefs might be better than most of the take from only Waterfront District.

Crookshank spat at Kayfer's feet. "Liar." He glared at everyone in the room. "You're leeches, living off the rest of us and feeding this oathbreaker!" His voice rasped with exhaustion. "Look at the lot of you!" He swung his hands wide. "Sitting here lapping up drink and food like caged birds. I curse him. If you take his orders and protect his throne, then I curse you in Rolond's name. You best mind your children!"

"Crookshank, you're mad!" Ulsa cried. "There is no such creature as the Shadow Snake!"

Kayfer snapped his fingers, calling his rushers. Four of them seized Crookshank's guards. Another grabbed the old man by the arm. Kayfer stepped closer to Crookshank. "It is terrible, what's happened. We all are sick with sorrow for it," he said, his voice quieter.

"But why you, Ammon? Why might someone callin' himself Shadow Snake target your house, your family? What tidbit has come into your hands of late? Why have you not offered a taste to your Rogue?"

Crookshank lunged at Kayfer with a knife he'd pulled from the folds of his tunic. The chiefs jumped to their feet with a roar, trying to get to the Rogue before his throat got cut.

But it was Rosto who got there first—he was a blur, as quick as Sergeant Ahuda. Had he been waiting for it? Or had he just been ready to move at need, like the Sergeant was always telling us to do?

"Quick little spintry, isn't he?" Aniki asked, her voice just reaching us Dogs. "You should see him swarm up a house wall. A thing of beauty, he is."

"I'll pass on the house wall, thanks so much," Goodwin replied, her voice the same kind of quiet. "I'd hate to arrest such a pretty fellow."

"He promises to be interesting, if he manages to live," Tunstall murmured as Rosto plucked the dagger from Crookshank's hand and gave it to one of Kayfer's rushers. Only after Rosto searched Crookshank did he let the old man up. He was very good. Those who didn't have the same point of view as we Dogs would not have seen Rosto slip something into his own left boot top.

"Oh, well, *living*," Kora said. "Aniki, a silver—

what's that local coin? A silver noble that the big red-headed chief is the first to offer Rosto a job."

"Done," replied Aniki.

"Two silver nobles it's Ulsa, the chief of Pretty-bone," Tunstall said without turning to look at them. "She likes handsome coves that know what they're doing." He glanced back at them. "Even more if they have pretty mots who also know what they're doing."

Aniki reached up, offering her palm. "Bet."

Tunstall turned and clasped it. "Bet."

Rosto was sauntering back to us, hands in his pockets.

"Puppy, fetch," Goodwin ordered me in a voice that just reached my ears.

I couldn't believe she would say that to me, after the night before. Then I steeled myself. I knew what she wanted. I had to redeem myself. Goddess, please don't let me fumble, I prayed, turning my baton in my fingers. I went to rearrange it on my belt. As Rosto drew level with me, I dropped it on the floor and lunged for it, right across his shins. Quick as he was, with my body in the way he didn't see I'd put my baton between his feet. Down he went as I turned, making us a tangle of baton, Puppy, and Rosto.

"Dear, if you'd asked, I'd've considered it," he muttered as he tried to undo us. "You're a pretty thing when you look a cove in the eye."

I stammered apologies, seemingly trying to get my

baton untangled from his legs. That was a trick to manage, with him being so nimble. He almost freed himself twice before I thought we'd been at it long enough that he'd be too flustered to think to check his boot top soon. By the time we stood, Dawull of Waterfront led the guards as they dragged the screaming Crookshank from the hall. The chiefs now went to Kayfer to congratulate him on his escape. Goodwin came over to straighten my clothes and scold me for my clumsiness. As she did, I passed her the leather-wrapped lump that had been in Rosto's boot.

"Now, Clary, the Pup can't help it," Tunstall said, watching us. "Her second day, after all. She's yet to get used to things breaking out sudden-like." He knew something was up. I saw it in his eyes. I met his gaze and raised my brows, flicking my eyes beyond his shoulder to warn him we were about to have company. Goodwin saw me do it and turned. So did Tunstall.

Kayfer nodded to them as he passed us. He offered his hand to Rosto, whose mots fussed over him, tugging at his clothes. With the Rogue standing there, they stepped back to take positions just behind Rosto. Aniki hooked her hands in her sword belt. Kora folded hers before her, lowering her long lashes.

Rosto took the hand that Kayfer offered. "The least I could do, Majesty. I saw the knife's shape against the old cuckoo's tunic. Sad work your guards done searching 'im, you ask me."

Kayfer's smile had a lot of friendliness in it. "You've a good eye. Are you and your gixies here lookin' for work? My gate crew goes for a swim tonight, unless they convince me they can make their way back into my good graces as wounded mumpers."

I winced. A choice between death and life as a maimed beggar was a hard one.

"Majesty, you're not talking of breaking the law in violence before three Dogs, are you?" Tunstall asked. His voice was so polite he might have been speaking of temple services. "We can't have that on our watch. Not when we're standing right here."

Kayfer looked up at Tunstall and laughed. "Never a bit, Mattes Tunstall. Why don't you and Goodwin come settle our business. Young Rosto and I can talk later. Maybe extra sweetenin' will make it into this week's Happy Bag, to assure you I'd never do violence with the Dogs out." He glanced at me and then pinched my cheek. "Leave the Puppy. She doesn't look like she'll last."

I clenched my jaw so tight I heard my teeth creak.

He led Goodwin and Tunstall back to his precious throne. I took the rest position, baton gripped two-handed before me, my feet braced a forearm's width apart. Those who'd heard Kayfer enjoyed a laugh at my expense before going about their other business.

"A nice trick, lifting that pouch from me." Rosto

stood at my elbow. "If you're a Fishpuppy like the gossip says, it's because you're so slippery. I don't suppose you'd take a silver noble to tell me what it is, once your Dogs have a look? From the feel it's gems, but it never hurts to be certain."

I forgot myself enough to glare at him. His eyes were mocking. I looked away just as quick as I'd glared. It was one thing to trip the cove on Goodwin's orders, and quite another to talk to him. Besides, I was on duty.

"Not taking offense over a bit of bribery, are you?" There was mockery in his voice as well as his eyes. "On the very night your Dogs are here to collect their bribes from the Rogue?"

I glared at the floor this time. I expected a cityman to talk so foolish, not an experienced rusher. "That's different. That's for all the work every one of us does, to keep the streets orderly. *You're* asking me to sell out my Dogs."

I saw his booted feet rock back on his heels.

"Hel-lo! It has a bark *and* a bite!" He sounded startled. "Here I was thinking you're a mousy little bit. But you're not mousy, are you?"

Seeing the start of movement, I blocked his arm before his slap touched my face. I turned my hand around to grip the inside of his wrist. When I found the gap between two of the tendons there, I dug my thumbnail deep into it.

"Ow," he said, trying to yank free. I'd put my hand so the harder he tugged, the deeper I could thrust my thumbnail.

"Rosto, you take shy as fearful. Why would a coward become a Dog? There's easier ways for a pretty gixie to make a living." Aniki propped one elbow on Rosto's collarbone and leaned on him like he was a convenient post. She smiled down at me. "Normally he's not thick about mots, but he's slow when they're not in love with him. Me and Kora had to knock him around until he got us figured out. Say you're sorry, Rosto, and don't try to bribe the nice Puppy again."

"I'm sorry, all right? I'm *bleeding.*"

I had broken his skin. I took my hand away and wiped my thumb on my breeches. That was the good thing about black. It didn't show stains.

It was easier to look into Aniki's smiling blue eyes than Rosto's. I told her, "Two days as a Dog and I've my first bribe offer. I think it's a record."

She laughed and cuffed Rosto lightly. "She's *shy,* cabbage head, not stupid."

Rosto had a handkerchief pressed to the wound I'd left in his wrist. "So I'm learning. What's your name, then, shy-not-stupid Puppy?"

I told him my name. There was no reason not to. Besides, I had a feeling that I'd see these three again. If Kayfer didn't decide it was to his advantage to kill such talented new people, they might rise high in the Court of the Rogue.

I saw movement at my side. Kora stepped in next to me, cuddling Pounce in her arms. "I heard folk say last night that your mother was an herbalist." She had a soft, pretty voice and demure eyes. "So then you might be able to tell me where I could get good dried and fresh herbs, the reliable sellers? We're still learning our way around. With so many markets I hardly know where to look."

It was odd to speak of something innocent. Odd, but nice. Rosto had an interest in the subject of herbs, more than I expected of a cove. He even argued with Kora about the benefits of dried chamomile against fresh for lightening hair. Aniki drifted away to play dice with some of the rushers.

"So, Cooper," Rosto said after Kora had thanked me, "how quick is this Rogue to wield the whip?" When I looked at him and waited, he explained, "That Crookshank fellow. What did the Rogue call him?"

"Ammon," I said. "That's his birth name, Ammon Lofts. In the streets he's Crookshank, scale and landlord."

"Ammon Lofts," Rosto said. "Him. Your Rogue daren't let him go unpunished, can he? Not after Master Lofts called Crookshank spits at his feet in front of his whole court."

I know as well as anybody Crookshank must pay for what he's done, but it's been three years since Kayfer pulled up and belted his own breeches. It was folly to say as much, though. "You'd have to ask the Rogue," I said at last. "How was it done in Scanra?"

"Right then and there," Rosto told me. "The one time I saw it done. Poor fool was drunk. Not that it stopped our Rogue." He went on with the story, with Kora to put in the bits he left out, about the Rogue for Scanra. At last my Dogs returned, their packs with the Happy Bags heavy on their backs. Rosto and Kora nodded goodbye as Pounce and I fell in behind them.

As we walked out of that house, I felt visible. The Rogue's Happy Bags had more than just the coin in bribes paid to the Jane Street kennel. They also held gems, fine statues, magical devices, and other items. Now we walked into the Cesspool with fortunes on the backs of my Dogs. They do this every week and live? The hair prickled on the back of my neck. Surely this was asking a great deal even from them.

Usually pairs took the Bags to collection points, where armed crews gathered the week's earnings to be split among the Dogs. Did we have such a crew? I wanted to ask. Or did we carry the Rogue's Bags alone, to make a point about his power in the Cesspool and ours? What if the Dogs thought that no one would dare try to rob the Rogue's own Bags?

"Stop sweating, Puppy," Goodwin told me as the

gates closed behind us. "It's a thing of pride, to go in there and come out on our own. The Rogue's always known that, if anything happens to the Dogs who call for the Happy Bags, his stronghold will be ash by dawn. Some laws a madman breaks. But we're not stupid."

A block away, five Dogs with horses waited for us. Three were mounted and armed with crossbows. I knew them: they were part of the guard who served my lord Gershom personally. Jakorn had taught me to use a crossbow. He grinned and nodded to me. The two guards on foot I knew from the Jane Street kennel. They took the packs from Tunstall and Goodwin with a little conversation, then looked at me.

"She manage her first visit with the Rogue and his milk-fed geldings?" asked one of them.

"She did well for us. We'll keep her," Tunstall told them. "Run along, children. We have work to do yet. And Ahuda doesn't like to wait."

They trotted off into the darkness of the Lower City. Goodwin was still watching them when she asked me, "So did he try to bribe you? Rosto?"

"Yes," I replied. "He wanted to know what was in the thing he took from Crookshank."

"We'll have a look over supper," Tunstall said. "*Very* nice work with the baton, Cooper."

"I liked how you shielded it with your body, so he couldn't see you use it to tangle him up," Goodwin said. "You outthought him."

I shook my head, and Tunstall saw it. "You planned for him being better than you?" I nodded. "Smart Puppy," he said with approval. "You earned your supper again for the night."

"Well, she has a while till she gets it," Goodwin said, making sure her gorget was fastened. Tunstall was doing the same. "We've a way to go before we can think of eating." She pulled out the gloves tucked into her belt and put them on. They had mail stitched on the backs and palms. She then strapped her wrist guards over the edges of the gloves. Tunstall's gloves had metal straps on the back instead of mail, though he had mail over his palms.

Goodwin looked me over. "We need to get you a gorget, Cooper. And proper gloves. Leather isn't good enough in the Cesspool. Stick close to us for tonight."

"I'll see to the gear," Tunstall added. He clapped me on the shoulder. "It may take a couple of days. Should be quiet, with all their chiefs and rushers in for the Happy Bag, Cooper. They like to frolic in the Cesspool once Kayfer turns them loose, to show who's on top and who's low-down. Most folk will keep out of sight."

I soon realized that Tunstall's idea of a quiet night and mine are different. By the time we reached Mulberry Way, we'd stopped three robberies, two casual beatings, and two tavern brawls. At least, my Dogs did. I was ordered to stand off and watch. It was an honor, so neatly did they work. We hobbled no one. My Dogs found no one worth the trouble. They explained what they did as they did it, so I would learn. The robbers got a broken arm each, since they attacked only for coppers. They would pay more to healers than they had hoped to get from their victims, who fled as soon as my Dogs stepped in. In the cases of the beatings, Goodwin and Tunstall administered broken fingers to several of the rushers involved. They broke one rusher's hand, because he worked for a slave trader who liked to force folk to sell to him. Those victims ran away, too. In the case of the tavern brawls, my Dogs simply kicked everyone out.

They did let me hold on to two of a gang of boys who thought torturing a piglet was a night's fun. Pounce led the piglet away while Goodwin delivered businesslike paddlings with her baton. I gave her my captives when their turn for a lesson came. Those scuts would wish their mothers had taught them better, limping for some weeks after the unkind kiss of a Dog's weighted stick.

On we wandered. Most of what we saw up this way was owned by Crookshank, Tunstall said. Thousands of families had him for a landlord. He could be rich on their coin alone and never go near stolen goods.

"His greed don't stop." Goodwin said it with the strictness of a Mithran priest speaking for the good of our souls. "Could I but catch one of his bookkeepers and make him sing, we might be able to roll the monster up. Speaking of monsters, what was that gabble about the Shadow Snake?"

"I've been wondering about that myself," Tunstall said. "Crookshank's so cracked with grief he's making up babies'-tale creepies."

"He got the idea someplace," Goodwin said.

I'd been hearing a fight for the last moment as we walked along, a mot's shouts and children's shrieks. Then a cove bellowed. We heard crockery shatter in the building just to the left. Someone screamed, "Goddess save them, she's got a blade! Come on, Jack, stop 'er afore she does yer babes!"

A mot yelled, "She's curst near done *him*!"

A shutter flew open on the ground floor. A cove leaned out. He looked around and saw us. "She says she'll crop the littles' nobs, an' she's a knife in her hand! Two stories up!"

Goodwin and Tunstall traded looks. No Dog likes to be caught in a family brawl, but if the neighbors were right, this mot was threatening to cut her babes' heads off. They charged through the house's doorless entry and up the rickety steps, me at their heels. We had to shove our way past clumps of neighbors at both landings. None of them wanted to get caught in this, not when knives were involved. They did point to the door where the worst of the noise came through.

It was the babble of children pleading for their

mother to stop, to be nice. They told her they loved her. She screamed she would cut their throats if they didn't shut their gobs. A cove was telling her to calm down.

"In the name of the King's law!" Tunstall shouted as he tried the latch. The door wasn't locked. He shoved it open, showing up a middling-sized main room. Here was their hearth and table and the children's pallets. The little ones stood in a corner on the far side of the window, two girls and a toddling boy in a dirty napkin. Their papa stood closer to us, near the tiny hearth in the wall. Between them, at the center of the room, was the woman. She had a long knife in her hand, and she swayed where she stood. I could see her small brown eyes, flicking quick like a bird's from Goodwin to Tunstall. My Dogs spread apart to make it look like she could dart between them to reach the door. I was in that opening, but she might think she could shove by me.

The oldest of the little ones had a black eye. Another had a scratched face. The cove had blood on his face from cuts around one eye. His lip was split and his patched shirt ripped. From the broken crockery at his feet, she had thrown a jug at him. I knew by the vinegar and mint smell that it had held hotblood wine.

Goodwin sighed and scratched her head. "Mistress, what do you think you're doing?" she asked. "You've gone and upset your neighbors. We can't have you disturbing the King's peace. Your man will need a healer for those cuts, and you know what healers cost these days. Added to that, you'll have the cost of the Magistrate's fine. Don't make it worse for yourself. Put the blade down. Come with us."

The mot replied with a suggestion so foul I was impressed.

Goodwin didn't even twitch. "That's very nice. The blade, Mistress— What's your name?"

She cursed us again.

"Orva," the cove told us wearily. "You've gone too far this time. Put down the knife and do as you're told."

I hadn't seen her other hand or guessed she might have something in it, like a little stone mortar they'd use for grinding herbs. I saw it now, when she threw it at her man's head. Tunstall knew it was there, because he caught it easily. And Goodwin knew that it was there and that Tunstall would catch it, because she lunged for Orva's arm, the one holding the knife.

The mot was quick enough to have been a good Dog. I saw her move as Goodwin lunged. Orva struck backhand, her fist turned sideways. She caught Goodwin with the butt of the hilt square on the hinge of the jaw. Goodwin dropped, her eyes rolled up in her head.

The children screamed. Then Tunstall said very quietly, "Orva. You struck a Dog with a blade."

She turned and leaped through the unshuttered window. I went after her. I didn't even think, or it might have occurred to me that I was jumping to a pair of broken legs or a broken back. It turned out this window opened onto stairs that went down the outside of the house. I hit on the landing with a jarring of my ankles. Orva was racing down those stairs. I scrambled to my feet and followed.

She took me through the Cesspool, alley by alley, through puddles of slop and hollows of mud. The only light leaked from the open doors of drinking dens and brothels. Hotblood wine, filled with herbs, kept Orva going long after a mere drunk would have dropped. I slipped and stumbled into a tumbledown fence somewhere behind the Court of the Rogue. Orva was nowhere in view. I blinked, listening for her running steps rather than trusting my eyes. I heard the rustle of cloth behind me and jumped away just as she thrust that knife through the gap in the fence behind me. She had circled around. I found the opening she used and darted through. She was off again, plunging between two dark houses.

I was closing the gap between us when she dove into the back door of a tavern. I followed, ignoring curses and swerving to avoid a cook chopping rats for stew meat. I dodged a serving girl who tried to smack me with a wooden tankard. In the common room Orva made for the door, jumping over drunks and showing her knife to the ones who didn't get the message.

I saw my chance and leaped onto the tables as a shortcut to the door. I ignored the yells of fury. I was a

Dog in pursuit. If these tosspots couldn't see my uniform under the muck, they could see the baton in my hand.

Orva was through the door just before I reached it. She slammed it shut. The bar on the inside thumped down the moment the slam shook it from its position. I wrestled the bar up and got the door open in time to see Orva turn a corner a half block away, where torches from a cockfight lit that part of the street.

She took me through another drinking den. The third time, I skidded around to the front door. When she came dashing through, I swung my baton around, straight into her middle. She doubled over, dropping the knife. I kicked it out of the way and wrenched one of her arms up behind her back.

"Kneel," I said between gasps for air. "I arrest you in the name of the King." As a Puppy, I wasn't really allowed to arrest someone, but I doubted that Orva knew as much.

She wailed. "I di'n' do nothin'. Why di'n' you lemme *go?*" She was even more out of breath than I was. Her head lolled on her neck.

"Orva, *you struck a Dog,*" I reminded the stupid drunken creature. I tightened my grip. "Now will you kneel, or will I dump you on your front?"

"I want to see my children," she whined.

With a sigh I levered my strength down on her captive arm. She had to kneel or get an elbow broken. I didn't want to use my baton, in case some looby decided to help her. As it was, people were coming out of the tavern and gathering on the street to watch.

Orva knelt, babbling about her little ones. I thought that if they and their papa had any sense, they would be halfway to Barzun by now. But I wouldn't bet a copper that papa and the little ones wouldn't beg the Magistrate to free Orva.

I tied her wrists with my rawhide cords, their first use. Then I used a pair of cords to tie her ankles so she could walk, but not so well that she wouldn't fall if she tried to run again. Not that I thought she might. Her legs trembled even worse than mine.

I looked at my surroundings. Mithros, we'd come almost to the North Gate! There was no point in going back to her house. Tunstall would have taken Goodwin in for care. He'd know I would report back to Jane Street if we were separated, so Jane Street was where we'd go. Orva was bound for the cages anyway.

I looked for the knife. Someone had taken it. "I want the blade and I want it *now*," I said, feeling more than a little cross. It was easier to talk with my face in shadow and a Dog's uniform, even a Puppy's, on my body. "It's evidence in a crime. In the King's name."

Some of the watchers chuckled. I gripped my baton hard. Did I have the strength to break a few heads like a good Dog, to make my point, or should I just let it go? Then, to my surprise, a little one came forward with the knife and offered it to me. "I di'n't mean no harm by't, Guardswoman," he (or maybe she) mumbled.

I swallowed an odd feeling in my throat. I'd never been called "Guardswoman" before. "All right, then," I said, sounding properly gruff in my own ears. "You've done your duty."

The child touched a knuckle to his, or her, forehead for respect and went back into the crowd.

Still feeling strange, maybe even proud, I poked Orva with my baton. "Walk," I told her. "And walk silent."

The crowd parted so we could pass through. Now that I was calming down, I could feel every bone in my feet, because each of them hurt. It was going to be a fearful long trip back to Jane Street.

It was well past suppertime and my belly was growling by the time I hauled Orva into the kennel. Only the threat of my baton and a ride partway on a chance-met wagon had brought her this far. She had the gall to drop to her knees and cry, "Thank the Goddess!" when we walked through the door. "I'm weary to death!"

I swore never to turn into one of those Dogs who hit their Rats as easy as talking to them. I was sore tempted, though.

We were halfway to Ahuda's desk before I thought to look for Goodwin and Tunstall. They were in the corner by the healers' room. The beds inside were full. Tunstall watched as a healer worked her magic on Goodwin's swollen face. Then all three of them turned to stare at me. Tunstall's mouth fell open. I looked around the room. Everyone there—Dogs on duty, visitors for those in the cages, hangers-on—gaped at me and my first captive Rat.

Then I heard Ahuda, high on her perch, say, "Great Mithros bless us, you actually *caught* her."

I was so startled I looked at the Sergeant. Wasn't catching her what I was supposed to do? "Sh-she hit a Dog with a blade," I stammered.

Tunstall came over. "And I didn't even have to say 'fetch.'"

"Here we were thinking you were naught but a Fishpuppy, and you turn out to be one stubborn little terrier." Ahuda was shaking her head as she opened the thick arrest book. *"Lockup!"* she yelled. "Rat coming in!"

"I want to see my children," Orva whined. "I want my Jack. He'll be tellin' you—"

"Shut your gob," said Ahuda. I thought I'd seen her at her worst when she dealt with us trainees. I was wrong. "You tell me nothin' in my kennel. Here, I am Queen Bitch, and you will muzzle yourself." She turned to the cage Dogs. "Get her out of my air—she stinks of hotblood wine. And make sure Cooper gets her cords back, *uncut.* If you have to cut them, give her good replacements." She turned to me now. "Cooper, you

don't leave till you get one or the other and sign my supply book to claim which. Cords cost money."

My knees were frightful wobbly, from work and from talking before all those pairs of eyes. "Yes, Sergeant."

Ahuda pursed her lips. "Sit, girl, before you fall. Over by the healers. Tunstall, get her a cup of that restorative tea, the one that tastes like hay."

I sat on one of the benches near the healers' room. Then I had to change positions. Tunstall was pointing me to a seat directly across from Goodwin and the healer who tended her jaw. I took a quick glance as I settled into the new place. A huge bruise went from Goodwin's cheekbone under her chin on that side, but there was no swelling.

The healer stood back and looked at it. "You'll be sore for some days, and you'll need to eat on the other side, but given you'd a cracked jaw and a knot the size of a walnut, you'd best not complain. You're lucky I do bones so well or you wouldn't talk for a week. What were you hit with, a hammer?"

"The hilt of a butcher knife," Tunstall said when Goodwin opened her mouth and winced. "I don't suppose you have it, Puppy."

Given all her whining and foot dragging, I'd needed the hand that didn't hold the baton to keep Orva moving. Thrusting the knife into my belt would have meant the tip pricked my thighs. I reached inside my tunic and fished it out. I'd prayed all the way to the kennel that I wouldn't fall and stab myself.

"Mithros," whispered Tunstall. "The thing's a pig sticker."

Goodwin smiled crookedly and beckoned for the knife. I gave it to her, hilt first. It was black, heavy wood at the hilt. The thing had been valuable once, before a thousand sharpenings had made the blade as thin as a lock pick. The healer whistled, looking at it. "The Mother blessed you tonight, Guardswoman. Had this struck you a little harder, your jaw might well have shattered beyond my skill."

Tunstall got my cup of tea. I looked at it, wishing I had the gumption to ask for food instead.

"You're starvin', an' so'm I," Goodwin said. "Knock that back, an' we'll get a proper supper."

"Soft foods for you," the healer warned Goodwin.

"May I feed our Puppy now?" Goodwin asked with frightful patience. "She d'serves a treat."

I looked at her, shocked.

"Don't worry," Tunstall reassured me. "She'll get over it eventually."

I hoped so. I couldn't have Goodwin changing her nature on me from day to day. I liked to know where I stood with people.

Most of the usual Dog trade had been and gone by the time we reached the Mantel and Pullet. Now my legs ached. I hoped it wasn't the run. As a message runner I had covered the city at a trot. I'd hate to think I was so out of trim. True, even a run from Unicorn District to the palace was not the same as chasing a half-mad female through the Cesspool, then dragging her back to Jane Street.

Tunstall beckoned one of the server girls over. "A quiet room," he said. Silver passed from his hand to hers. "No fuss about it," he added.

The server girl led us into a narrow hall. Along one side were four doors covered with flimsy curtains. She pointed us through the third. We ordered our food. Poor Goodwin requested pease porridge, which made the girl take a step back. Once she'd brought it all, she closed a wooden door behind the flimsy curtains.

"No magic in these rooms," Tunstall told me as he cut a thick slice of ham into tiny pieces. "The host is paid extra to make sure of it." He looked at Goodwin as she poked the contents of her bowl. "Mayhap you should go home after this, Clary, leave me'n Cooper to finish the night."

"Curst if I will," she muttered. "We'll go back to th' Cesspool. If I get t' break s'm heads, I'll cheer up."

"If you bang your jaw, you won't be cheery," Tunstall warned. "Cooper, take more of them parsnips. You need some meat on your bones."

"Mother hen," Goodwin said.

"Will you gabble till the giants return, or will you show us what that canny lad Rosto foisted from Crookshank?" Tunstall asked. Then, slowly and with great care, he buttered a fat roll bursting with nuts and raisins and ate it, making sounds of delight.

Goodwin swiftly took a spoonful of porridge, levered it back with her free hand, and released it like a catapult. The porridge flew to land on Tunstall's forehead.

I covered my mouth with both hands that I might not giggle. The toughest Dogs in the city still have some play in them!

Tunstall used an unbuttered piece of roll to wipe his forehead. He popped roll and porridge into his mouth. "*You've* been practicing," he mumbled with his mouth full.

Goodwin smirked and dug in her breeches pocket. "Don' torture me wi' what I can't eat, Mattes," she warned. "Not wi' my belly growlin' like menag'rie bears." She fetched out the leather pouch as Tunstall and me shoved plates aside. She spilled out five stones.

They were like the rock in my breeches pocket. When Tunstall drew the oil lamp closer, they showed brilliant flashes of color. One had a bulge of glasslike stuff. Within the glass were dark orange flecks, some clear patches, and a strip of deep, green blaze. One had a lump of clear stuff the size of my thumb. In the lamplight it flashed lilac, blue, and palest orange. Another threw off green fire in a rippling strip along its spine, a fourth shone with tiny yellow, green, and blue sparkles.

A fifth showed spots that looked like deep glass wells, one green, one dark blue.

"Oh, we *got* t' get a mage," Goodwin said. "Tunstall, we need you-know-who. First thing tomorrow."

Tunstall raised his eyebrows. "You're certain?"

Goodwin nodded. She gently slid each stone back into the pouch. "We've seen plenty a' gems in our day, Mattes. These're diff'rent. Goddess, m'jaw hurts. Crookshank took these t' Kayfer."

"You think he meant to bribe the Rogue? He went about it strangely." Tunstall offered Goodwin the tiniest bit of ham on the tip of his knife. She took it, chewing carefully.

"One of the chiefs?" I asked. I didn't look at them for fear they might scowl.

Then I heard Goodwin say, "Go on."

"Dawull of Waterfront—he helped the guards take Crookshank away last night." I drew patterns in the gravy on my plate. In my mind's eye I saw the big redheaded Dawull chivvy the rushers along. "Since when does one of the Rogue's own chiefs take out the trash? Were me, I'd worry more that Crookshank might remember me when he got his feet under him again."

Tunstall rested his chin on his hand. "Good point."

"Dawull's first 'mong the chiefs. All them waterfront toughs t' call on," Goodwin said. "Strong fellow. When he was movin' cargo in Port Caynn, he'd knock an ox down, f'r bet money. He c'n stand a few challenges if he's Rogue."

"Crookshank's money, he could buy some of the other chiefs," Tunstall said. "Enough to overset Kayfer, though?"

"Might Kayfer actually claim to be this Shadow Snake?" I asked. "If he did and he killed Rolond, the chiefs might turn on him. Crookshank could buy them then."

"You b'lieve that?" Goodwin asked. "No, Crookshank's been at th' bottle, t' yelp of th' Snake. My nursey tol' me that one. Waits at th' crossroads an' swallows bad children. It's a bogey story, Cooper. You never heard it?"

Of course I'd heard of the Shadow Snake. I'd just never known anyone cracked—or hard—enough to use the name for anything, let alone the murderer of a child.

"Someone calls himself the Shadow Snake, to do business," Tunstall said, thinking out loud. "They *use* the bogey story, to put the fear into him. To pay Crookshank back for something. The old man's up to his skull in enemies. Now he knows someone's out there who's so full of hate they'll not stop at child murder. So Crookshank pays to buy all kinds of guards."

"But he doesn't trust the Rogue. He thinks the Rogue is the Shadow Snake," I said. "And he's got enough coin to buy one of the Rogue's chiefs. That's a *lot* of coin, even for Crookshank—where's it from?"

"I'm bettin' it's these rocks," Goodwin said as Tunstall picked up the leather bag. "What are they? How'd Crookshank come by 'em? Too many questions. I don' like questions."

"Dogs don't like questions," I said, the first half of the saying. Tunstall finished it with me as he stuffed the bag inside his tunic. "Dogs like answers."

Goodwin asked, "What'd Rosto want of you, Cooper? While we were up greasin' Kayfer's vanity?"

I spat out a mouthful of buttered greens beside my bowl so I wouldn't talk with my mouth full. "He wanted to bribe me to know what was in that leather bag."

"How much?" Tunstall asked.

"A silver noble. I told him no," I replied.

Goodwin slapped the back of my head smartly. I gaped at her. "Don' be a fool, wench! One an' a half, an' you tell 'im!"

"Then split the takings with us. That's how it works," Tunstall said. "Personal bribes don't go in the Happy Bags. They're for the Dogs who earn them. Sooner or later word of these stones will get out. So we'll control who hears of them. Then we follow the rumors. Maybe learn something. Never turn down a bribe, Cooper. It's bad for business. Bad for you, and bad for us, because *we* get half of everything *you* get. We train you, after all."

"Folk don' trust a Dog what don' get bought," Goodwin told me. "You're too good t' be bought, they start thinkin' maybe you got some other angle—"

"Or some other master. Then it gets bloody." Tunstall stuffed a sweetmeat into his mouth.

I ate the vegetables I'd spat out. I never waste food.

"No sense lettin' you get yourself killed if we're puttin' work into you," Goodwin said, glaring at her bowl. "This Rosto, if he survives, might be a good connection. Aniki and Kora, too."

"If the Rogue don't kill them for being too good," Tunstall reminded us both. "Eat up, girls. We still have the rest of the Cesspool patrol."

As I stood, I heard crackling. I'd forgotten about my clothes. They were covered in dried muck. I'd need a bathhouse at the end of my watch *again*. I'd need to pay a laundress to get these gummy stains from my uniform. My hoard of coins dwindled in my mind's eye. I'd saved plenty, from my allowance at Provost's House and the tips I'd made as a runner, but buying furnishings and taking rooms ate into it. Laundry and baths ate still more.

I put it from my mind. I had to be alert on the streets, doubly so if Goodwin's pain distracted her. A mage's healing was all very well, but after a point, the Dog's body had to do the rest. That bruise looked like it hurt.

So on we went as the clocks chimed eleven. Once more I stood by and watched as Goodwin and Tunstall broke up tavern fights. Finally it was time to return to Jane Street. If Goodwin's pain had an effect on her work, I did not see it. My sole bit of excitement was when one looby crashed into me. I tripped him with my baton and smacked his ankle so he'd remember me.

My legs were filled with nails by the time we mustered off watch. The thought of reaching a bathhouse was as lowering as paying for it.

Once we'd told Ahuda that we'd finished our evening alive, she dismissed us. I was about to drag myself out the door when Goodwin put a hand on my arm. She gave me a circle of wood with the Provost's mark on one side and her name on the other. "Where's the Dogs' bathhouse, Cooper?"

I blinked at the piece of wood. "Stormwing Street, right around the corner." I was so weary the marks on the wood smeared in my vision. Goodwin was sore, too. I had to listen hard to understand her because her jaw was so stiff.

"Good Puppy. Go there. Show 'em this. Tell the 'tendants I said clean you'n your clothes, 'n give you a spare uniform for t'morrow. Yours'll need soakin'." She thrust the piece of wood closer to my face. "*Take* it, Cooper. They won' let you inna Dogs' bathhouse till you're no Puppy, 'less you've got one of these."

"But I can't afford—" I reached for my purse. A spare uniform cost money. I'd have to take the coin from my food budget. I couldn't take it from the rent or my pigeon money. Those birds were my informants.

"Pay me your share of Rosto's bribe, if it makes you feel better," Goodwin snapped. "*I* don't need a bathhouse. I'm goin' home t' let my man scrub my back. An' you need spare uniforms if you keep gettin' muck on you. Now scat."

I wanted to argue, but pride is something only folk with money can afford. I scatted. As I moved off, I heard Tunstall ask, "*All* the bribe money? That's hard."

"I'm short of coin this month," Goodwin said, her voice tart. "Maybe she'll be wise and make 'im pay 'er two silver nobles, keep th' extra half for 'erself."

The bathhouse attendant made me leave my clothes in the rinsing room. I wore a robe to the hot pools. Dogs were coming in, looking strange without their uniforms. Two of them started to come toward me. Each time an attendant grabbed their arms and whispered in their ears. Did they tell their friends that I was here with Goodwin's permission or just to let the Fishpuppy swim alone? Once I'd soaped and rinsed my hair, I slumped on my underwater bench until I was hidden up to my lips. If they couldn't recognize me, they wouldn't think about me.

The next thing I knew, the attendant was shaking my shoulder. The Dogs had gone. She lifted me out. I

131

was pink and wrinkled like a new babe. She'd found a spare uniform and stitched on white trim while I slept. She even helped me dress. I found a couple of coppers for a tip, but she pushed them away.

I managed the walk to my rooms. Pounce jumped to my shoulder as I let myself in, leaping on and off me as I undressed. He talked like mad in plain cat, attacking my braid as I stripped off my clothes and got into my nightshirt.

At last I fell into my wonderful bed, curling up under my divine blankets to write in this journal. Somehow I woke up for that, as if I live the day afresh to record it. Now, though, my eyelids are heavy. Pounce is purring in my ear. It's a soothing sound. I will end this, before I sleep and get ink on everything.

On the whole, a better day . . .

Friday, April 3, 246

When I stood this morning, I nearly fell, my legs hurt so bad. Even the hot soak last night did only so much. I kneaded them like Mistress Noll taught me to knead bread, biting my lip to keep from yowling like Pounce. As I worked on one leg, stretching it out in front of me on the floor, he draped himself over the other. He understood his warmth eased the muscles.

Once I could move without crying, I unlocked my trunk. Back when I was a runner, Mama made a big jar of ointment for my legs. I think my lord's cook paid a mage to charm it, because it worked the best of all Mama's concoctions. I only used it when I could do nothing better for myself, because it worked and because Mama had made it. This was one of those times.

"How far did I chase that addled creature?" I asked Pounce as I rubbed the ointment in. As I got dressed, I muttered about getting new work, where I spent my time on my back.

Today my landlady said naught as I left, though she was there at the window. She nodded, but there was a strange expression on her face. Pounce looked up at me, as if I might know why she was so quiet. I only shrugged at him.

That was when the rotten vegetables hit me, one turnip square in the shirt, one old onion glancing off my shoulder. I reached for a baton I didn't carry just then and looked for my enemy. Orva's two gixies stood in the street, their bruises highly colored in daylight. As I spotted them, the older girl threw a cabbage. I dodged. It splatted on the front of my lodging house.

"Y' took our mama!" she cried. "Give 'er back, y' stinkin' puttock!" The other one started to cry. They were bony, ragged, and sad. With rotten onion stink in my nose, I should have been furious.

Mama only paddled us when we'd done wrong. She always told us why. She wouldn't let her men knock us about. She sang to us, when she had the breath for it, and went short of food and clothes for us. Yet these little ones loved their mama, too. Like me, they were going to lose her. Never mind it would be for a shorter time than I had lost mine. It didn't matter that last night their mama had threatened to cut off their heads. Mamas were such strong creatures to their children.

"Your mama did a bad thing when she struck a Dog with a knife," I told the older gixie. "There's no forgiving that under the King's law. You draw a blade on a Dog, the Magistrate sends you to prison. If your mama behaves, she'll come home one day. But she was going to prison the moment she attacked Guardswoman Goodwin with steel."

"Here, you beggars—you've done enough damage! Scat!" It was Rosto the Piper. Somehow I don't think he'd come along by accident. "Be grateful you're still alive to cry for your ma. Be gratefuller still your da has two eyes in his head yet."

I wasn't surprised that Rosto knew of their case, either. But I *was* surprised when he flipped each of the girls a copper. They jumped to catch the coins before they got lost in the street muck. Then they ran off before he could change his mind. He sauntered up to me, more graceful than Pounce, hands in his pockets, the folds of his tunic loose, the dark blue cloth clean. Even his leggings were barely touched by street dirt. I marked the print of six knives against his tunic. The flat blades hidden on the insides of his wrists made me itch to handle them. I do love a good weapon.

"Here." He took a cord with a wooden disk on it from around his neck. There were magical signs carved deep in the wood. "Kora made it for me, to get stains out of my clothes. She does very good charms, our Kora." He looked behind me at the rows of houses. "Nice neighborhood, this. Handy to the markets and the riverfront."

I hesitated and looked the street over. My own charm against bad magics didn't warn me by turning warm against the skin of my chest, so I took the thong from his fingers. Slowly I passed the disk over the places where the vegetables had smeared my shirt. The wood glowed for a moment, then went dark. The muck dried and fell from my clothes.

"Thanks." I gave the disk back. He'd just saved me

three coppers' worth of laundering. "Appreciate it. I don't owe you anything, though."

He waved that aside. "Look, Cooper, I insulted you, offering a noble last night—I see that now. I was naughty."

I glanced at him sidelong and waited. Pounce wandered over. He stood on his hind legs, stretching until his paws were braced on Rosto's thigh. Then he flexed his claws, hooking them into Rosto's leggings.

"Look here, you, whoever you are, I am *not* a scratching post." Rosto crouched, taking care not to startle Pounce into ripping his clothes. Gently he rubbed my cat's ears. Then Rosto looked up at me, his dark eyes wicked. "A noble and a half."

I nibbled on my lip, then said carefully, "You don't want to know bad enough, I suppose. Pity."

Rosto made a face like he'd eaten some rotten onion. "Two silver nobles. It had better be worth it."

I thought about driving the price higher, just to prove I could. Then I decided not to get greedy. After all, we didn't know what the stones were. "Pay up."

Pounce turned out of Rosto's hold and jumped to my shoulder.

"Interesting cat, he is." Rosto reached over to scratch Pounce's chin again and let two silver nobles slide into my fingers so no one could see.

"Rough, sparkling stones, very colorful, tucked in reddish rock like the kind you find all over the Lower

City," I told him softly. "My Dogs have never seen any like them. We had another stone like these. Crookshank's grandson gave it to his wife, who's a friend of mine. My Dogs will find a mage to see what they are." I wondered if I should tell him Fulk had tried to steal the first stone. I chose not to. He'd only paid to know what he'd stolen from Crookshank, after all.

"Stones that two experienced Dogs can't name? That's a curiosity. This Lower City of yours is all tied in knots, you know." Rosto looked down at me. "You take care, Cooper, before you get strangled."

"I'm not a cove who's a bit too interesting and a bit too fast at Kayfer's Court," I said. But Rosto was on his way already, whistling a jig. I wished I'd thought to ask if he'd sworn to one of the Rogue's chiefs or not.

I looked at the sun. Perhaps if I rushed, I could still see my pigeons as well as the spinners. . . . No. It was near eleven o'clock. Dust spinners it was. Pigeons are everyday birds who leave scummer on my clothes and puke on me sometimes when I cut thread from their feet. Dust spinners are magic. They're exciting. Some corners always have a whirlwind of dust, leaves, and bits of this and that. Even on days when there's no breath of air anywhere else, the spinners will be stirring on their cobbles. They won't cool folk off on those hot days, though. Their touch is always dry as bone.

They don't only pick up solid things. They gather talk that comes their way. With work and thought the information I collect from them is useful. Best of all, I don't have to give them bribe money from my wages. The spinners are happy to give up their burden of talk for nothing. The weight of our joys and sorrows, even in the small bits carried to them by the city breezes, bears them down. They can hand that burden over to me and be free, at least for a time.

I can't see them all in one day, of course. I try to get to them all once a week. Today I went to those of the Lower City. I started with Shiaa, the dust spinner just a block from me at the corner with Koskynen Street. She's lively, spilling all kinds of talk straight from the slave markets into my ears as she tugs at my tight-braided hair and my well-tucked clothes. I'd brought her grit from Charry Orchard Street so she'd have something new to taste. She liked that. I memorized what she'd given me to go over later, then went to see Aveefa at Messinger and Skip. She usually collected the talk of the Northgate Guards and travelers. For her I had grit from the Jane Street kennel.

I could see Hasfush as I approached the corner of Charry Orchard and Stormwing. He was eight feet tall, the biggest I'd ever seen him, and solid gray. Something was wrong. The spinners hate to do anything that might make folk think they're more than just bits of wind at corners. My tripes clenched. Pounce yowled.

"I don't like it, neither," I told him. "But there's only one way to know what's bothering him." I gritted my teeth and stepped into Hasfush.

My ears filled with cries for mercy. They were cut off with dreadful sounds. I had heard murder done in my visits with the dust spinners, but never so many at once. No wonder Hasfush had picked up all the dirt and litter he could, to stop more sounds from entering his sides. I hadn't seen him in, what, two weeks?

"I'm sorry, old fellow," I whispered as he dropped the mess he'd picked up to protect himself. "I've been starting a new life." Guilt was pricking me. I hadn't been that far from here last night—but no. I'd been off chasing Orva before I would have come any closer.

I opened the bit of cloth I'd carried my gift of Rovers Street grit in and let it trickle to the ground, thinking. Sorting out the sounds, I decided there had been seven killings, maybe eight or nine if some sounds covered more than one death at a time. People disappear all the time in the Cesspool, but not like this. Moreover, it must have been very recent. Elsewise the pigeons would have told me. So seven, eight, or mayhap nine had been killed, for what? The killers had been professionals. They'd said nothing at their bloody work. Before Hasfush had blocked out more of what they did, they'd begun to dig. Grave and killing ground were the same. They were upwind of Hasfush.

How could I tell my Dogs? Was there a way to shake up a few Rats here in the Cesspool? Surely someone had heard of folk gone missing.

Wake up, Fishpuppy! said a scornful voice in my head. Half the Cesspool could go missing and folk would make it their business *not* to notice!

The spinner at the corner of Holderman and Judini held more screams and deaths. These were fainter, being downwind of Hasfush, thank the Goddess. I forced myself to walk up Holderman to the spinner who lived where Holderman crossed Stormwing. That spinner was across from Hasfush, in the same wind. It was dreadful to hear the murders again, almost as strong as Hasfush had heard it, but I was rewarded despite my fear.

"You three tell a living soul of what you have done, even your fellow guards, and you will join the dead." The voice was silky and female. "When I clasped your hands at the start, when you hired on, I put a mage mark on each of you. Talk of this, and you'll want to lop your own hand off before you die."

Seven to nine dead folk buried where they fell, I thought as I turned my steps toward home. Add to them three killers with mage marks on their hands, fatal ones. And a woman who's a mage. How can I tell my Dogs about this so they might take it serious? It would help if they already knew folk are missing from the Cesspool, *if* those missing folk didn't just vanish as so many people do. If those folk have names and families who seek them.

So deep in thought was I that Pounce had to claw my shoulder (startling me nearly out of my boots) for me to hear someone call loudly, *"Cooper."*

I spun around, yelping as Pounce dug in. Tunstall stood behind me, wearing a cityman's dark brown tunic and leggings. Off duty, he wore a sword as well as a dagger. He knew better than to walk out unarmed.

"Cooper, did you get street muck in your ears? I've been calling you for the last block." He looked me over and raised his brows. "Puppy, what have you been rolling in?"

I looked at myself while Pounce insulted him. There was grit on my shirt and breeches. Leaves and other trash stuck to my clothes. My hands were smeared with dirt. I felt my hair and pulled away a twig.

"I'll wait while you change," Tunstall said. "Wake up, Cooper. Our work doesn't end with the watch. Do you want to learn what those sparklers are? We're going to talk to a mage. A good one."

"I'll hurry," I said, and walked home as fast as my poor legs would take me. The clocks were chiming two. I might well not make it back before it was time to train, so I tucked my Dog's gear in my pack, changed shirts, and brushed off my breeches. I washed my face and hands and combed out my hair. Dirt and clutter fell to the floor. I'd never come away so filthy from the spinners before. Upset as they were, I couldn't be surprised.

Ready to go, I looked at Pounce. He stared at me, purple eyes slits, as if he was thinking, Are you going to tell me I may not come?

I opened the door and bowed for him to leave before me. He trotted past, tail high like a victory flag. At least I'd spared myself the shame of having him appear when I'd sworn I'd left him behind.

Tunstall let us walk alongside him for a block or so before he said, "I followed you for a while. You stood inside dust spinners. Everyone else avoids them. Most people think they're bad spirits. But you stood in one, your face turned up as if you were happy to be there."

I stared at the muck under my feet, my brain scrabbling for something to say. Time stretched, too much for it to seem as if I did anything but refuse to answer a Senior Dog.

Tunstall put a hand on my shoulder. "Tell me when you invent a good lie, Cooper." His voice was kind. "Or if you respect me, the truth. The truth is better if it's something me and Goodwin ought to know. Elsewise, keep it to yourself. We all have our odd habits. I have a little garden I keep in window boxes in my rooms."

I gawped at him. Tunstall just doesn't seem like the gardening sort.

"Oh, yes," he said with a nod. "It's soothing. I grow miniature roses. A Yamani friend taught me. Red ones and yellow ones, the size of your little fingernail. Even a normal fellow like me has a surprise or two." He took out a toothpick and turned it over in his fingers. "You're not limping as bad as I expected."

"I had an ointment, sir," I mumbled.

He led us onto Jane Street. It was busy with the carts that supplied the businesses of the Daymarket. We kept to the high stone walkway that lifted us clear of most of the splashings. Even though we didn't wear our uniforms, everyone gave us clear passage. From the way many of them looked at him, I think they knew Tunstall, or there was something about him that said "Provost's Dog."

He tucked the toothpick into a pocket. "The spinner. Is it like Mistress Noll said, that night we went to Crookshank's? She told us your grandda and da had strange magic with birds, and pigeons follow you. Is it like that? Or does it just feel good?"

I swallowed. He was my training Dog. "The spinners collect things that folk have spoken, the really hurtful things, the wondrous things, the big things that get caught on breezes."

Tunstall halted to stare at me. "For true?"

Three people dodged around us. The third was a big fellow, even bigger than Tunstall. He opened his gob like he was about to say sommat. Tunstall's head snapped up. He stared at the bigger cove with no feeling in his eyes whatever. The big man blinked, then hesitated. Tunstall shifted the tiniest bit.

The other cove hurried on his way.

I thought to memorize just how Tunstall had looked and moved so that I could do the same. Then I gave it up. I was no owl of six-odd feet in height. And for all of Tunstall's humor, he had a deadly look.

"I hear all manner of things in the spinners," I told him, to answer his question. "Mostly nonsense. Not always."

He drew me against a shop's wall so folk could get by. "Do they listen? Do they know you hear?"

I shook my head. "They're just happy I carry it away. It's like weight to them. They don't want it."

I watched him as he went to tap the end of a baton he wasn't carrying. I wondered if I'd do the same after years as a Dog.

"Did you hear anything of use today, Cooper?"

I licked my lips. This was a great matter, not passing bits to my lord Gershom, but using them on my own account. "Three spinners heard at least seven folk doused one or two nights back. They're buried secret where they were killed. Mots and coves alike. Them that killed them are mage-marked. If they talk, they die. I heard the mage tell them that—a woman mage."

Tunstall began walking again, rubbing his chin. I had to step double to keep up. "No names, no faces, just seven folk. We don't know where they're buried. They've just vanished. Cooper, ten times that vanish from the Cesspool any night of the week. Run off, die."

I nodded. It sounded like a mumper's brag—all

noise, no coin. "But those folk go one at a time, not all together." I had to say it, even if I half choked to do it.

Pounce leaped to Tunstall's shoulder and delivered a good scolding in cat. I was afraid Tunstall might dump him in the street muck. Instead he began to laugh. "Master Pounce, give us names or a place to dig, and we've somewhere to start," he said. "We'll tell Goodwin. We'll talk with our Birdies and ask around. Mayhap someone out there knows more of this story, if your spinners didn't just blend tales together. Magic is a chancy thing, Cooper." He looked at me sidelong. "When you led my Lord Provost to the Bold Brass gang, you may have been only eight, but you knew to track a *man,* not whispers on the wind. That's what good Dog work is. Rumors and what your Birdies say are useful, but in the end it's the Dog work that matters."

I nodded as I looked at the ground. He was right, as far as it went. He didn't know the pigeons served the God of the Dead. And mayhap he didn't know it took Dog work to seek out the voices heard by a spinner as well as it did to chase down a scummernob who thought he could smash any woman he liked.

Tunstall went on, "My lord Gershom didn't place you with Goodwin and me. Ahuda did that, though gods forbid anyone say she's got a soft spot for you. But I wasn't brokenhearted to have you with us. I always wanted a Puppy. It's Clary who needs convincing. She always fusses over what's new. I *was* startled you picked the Lower City, though. Being my lord's foster daughter, you could have gotten any district you asked for."

I shrugged. "It's what I understand," I mumbled.

"With your chances, I'da picked Unicorn District, or Prettybone. Hold up, Puppy. We're here."

"Here" was the Gem Merchants' Guild Hall in the Daymarket. The windows were barred, with magic symbols writ around them and on the bars themselves. Signs were even carved into the stone walls. The doors were solid oak with iron fittings bespelled in their turn. Tunstall took me to the front entrance.

"Who's that?" One of the guards swung her ax down to block Pounce's way. Pounce clearly had it in mind to vex the great dolt. He batted at the ax as if it was a toy, then leaped over it as if it was three times as big.

"It's our cat," Tunstall said. "We've heard you've a terrible mouse problem. Our cat is so excellent he'll do for all your mice and some of your bigger rats, too. Don't bother to thank us." Tunstall scooped up Pounce. Then he smiled. In some strange way all the friendliness in his manner until that moment vanished with his smile. "We're on the King's business, and you know my face. This is Guardswoman Cooper, my partner. We've an appointment with Jungen Berryman."

He called me "Guardswoman"!

"Let 'em go," the man on duty told his partner. "I

know Tunstall. And Berryman'll just bore them to death." To Tunstall he said, "Try to walk out afore you die of his gabble. I don't want the work of haulin' your carcasses away. Even the cat's."

I followed Tunstall inside. Pounce draped himself over Tunstall's shoulder, pointing his whiskers at me in his smuggest smile. I wished I could say he'd never been so venturesome before I became a Puppy, but it would have been a lie. Pounce is a venturesome stinker.

The short hall was marked with frescoes showing folk in the gem business, measuring, inspecting, setting, weighing. Up beautifully carved stairs of fine wood we climbed, passing windows with pieces of colored glass set in to make pictures. I was awed. Surely even the King's palace was not so grand.

I might have gawped all day, but Tunstall hustled us onto the second floor and down a hallway. At the very last door on the left he stopped and knocked hard, then thrust the door open.

"I was meditating on a very important spell!" A man was seated at a big desk by an open window—one with no glass, only shutters. His round cap was crooked on his bald head and he fought to sit upright, which made his meditation look more like a nap. He had a weak chin and looked like he rarely saw the sun. When he recognized my partner, he dropped back into his seat. "Tunstall, you wretch! I thought you were some idiot wanting me to check yet another load of pearls."

"Then put out a warning sign before you take your nap," Tunstall told him.

"I but closed my eyes for a moment!" the mage protested, smoothing his well-made tunic. "So would you, if you'd tested three dozen pearls in a week!"

"Pearl fakery's become a problem to the guild?" Tunstall asked. "Cooper, bar the door. Put that card on the string on the latch outside first so we're not interrupted."

I did as I was told. When I turned around, the mage Jungen Berryman was squinting at me. "What's happened to Goodwin?" he asked worriedly. "I hadn't heard—"

"Goodwin's fine. Cooper is our Puppy. Rebakah Cooper, Master Jungen Berryman."

He flapped a white hand at me. I gave him enough of a bow for a guild mage. I could have bowed deeper, I suppose, but he wasn't my lord, and he was nothing in the Provost's ministry.

"Pull up a chair and tell me what you want, Tunstall. And if you've got any good stories, I'll even feed you and your Puppy—whoa!"

The "whoa" was Pounce's fault. He leaped on to Berryman's desk and batted a cloudy blue, gold, and black stone with his paw. Berryman saved it from falling.

"That's Pounce," Tunstall explained. He took a chair. "He's going to be the first cat to earn pay as a

Dog. Cooper, close the shutters. You might want to light the lamps, Berryman."

Berryman took another stone from Pounce. "That's an uncut ruby you're chewing on, my friend. Tunstall, not the shutters! I kept them closed all winter—it's spring, in case you haven't noticed!"

I closed and locked them anyway. I answered to Tunstall, not some goggle-eyed bead counter. When I turned around, there were fires in all the room's lamps. Berryman had good ones, with bright-polished brass in back of the flames to cast triple the light.

"There's dark doings in the Lower City, Berryman," Tunstall told the man. I went to stand behind my Dog. As if he took that getting-paid folly seriously, Pounce sat at Berryman's side, tail curled around his forefeet. "Murder and vanishings. We think these stones may be involved." He upended the washed leather pouch on the desk. The stones spilled out.

I remembered the stone in my breeches pocket, pressing against my leg. I wondered if I should remind Tunstall I had it. No, I decided, he wouldn't forget there was one more in my keeping.

Berryman pushed the stones apart with a rod he kept on his desk. Pounce reached out and drew away two. Then we all watched as Berryman's eyes got wide. Would he do as Fulk had and pretend the stones were unknown to him or worthless? He would be a looby of the noblest class if he did, because his face gave away even bigger fortunes than Fulk's had.

He reached out a hand. A lamp sailed over from a shelf nearby. The lamp was made special, the flame protected by a glass chimney so it didn't gutter in the air like others did. Half of it was backed with silver polished so bright it reflected an image of the flame. It did even better than brass to make the light brighter.

Berryman lifted a pitcher that sat on his desk and started to pour from it into a cup that was there, but his hand shook. He tried to steady the pitcher and slopped the contents on his papers.

"Cooper," said Tunstall.

I stepped around to take the mage's pitcher. I could see we'd been right about the stones, and Fulk had made a mistake in lying to us. They had to be greatly important if a mage who handled pearls and rubies got the shakes so bad over them. Carefully I poured water from the pitcher into the cup. Berryman dunked two fingertips into the cup and let them drip onto the rock with the biggest bulge of clear, jelly-like stone. Then he held it up before the lamp. The green stripe blazed out of the orange, brighter than we'd ever seen before. Tiny bits of red and blue sparked out along the edges. Now we could see a small pool of purple on the back side of the thing.

"Shakith's scales," said Berryman. He put the stone to one side. He did the same thing with each rock, showing us darts and blazes of color that appeared only when they were touched with water and held up to the light. He drank off the water in the cup, then motioned for me to pour him another. I did so, though I considered dumping the pitcher on his head to remind him I was no serving wench. He looked so rattled I changed my mind.

Berryman sat back in his chair. He ran his fingers over his lips time after time, staring into the distance. Finally Tunstall began to tap his foot on the floor. Berryman came to himself with a start. When Tunstall opened his mouth, the mage shook his head. First he snapped his fingers four times. Signs appeared in glowing yellow light on the walls, ceiling, and floor, then on the doors (there were three) and the window shutters. They faded away. More yellow light appeared in keyholes, in the gaps around the doors and shutters, on the doors, and on the sides of the room's standing cabinets. That too faded. Then I yelped as yellow light coated Tunstall, Pounce, and me. My skin tickled. Then the light was gone.

"Forgive me, Cooper, is it? But it's easy to attach listening spells to someone," Berryman said. "Please, sit down. I assume Tunstall here trusts you." He looked at Tunstall. "You'll understand my caution in a moment. *Is* there a problem with Goodwin on this?"

Tunstall shook his head. "She'll hear of this meeting when we go on duty. We've talked about these baubles. Far as we know, we're the only ones who have them, apart from Crookshank. Fulk handled the first one, that Beka got. Give it to him, Beka. And then you can sit down."

I tried not to let my dismay show as I winkled the first stone from my breeches and placed it before the mage. It was so beautiful, I didn't want him to take it from me. But orders are orders. I knew I'd have to give it up sometime. Once I put it down, I sat on the edge of the chair.

"Beautiful," said Berryman, holding it before the light. "Even without water or proper grinding to bring out the inner fires. So we'll assume Master Fulk knows there's one of these stones about, but not more."

Tunstall and I looked at each other. He wasn't about to tell Berryman of Pounce's aid in stealing this one.

Berryman put my stone down and opened a desk drawer. From it he removed a black cloth bag embroidered with gold signs. Carefully he placed all of the stones in it but the one I'd been carrying. "I'll ward these against magical prying," he said to Tunstall. "That will keep the likes of Fulk from calling them to him. It's not worth it with this one." He tapped my stone and did nothing when Pounce nudged it. "There's no piece of gemstone in that one big enough to be worth money. There are just tiny pockets of the gem in the matrix—the surrounding rock."

"You may as well keep it, then, Cooper," said Tunstall. "A good luck stone, since it came to you your first night as a Puppy."

Pounce had pushed it to the edge of the desk. I grabbed it before they could change their minds. I love the pretty thing.

Berryman traced each gold sign on the bag with his fingernail, yellow light trailing as he did so. Then he pulled the drawstring tight and thrust the bag across the desk to Tunstall. It only went halfway. We all watched as Pounce walked over, grabbed the bag, and dragged it over to my Dog.

"Thank you," Tunstall said as he picked it up.

"What an odd creature." Berryman didn't seem much interested in things not involving gems, even cats who weren't catlike. He leaned back in his chair and said, "Those stones are raw fire opals. The smallest fire opal that can be separated from its matrix without cracking is worth more than I earn from the guild in a year. They are very, very rare, partly because they are hard to cut. There's a mine that's almost played out in Legann, another in Meron, five more in Carthak, and none have pink-colored matrix stone like this. Only a trickle of new gems enters the market in any one year." He bit the nail on his little finger.

Going on, Berryman said, "Two finished stones and a pound of rough ones like these have come to this guild hall in the last two months. The seller is keeping his name secret, and the broker is sworn to him. The stones are . . . extraordinary. An auction of fire opals is to be held at the end of July—a big auction. So big that gem merchants from fifteen countries are either here already or on their way. I thought the auction talk was just gossip." He sighed. "I was wrong. If you sold those rough stones in the bag there—a good cutter could get at least one finished stone from each—you would be wealthy."

Tunstall smiled. It was his turn to lean back. He put his palms together before his face, then cupped them and began to tap his fingertips together, one, two, three. . . .

It seemed Berryman wasn't the sort of fellow who needed folk to keep asking questions. "All opals are powerful magical stones. Fire opals are fascinators—bewitchers. Properly enchanted—which these aren't, you'll be glad to know—they'll take and hold the attention of anyone the mage shows them to. They leave people open to suggestion from the mage or the person he works for. Fire opals don't hold spells for more than three or four days. If you leave them in water for a time, then let them dry out, the stone will crack. It will be useless for spell making after that. Most people love them for their value, because their magical uses are so limited. It's better to sell the stones and get very rich." Berryman rubbed his eyes. "Where are they coming from, Mattes?"

Tunstall's tapping fingers slowed to a stop. "We

don't know," he said. "But the native stone is very like that of the Lower City."

"Surely not!" Berryman said. He seemed horrified and amused. "That—it would be like finding pearls in dung! We would have found any stones of value there centuries ago."

I fidgeted. The Lower City, so the tales went, had been good farmland when Corus was first built on the Olorun River. Then had come the Centaur Wars. The first way to halt the armies was with huge earthworks, built from our soil. They were carted away when the Annste kings built the first city wall. The Lower City's farms were less fruitful after that. In the Decade of Floods, the Olorun swamped the lower ground, where folk still farmed, and carried much of it back to the riverbed with it when its waters shrank. With each flood there was less black soil in the Lower City. By the time the wall encircled the Lower City, the rich black soil was but a couple of feet deep, and beneath it was the stone that shaped the ridges of Corus. So Granny Fern's tales explained how we spent as much of our summers yanking twice as much reddish rock from our small garden as we did vegetables.

Tunstall caught me thinking. "Cooper?" he asked with a smile.

I did my best to look at him, who I knew. "The old stories say the Lower City used to have beautiful farms for all the good dirt there." I tried to say it like they taught us for Dog reports, firm and clear. "But it got taken away, and now all we've got is scrapings and rock. Rock like the rock in the stones."

"What does a Puppy know of such things?" Berryman asked. He was surprised Tunstall even let me speak. "Maybe she's been educated to be a Dog, my dear Mattes, but I should think *I* have the advantage in knowledge of the land!"

"She grew up in the Lower City," Tunstall explained.

"A Lower City wench," Berryman said flatly. "Lessoning me on whether or not opals may be found in the disgusting sewer they call the Cesspool."

I clenched my fingers, wondering if his head would split like a melon if I hit it right with my baton.

"No offense, girl," Berryman told me. "But you must leave the matter of what stones are found where to those who are educated to these things."

I looked down. He might be one of those mages who could read murderous thoughts in my eyes. What did this underbaked flour dumpling know of the Lower City and the people who lived there?

Tunstall slapped the desk. I was on my feet before he was. "Berryman, thanks," Tunstall said. "You'll keep news of the stones to yourself?"

"But you haven't *told* me anything about them," Berryman complained. The man was actually whining. "They're part of a crime, aren't they? A robbery? No, it must be a murder, for Lower City Dogs to be holding a fortune in fire opals. How many were killed? Where were they from? Carthak? Why haven't I heard of a hijacked shipment of gems? As far as I know, there aren't any Carthaki gem merchants in the city yet, and they're the only ones who could have so many fire opals. And they usually—"

Tunstall put his finger to his lips. Berryman pouted.

"It's an investigation, my friend," Tunstall explained. "A secret one. Even my Lord Provost doesn't have the details. Lives are in the balance and depend on your discretion."

"You *always* say that." Berryman had turned from a man of power to a child who can't have a sweet.

"Have I ever lied?" Tunstall asked him.

The mage still pouted. "No."

"Goodwin or I—or Cooper here—will tell you all of it, depending on who lives and when the Rats are caged. Right now it is a thing of blood and theft and dark deeds in the Lower City." Tunstall said it like a corner storyteller. From the shine of Berryman's goggling eyes, he drank it like the storyteller's audience. Had there been thunder and lightning outside, I think Berryman would have paid Tunstall for the pleasure of hearing him.

"Promise?" Berryman asked.

"Promise," Tunstall replied. "Cooper promises, too," he added. "Don't you, Cooper?"

"I promise," I said to the desk.

"I should have been a Dog," Berryman told us. "You have such dashing lives. All I do is a bit of magic here and there and then off to home." He sighed.

I started. He believed our lives dashing? What would he have thought of jumping through Orva's window with no inkling of what lay on the other side? Would he have found landing in fish guts dashing?

Tunstall kicked me lightly on the ankle. I don't know if I would have said what I truly thought. Mayhap Tunstall was used to Goodwin and kicked me to keep me silent just in case.

"Berryman, we could not do this without your advice," he said, as solemn as a priest. "Be sure your name will be in our final report to my Lord Provost."

Berryman was so happy with this that he walked us to the guild hall entrance. Though I wondered if he didn't do it so the guards could hear him call Tunstall "my friend" and watch him clap my Dog on the shoulder. I'd seen people like Berryman at Provost's House, folk who thought it daring to be friends with Dogs. I was just surprised to see any of them could be of use for more than buying supper and drinks.

"He's a very good mage," Tunstall said as we went on our way. "And he'll do all kinds of mage work for Dog gossip. You need folk like him, Cooper. He's a useful cove to know."

Pounce cried, "Manh!" as if he agreed.

"Good cat," Tunstall said, and picked him up. "Between you, me, and Goodwin, we'll get this Puppy licked into shape."

Tunstall had an errand to run. He left me at the kennel gate so I could go to the training yard and stumble through an hour of practice on aching legs. When I saw him at muster, he was giving Ahuda the bag of fire opals to be logged in. I had a feeling *that* wealth would not go into the Happy Bag for the street Dogs, but I could only shrug. Unlike scummer, gold flows uphill.

Goodwin was in better spirits when we mustered for our watch. She listened close as Tunstall explained what Berryman had told us on our way to the Nightmarket. "So we just kissed our fortunes farewell." She also sounded better after a night's sleep and time for the healing to work. The bruise on her jaw was still astounding, but I could understand her well now. "That will teach us to be honest. Maybe we ought to take Berryman on rounds sometime, Mattes. He'll probably faint before we cross into the Cesspool, though." She looked back at me as we ambled up Jane Street. "He's not a bad sort. He just sometimes lets being a merchant's mage do his talking for him. When you smarten him up, he improves."

I glanced at her. Had *she* gotten the temptation to hit him, too?

"At least we know what the rocks are now," said

Tunstall with a nod to a passing ragpicker.

"I'd like to see *where* Crookshank gets them. I hate to know that old spintry is getting any richer." Goodwin spun her baton on its rawhide cord. "If they were clean and legal, Berryman would know. They'd have come through the guild hall. Which means they're smuggled or local. Either way, too many big money stones could set up a robbers' ball down here."

I cleared my throat. Without looking back at me, Goodwin held up her hand and twitched her first two fingers, telling me to cough up. "Why didn't Berryman try to keep the stones?" I asked. "He's a mage. And he said they'd make us rich."

"Addled, poor cuddy," Tunstall told me over his shoulder. "Doesn't care about fattening his own purse. *I* think he's spelled so he's never tempted to pocket all those gems he handles."

"He's got a rich wife," Goodwin said. "Some folk just aren't greedy."

"Don't say that where the gods can hear," Tunstall whispered. "They hate talk of things unnatural."

"Then they should've stomped Berryman years ago, because it's unnatural for a man not to want to lift a ruby here and there."

The first half of the evening passed easily enough. Plenty of drunken loobies greeted me by trying to say "Fleet-footed Fishpuppy." Orva's man (Jack Ashmiller, he was called) came to apologize for his woman to

Goodwin. She was gentler to him than she'd been with anyone but Pounce that I'd seen. The cuts on his face were swollen, the one over his eye holding it shut. He had no coin for a healer mage or even a hedgewitch's stitching, poor mumper. Whilst Tunstall and me waited for them to finish talking, something rotten hit the back of my uniform. I heard a hiss from the shadows. However their papa felt, the young Ashmillers wouldn't forgive me for my part in their mama's hobbling.

On we walked, my muscles groaning with each step. I got to stand off and watch as my Dogs put a halt to three purse cuttings, four pocket pickings, and five thefts from shops. It was wonderful to see how quick they moved, how smoothly they broke up trouble. Tunstall asked me what they looked for on the purse cuttings and pocket pickings beforehand, until even Goodwin said I could spot cutpurses and foists better than most second-year Dogs. Whenever we had three or four Rats in hobbles, we'd take them along to the cage carts positioned around the Lower City for transport back to the kennel.

"Just a swing along the Stuvek side of the Nightmarket," Tunstall said at last. "I'd say all three of us have earned our supper good and truly tonight."

"I can pay for my own," I heard my fool self say. "And I owe you a silver noble and five coppers from Rosto's bribe. I got two silvers out of him."

"I'll take those coins," Goodwin said, putting out

a hand. I turned them over to her.

As I did, Tunstall said, "Crown pays for half of our meals wherever we feed. And me and Goodwin say who pays the rest."

"You're a good Puppy, you do your work, we feed you," Goodwin told me. I blinked. Tunstall was supposed to be nice to me. Goodwin was supposed to be gruff. "After last night, you've earned your meals for a while, so be quiet about it and— Goddess!"

We were half a block from Crookshank's house by then. What startled Goodwin was the crack of breaking glass—and aren't glass windows stupid and gaudy for a man living right on the edge of Nightmarket?

A moment later flames shot out of the front of Crookshank's house from a hole where a window had been. The front door slammed open. Folk threw themselves out onto the steps. We saw orange glare over the wall around the house's side. The fire starters had struck there, too.

We took out our batons. "Now we know the Rogue's revenge," Goodwin said as we started to run. "Cooper, wet your handkerchief in the fountain, keep it over your mouth and nose. Fountain." She pointed with two handkerchiefs in that hand, hers and Tunstall's. I grabbed them, yanked mine out, dashed over, dunked them, and fetched them back, soaked. Tunstall grabbed his and ran. Goodwin waved me to the front door. "Upstairs, Cooper, the garret. Get whoever you can, get them out. Send them through the side doors. I'll be on the second floor. Don't be stupid."

I clapped my handkerchief over my mouth and nose. In we went, under the plume of smoke that came from a burning room off to the side. I smelled cooking oil before I followed Goodwin up one set of stairs and ran up two more on my own. A couple of maids darted past me. I ran on up the tiny steps to check the rooms under the steep roof—empty.

Back down one flight I went. Tansy was dumping her jewelry case into a pillow slip. I boxed her ears for wasting time, shoved the case into the slip, and knotted it. Then I poured her water pitcher on the sheet, threw the sheet over her, and shoved her out the door. Her maid was huddled, forgotten, in the corner, stiff with terror. I couldn't get her to stand. I finally dragged her from the room and down the steps until she scrambled to her feet and ran out.

Back to Tansy's floor I went. I checked room after room. Looking out a window, I saw folk down below had formed bucket brigades to douse the fires on the ground floor. Once I was certain everyone on the third floor was gone, I went to the second floor to look for Goodwin. I'd had a notion she wasn't clearing the household out. My notion was right.

"Cat, this is a bad time and place. Do your business outside, you idiot creature!"

Her voice led me to rooms that had to be the ones

shared by Crookshank and his wife. It looked as if she'd been searching his papers and cupboards. She stood in the middle of his workroom with a ledger in her hands, taken from a table stacked with them. Pounce stood on the big desk, digging fiercely in a pile of letters.

Goodwin shut the ledger with a snap and put it with the others. "Crone's teeth, if he ruins anything useful, Cooper—"

"Pounce, stop that," I said, though I could tell he was looking for something. He knew I wasn't serious. I helped Goodwin pick up some papers that had fallen to the floor. "It looks as if they've got the fires controlled. Though the smoke's still nasty."

Pounce *mrt*ed. With a snap a wooden panel in the desk's surface popped open, almost smacking him. He jumped back, tail switching, and yowled in triumph.

Goodwin straightened, papers in her hand. "You pesky little beast, how did you even know that compartment was there? Cooper, you saw him, same as me. He deliberately went after it."

Goodwin went to the desk and checked the compartment for booby traps before she removed what it held—a small sheaf of notes.

"He does things like that," I told her with a shrug.

Goodwin set aside the other papers she'd gathered. She looked over the notes from the compartment, swore, then closed the lid and stuffed the notes down the front of her tunic. "Let's get out of here before they come looking for us." She picked up the things that Pounce had scattered and tossed them on the desktop so it looked like it had never been disturbed.

I followed Goodwin. The fires were almost out. Smoke had ruined Crookshank's fancy things downstairs, but he could well afford to replace them. Hardly a person in the crowd that had gathered didn't wish the house had burned to the ground.

I found Tansy on her own, shivering in her wet sheet. The spring night had gotten chilly. I peeled the sheet off. "You'd think they'd pity him, losing a great-grandbaby," I said. I looked around to see if anyone had fetched blankets. Tansy's belly was a mound against her thin housedress. At least she wasn't in bedclothes at this early hour.

"Why should they?" she asked, hugging the pillow slip with her jewels. "Enough of them have lost a child lately, and no one's raised a fuss about theirs."

I guided her to a fountain bench, but it wasn't all from the goodness of my heart. On our way I grabbed a blanket from a maid's hand. She yelped and yanked, then let go when I glared at her. *She* wasn't wet and pregnant. I got Tansy wrapped around before I made her sit, whispering as I did, "What do you mean?"

She rolled her big blue eyes at me. "Everyone says it's just slave catchers calling themselves by a nightmare name. They say little ones always go missing down here. But some are different. See that thin mot over there?

With the round scar on her cheek? Her ma left her a spell book, onliest bit of value the poor thing ever had. Middle of the night a cove's voice beside her bed tells her where and when to leave it for the Shadow Snake, elsewise she'll weep for it. Gave her a week. She didn't do it, not the only thing she had from her ma. After the week, her little girl, only four years old, vanished. Just like that." Tansy's lips trembled. "The Dogs say little ones vanish all the time in the Lower City, did she try the slave traders? Of course she tried the slave traders, for all the good it did. She searched for months. She still looks at girls that age with white blond hair, just in case. It was fifteen months ago."

"But it could've been anybody," I said. "Just 'cause someone *says* she'll be sorry—"

"They drew a snake in ash on the little girl's apron and left it hung on the clothesline for the mother to take down," Tansy whispered. "They left it on her pillow inside the house, too. When the whisper in the night came again, that poor creature thought of her two younger children and left the spell book where she was told."

I clenched my hands. Preying on folk who had so little was more than bad, it was vicious. "But it's only one time this cove says he's the Shadow Snake, Tansy."

"Watch my finger, Beka. I'm not going to name them for you." She pointed again and again and again. Twelve times she pointed at different people in the crowd. "It's been going on almost three whole year. All of them have a piece of their child's clothing with that Shadow Snake on it. They had something the Shadow Snake wanted. Them that didn't give it up right off, well, some of 'em got their little one back, all right—as a corpse. Some never saw their little one again. Grandpa Ammon got a bit of paper asking for something. He said no Snake would ever wring him like a three-month-old hen. Only they didn't wring *him*, Beka." Tears rolled down Tansy's plump cheeks. "They wrung my little Rolond."

"I pay for *protection*!" I recognized Crookshank's ragged screech. He was yelling at my Dogs. "I pay more into that Happy Bag than anyone on this street. For that I expect *protection*!" He swayed on his steps, shaking a bony finger at Tunstall and Goodwin. Three of his rushers stood at his back, hands on their weapons. Smoke still rolled out of the broken window behind them.

I belonged up there with my Dogs, but I didn't want to leave Tansy. I looked around until I spotted Annis. She came over. "Come on, girl," she said, gathering Tansy up, blanket and all. "Let's stop Father from making even more of a fool of himself."

Tansy yanked free. "Why? I don't owe him. He got Rolond killed."

Annis grabbed her arm. "We're stuck with him." She spoke in Tansy's ear. The words were not meant for me, but I have very good hearing. "And we have more to lose. Don't think we're free just because Rolond's gone. You need to think of the babe that's coming. Now be an obedient granddaughter-in-law."

As she tugged Tansy over to the steps, I cut around them to stand behind my Dogs. Tunstall was saying, "You'd have to pay ten times what you do to get enough Dogs to guard against the Rogue's wrath, my friend. These lads know it as well as we do." He nodded to Crookshank's rushers. "Did you think Kayfer Deerborn would let your speech last night go unspanked?"

Crookshank stared at him, trembling in fury.

"Why do you think he had a hand in killing your great-grandson?" Goodwin asked, her arms folded over her chest. "Last night you accused him of it. What have you got that he might want that bad?"

Crookshank went dead white under the soot on his face. He spun and rammed through the wall of guards behind him to dash into his house, smoke and all. The rushers looked at each other, then followed, covering their noses and mouths with their arms.

"Well, that shut the old vulture up," Tunstall said cheerfully. "Where's Cooper and the cat?"

"Right in back of us," Goodwin said. "Let's go. I'm past hungry. We'll be lucky if there's any ham left at the Mantel and Pullet."

I moved so they could pass us and muttered, "They could've waited to burn the place till we had supper."

Both of them turned to face me. Pounce looked up at me and meowed.

"She spoke," Tunstall said. "Goodwin, did you hear? She actually made a joke. It was practically conversation."

Goodwin elbowed him. "Don't let it go to your head. Look, she's going shy again."

It was true. I could feel the ground draw my eyes toward it. Pounce jumped onto my shoulder and settled across my back, just behind my neck. To console me for making idiotic remarks where my Dogs could hear, he began to purr.

We weren't lucky. There was no more ham at the Mantel and Pullet. The chicken had been on the spit so long it was dry. The bread, warming by the hearth since before the supper rush, was also dry. At least the fried greens were passable. The cook was so heartbroken at putting such a poor meal before longtime customers like Tunstall and Goodwin that she quickly fried some almond cakes and served them drizzled in honey. The ale was free. The cook brewed rose hip tea for me.

Once they had done hovering, Goodwin fetched the papers out of her tunic. All four of us, including Pounce, leaned in to look. Goodwin placed each piece side by side, the back of the note face up. Each was signed with a long double-curved snake writ in ash.

"'When you grub in the Snake's earth, you owe a payment to the Snake,'" Tunstall read softly. He pulled a second note over to read it. "'Fifteen stones to the Snake, left in a leather purse behind the Lonely Journey altar, Death's temple on Glassman Square, a week from today, or you will pay with your own kin.'" He whistled. "Not very nice."

Goodwin leaned her head on her hand. "I thought maybe I'd mistook it when I glanced at it in the house. We were wrong, my buck. There *is* a Shadow Snake, a real one. We've the evidence right here." She smiled crookedly. "The bogey is real."

"I'd druther he wasn't," I said. "Are the other notes the same?"

"'You think yourself safe,'" Goodwin read from the second one. "'A Snake finds gaps in every wall. The child is now in the Snake's coils. One week from today, thirty stones in a leather bag, behind the Lonely Journey altar, Death's temple on Glassman Square, or there will be blood.'"

"He didn't pay up the first time, so the Snake doubles the tally, takes Rolond, and gives him a new week to pay," Tunstall said. "I'm surprised Crookshank didn't have an apoplexy. He gets half mad when folk give him orders. Arranged for his rushers to beat a Captain of the Guard who turned him back from the palace gate. The cove was crippled when they'd done."

Goodwin read the third note. "'You have more to lose. Forty stones, you know where to leave them, the night of the full moon.'" She made a face. This Snake isn't done with Crookshank, and the old man knows it."

I was cold. I gave Rolond horsey rides in the Daymarket once. I let him chew my braid when he was teething, the times Tansy escaped Crookshank's watchers. Might I have put a stop to this, had I known? But I hadn't. While Crookshank was getting those notes, when Rolond was taken, I was moving into my new home. After, when I heard, the old man had the house under such tight guard that Tansy couldn't get out, nor I get in. My first real talk with her in three months was on Monday. Why didn't she tell me then about the Shadow Snake? I wondered. But I knew the answer already. Tansy was so much happier, and sillier, before Rolond was killed. After, she had learned to keep secrets.

"But I think Crookshank did know the Snake meant business," I said, clenching my hands.

"What?" Goodwin asked.

Pounce crawled into my lap and began to purr. I stroked him as I told Tunstall and Goodwin what Tansy had told me about the missing children and the sign of the Snake left behind. Of the things the Snake had wanted from those parents. I even said, "She told me some of them went to the kennel and reported it, but nothing was done. Did you know?"

I mustered my courage to look at them. Surely they

didn't turn their backs on the poor of the Lower City, not Tunstall and Goodwin. But Tunstall was carving a piece from the table as a toothpick.

Goodwin frowned. "What do you want from us, Cooper?" she asked. "Do you know how many robberies there are in a day in the Lower City, how many burglaries, how many purse cuttings, rapes, brawls. . . . Folk disappear or die all the time, children in particular. We don't have a third of the Dogs we need to cover the Lower City alone. We do what we can."

I wanted to ask, You didn't seek on any of them? but the words stuck in my throat. I know the numbers. We were made to memorize them our first day of training and to repeat them when asked. We learned them by district. Each district, from Palace to Highfields, had a particular place in every Puppy's memory, with its numbers for disorder and crime, its numbers for Dogs and for mages who might be problems, and its chiefs under the Court of the Rogue. I could say them in my sleep.

"It could have been me that went missing," I said. "My brothers, my sisters. Any of us. Vanished or dead in a gutter, a snake on our pillows and Mama heartbroke. She was so frail. It would've killed her before her time." I looked at them. "It could still be one of them, if they wasn't safe in my Lord Provost's house."

"Wake up, Cooper." Goodwin said it, but she did not seem angry. "Do you know how many mothers drown newborns and tots in privies or rain barrels? How many fathers and uncles toss them into the rear yard with broken skulls?"

"Someone they know or some stranger who offers a solid meal hurts them and leaves them to die." Tunstall's eyes were sad. "And plenty sell 'em to the slavers. Instead of telling folk and face the shame, they say the child just vanished. Savor your good luck, Cooper. Savor it for you and your family. If we catch this Snake, we'll catch him. But there aren't enough of us to chase every vanished cove, mot, and child. Not near enough."

Goodwin rubbed the scar on her cheek. "Tunstall says you've word of seven missing mots and coves. We haven't heard anyone hunting for *them,* let alone the odd vanished child. Let's get moving. And toughen up, Cooper, that's my advice." She got to her feet. "Before you jump into the Olorun or slice your wrists. We lose five Dogs a year to the Black God's Option. Don't you be one."

"We look around on patrol, Cooper," Tunstall said as he stood. "But it's harder once it gets dark. Not many littles around, and their faces aren't clear. And it hurts. You find enough dead ones, you don't want to know, after a while. The older ones, they went looking for it most of the time. Not the dead children."

In the Lower City we're supposed to give up pretty ideas and dreams. I'm vexed with myself, to find I've nursed some about these two. They are only human.

And their people aren't from here. Tunstall is a barbarian from the eastern hills. Goodwin's family are respectable members of the Carpenters' Guild. My Dogs don't know what it's like to have no one fighting for them. They do their jobs and that gives them plenty of work, looking out for them that fill the Happy Bags.

I won't content myself with filling the Happy Bags. Not ever. The Lower City is mine. Its people are mine—its children are *mine*. If I find them that's doing all this kidnapping and murdering, they'd best pray for mercy. Because once I get my teeth in 'em, I will *never* let them go. And I start with the Shadow Snake.

We washed up from supper and left for the last two hours of our watch. I had plenty to think on. Luckily we returned to the Nightmarket, where it was too busy to give me time to think. I was taken up learning to tell the differences between minnows and pikes, and learning how to spot the best of the Nightmarket foists and sutlers. I came home with eyeballs that jumped from trying to look everywhere at once, to write in this journal.

I have only been a Puppy three days, yet it feels like three year. I feel I have changed so much from the mot who wrote her account of that first day. Who will I be by week's end?

Saturday, April 4, 246

Afternoon, before training.

What woke me this morning wasn't Pounce's washing, but a pigeon's good hard peck on my cheekbone. I yelped and threw the beast off. Back he came, landing on my crown and digging his claws into my hair.

Pounce had opened my shutters. I forgot my gratitude. "Y' mangy fleabag!" I yelled through a mouthful of cover. "Y' want us murdered in our sleep?"

"She'll think I run off," a cove whispered. "She'll think I di'n't love 'er an' the girls. She'll think I got a decent job an' pay an' run off with it."

Goose bumps raced over my flesh. I reached up slow with both my hands. A hard beak fastened in the tender skin between my thumb and forefinger and twisted. I closed my fingers around the bird, growling from pain, and brought him around where I could look at him.

Slapper.

I worked his beak free of me and tried to shift my hold so we were both easier. For my trouble he got a wing free and smacked me full in the face. It was a pigeon's punch. He clipped me on the nose as the spirit that rode him said, "She'll think I run off."

"I heard you." I took hold of Slapper's wing and tried to wipe my watering eyes on my shoulder. That blow *hurt*. "Tell me where I'll find your corpse. Then

175

she'll know you're dead and can't go to her."

"She'll think I run off," the ghost moaned. "I'm dead in the ground."

Slapper turned his head and bit my cheek. I yelped and let go. The curst bird took off out my window.

He would be back. Or I would find him, and his rider, with other pigeons. Should I feed them? Or try to find the murdered folk the dust spinners spoke of? I checked for my clothes. I looked out the window. From the sun's angle, it wasn't quite yet nine in the morning. I had time, and I needed to do chores.

I had to wash a uniform today. At least I had a clean one ready now, thanks to Goodwin. I would soak the soiled one free of wrinkles, then hang it with weights on overnight. If I mucked up today's uniform, I would have a clean one for the morrow.

I was pulling on breeches when I heard a mot's shriek. Something crashed on my stairs. I beat Pounce to the door and pulled it open. The door to the rooms opposite mine was wide open: moving day for a new neighbor. Someone came up the stairs backward and half bent over, carrying a wooden table legs up. Atop the table were some packs and a small trunk. Another person down below supported the other end of the table as it bobbed and swayed.

The bearer who was almost to my level looked over her shoulder and grinned. It was the swordswoman Aniki, wearing breeches and shirt, her sleeves rolled up.

She looked back at the other end of the table. "Rosto, leave that box! Kora can get the curst thing. If you try to grab it, you'll dump everything else down the stairs!" She told me, "I think we overloaded it." She backed up again. Here came the rest of the table, with Rosto the Piper holding up the wobbling end.

"Told you I liked the look of the street," he said to me. "And here's this place, with three sets of rooms nice and empty, for cheap. I rented 'em last night—me and Kora have the two just downstairs, and you've got Aniki for a neighbor."

I blinked at Rosto. Trouble has just moved in, I thought. Then I remembered I stood there in no more than breastband and breeches. I shrieked and slammed my door. I cleaned up for the day and put my uniform to soak in a washtub, my poor brain racing. Aniki and Kora seemed like good sorts, for mots clearly on the other side of the law. Truth to tell, it would be nice to have friendly folk here. But *Rosto* . . .

"Aren't there other lodgings?" I asked Pounce as I felt my hair. It was all tangles. I brushed it out, then wet my comb and worked to make a smooth braid. By the time I was done, the moving noises had ended with a clattering of feet down the stairs. I can't say how I might avoid Rosto after him seeing me half naked if he is to live here, but knowing he wasn't right outside my door was a start.

Someone knocked. I peered through the eye cheat

to see that Kora and Aniki were outside. My nose twitched. I smelled spiced turnovers. I opened the door. Kora, neat and tidy in a green cotton gown fit snug to her hips, held the covered basket that gave off the wonderful smells. Aniki stood behind her, two flasks in her hands.

"We fetched breakfast to begin well as your neighbors," Kora told me with a wicked smile. "The turnovers come from a baker named Mistress Noll. They say at the Court of the Rogue she's the best. And I warmed up everything with a bit of magicking."

My belly growled. It had been a very long time since last night's dry chicken. Both of them laughed.

I ducked my head and let them in. It felt like they brought sun and fresh air with them. Aniki set aside her flasks and lay down a cloth on my floor. I fetched three cups and plates from my shelf and set them down at the cloth's center whilst Kora whisked the napkin away from her basket. We sat cross-legged, spearing pasties with our belt knives.

"It's partly our own celebration," Aniki explained with her mouth half full. "Me'n Rosto have work. Me with Dawull—"

I nodded. Dawull was the redheaded chief of Waterfront District. It ran from the South Gate to the North Gate along both sides of the river.

Kora took a gulp of barley water. "And Rosto with Ulsa, who runs the Prettybone District." She gave Aniki a pert smile. "You owe Cooper's tall Dog two silver nobles. You bet him Rosto would hire on with Dawull."

"I know, I know," Aniki said, grabbing another pasty. "And now I can afford to pay him."

I looked from one to the other. Kora and Aniki are so relaxed and friendly that it doesn't seem to matter if I talk or no. They act as if we've known each other all our lives. I know there are Dogs who are friends with folk on the far side of the law. It can be done, so long as everyone observes the rules. If they do not give me knowledge of acts against the King's peace, so long as I do not catch them breaking it, we can do this.

"You're wondering how Aniki can work for one chief and Rosto another?" Kora asked. In a way I was, since my problem was similar. She offered a scrap of pasty to Pounce. "We've never turned against one another. Masters come and go. Friends remain always."

"Besides, where's the problem?" Aniki stretched her long body and leaned against my wall as if she sat in the most comfortable of chairs. I tossed her a couple of pillows. "Thanks." She stuffed them in around her back. "Kayfer's chiefs spend all their time protecting Kayfer. They don't battle each other." She grinned, but it was a wolf's grin, showing teeth. "So me'n Rosto don't have to worry about fighting. Not that we would. So what's your Dog's name, Cooper? The one I owe money to?"

"Tunstall," I replied, watching her hands as she

flexed them. She didn't even look like she noticed she did them, the exercises swordfolk were always about to keep their hands limber. "Matthias Tunstall. The other one's Clara Goodwin. And I'm Beka."

Aniki wove the fingers of both hands together, turned her palms out, and stretched her arms as far as she could. I gave it a try. "Easy," she warned me. "Push too hard and you hurt yourself fairly bad. I'm Aniki Forfrysning. That's Koramin Ingensra. You heard Rosto say we've all moved in."

"And *you* are a very fine fellow," Kora told Pounce, gathering him up in her arms. "Aniki, feel his coat! It's like velvet!" She looked at me. "I've never felt a cat's coat so clean and so soft. How do you do it, when he runs in the street?"

Pounce looked at me. *Make her stop,* he said in cat.

I looked back, telling him silently, *She's a mage. You make her stop.*

Kora had just found his favorite place to be scratched, right under the point of his jaw. Fickle Pounce began to purr instead. Aniki scooted over to scratch him herself.

"We've been on the road too long," she announced with a sigh. "I'd like to settle here and have a cat. Maybe I'll steal this one."

"Pounce doesn't take to being stole. I should just mention it," I explained. Shadows broke up the light from the window. All three of us looked up. Kora freed a hand. I could see a pale green-blue gleam around her fingertips. I shook my head at her. Pigeons lined up on my sill. There were three, Slapper, Pinky, and White Spice. Slapper, with no more sense than the average cracknob, hopped onto my floor and limped to our cloth. He glared at us all like some prophet out of legend.

"Friends of yours?" Aniki asked mockingly.

I shrugged.

Slapper began to peck at our crumbs. Seeing their flockmate was getting away with something, the other two flew over to us.

"Look at this," Kora whispered. "He's not so much as twitching."

Pounce sat in her lap, purring away. He wasn't about to give up being petted.

Since they weren't crying out and demanding the dirty birds be chased off—like my sisters, Diona and Lorine, often did—I crumbled some of my pasty and held out my crumbs. White Spice came over.

"My little boy's lame," his man ghost mourned. "Who will look after 'im? Slavers took 'is ma. She was so beautiful I knew we wouldn't be let keep 'er, but we did our best. Who'll look after 'im now?"

"This wasn't s'posed to happen," cried Pinky's ghost. "We was supposed to dig a well, that's all, just a well, and we dug it—"

"Beka! *Beka!*"

181

That living cove's yell jerked me from my listening. I spilled what was left of my palmful of crumbs. My pigeons took flight, leaving droppings on my floor before they fled through the open window. Aniki and Kora both grabbed their daggers.

"Beka, you are *not* hiding in your rooms all day! You are having fun with your friends! You know, *friends*?"

"Ersken," I said with a sigh. My head ached as he pounded up my stairs. He had others with him, too, unless he had brought a herd of horses. "It's my friend Ersken," I explained to Aniki and Kora. "He's another Puppy. And one, mayhap two, of the others."

"This could be interesting," Kora murmured.

"Beka, they's more to life than sleepin' an' walkin' your watch!" Verene is from Blue Harbor and still has the accent to show for it.

Pounce muttered in cat. At least, Aniki and Kora heard it so. Aniki petted and admired him for being "such a talky little pippin." I heard, *Humans. Always getting good ideas and interrupting important business with them at the stupidest times.*

I would have said he had a poor idea of them who fed him, but Ersken was almost up the stairs.

"Beka, I mean it! You will open this door and—" He halted in my open doorway, blinking. Verene and Phelan collided with his back. Phelan was a second-year Dog who'd befriended us Puppies. "You're—

Hello," Ersken said to Kora and Aniki. "Bek, you—um . . ."

Kora looked at him sidelong and smiled. That was it for Ersken. He turns as shy as me when a pretty girl bats her lashes at him. Then Aniki got to her feet. She is half a head taller than Ersken, more woman than he knows what to do with.

Verene started to giggle. She came in and offered a hand to Aniki. "We're Beka's friends. We came to keep her from turnin' into a mushroom. I'm Verene, tha's Phelan, and th' spaniel Pup is Ersken. He's sweet. Don't bruise him." Ersken turned beet color.

"We're moving in, so we invited Beka to breakfast," Aniki explained as she shook Verene's hand. "That's my friend Kora on the floor. She's living downstairs now. I'm Aniki. We met Beka at the Rogue's Court."

"You were there when Crookshank pitched his fit?" asked Phelan, his eyes bright with interest. "The word is he tried to kill the Rogue. Some Scanran pretty boy saved ol' Kayfer's life."

"That 'pretty boy' would be me," said a slow voice from my doorway, behind the group.

My friends turned. Pounce gave the *mrt* that served him for a laugh.

"I brought fresh food," Rosto said. He eased his way in. The next thing I knew, I had six guests on my floor splitting up fresh-baked oatmeal and rye bread.

Rosto had bought soft cheese to put on the bread, which made him a good fellow in my friends' eyes.

"So why do they call you the Piper?" Verene asked when he'd been introduced around. She'd taken care to get the seat beside his. Verene had an eye for a good-looking cove.

"I play well enough, don't I, girls?" he asked. Aniki and Kora nodded. Rosto smiled. It was a razor blade of a smile that made me wonder if he was thinking of Kayfer Deerborn. I was sure Rosto and his mots had come to take the Rogue's throne. They couldn't do it alone. Three young rushers new to Corus would stand on that platform for less time than it would take to mop away the old Rogue's blood before they'd be over-whelmed by his followers. But being new, they didn't have the old feuds and hates built up among the folk in the present court. If they made friends, Rosto might well be on the way to a kingship.

To make his point, Rosto took a flute from his tunic and began to play. He *was* very good. Then Verene rec-ognized one of his tunes and sang it. She had the pret-tiest voice in all the Provost's Guard. Kora danced for us. Rosto and Phelan discovered they had met the same old wandering mage in different towns. Finally we de-cided someone had to go for lunch before all of us but Kora went on duty. Everyone put in some coppers. Me and Ersken went out to get sausages, more cheese, and some spinach tarts.

"Be a shame to hobble any of them," he said after we'd walked in silence for a bit.

I nodded.

"You think that Rosto likes you?"

I gave him a shove.

"He moved into your lodging house, didn't he?"

"He said he liked the location. And he's got Aniki or Kora."

"I'd say both."

"That's his business, Ersken."

"What if he's looking to add you, Beka?"

"That's *my* business." I kicked a rotting vegetable away from me to hide my blushes. "Besides," I said, keeping my eyes down, "he's got to be twenty-two if he's a day."

"Oh, *ancient,*" Ersken said, scoffing. "Handsome as the sunrise, if you like that sort of cove. Don't look at *me,*" he said when I stared at him. "Well, look at me, but not that way. I have older sisters, remember? If I don't know what makes girls wiggle their toes, I've had my head in the Olorun for seventeen years."

To distract him, because I didn't want the talk to come round to whether I saw Rosto that way or he saw me the same, I asked, "Have you heard of the Shadow Snake?"

Ersken frowned. "Shadow Snake? You mean, what they say Crookshank and the Rogue were talking about that night you were there?"

"The same, but before then. Stealing children from the Lower City. Threatening folk who had something of value and taking a little one if they didn't pay it over. Have you heard aught?" I never had trouble talking with Ersken. He made it that easy. The other girls said he was too nice, but what was wrong with that? Better that than Rosto's sword-edge self.

"Me? Heard anything?" Ersken began to laugh. "Beka, we've only been on the prowl three days! I'm *new* in the Lower City, remember? I've not got my ear to the walls like you!"

If I had my ear to the walls like you think, I'd've known about the Snake when he took Rolond, or a year ago, or two. I thought it, but did not say it. I was too ashamed.

I stopped dead in the street to glare at him. "Your Dogs mayhap said sommat when you heard about Crookshank."

He made himself stop laughing. "They did not. Come on. Tell me what you've heard, and I'll see what I turn up."

And so I told him. Now two of us will be seeking this snake.

After my watch.
It was a beautiful spring evening. I felt a bit of a twinge when Tunstall greeted me at muster with "We're back to the Cesspool tonight, Cooper." Not even spring im-

proves the Cesspool much, though the weather was perfect. Not too cold, not too hot.

An hour in, we raided an illegal slave auction. One of Goodwin's Birdies brought the word to her and carried away her coppers for thanks. It was being held in a ramshackle barn. As big as the place was, my Dogs had no choice but to post me at the side door, since they had to go in at the front and the back.

Lucky for me I had my baton out and was ready for trouble. A Rat came dashing through my door. He was a giant fellow a head taller than me. When I called, "In the King's name!" and grappled with him, he turned and caught me one on the cheekbone with his elbow. For all that, I hung on and got my baton placed so he went quiet and gave me his full attention. I got the hobbles on his wrists, then made him kneel so I could get his ankles.

Goodwin came out the door to see what had become of me. Seeing us, she gave me a nod and a quarter smile. It turned out my Rat was the ringleader, a crooked cove who'd tried to sell a dozen slaves without paying the King's tax. Even with the knot on my cheekbone, I felt as good at dropping him as I had Orva Ashmiller.

Around nine we took supper in an eating house by North Gate. For the rest of our watch we worked that part of the Cesspool. It was quiet.

"Such nights happen," Tunstall said as we trudged

down Rovers Street on our way back to the kennel. "I like to give Mithros a bit of an offering before I go home, to show him I'm proper grateful—"

We were passing the Barrel's Bottom. It was one of the worst riverfront taverns. It proved its reputation now as the double front doors blew open and a knot of brawlers fell into the street.

"You had to tempt the Crone," Goodwin muttered. We drew our batons. "Cooper, just keep anyone we pull out from piling back in."

They were splendid to watch, my Dogs. To dishearten the brawlers they yanked from the knot, they hit them neatly with the fist end of their batons. The blows caused so much pain even these drunken swine felt it.

The problem began when the river dodgers fighting inside learned someone was pounding their friends outside. Bees hummed in my belly as they came stumbling out of the tavern. I knew my Dogs were tough, but this looked like a lot of scuts and not enough batons. My mouth went wool dry.

When one mot whose arm muscles were double mine seized Goodwin, I don't even remember deciding to disobey my orders. I smashed her aside like Sergeant Ahuda taught us to do. That brought me to the river dodgers' attention. I got caught up in a tide of bodies. Somehow we were pulled inside with the fight. I laid about me as my Dogs did, feeling my baton hit. I remember trying to get my whistle to my mouth to call for other Dogs. Someone cut the cord from my belt and sliced my arm in the doing. I was scared. Sooner or later I was going to fall and be trampled. Try as I did, I couldn't get close to Goodwin or Tunstall.

I don't think Tunstall remembered he even had a whistle. He pounded heads with his baton, roaring. Goodwin blew her whistle even as she laid out coves and mots alike. Sometime in that fight, I decided I wanted to be Clara Goodwin if I lived. I don't know if that was afore or after someone laid a very hard fist in my left eye.

I kicked up as I was taught. My reward was a yell of pain. Then I heard a cat's battle scream. Pounce landed on the head of a cove who'd drawn a blade on Tunstall. My cat blinded the knife wielder with scratches that bled into his eyes. Then Pounce was on to his next Rat before that one could grab him.

Curse all Dogs who can't hear a whistle! he yowled.

Someone pushed me against a table. I smashed him across the head hard, then shoved him behind me. I heard him smack into furniture. Somewhere in the corner at my back I heard a woman's voice, a low and pleasant one.

"All I want is to get peacefully drunk after eating hill dirt in my ale for months. Goddess, was it too much to ask?"

I didn't think the Goddess was anywhere present.

I glanced back, in case the woman who was getting up from her table might need a baton smash on *her* head. She was near as tall as Tunstall, brown-haired, brown-eyed, long-nosed, broad-shouldered, slim enough for her height. She wore a brown leather jerkin and breeches and a shirt that mayhap once was white. The leather scabbards of her dagger and sword were just as beat up as her clothes and boots.

The tall mot battered her way to the bar. She dragged the barkeep up by the shirt, seized the well-polished club he clutched, and shoved him back into his hiding spot.

Hands grabbed me. I was busy again. I did my best, but I was getting tired. I finally remembered Ahuda's teaching and fought my way to a wall. I put it at my back so no one else might grab me from behind. Taking care, I got into a corner, with a wall on the side of my black eye. I didn't like having my arm restricted, but it beat fighting on my blind side.

Goodwin was backing up to me, using a lull in the fight. The woman in brown wielded the club like a blade. Behind her lay a trail of collapsed river dodgers. Some even decided they'd had enough fun. They were sneaking out the side doors. More crawled through the doors in front.

By the time the lady and Tunstall met at the center of the room, Goodwin had reached me. She leaned against the wall, panting. "You're a mess," she said. "You're bleeding where?"

I showed her my arm. She cut a strip from the shirt of a cove I'd downed and bound my cut with that. "Carry spare handkerchiefs and strips of linen. Bind cuts right off," Goodwin told me as she knotted the bandage. "Elsewise you'll as soon die of blood loss as someone's shiv in your ribs." She grabbed a pitcher from a table that had survived the jostling and took a huge gulp of the contents. Then she made me take a few swallows. It was ale. For a moment we watched as Tunstall traded blows with a nimble, fat cove.

"Cooper, nice baton work. Very nice." Goodwin took a deep breath, then looked away. Finally she leaned in and spoke quietly. "Me'n Tunstall got lucky here, Cooper. You're good in a fight, thank the Goddess. We didn't look out for you as we should have done. Most Puppies would be dead right now, understand? Because this isn't the kind of fight Puppies survive without their Dogs watching out for them. We'll look out for you better in future."

"I was doing the job," I said.

"Shut up. *We* weren't doing *ours,* me and Tunstall. We were doing the job we used to have, just breaking heads. We can't do that anymore. Now we have you to look after." Goodwin nodded. "We're learning this teaching Dog business same as you're learning a Dog's work, but that's no excuse. Older Dogs look after younger ones, that's the rule. Now, who do you suppose our lady knight is?"

"That's a knight? How can you tell?"

I was glad to see Goodwin's hooked half smile. "I saw her and four other knights riding down Messinger on my way to the kennel this afternoon. I didn't see more than the shape of the shield, but she had the armor and trappings. And knights have a way about them, chin so high in the air they're just begging for you to give them the nap tap."

I grinned. All of us love that hammer blow of baton against jaw, even if it doesn't always knock a Rat out. Goodwin has the city's record for the highest number of perfectly delivered nap taps that end with a Rat carried away, stone unconscious.

The scrape of wood got our attention. A mot with one eye picked up a wooden bench, meaning to throw it at the lady knight. Goodwin started forward to help, but the lady turned and caught sight of her danger, and Tunstall's. She didn't even waste the breath to shout. She slung her free arm around Tunstall's neck, hooked one of his legs from under him, and dragged him down and to the side. They fell as the mot hurled the heavy bench. It went over their heads and smashed into the three river dodgers who'd been moving in on Tunstall. As he and the lady struggled to their feet, Goodwin returned to lean against the wall.

"They're all right," she said. "They don't need me."

Pounce wandered over to us. Sitting on the floor, he began to wash his paws. I bent over to pet him, only to see the floor yaw away from me. "Pox," Goodwin whispered as she grabbed me.

I straightened with her help and let her get me to a bench. "Sorry," I muttered, feeling miserable.

Pounce jumped on my lap and began to talk to me. *Cheer up, you're doing fine. Learning hurts.*

"It's the blood loss." Goodwin half sat on the table next to me and crossed her arms over her chest. "It makes a girl feel giddy, and no mistake. The healer will set you right, Cooper."

Tunstall and the lady knight had come to the last pair of foes. Neither Rat looked sharp, but seemingly they were clever enough. With no friends left, they ran.

The lady looked at Tunstall, then at Goodwin and me, and leaned on her club. "Well," she said, a little winded. "This was refreshing. That's a fighting Pup you have there, but she nearly got killed. I know better than to take a squire into a fight where I'm outnumbered seven to one. It's one thing to dice with your own life and another to dice with that of someone you're training, Master Dog."

Tunstall scowled at her. "Cooper can take care of herself, and if she can't, we can take care of her, whatever your name is." Then he took a look at me and cursed. "Ox's eggs."

I swear it was the blood loss that made me say, "I am *fine,*" loud enough that even the lady heard me. As a lie it was pitiful. My head spun in the speaking of it.

The lady threw back her head and laughed. It was no well-bred laugh, but a full-throated guffaw. "A fighting Pup indeed." She strolled over to Goodwin and smiled. "I am Sabine of Macayhill, lady knight."

"Clara Goodwin of the Provost's Guard. My partner is Matthias Tunstall, and this is Rebakah Cooper." Goodwin smiled up at the lady. "Thank you for helping us deal with this lot. I'm curst if I know why no one responded to my whistle—"

Four Dogs walked in the front door, none of them people I knew well. Tunstall was coming toward us, so I could hear his mutter of "Pig scummer."

"Some 'un said they heard a Dog whistle a-blowin' down this way. We come as fast as we could," the biggest of the four said, looking around. "Seemingly you didn't need us, then."

"Change of the watch," Goodwin said, and sighed.

Now it made sense. It must have been later than we thought. The fellows of the Evening Watch were on their way to the kennel or already there when Goodwin blew her whistle. Night Watch is made up of the district's dregs, the slow and the sullen or the plain lazy. Someone carried the word of our alarm to the kennel because they got a copper for doing it, and the Dogs of the Night Watch took their time in coming.

For a moment the anger rose up so bad it choked me. I didn't know about dying, but these scummernobs could have saved me a beating. If I'd had the strength, I don't know but I would have flown at these four lazy scuts and tried some nap tapping of my own.

Pounce fluffed his fur out until he looked three times as big as normal. He jumped at the lummox Dog's chest. He howled like something from the Realms of Chaos, scaring the Dog and his friends so bad they went scrambling to get away from him. They tripped and fell over the river dodgers on the floor. Sadly for them, those folk were waking up, and they were vexed.

"Quick," whispered Lady Sabine. She pointed to a side door.

Before I knew what happened, Tunstall had scooped me up in his arms. He, Goodwin, and Lady Sabine ran out into the alley. Behind us we could hear a new fight break out.

Pounce caught up with us on Rovers Street. He took the lead, his tail a flag. He was very pleased with himself.

Once the healer had seen to me, Goodwin, Tunstall, and Lady Sabine walked me back to Nipcopper Close, Pounce riding on either Goodwin's or Lady Sabine's shoulders. The three of them wandered off to find a meal. It seemed that Tunstall had forgiven the lady her disapproval, at least enough to eat with her. My cat and I went in search of my bed.

Sunday, April 5, 246

This morning I opened my door to Kora, Aniki, and the wonderful scent of heated pasties from the basket on Kora's arm. Despite my weariness and the pain of my half-healed bruises, I smiled to see them. They looked full of mischief, and I have a sad liking for mischief. Why else would I prefer to live in the Lower City? My lord says that the best Dogs are half crooked at heart.

"Breakfast?" Aniki asked. "We heard you were dancing with river dodgers last night. You will need to build your strength back up."

"That's a splendid black eye," Kora said. "I like the cheekbone bruise, too. Before or after healing?"

"After," I said. My belly growled. I was always starved for a day after healing. Kora handed me a mutton pasty. I ate it then and there, standing aside to let them in. "How did you hear?" I asked them as Aniki put down the cloth and Kora laid out my plates.

"I was at Dawull's," Aniki said. "We got the news straight off. Some of our rushers wanted to go help the river dodgers, but Dawull wouldn't allow it. He won't let his people take on your Dogs if he knows about it beforehand, I found out. He says they're too tough."

I confess it, I was flattered. Aniki and Kora have plainly lived a hard life. To have them speak of my bruises and my Dogs as if I belong to that world—it seems as if I am accepted into it. As if I wear a Puppy's trim but have a Dog's standing. And I *have* paid a hard price for those bruises. Even with healing, they will linger on my face for days. It's good to get respect for them in the wake of the pain.

I found the bottles of twilsey and barley water from yesterday and put them down, then opened my shutters. The pigeons with the ghosts of the dead diggers waited for me. I fed them their corn as Rosto arrived with more food.

"I'll kiss them and make them better," he said when he saw my bruises.

I slid one foot back to balance myself and raised my arms, hands fisted, into blocking positions. "Try and I'll bruise *you.*" I actually said it out loud. "Then Aniki and Kora can kiss *you* better."

Kora smiled. "Aniki can do the kisses. Rosto, don't pull Beka's tail. She doesn't like it."

Pounce wandered over to Rosto and stood, reaching up delicately between his legs. He said, *"Mrt?"* just loud enough to make Rosto look down, then patted the inside of Rosto's knee.

Rosto sighed. "I was being *friendly,*" he complained. "Modern times are cruel when a cove can't be *friendly.*" He stepped around Pounce and settled on the floor cloth. "See if I bring you a treat tomorrow, Master Cat." He looked up at me. "Is there a tomorrow? I think this little breakfast idea is quite nice, even with threats and the nasty birds coming and going."

The "nasty birds" ignored him, being too busy fighting over the corn on my ledge. I eased off my fighting pose, dizzy from healing, and sat on my stool.

"Not tomorrow, Tuesday's my day off. I leave early to visit my family," I said. "And tomorrow is our day in Magistrate's Court. It starts the hour after sunrise."

"Ugh!" Rosto said, grimacing. "They don't pay you enough, sweetheart."

I scowled at him. I'll never tell him that I like his company. The extra food is nice, of course, particularly at the start of the day. I'd bite my tongue off before I said it, but Rosto *is* funny.

Very well. The truth, since I am the only one who reads this.

He makes my skin, my peaches, and my other parts tingle in an agreeable way. Naught will come of it. He's clearly meant to be more than an ordinary rusher, which means that one day he and I will be on the wrong sides of an argument. Besides, he's got Aniki and Kora. I'd druther be their friend than their rival.

But it's good, after the dark and the scares of night duty, to sit in daylight with food and interesting folk. Clever folk, who know how to laugh. Who know how to make *me* laugh, when doing so doesn't make my cheek hurt.

Ersken and Verene came not long after Rosto with sausage rolls and gossip. One of the barons in Unicorn found out his lady wife was canoodling with an Earl.

Rank or no, a challenge had been issued. Mistress Bircher, wife of the head of the Silversmiths' Guild, presented her man with twins. That was Flash District. Flash Dogs would have the joy of guarding that celebration when it happened. We would have a quiet night, as many of our foists and thieves went to help themselves there.

"Remember Alacia?" Verene asked me. To our crooked friends she said, "She's another Puppy, named in tribute to His Majesty's first Queen. Well, till yesterday she was on Day Watch in Unicorn. Then my lord of Olau got word that his youngest and only son has been flirtin' with a pretty Puppy."

"Fast work," Aniki said with respect. "You lot have been on duty, what, five days?"

"Four, not counting today," Ersken said. He's a stickler for numbers.

"*Anyway,*" Verene said. She hates it when wonderful gossip is interrupted. I never interrupt, because she has better gossip than most Dogs. Her mother is a barmaid at Naxen's Fancy, where they hear everything as soon as it happens. "*Anyway,* the lad's noble father pitched a fit at the Unicorn kennel, and they switched Alacia with Clarke. He was on Night Watch at Prettybone. So now *she's* on Night Watch."

Rosto rubbed his chin. "So this Alacia's a sweet armful? I'll look out for her, Dog or not."

Aniki gave him a hard elbow. "Don't you have

enough women in your life, Rosto?"

Rosto gave me what he thought was a sober look. "Not without Cooper, I don't."

"Cooper will never go with anyone crooked," Ersken said. "A rusher was mean to her mother. She's never forgiven them."

I could pretend not to hear what he said, because Slapper was making way for a new pigeon, one I'd never seen. This one was a sad case. He was a caked-feather fellow I instantly named Mumper. Mayhap he was gray under the dirt and grease on his wings and belly. His ghost, like those of the other murdered diggers, complained about being buried whilst his people believed he'd run off.

Once I'd gathered aught new he had to say, I heard Verene call my name. "You remember that Dog who taught us to tell dice that have been meddled with? He was on Night Watch?"

I knew him well. I remembered the sight of his fingers, handling the sets of dice he'd used to teach us. He could hold five in one hand and throw them so they'd all land in one circle drawn in the dirt.

Verene drew her finger over her throat.

My chest went tight. "Dead?" I whispered.

Ersken nodded, his face grim. "And we're not to go to the burying. There's a notice up on the kennel gate. We saw it on the way here. They found him with his dice in his mouth—all rigged. All crooked. My lord's order, under his seal: "Bury him with the Dogs, but not *as* a Dog."

We all made the sign against evil on our chests. Pounce came over and sat on my crossed legs to purr at me. Of course there are crooked Dogs. I can name two handfuls myself. But this is the first Dog to die since I entered the ranks. That is a sad thing.

I will buy prayers for him. I do not like that he was crooked. But he'd still been a Dog.

We sat and talked of other things as the sun rose higher and the room got warm. I wanted to get out and feed more pigeons. There might be others who'd been killed along with the ghosts who rode poor Mumper and Slapper. Mayhap once I had all of the murdered ones together, they could lead me to where they were buried. But healing had left me dozy, as it often does the day after, especially when I lose blood.

"You need a nap," Kora said when she saw my eyes start to flutter. "And I'm taking your clothes to wash. You can pay me three coppers for each wash I do."

"*Wash?*" I asked.

Kora had picked up my basket. "The herb women aren't hiring as yet. I have my charms to get clothes clean faster than most."

"You'll charge three coppers?" Verene asked.

Kora looked at her. "Five for those who don't live in my house."

"How about mine?" Ersken asked. "I'll pay five

and pay it more than gladly."

Kora smiled at them. "Hurry and get your things."

Ersken and Verene ran to fetch their wash.

"It doesn't seem right," I said. I didn't have the strength to argue much, I was so tired.

"I do a bit of magic with the soap and they're clean, a bit more and they're dry. I could make a fortune as a washerwoman," Kora said. "The worst part is carrying wet things."

Aniki and Rosto were clearing up the remains of breakfast.

"Get some street children to help," Aniki said. "A copper each and they'd wash the things themselves."

"I can imagine," Kora said. She looked at me. "Tell me you could do better yourself."

I yawned. "I can't."

"Then hush. Sleep till it's time for your watch."

I wrote this morning up during the afternoon, now I've woke up. When I opened my door, my clean wash was there in a basket, neatly folded. On my way to training, I will put three coppers under Kora's door.

After my watch.

Tonight Tunstall, Goodwin, and me were back in the streets around the Nightmarket. And I will write details now, truly. There were tavern fights, robberies. We broke up a fight among gamblers as a man claimed a mot had cheated him. I stopped five cutpurses and three foists on my own, but they were not stealing anything worth the trouble to hobble them.

We caught a cove trying to sell children who were not his to sell and fetched him and the slaver who was about to pay him back to the kennel. We took the three nearly sold children home. One mot didn't even know yet her little boy was missing. She had been sewing on a fancy gown for a fine lady that had to be finished in the morning. She thought her neighbor still had charge of her son.

I think that is all the work we did. I obeyed my orders and came home as soon as we mustered out, to write this little bit. I am bone weary with the work of this week, and there is Magistrate's Court yet tomorrow. So much for good intentions and keeping a record of everything from my first week on duty.

Monday, April 6, 246

Court Day!!

This last day before our day off, I had no time for breakfast. I gobbled stale rolls and cheese, then reported at seven in the morning to the Magistrate's Court for the Lower City. On Monday the Dogs of the Evening Watch account for those Rats they've bagged that week. They say what the Rats have done to warrant bagging and defend their actions in the bagging if need be. Tunstall and Goodwin will give the reports at the bidding of the Provost's Advocate and answer the questions of the King's Magistrate. The way it should work, the Puppies have little to do but pay attention against the day when they have to do the same. It's up to the Dogs who write the reports and who are there as each case unfolds to present the whole thing before the court.

I had most of the long day to see that all I'd heard was true. Magistrate's Court is simple enough. Some Rats with a little coin or patrons have advocates to speak for them. These lawyers sometimes persuade the Magistrate (Sir Tullus of King's Reach covers Evening Watch's arrests) to order fines, lashes, time in the stocks or Outwalls Prison, or work inside Corus or on a farm instead of something worse. Hard sentences go from labor on the realm's roads, mines, docks, or quarries to death for the murderers and arsonists.

I was familiar enough with the Jane Street court, having run messages there before I started my training. Still, it was odd, sitting in the Dogs' benches with Tunstall and Goodwin, my fellow Puppies, and their Dogs. Ersken had managed to slip into the seat next to me. Together we read what bored Dogs had carved into the low backs of the benches in front of us.

Not that we spent all of our time hearing reports and admiring the history. Behind the Dogs' seats was the wall of bars that separated the business side of the court from the visitors' side. Plenty was going on back there. Some of the folk on that side were family, friends, and sweethearts of the Rats who took their sentences that day. They had all matter of things to say, whether we were the Dogs who had vexed them or no. Then there were those who'd come for amusement's sake. Along the wall behind the bars stood the Dogs whose work it was to keep order.

When I got bored with the crowd, I watched the court officials. They were set up in front of the Dogs' benches. There was a table for the Provost's Advocate, where he kept his many lists and notes, and another for any advocate hired by the Rats. We saw few advocates that day. The mages who served to keep order against any other mages sat on benches at the front of the room. The Magistrate's Herald sat next to just such a mage, his list in one hand and his staff in the other, when he was not reading out the name of the Rat, the names of the Dogs involved, and the charges. And at the great desk, higher than the rest of us, flanked by two uniformed soldiers to represent the King's authority, was the Magistrate himself. Sir Tullus had ruled on Evening Watch cases for six years. My lord said he was fair and knew more law than most. The Dogs said he was a bit impatient with dithering.

Around three in the afternoon they brought Orva Ashmiller up. She was a sorry-looking mess in the light of day, with cage muck on her. And she was chained, which was a puzzler. She was so skinny the shackles seemed like to drop from her wrists. If not for the memory of that big knife, I almost pitied her. Then she caught sight of me.

"You *bitch*!" She threw herself at me. She'd caught the cage Dogs napping. Before the lackwits collected themselves, Orva fell headlong, her ankle chains tripping her. She scrabbled to her hands and knees to shriek, "You took my children from me! You turned my man agin' me, you puttock, you trollop, you trull—" She lunged and fell again. Now I knew why they'd chained her. "I'll cut your liver out, you poxied leech! Why wouldn't you let me go! You ruined my life!"

The crowd who had come for entertainment hooted and whistled. I wanted to vanish. I didn't feel even a little sorry for Orva anymore.

"Steady," whispered Tunstall.

I looked into the air over Sir Tullus's shoulder.

What a splendid omen for my very first day in the court. A drunkard who blamed me for the mess she'd gotten herself into was making a spectacle of me.

The dozy Dogs who'd let her escape ambled up to her, grabbing her arms to haul her to her feet. I just kept telling myself that with no coin and no advocate, the best she could hope for was a couple of years on a farm for striking a Dog. She'd be gone a long time, and maybe she'd get the hotblood wine out of her veins.

"Mama!"

I closed my eyes then, wishing I could trickle through the cracks in the floor. Why had the children come? I glanced back, where the crowd was. Of course her man had brought them, all three. Master Ashmiller wouldn't look at me as he carried the little lad up to the bars. What had he been thinking? Why would he want them to see their mama like this? She was still screaming, spittle flying from her lips, calling me every vile name there was, not once looking at the little ones calling for her.

The herald banged his staff on the floor without it doing any good. At last Sir Tullus ordered the cage Dogs to gag Orva and the court Dogs to take the screaming children out of the room. I finally drew a breath. Folk were yelling at the court and cage Dogs, their attention taken away from me at last. The two loobies who'd lost control of Orva in the first place silenced her.

I began to relax.

"The case of Mistress Orva Ashmiller, resident of Mulberry Way." The herald had a fine, ringing voice that bounced from the worn, smooth wood of the floor and walls. "Charges—striking Provost's Guardswoman Clara Goodwin while Guardswoman Goodwin acted to uphold the King's law together with fellow Guard Matthias Tunstall and trainee Guard Rebakah Cooper."

Sir Tullus scowled. "Struck a Guard? Report."

Tunstall nudged me with his elbow. "Cooper."

I must have stared up at him like a snared rabbit. "None of the other trainees had to." I think I whined.

"Cooper, he hates Dogs that waste time," Goodwin said. "Report. The Dog that was there for the whole thing does the report. That would be you."

Ersken actually tried to push me to my feet. "You can do it, Beka!"

Some nightmares do not end. I peered at the Magistrate through my bangs and dug my feet in against Ersken's push. To my scrambling brain Sir Tullus seemed very like the smoked boar face the butchers hang before their shops to advertise. His face was that beet-like red, his jowls dark with beard-shadow. I believe he had but one very long eyebrow.

His mouth gave the oddest of twitches. By then I was in a complete, blind panic. I couldn't speak before all these people. I didn't care if most were behind the onlookers' bars!

"This day comes to all trainee Guards, Rebakah Cooper," Sir Tullus said. "Your day has only come earlier than most. Speak up. The sooner you begin the telling, the sooner you may go."

"We were walking the rounds when we heard the sound of violence," Tunstall said quietly. It was one of the beginnings we committed to memory in training. Now Goodwin had a grip on my other arm, far more painful than Ersken's.

"Stand up or I'll poke your wound," she muttered. "Do *not* embarrass Tunstall and me in front of the Magistrate."

I stumbled to my feet with that, but my knees wobbled. "I—We were w-walking the—the rounds when we, um, we heard violence. Milord."

"Look up, Guardswoman, and speak up." For a man supposed to be peppery, he sounded almost kind. "Just tell it. What happened?"

How could I say I could not speak before this whole hooting chamber? I stumbled and stammered and got no more along than explaining the mess Orva's man was when Sir Tullus took pity on me. "Enough. Tunstall, continue."

I dropped onto the bench and put my face in my hands, feeling the heat of my shame against my palms. Why must I be unable to speak before strangers? It is my biggest fault as a Dog, and I must find a way to fix

209

it, but how? They were all laughing at me. Who could blame them? From fish guts to drooling cracknob, I'd had a glorious week.

Nor was it done. I heard Tunstall say, "Orva escaped through the open window." He stopped then and cleared his throat.

"She knew there were stairs without? Go on," Sir Tullus urged Tunstall. "I assume you captured her outside."

"No, Sir Knight," Tunstall replied. He cleared his throat again. I saw where this was headed. My tripes clenched. For a moment I thought I might throw up.

"But you have said that Goodwin was unable to give chase," Sir Tullus reminded Tunstall.

"I did, Sir Knight." Tunstall started to rub his beard, as he often did when he wasn't sure what to say.

"Ah." To my sorrow, Sir Tullus was a quick-witted man. "Stand up and try again, Cooper."

I actually heard a moan from the onlookers.

I stood.

I was dizzily trying to remember my own name when someone walked between my trembling legs.

Pounce.

He curled up on the toes of my boots. I could feel his purr rumble through the leather.

"Sir Knight, I went after her," I told the floor.

"Louder," Ersken whispered.

"Sir Knight, I went after her," I repeated, as loud

as I could manage. "She would not halt when I bade her to, so I gave chase. I caught her."

"Where, Cooper?" The Magistrate sounded *very* patient.

I swallowed. "At the Sheepmire Tavern, Sir Knight."

"He won't know where that is!" Ersken whispered. So eager he was to help me that his voice was just a bit too loud. Folk heard and laughed.

Goodwin took out her baton, went back to the bars, and walked along, banging them hard. The ones hanging on to the bars had to jump away to keep from getting their fingers smacked. Of course they hit those crowding behind them. Some went down in a heap.

"Silence!" she cried in her crowd voice. "I don't know what manner of Players' jollity you thought you came here for, you scuts, but you were dead wrong! This is a court of the realm's law. Shut your gobs or I'll come back there and crack skulls!"

Goddess, how I want to be Clary Goodwin when I get to be a proper Dog, I thought with envy.

The court Dogs, them as were *supposed* to keep order, stirred. It had dawned on them that they ought to do some work. They moved out into the crowd, hands on their own batons. Goodwin thrust hers back into its straps and came to sit next to Tunstall and me.

"Thank you, Guardswoman Goodwin." Sir Tullus's voice was as dry as Crookshank's heart. "It is a pleasure to watch you restore quiet in my court. Continue, Guardswoman Cooper. The Sheepmire Tavern . . . ?"

For a moment I'd forgotten my own pain. I ground my teeth and tried to remember where the curst place was. "Spindle Lane, Sir Knight," I said at last.

"I have no idea where that is," the Magistrate said.

Tunstall stood. "It's but a short walk from the North Gate, Sir Knight." He sat down, giving me a pat on the shoulder as he did so.

I tried to forgive him for handing me to Sir Tullus. I knew nearly as well as he did that it was the Dog who stayed with the Rat who did the report. It was only because I was so curst tongue-tied before folk that he'd had to speak at all.

Sir Tullus's eyebrow shot toward his forehead. *"From Mulberry Way to the North Gate?"*

My tongue felt too big for my mouth. Ersken kicked me to make me speak. "I—I— Forgive me, milord, sorry, Sir Knight, but we went by back ways and through a few . . ." I clenched my fists and kept on going. "There was alleys and between houses and she went through a couple of drinking dens and I caught her by going around one, Sir Knight, then I hobbled her and we got a cart ride back to the kennel and I know I wasn't s'posed to arrest her but I had her and so I told her she was arrested and then my Dogs— 'scuze me, my Guards—they done it proper when I got her to the guardhouse." My mouth kept going as I said, "I'm sorry for her children and her man, but they're cracknobs for wanting someone who breaks crockery on their faces and tries to cut them with a dreadful big knife, with apologies, Sir Knight." Then I clapped my hands over my traitor mouth. It was a heady thing, reporting like that, with my heart pounding and my cheeks burning like one of Crookshank's houses. I think I went a little mad for just a moment.

Someone poked me from behind. It was Verene. She gave me a flask. I sniffed, but it was just warm raspberry twilsey, naught that would make me giddy. The tartness washed the dry coat from my mouth and made it tingle. I reminded myself to do something nice for Verene one day soon.

I looked at Sir Tullus through my bangs. His mouth was twitching, more this time than it had before. Then it steadied out. He scratched his head. "Better, Guardswoman?"

I nodded. This time it was Tunstall who kicked me. "Yes, sir, thank you, Sir Knight," I said, thinking that between Tunstall and Ersken, my legs would look like eggplants in the morning.

"Perhaps you would be so good as to explain *why* you went to such trouble, if you please," Sir Tullus said. "You show a degree of . . . enthusiasm that is unusual, even for a trainee Guard."

"Sir?" I asked. Now that the worst of it was done, I could meet his eyes, as long as he didn't want to be chattering until midnight.

"Why did you not let her go? You could have returned for her another day," Sir Tullus explained.

Perhaps it was Sir Tullus who'd run mad, not me. Except he seemed to be the same as when the day had started. Still, it was a crackbrained question, though I could not say as much to him.

"Sir Knight, she *struck* Guardswoman Goodwin," I said, wondering if I should talk slow, like a person did with the simple and the young. "With a knife. Not the sharp end, but it might've been. Orva couldn't be let get away with it, sir."

"And why not?" he asked, prodding again.

I wished I could scratch my head or sew or whittle to help myself think. Trying to explain with my hands hanging useless was like being schooled by the law masters in training or my teachers in Lord Gershom's home. Surely any Dog in this room could explain this to him better than me.

"Sir Knight, striking a Dog with a knife—it's a serious thing. A Dog is the face—we're the face of . . ." My thoughts scattered. I found them again. "The Dogs are the face of the law. We're so few. Nobody wants the work. So the realm says, *We* value Dogs. We set the price high for them as turn a blade on a Dog." I'd had about enough explaining. I looked at the floor again.

"If the realm values us enough to make the law and the penalties like we have, I must value us Dogs enough to catch them as breaks the law. Mustn't I, Sir Knight?"

No one said anything, or laughed, or hooted. I think they were trying to work out what I'd said and if it made sense. *I* wasn't even certain of the sense of what I'd said.

At last Sir Tullus told me, "Guardswoman Cooper, Corporal Guardswoman Goodwin is a true hero in the Provost's Guard. She has recovered large amounts of property, brought hundreds to justice, and saved countless lives. You are right. Her life and work are valuable to this court. You may be seated."

As I gratefully planted my bum on the bench, I heard Goodwin mutter, "Don't even *think* this makes me sweet on you, Cooper."

Hiding behind my bangs, I grinned.

"Orva Ashmiller, have you an advocate to speak for you?" asked the Magistrate.

"She does not," said the Provost's Advocate. "Her husband, Jack Ashmiller, begs the mercy of this court. He asks that his wife be granted a fine or work and imprisonment within the city. I have also gathered the complaints of Mistress Ashmiller's neighbors. They state that she has repeatedly given her husband and children bleeding injuries, bruises, and broken bones. They ask for the peace of their homes that Mistress Ashmiller receive a sentence to prison or to exile from the city of Corus." He walked up to the Magistrate and presented him with a paper.

Sir Tullus read the paper over. He looked at Orva. *Did I see disgust on his face? I* disliked anyone who mauled children so, but most folk thought that children grew up unruly, even wrong, without some touch of the strap or the slap. As for Jack Ashmiller, why had he not fought her when she got to breaking things on his head? Usually Lower City men gave as good as they got, or worse.

"Your neighbors should have come to this court long ago, Mistress Ashmiller," Sir Tullus said. Orva started to fight the cage Dogs' grip on her arms again. She knew she would not like what came next. Sir Tullus continued, "Orva Ashmiller, it is the judgment of this court that you go to the royal work farm in the town of Whitethorn. You will labor there for five years for disturbing your neighbors' peace, for violence to your family, and for the crime of wielding a blade against a representative of the King's peace. Should you try to escape the farm and return to Corus, you will be branded and sold into slavery."

He struck the bronze sun disk on his desk with his polished granite ball, the sign that judgment had been made. The Dogs carried Orva off to the cages to wait for transport. She had a long journey ahead.

I thought I would feel better about it. More victorious. Instead I just felt sad.

"Next case," Sir Tullus told the herald.

They'd lit the court's lamps well before all of those hobbled that week on the Evening Watch came before the Magistrate. Despite the food all the Dogs had known to bring, things like sausage rolls that they shared with the Puppies, my belly was growling like a four-footed dog by the end of it. I could hear everyone else's belly making the same complaints. Finally Sir Tullus struck the sun disk on the day's last judgment.

And thus went my first Court Day.

I think I am going to puke.

Tuesday, April 7, 246

At day's end.

I think even if I'd come home late last night, I'd have been up with the dawn, but I'd been to bed at a good hour. Today was my free day. I was going to see my family at Provost's House. I took my blue dress from my clothespress yesterday and let it air out, along with my underdress and a veil for my hair. Lord Gershom would only laugh if I wore lads' garb as I did most days, but Lady Teodorie would smile in that thin, ice on the puddles at dawn way. I would give her no extra cause to level that smile at me. The bruises that had gone purple-green on my face would be more than enough problem in that regard.

Each time I walk up Gold Street to Provost's House, I remember coming this way with Mama that first time. She rode in the cart with our few things, trying not to cough. I remember the roses bloomed on her cheeks. My lord's healer said later those were a cruel joke of the sickness. The sun struck red lights in Mama's brown curls, too, making them shine. She was so happy. "Had I prayed the Goddess, I would never have dreamed such a chance for us, Beka." She knew I was angry that my lord had tracked me home and waited until I was out to persuade Mama. "You cannot spit on the lady's gift, you mule-headed gixie! This is not only for you, but your sisters and brothers. *You'll*

218

never grow old in the Cesspool—you're meant for better things!"

The servants' gate was open and Jakorn was on duty today, as he was then. There had been more black in his long hair then, which was almost all gray now. This morning he grinned, showing the gaps where he'd lost teeth over the years. "Beka. Not wearin' yer uniform?" Jakorn came from the north. When he was angry, his burr was so thick it was that hard to understand his speech at all.

"I don't want to wear the same thing every day," I said, and kissed his cheek.

From the glint in Jakorn's eye, he knew very well I'd worn a dress to stay on my lady's good side. "And yer face, mistress?"

I hung my head before my first teacher in fighting. "You was a street Dog once, Jakorn."

He clapped me on the shoulder. "Di'n't I tell ye, th' idea be, yer *foe* walks away lookin' mauled?" he asked, but it was all teasing. "Run on in t' Cook. She's been worritin' about ye leavin' yer insides in some privy from the dreadful food down in th' Lower City."

I grinned at him and passed on through the gate. The servants were already at their work, of course. They smiled and called greetings but did no more. They had their duties, and my lady expected those to come before all else. My sisters, Diona and Lorine, just about worship my lady, and I dare say no word against her before them. I feel sometimes like my lady means more to Diona than I do. My sisters are turning into proper young mots, neat in their appearance and correct in their speaking. The days when we giggled together over Pounce's kitten antics seem to fade with every month since Mama's death.

I want them to do well in life. My lady is seeing to that. She is training Diona as a lady's maid, which had been the dream of Mama's heart. She has promised to find Diona a very good place when she thinks Diona is ready, and my lady keeps her promises. Lorine, though only twelve, bids fair to be an excellent seamstress one day. Already she does much of my lady's fine sewing, which suits my lady's personal seamstress well. She's getting old, and her eyes are not what they once were. She looks on Lorine as a daughter and teaches her those tricks of good stitchery my lady does not know.

Two of the dairymaids passed me in giggles. I wished just once that I could say, "You don't snicker when the lads come home for their day off!" Plenty of servants' sons have gone to be Dogs. It was only the girls who are given the raised brow.

The door to the kitchen wing was open. Only in the coldest winter is it closed, along with the door on the end of the hall that opens onto the kitchen proper. I walked in. A boy scrubbed tableware from the household's breakfast. Cookmaids sat at the chopping table, preparing vegetables. Cook stood with her back to me, tasting several different cheeses. She saw the boy grin at me and turned.

"Oh, my dear, what happened to your face?" she asked in her soft, kind way. She opened her arms, and I stepped into her warm hold. Mya had looked after our family from the moment our cart rolled through the servants' gate. She made soups that Mama kept down despite the cough that so often made her bring up other food. When Mama found the Black God's peace at last, it was Mya who held me. She was a tiny dumpling of a mot, rounded and sweet, her eyes up-tipped at the corners. So, too, was her nose tipped at the end. Kindness was what she gave as easily as she breathed, but she ruled the kitchen, and the children of the house, firmly. No one fooled her.

I put my hand to my healing eye and shrugged. "Doing work on Rovers Street, Mya."

She cocked her head to one side. "I thought your job was to duck," she said.

I giggled, because of course she was right. "I'll do better another time," I promised.

She sat me down and fed me. I couldn't escape that, no more did I want to. My belly had started growling on Gold Street.

"Now," Mya said once she'd put some food before me, "my lord says Kebibi Ahuda got you assigned to

Goodwin and Tunstall. Is it true? If Clary Goodwin is giving you a bad time, tell her I will be coming to have a word with her."

The thought of my kind friend scolding Goodwin made me grin.

Mya saw it. "You may think me a silly little cook, but Clary and I attend the same temple. We have been friends for twenty years. She is good at what she does, but she does not know how to handle young folk."

I swallowed my bite of cheese tart and said, "We do well enough. She's my training Dog, not my friend."

Mya sighed. "I'm sure you're right. You can't be in better hands. Mattes Tunstall is a feckless, overgrown lad, but no one argues that he's one of the best Dogs in the city."

Feckless? I thought, putting sliced ham on my plate. And how would she know that? Then a dreadful idea dawned and I stared at Mya. "Auntie." I swallowed, the pictures in my head making my belly lurch. "You— you and Tunstall."

She suddenly smoothed her apron over her lap. "I was once accounted a very pretty girl. We had so much fun together—but I wanted marriage and babies, and Mattes just wanted fun." She smiled at me. "Ulfrec has made me happy these fifteen years."

"My lady says Rebakah may visit her now." All unknown to us, my lady's personal maid had walked into the kitchen. The maids hurriedly began to chop again.

The boy splashed as he scrubbed like a madman. I half tripped over my bench as I tried to jump to my feet and brush the front of my dress at the same time.

The walk through the house felt strange. I'd made it only three weeks ago on my last visit, and yet the place seemed different. Smaller. No less elegant or well kept, but not the same.

I understood the difference as we passed through the door to my lady's part of the house. It was less important. Provost's House had not changed, but I had.

As if she'd heard my thinking and meant to say that I did not matter, the maid pointed to the workroom. "Wait in there," she ordered.

I walked inside. My sisters were there with the other mots of the house who did sewing. Diona had an embroidery frame set up before her. Lorine worked on a silk underdress so fine it was almost sheer. Both of them looked like tidy strangers to me.

Everyone looked up when I came in. The room went very quiet.

My sisters stiffened. I did not mistake it. I knew them like I knew myself.

"Goddess bless us, Beka, were you drinking? Or brawling with your Dog friends?" asked one of the older maids. She was favored by my lady for her embroidery. It meant that she gave herself airs. She made a game of saying something cruel to me, then claiming it was a joke when Lorine took her to task for it. "You might have covered those with face paint, you know." Most of the other maids giggled. Diona went red.

I let my gaze fall to the worn floorboards, then stiffened. Why did I let her speak so to me? What would this empty-headed mot have done on Rovers Street?

"I might have been mistaken for a doxie, too," I told the floor. The gigglers went silent. Then I looked up and held her eyes. Everyone else says that my gaze makes folk nervous. They tell me it's like being touched with ice. Let me see if I scare her, I thought.

She tried to stare me down. I made myself think of old Slapper and his crazed glare. She held firm a moment, then blinked and looked away. I waited. When she looked up again, I was still there, still staring. She got up. "Some females have gutter mouths!" she mumbled, and skittered out of the room.

I looked at each of them to see if anyone else wished to sharpen her wits on me. None would meet my eyes, not even my sisters. I went to kiss them on the cheek. Diona pulled away rather than let me actually touch her. Lorine held rock still. They spoke no word to me. I stepped back, not sure what to say.

"My lady will see you now." The maid had returned for me. It was the only time I was glad to be on my way to Lady Teodorie. I could think of nothing more to do with so many looking on.

Of course my lady's lips went tight when she set eyes on me. I'd known as much that morning when I'd looked in my bit of mirror and seen my bruises were still plain on my face.

I made my curtsy to her.

"And so you have begun work as a Guardswoman, Rebakah. Plainly you have found it invigorating."

I didn't reply. She didn't expect me to answer. Unlike Goodwin, neither did she expect me to look her in the eyes.

"Dare I hope that you have come to your senses? Your mother wished for you to better yourself." She took up the needlework that lay in her lap. She always had some about her. She had taught my sisters their first stitches, sewing and embroidery alike.

I never know what Lady Teodorie wants from me. My sisters and brothers are bettering themselves. Why does it matter to her if I am not what she thinks a girl should be?

She pursed her lips. "Tongue-tied as usual. Your performance yesterday before the Magistrate did my lord and me no credit."

I felt my shoulders twitch. So word of that had come here already. Splendid.

"Have you anything to say for yourself?"

I knew my duty. "Forgive me for disappointing you, my lady," I said.

"Your seeming meekness would serve you so much better as a maidservant than as an enforcer of the King's law," she remarked. "When you recover from your folly in your choice of livelihood, of course I will do my best for you. I promised your poor mother I would do my best for all of her children. You are dismissed."

I curtsied again. Why does she take it so personal that of all five of us, I am the only one who don't want the life she picked out for me? I can't understand why she hates the world of the Provost's Guard, either, but that's my lady. My lord has lived with it these many years. Maybe that's why my being a Dog is so vexing for her—of all the lads and gixies of this house who have gone into the Provost's Guard, I'm the only one who my lord shares it with, who he's raised to it. Who loves it as he loves it.

Feeling small and dirty, I returned to the kitchen. I certainly didn't want to see Lorine and Diona. The other maids would have been talking at them about me all this time, how low I'd seemed. Mayhap when we met in the afternoon, with none but our brothers there, my sisters wouldn't find me so common.

The kitchen was busy. Vendors awaited Mya's attention. There were geese to be put on the spit. The undercooks made plenty of noise as they put together other dishes for the noon meal. Mya, tending a weeping stable girl, thrust a basket full of bread odds and ends at me. I took it with thanks and fled.

This time of year the orchard is quiet. The trees are in bloom. They're pretty, but they're of use only to bees. They stand behind the hay barn, which is also left to it-

self so early in the year. No one sat on the bench behind the barn. I settled there, put my basket on the
ground, and enjoyed the warm sun for a moment.

A thought: Did I know, when I lived here, how often I
dodged folk I might offend with what I said? Or did I
just not notice because mostly I didn't talk?

Breakfasts these days will be the ruin of me. First I
start talking to Kora, Aniki, Ersken, and the rest. Who
knows where it will end? A party? A feast? Chattering
with strangers?

Tansy might like breakfast with us sometime. If I
can pry her out so early in the day, she might like to
meet my friends. Mayhap Annis will help.

But I was writing of my visit and of sitting behind the
barn. I ended my sunbath when a shadow passed over
my face. I opened my eyes. Of course it was Slapper. It
was here that I'd met him two years back. Since then
he's carried at least ten ghosts that I know of. A busy
bird.

For the moment he was actually alone, no other
birds at hand. Was this a pigeon miracle, a bird without a flock? He landed on my shoulder and pecked my
temple hard.

"Pox and murrain!" I cried, and grabbed him. In
my lap, he glared at me with poison-yellow eyes, fighting to free his wings. Pigeons are stronger than they

look, even one whose back is twisted like Slapper's. I held him gentle, second and third finger around his right wing, first finger along his neck, thumb around his left wing. With my free hand I dug out some of the cracked corn in my belt purse. I showed it to Slapper, and he went quiet. I settled him with a care to his clubfoot (I always fear it aches) and let him go. Instead of flying off, he began to eat the corn.

"Now listen," I told his ghost, "you got to give me more than you done. My Dogs need sommat real, not gossip pulled from the air." I spoke like Lower City folk so the soul he carried just now might trust me. "I been listenin' to you lot, but it ain't enough. Can't you name the street? Is there a stream nearby, or a drinkin' den? Sommat I can seek and *find*?" I didn't say that I'd never been able to get a pigeon and its ghost to lead me anywhere. Maybe these dead would be different, they wanted to be found so bad.

A new pigeon came. It looked as if it had been sprinkled in ashes and its tail dipped in them. "Th' wagon was covered, an' it were night." It spoke to *me,* or its ghost did! I found more corn and laid it down close to me so Ashes would come near. It waddled over to eat. "They put scarves on our glims so we mayn't see where they took us. We was led downstairs, t' the cellar. They took the scarves off. Our orders was, dig against the wall, down an' down. We thought 'twas a well, but 'twas too big. We was diggin' pick an' shovel through the pinky rock."

"The pinky city rock." White Spice's ghost whispered it as the bird glided down to sit with Ashes.

"Pinky city rock," Mumper's ghost said, landing on the dirt.

Slapper finished the corn. He jumped up, smacking me in the face with his wings, then landed beside his friends. "Ungrateful filcher," I mumbled.

"I was hired to dig a well," Slapper's ghost told me. "We was *all* hired to dig a well. There was a real well partway dug, but no water."

"They never let us out," said the ghost that rode a fresh arrival. That was the pigeon I'd named Fog. "Never once. They brung us food and drink and clothes, but we never left the cellar."

"The mage drove off the water in the well. The rusher with the bullwhip said so." White Spice's ghost didn't seem to mind that the bird preened while she talked. "It was dry, the hole where we dug. No water, but there was pieces that glittered in the torchlight."

"It sparkles, the rock, like nowheres else." The bird I'd named Pinky landed on my knee and left a large, warm present there. I swore, but I dared not shoo him off. I had no idea why they were talking so sensible, unless they'd reached some magical number (six of the same group of murdered folk) that let them speak more clear to me. "They have parts like glass as big as your thumbnail, bigger, that glow like fire with all manner of color. *Beautiful.*"

"Beauty in th' Cesspool, what a joke." Mayhap the magical number was seven. Here was a seventh bird, spangled in blue, green, and violet on white. Spangle's ghost was a woman who sounded as tough as any of the river dodgers I'd faced. "But when we'd spilled some of our water on the rocks—Mithros!"

"Mithros," the other birds said. The ghosts sighed. Two more arrived to sit with them. One was dark gray about the head and tail and pale gray in body, the commonest coloring of all the city's pigeons. The other had a purplish gray head, a white bib, and purplish gray shoulders on a gray body. So there were nine in all.

Pinky bit my hand and jumped down to be with the others. Now they were cooing, pecking the dirt, looking for food. I grabbed the basket and started crumbling the bread for them.

"Where *are* you?" I asked. I was certain now that these were the ghosts of them who had dug Crookshank's fire opals for him. He'd had them killed to keep the stones' location a secret. I'd wager the cellar where they'd dug was in a house of his, but *which*? We'd need the army to search them all. And every mot, cove, and child in them would be doing their best to put a stop to it, for sheer contrariness. "You'd think you'd *want* your grave found!"

Well, I'd offended them then. Off they flew, leaving me to try to get pigeon scummer off my dress. Then other pigeons came, the flock that lives here and any pigeons who'd been drawn to them or to me. I forgot my clothes and crumbled bread fast. I put the diggers from my thoughts and listened to what all these birds had to say. There was always something going on, something I could piece together for my lord or the kennels.

When I'd finished with the pile of bread ends Mya gave me, I propped my chin on my hands and watched the birds. They'd quieted, but few had left, despite the food being nearly gone. They eyed me. I think they knew I liked them even if I didn't hear their ghosts. They were beautiful, when they weren't dirty. And whose dirt was it but the human folk of the city's?

They have such silly faces, pigeons.

I held out my hand. One of them landed on it. When I put up the fingers of my free hand, the cracked bird tried to eat the tips.

"I don't suppose any of you are here because the Shadow Snake doused you?" I asked, keeping my voice quiet. "Kidnapped you and killed you?"

The bird on my hand took off. More of the flock left—most of it. Nearly three dozen remained, all staring at me. One that was white but for drips of black on the ends of his wings and tail came toward me. "Mama? I'm lost, Mama."

I leaned forward. "Rolond?" I asked. "You know

me. I've held you sometimes, lad. Your mama is my friend Tansy." My eyes were stinging, but I kept my voice calm. Spirits are all emotion. I get upset and they take off. "Your papa is Herun Lofts. And I know your grandmama, too, Annis."

I didn't know if he understood me, but I had to try. Mayhap today was a day of miracles.

Mayhap it wasn't. "Mama, it's dark and I'm lost," he said, deaf to my words. "They took me away. Where are you?"

"Mama?" That was a little gixie's voice. "The mot said yez wouldn't give the Shadow Snake what the Snake wanted. Yer lily necklace was more important— tha's what the mot said."

"Da, the Shadow Snake said ye wouldna give o'er what ye won at the gamblin', so he took me. . . ."

"It was just a poxy book you can't e'en read, you stupid puttock!" That girl was older and furious.

"I don't understand. Why does someun called a Snake want yer brass box, Ma? Ye said it only had writin' from some noble ye danced fer oncet."

I finally put my face in my hands. Mama had always said there'd be a day I'd be sorry I asked so many questions. This was that day.

When I couldn't bear it no more, I jumped to my feet and threw up my arms. They all took off in a cloud of feathers and a clap of wings.

Goddess, let me make something good of so much

that is bad. Let me take from these birds some piece of knowledge. Something that will help me seek the Rats that killed those diggers, or the Shadow Snake. The feeling I'd had that day I led my lord to the Bold Brass gang would be naught compared to hobbling *them*. Knowing that two killers ran free in the Lower City was an itch I couldn't scratch.

I rubbed my hands on my thighs and felt a lump in the pocket of my underdress. I had the fire opal still. I fetched it out and turned it over. It was so lovely as it was, I had to wonder what it looked like all polished and clean. Probably the nobles and the rich would want it more so, with no hint that it had come from the rock of the Lower City. I grinned. I liked the pinkish stone that cropped up everywhere, in our walls and walkways and little gardens.

Berryman had called them "fascinators." Folk with gold in their purses would be fascinated with those bits of cherry and blue fire, the blaze of green. . . . I turned the stone now and then, shifting to new bits of color, and let the moments of the last week drift in my head. I let my questions come to the surface of my thoughts, bubbles in a well. Who would notice nine healthy mots and coves all gone missing together? Who would notice the vanishment of one child here, one child there, gone seemingly by magic from bed or street or plain daylight?

I had all manner of thoughts while I sat there. One

of them was something Tunstall had said to Mistress Noll on my very first night of duty—"You sharp old folk are everywhere, aren't you? You're everywhere, and you see and hear everything."

I came alert with the sun in my eyes. I know old folk. Mistress Noll herself, for one. Granny Fern, for another. And there were others throughout the Lower City, beggar women who sat their corners like my dust spinner friends, laundresses who used the same fountain squares, doxies who spent all their working nights in the same part of Corus. Folk talked in front of them like they was sculptures.

"I knew I'd find you here."

I scrambled to my feet. So lost in thought was I that I hadn't heard Lord Gershom's steps in the grass. I bobbed my curtsy too fast and almost fell, which would have earned me my lady's iciest gaze. My lord only chuckled and seized my elbow to steady me. "Beka, I hope the other fellows look far worse." He waved his free hand to show he meant my eye and cheekbone.

I looked down and stammered, "I—I wish I could s-say as much, milord. I g-got the worst of it."

"But I hear you did well. You and your Dogs were outnumbered nearly seven to one even after Lady Sabine stepped in, yet here you are." He was dressed for a day at home, his steel-colored hair combed back in a horse tail, his clothes an embroidered short tunic (my lady's work) over loose leggings tied around his calves. "I wish I'd seen it. You did well—a brawl in a place like that would have been the death of most trainees. So tell me, what happened that first night?" He sat on the bench and drew me down next to him. "How'd you miss the lookout? I know I taught you better, and I'm sure Ahuda did."

I hung my head. "My lord, I got excited."

"Ah," he said, crossing his legs at the ankle and leaning back. "It's to be expected, when you're starting out. I warned you it would take time to season. All the talent in the world doesn't take the place of good, solid experience, Beka."

I nodded. *It just seems to take so* long *to get experience when I need it* now.

"You know what happened to Tunstall, even after he was voted a Dog by his kennel?"

I shook my head, but my ears perked up.

"He fell off a roof. He was chasing a Rat who'd gone and killed a man over in Prettybone, where they have houses built next to each other, except there was one that was two stories higher, with a steeper roof. Tunstall made the climb and had the cove by the ankle when the cove scraped his hand in the chimney and threw soot in Tunstall's face. Off the roof Tunstall went. Straight into a pile of dung, three stories down."

"Ouch," I whispered.

"Other Dogs have made mistakes, Beka. It's what you learn." He patted me on the shoulder. "So what do you make of our Rogue?"

I told him everything. I knew I could trust him with the information about the fire opals, how Goodwin and Tunstall were looking into them, and about the Shadow Snake. I knew he would leave those things to my Dogs and not interfere himself unless he felt there was a need. He was famous for that.

When it was noon and the bell was ringing for the house's big meal of the day, I also knew that I felt better. In telling him how I had fallen in fish, sought Orva in the Cesspool, fought to keep my feet among river dodgers, *and* faced Sir Tullus and the Magistrate's Court, I saw my days for what they were, my first week. I had not shackled the worst foist in the Nightmarket nor caught Kayfer Deerborn himself with the crown's jewels in his pocket, it was true. I had not rescued the Queen from a pack of robbing coves or caught the slavers trying to pass off some Sirajit princess as a kitchen slave. But I was alive, and hungry.

My lord got to his feet and I scrambled to mine. As we walked toward the house, he said, "There is one thing in which you did not obey the letter of my instructions, Beka."

"My lord?" I asked, dazed. Whenever did I not follow his rules and orders as he gave them?

"I said to outfit yourself properly from our gear

room," he told me as we stopped near the kitchen door. The servants streamed by, bowing and murmuring greetings. I looked into his face. His brows were drawn down over his nose, but there was no vexation in his eyes, only a bit of fun. He knew me proper, did my lord Gershom. "Whether you didn't do as you were bid from pride or from a desire to go easy on my purse, you were in error. You left us without enough gear. Before you go back to your lodgings, I want you to draw three more items. And I want you to think about the week you've had as you do it. Now, you mind me, Beka Cooper."

I bowed my head. He was right, about everything. "Yes, my lord."

He clasped my hands in his. "Mithros and the Crone watch over you."

I curtsied as he went inside. "Gods all bless and keep you, my lord," I whispered. He is the best man I know. I felt that way when I was eight and he had chosen to listen to me in the street. My feelings now only go deeper, not different.

I wondered if I should stop first in the gear room, but then my belly growled. Wonderful smells drifted my way. Mya's cooking was calling to me.

Noon dinner is the big meal of the house. Everyone eats together, even the servers, once the food is set out. My lord and lady sit with their children and guests on the dais. They had noble friends with them today, four of the haMinch family, that has more branches than most trees, and a mage in the royal service. The mage and my lord had their heads together: business, then.

My friends among the dairymaids and laundresses made a place for me. That put me across the room from the stable hands. Most of them grinned or gave me a tiny wave. I didn't see my brother Will. He might have been off riding errands. I thought my younger brother, Nilo, might bounce clean from his seat, he was so glad to see me. He put a finger to his eye and mouthed, "What happened?" I frowned at him, not that it managed to cow him any. When we were dismissed for our noon rest, at least he waited until we were outside and beyond my lady's view before he seized me around the waist and spun me sunwise.

"Beka, lookit you! Black eye, who done it! And your whole cheek gone green! Did you kill anyone? Did you hobble anyone? Did you miss me? I learned to drive a pair, well, around the courtyard, anyways!" Nilo is the picture of Mama, with her brown curls and snapping brown eyes, and her dimples. He is only ten, but his head clears my shoulder. "Will was sent clean on up to the palace with a message, he said not to let you go back 'thout he saw you. Do you like being a Dog?"

The only way to silence him was to put him in a headlock. "Listen to you, you'd think you was brought up in a chicken coop," I scolded. "Let a person talk!

I'm not a Dog, I'm a trainee, a Puppy, you empty-headed looby! I don't know who blacked my eye. There was too many of 'em. Of course I missed you." And I threw him over my hip into the courtyard dust.

He went with a whoop, little mumper that he is. Him and three other stable folk—two lads and a gixie—begged me to teach them the headlock and the throw. Of course they were thinking about training as Dogs one day. I'd thought maybe Nilo might follow me to Puppy training, until I saw how much he loves to work with horses. I hadn't even time to daydream about Will. He'd taken to hanging about the stable as soon as he was big enough and rides like he was born on horseback. There's naught magical about it. The stable master is a fine teacher, and my brothers love horses as my mother loved other animals.

Once the youngsters were covered in dust and exhausted from my quick lesson, they scattered. Nilo and me went to the stable to wait for Will. We had no private place of our own to sit. My sisters slept with my lady's maids. The boys went to the stable quarters. Mya gave me a place with the cookmaids and stable girls until I went to live in the Puppy training barracks.

Now, listening to Nilo chatter about all that had gone on since I had taken lodgings in the Lower City, I was glad to have my own home. I can move about without waking someone, and no one objects to Pounce. I tried to bring him today, but he flat-out refused. He crawled back under my blankets after I made my bed. Nilo grumbled over my cat staying away, so I made him laugh over tales of Pounce on duty in the Lower City.

"Nilo, Nilo, guess who I met!" Will came in, leading a sweating horse. He and the mount were covered with road dust, but Will grinned ear to ear. He showed us a silver noble. "The King gave me this! King Roger himself! I took a message from my lord to the Lord High Magistrate. Then my Lord Magistrate has *me* take a message behind the palace to King Roger himself, because the King has taken the Queen riding! The King gave me this, and the Queen smiled at me." Will was giddy. "Beka, you look like you've been in a war." He kissed me, sprinkling dust on my dress. "She's *so* beautiful, the Queen, so much younger than His Majesty, with hair like dark clouds. . . ."

"Bleah," Nilo said, rolling his eyes.

"What do *you* know?" Will shoved him. "Let me care for Ladslove, and then I can sit. Nilo, will you beg something for me from Mya? His Majesty and the Magistrate had me go back and forth twice." He wandered off, the horse following him patiently.

I looked at Nilo, who pretended to puke. "I'd get him some food. I think he's addled," I said.

"I'm going. 'The Queen's sooo beautiful,'" Nilo said with mockery, twirling around. "'She has teeth like stars and hair like sheep fuzz, the Queen is sooo beautiful!'" Half singing it, he went to get food for Will. I tried not to laugh.

The boys and I were playing mumblety-peg with our belt knives when my sisters found us. They came through the stable door like great ladies and frowned at the three of us on our knees in the dirt.

I gazed at them and felt strange. When we were young, the little ones, including these two gixies in their neat dresses, wore patched shirts only and no shoes. I had but one thin dress. I went barefoot like them, trying to mind all four when Mama was busy. There was always a baby or two in hand, a basket of mending, rag toys, and the streets when we annoyed Mama's herb customers or her latest man. Our noses ran and our bottoms, too, when the meat was bad, if we had meat.

Now we wore clothes with mends not even showing, though Nilo's and Will's breeches had been let down three times apiece. The boys had good, sturdy tunics that would take horse dirt and wash up without going to pieces. Our feet were shod against all but the deepest street mud.

Our sisters were dressed a world away in respectable wool dresses with embroidery for decoration. They wore round caps on their heads with more embroidery still. Unlike the lads and me, they were so clean they shone, their skin fair and soft-looking.

The silence between us got uncomfortable, but I

didn't know how to break it. The boys scowled and sheathed their knives, our game of mumblety-peg plainly done. I picked up my knife. Feeling that if I sheathed it right off, it would look as if I'd been ashamed of our game, I spun it on my fingertip. Sadly, I fumbled the catch when I popped the knife in the air. I dropped the blade before it cut me.

Lorine made a face. "Now you are *dirty* as well as bruised."

I looked at my dress. It was streaked with grime. Good, I thought, it will cover the pigeon mess. I looked at Lorine. "I did the pretty for my lord and my lady," I said, deliberately talking Lower City to their Patten District. "I had dinner in the hall and didna slurp my soup. I won't be stayin' t' supper, so it's pigeon feed to a starvin' bull what my dress looks like."

"You like doing this, don't you?" asked Diona. Her cheeks were turning red. "Shaming us before our friends. Turning Will and Nilo into street urchins when they know how to behave themselves, like young men moving up in the world!"

Will got to his feet. "Lucky for me royal messengers can act like real folk when they're not before the nobility," he said, his green eyes flashing. He takes after his papa in looks. One day the gixies will all dance to his tune. "They're not silly enough to pretend the nobility rubs off on them—"

Diona went to slap him. I realized that *after* I'd

moved, coming off the ground to grab her wrist as I rose. I held on to her as I stood between them. "You're not my lady," I told her, keeping my voice down so no one else might hear if they were close by. "You don't go slapping people's faces. Shame on you!"

"She don't mean nothin', Beka, don't hurt her." Nilo sounded like he might cry in a moment.

I let Diona go and hugged him. "I didn't hurt her. I remember who I'm dealing with, even if she don't."

Lorine sighed. "Diona, Beka's right. Don't think I haven't seen you push Nilo when no one's about. You get above yourself, girl."

Diona rubbed her wrist. I hadn't even grabbed it hard enough to make it red. "My lady's maid is right! You're trash, Beka! Look at us! We've been fine ever since you left. You're not back half a day and the boys are filthy and ill-mannered and you've turned them and Lorine against me." Anger made her pretty face ugly. "My lady gives us a chance for a decent life and you *throw* it back in her face—"

"Who keeps your decent life decent?" I asked, losing my temper. "Who makes sure you hardworking folk stay safe, Diona? Not a lot of maids and footmen. River dodgers would kill the lot of you for a pair of weighted dice! Who puts murderers in cages and keeps your necklaces on your necks, eh? Who—"

"*Enough!*" The head hostler had heard us and was standing in the open door, a carriage whip in his hands.

243

"You'd think it was noon in Rivermarket and the fish startin' t' go off! Where did the lot o' you learn to make such a noise in a lord's house?"

My brothers and sisters looked at each other. And then they all did a sad thing, even Nilo. They edged just the tiniest bit from me. Of course, mayhap it was on account of me being the one to get caught. Or mayhap it was me being so ill-kempt, with the dirt and the pigeon stain and all. But they were of a set, four servants-in-training. I was the one what didn't match.

I curtsied and mumbled apologies as they did. After a last frown, the hostler left us. Diona and Lorine followed him, their hems and veils fluttering. To give them their due, they probably thought they'd see me later, at supper. The boys hesitated, shifting on their feet.

"I must visit the gear room and then go home," I told them. "You'll be working till supper, so we won't have time to talk. And I must return to my lodgings before then. It'll be drawing down dark in the Lower City. I shouldn't walk the streets alone with no weaponry."

"But it isn't dark when it's suppertime!" said Will, confused.

"You're up on the hill below Palace Ridge," I explained. "The Lower City's at the bottom of the rise. The wall's higher than anything down there. It shuts out the sun early."

"Oh," Nilo said. "When will we see you next?"

"I'll try for my next day off. Now go clean up. I'll say farewell here." They hesitated again, and I took the burden from them. "No hugging. You don't want those nice shirts wrinkled more than they are. Just a kiss on the cheek, one each." I gave and got them. "I love you both. I even love our sisters."

Like boys, they grumbled and walked away. I went over to the stable wall and rested my face against its rough boards, having a care for splinters. I have a bit of sense, so I didn't think it was my family that changed so much in the three weeks since I'd moved to Nipcopper Close. Was it?

I took a breath of stable smell: horse dung, hay, dirt, leather, polish, the oils needed to keep the leather smooth and limber. It smelled clean. Empty clean. So, too, did the big house smell, with its added scents of flowers and soap and cooking, though without horse dung or horse. No rotting vegetables or animal carcasses, no frying turnovers and heaps of fresh-cut flowers. No herds being driven to market or crates of birds and rabbits. No slop pots emptied into the gutter and flowing into the soup of mud that is the Lower City.

The clean, tidy folk who live and work at Provost's House don't smell so good to me as the dark streets where I live now. I put my thumb on what I'd felt all day. It was distance. I'd been glad to see Mya and my lord. I am hurt by my sisters and some by Will. Nilo is still a little boy. Besides, I remember that greeting he gave me. But I'm no part of their household. I am a Puppy, one who belongs in the Lower City. It was time to go home.

I chose my three extra items of gear, then set out. Of course, I didn't go back the way I had come. I never do. It's boring. I also remembered that tomorrow morning comes and breakfast with it. For once I might supply more than coppers for our gathering. It was too early for the Nightmarket, but the Daymarket was open. Mistress Noll's shop there would be a good place to buy some breakfast bread.

I walked down broad Palace Way, with its flat white cobbles. My clogs clattered like the hooves of the horses that rode by. Like my brothers, I could admire a good-looking animal. Some of these were bound for the palace rising behind me, atop the ridge. Others paced like I did, down north toward the river.

Despite the goldsmiths' banks and expensive shops between Provost's House and the Daymarket, no one blinked at my wrinkled dress. I walked with servants, message runners, soldiers, and merchants and their families. Mithran priests in their orange or yellow robes passed Daughters of the Goddess in white, brown, or black. Now and then I'd see Wave Walker priests in blue robes or the Smith's servants, their leather aprons stamped with holy signs. Bazhir in their burnooses walked with hands on weapon hilts. The folk of

Carthak, Galla, Tusaine, and the Copper Isles simply tried to pretend they were not staring.

This was more of the Corus I love, prettily dressed. A mix of high and low folk came this way to do business or to see the King and his new Queen. They'll hold the first festival for the young prince next year. Then neighboring kingdoms will send their finest to greet the babe, and to get plucked in the Lower City. We all look forward to having the world salute our young heir.

One thing I didn't see today was the usual number of mumpers. The Palace Way Dogs, who answer to the Patten and Flash District kennels, must have cleared them out. Fine ladies sometimes complain if there are too many cripples to ruin the view on the main road to the palace. By my guess, the clearing out happened around noon. One mumper had already come back to take a place on the edge of the street near Provost's House. She was fearfully thin, with a babe at her empty breast. The child was crying.

I walked by. She'll seek help at one of the Goddess's temples if she is serious about feeding the babe, I told myself. Despite my common sense, I added and re-added my budget of coin for the week to see if I could spare aught. Behind me I heard a passing rider tell her she'd earn more on her back than by putting her hand out.

I halted, angry, and took a copper in my hand.

Then I saw a newly come beggar grab a richly dressed nobleman's jeweled horse by its tack. The old mot gabbled at the man, offering to tell his fortune. He kicked her away.

I ran forward, cursing him in Cesspool talk as I tossed my copper to the skinny beggar with the child. She grabbed it and fled. I forgot her and spat at the rich man, who rode off, ignoring me. "Pig scummer," I muttered, grabbing the old mumper to help her up. She was annoying, but kicking a granny was the act of a beast.

To my surprise, she fought me. She was strong for one that was just skin over bone. There was no bruise on her face from the noble's kick, she had no bloody nose. She'd dodged him.

She also had three of the gems that had been sewn onto the horse's trappings in one hand, and a sharp-looking blade in the other. I snatched the blade and stuck it into the sheath behind my own belt knife. It wedged tight there. Even she would need a moment or two to winkle it loose.

I looked to see if the noble had noticed his missing gems. He was turning onto a side street, cursing a priest who crossed in front of him. No, he was too stupid to spot the theft. I disliked him too much to tell him.

I looked at her. She was lean and weathered, but sharp-eyed, to bag three gems with that little knife. I was sure I'd seen her around the Lower City, begging in the markets and temples. Her name came to me. Mother Cantwell.

I could turn her in for the stupid noble's vengeance, or I could make use of this opportunity.

I rolled the gems in my hand, letting her hear them clink. "Mother Cantwell. This here is a caging offense. Mayhap that fat lordling back there will reward a good Dog like me for giving him his sparklers. Or I could reward myself."

"You talk like a Dog as wants sommat, and you only a Puppy," she said, watching me with sharp old eyes. "It's shockin', how young folk grow up too quick anymore."

I felt a quiver around my belt knife. I gave the wrist I clung to a slight turn so she'd know I was paying attention. Then I looked down. She took her hand from my belt. That was the trouble with talking close together. Still, I had to admire how limber she was, especially at her age.

"I'm a Puppy as wants sommat. I'm willing to be forgiving in return," I said. Where had all my shyness gone? Was it that she reminded me of Granny Fern, and that gave me comfort?

No, it was that I felt so comfortable doing a true Dog's work. For I'd never worried about shyness hobbling Orva and getting her knife back or fighting river dodgers.

Now Mother Cantwell's eyes were on my free hand, the one with the gems. "Forgivin'? You mentioned forgiveness. I'm old, but I have my hearin' yet."

I thrust the gems into my belt purse and twisted my belt to put the purse behind my back. "Not that forgiving, Mother. Besides, you'd just sell them to Crookshank for not even a quarter of the value. Trust me, he's rich enough. He don't deserve your custom."

"You'll keep 'em for yourself. There's wickedness! Stealing from the Happy Bag already!" She shook her head in disgust.

I tried my best not to grin. Being schooled in morality by this old mumper was the funniest thing to happen to me all day. "Mother, if you strive not to vex me, you'll not spend the next six days in the cages or however many years you've left working for the King. May we get to business?"

She cocked a knowing dark eye at me and waited, like street sparrows wait for crumbs.

"Nine men and women got a digging job in the Cesspool, Mother," I told her, keeping my voice down. The street wasn't busy, but I wanted no passerby to overhear me. I drew her partway into Meadowsweet Alley. "They were told it was a well, but it wasn't. They were killed maybe a week ago. They've families that only know they vanished. Have you heard aught of them?"

Mother Cantwell curled her lip, disgusted with me.

"Gixie, your nob is cracked up and down and side to side. Folk—"

I cut her off. "I *know* folk vanish all the time in the Lower City! But this is different. Nine at once, all together. Even for the Cesspool that's a clutch. If you've heard naught now, that doesn't mean you won't hear it later, if you keep your ear flaps clean and turned."

She smacked her lips like she was thinking.

"Listen, Mother. They dug in a building somewhere. Think on the sparklers I took from you. A mage can put a truth spell on me to know I didn't take them, and you did. When that happens, you are on your way to royal justice." I smiled. "And I'd hate that. We could help each other."

"Seemingly it's more me helpin' you," she said.

"I'll have the odd present for you now and then." I'd have to manage extra sweetening somehow down the road, when her gratitude ran cold. "I'm not some Dog as will ask you to cough up for love of me."

She grinned, showing naked gums. She'd been afraid she'd have to do it all for free. "You'd get spittle if you did, Fishpuppy."

I·do not want folk calling me that forever. "There's one more thing, Mother," I said as she tried to shake my hand off her arm. "The Shadow Snake."

She drew the sign against evil, the light that drives back the shadows. I almost copied it but tightened my grip on her instead.

"You don't know what you're askin' for, Puppy Cooper," she said, all serious now. "I know naught. I'll ask no questions as will get me floatin' bum up in the river. I've nothin' the Shadow Snake wants. Long as I keep from his business, we needn't even bow in the street. Not that anyone knows who to bow to." She turned sideways and spat.

The Crone Goddess lit the tiniest witch light of a thought in my brain. "I can see not going to the kennel with this," I began slowly, choosing my words. "But what about the Rogue? Surely this Snake is poaching on the Rogue's ground, on the folk the Rogue is supposed to look after."

The old mot actually smirked at me. "In long-ago tales, mayhap. You truly think Rogue Kayfer and his chiefs care for little bits of things like spell books and jewelry? He's booted so many poor folk from the Court they don't even go to him no more. His chiefs are the same. The last cove whose babe was took that went to Dawull got tossed in the river for a swim. Folk were laughin' and kickin' 'im back in when he tried to climb out. Long as the Snake don't go slitherin' around no big score, the Rogue and his chiefs will leave us low folk to manage as best we may."

There is knowing and then there is *knowing*. "Folk *went* to Kayfer?"

"More'n one, girl. Now d'you see? There's no tellin' who's the Snake, and none to care if I'm doused for nosin' about the Snake's business!" The mot yanked on my grip, and yanked hard.

"But you can listen, can't you? You older folk are everywhere and hear everything. Listen and ask about the nine that went all at once. Mayhap someone's looking to hire more diggers. I'll need to know of that, too, soonest. I'll see to it you're paid."

"Not much, I'll wager," Mother Cantwell said.

I smiled. "I can give those gems to our mage. He'll find you *and* the owner."

"Of course, I'll be happy to listen as I may," she told me, and sighed.

"I'd appreciate your courtesy, Mother," I replied. "I'm hopeful you won't make yourself hard to find." I was certain any Dog at Jane Street could tell me where to meet her.

"Of course I won't, for so sharp a wench as you," she said, her voice sour. With that I let her go.

She went her way and I went mine, turning my belt to set my purse where I could see it. The Crone had put Mother Cantwell in my path, I was sure. I went straight to the Crone's shrine on Healall Close. There I left Mother Cantwell's sharp blade as a thank-you offering. The gems would go into the kennel's Happy Bag when no one was looking. It happened that way all the time when no one wanted to hobble a personal Birdie.

Then I went in search of Mistress Noll's Day-market stall.

I didn't expect to see her there. Not when she worked at the Nightmarket all last week. Her children minded the Daymarket place. The stall was new, and easy enough to find, since it was on Bakers' Row. I was impressed when I saw it. This was a true building, no three-sided shed with room only for warming ovens and braziers. There were shelves with pasties, buns, and pies on display, with muslin over them to keep off the flies.

Mistress Noll's youngest daughter, Gemma, was working the big paddles, pulling finished round loaves from the ovens and putting fresh ones in to bake. Her brother Yates leaned against the counter, talking to a blond cove and a brunette one who'd just placed sacks of flour on the floor. My hackles stiffened. I didn't like Yates. He was a bad Rat, in and out of the cages for brawling and theft. The other Noll sons were well enough, but Yates was trouble.

I made choices for breakfast, small fruit loaves that could be split, depending on how many of us gathered at Nipcopper Close. I made sure to get spice buns, favored by Kora and Rosto, and the ones with plenty of raisins for Verene and me. Then I waited for those who were ahead of me to put down their coin. They were servants in good houses from their talk, who treated Yates like he was hardly there. He smiled like a sick fish at them and spat on the floor when they turned away.

One of Yates's friends who had been with him and

his mother at the Court of the Rogue made some whispered joke that set the three coves laughing. Mistress Noll hired hard men to make her deliveries.

"Gemma, 'member me?" I asked, quiet enough that she would be the only one to hear. "Beka Cooper."

She smiled. "Everyone knows 'bout you. Livin' up in Provost's House and all. Lookit you, dressed all nice, like you wasn't from Mutt Piddle Lane."

I looked down at my wrinkled and stained dress. "Mayhap you could say that," I said, watching her from the corners of my eyes. She had a bruise on her forehead, a healing cut on her lip. There were bruises on her arms, left bare when she'd pushed up her sleeves to work. Was her man knocking her about? Did she have a man? She was forty or so, old enough to be a grandmother at least, with plenty of gray in her brown hair.

"If you're buyin', you're buyin'." Yates smashed a fist down on the counter. "You don't need to be botherin' my sister, wench."

Gemma's eyes went from him to me and back like we both of us was monsters. "Yates, don't! You remember Ma tellin' us 'bout Beka Cooper—this's her!"

"I don't care if she's a knight in armor. We're workin' folk here, and my sister's a respectable mot, not some Rovers Street trull." Yates smirked at his friends. He thought he'd become a wit. "Buy or shake your wares someplace else, wench."

I set my loaves on the counter and my coins beside

255

them. "Gemma, have I got the right change?" I asked. I began to tuck the loaves into a pack I'd got at the house, settling them careful so they wouldn't be crushed.

She counted and gave back a copper. Her hand was shaking. "Don't mind Yates, he's got a rough manner," she whispered. "He don't—"

He knocked her sideways, sending her sprawling on the floor. Now I knew where her bruises came from. "Shut yer gob," he ordered her. He turned to me and raised his hand.

I blocked his swing with my forearm, though it jarred my teeth. While he gaped, I grabbed that wrist with my free left hand and yanked him toward me over the counter, jamming my right hip into it to steady myself. When he grabbed at me with his free hand, I seized it and twisted so he'd stop thrashing. Then I rested my weight on my left hand, using it like a lever. The problem for him was, it was his elbow on the edge of the counter at the end of my lever. If he moved, I could throw all of my weight on his wrist and see what happened to that elbow, or keep turning his other hand. If he behaved, all that he got was cramps in his wrists and his right elbow, and some shame before those looking on. If he misbehaved, he would suffer the consequences.

His friends seemed to think he ought to do something. "I've not hurt Yates yet," I said to them. I felt that same clear-headed bravery that had come on me as I'd chased Orva and fought the river dodgers. "I will if you hurry me. I'm surprised this place gets any custom whatever, with Yates and you being so friendly with customers."

Just then I heard a familiar woman's voice say, "I have to say, *I'm* not impressed." Sabine of Macayhill walked to the counter, putting herself between Yates's friends and me. "I was told I might buy Corus's best apple-raisin patties at Mistress Noll's. Nobody warned me about the service." She looked at me. "Maybe you should kill him. I would."

"It's against the law," I said, keeping the pressure on Yates. I wasn't at all sure if she was joking.

"Oh, I forgot—I'm in Corus again. People care about things like that here. You being a Dog, I suppose you care more than most." Lady Sabine smiled crookedly at me and looked down at Yates. "She's a Provost's Dog, you know."

I let him go as I said, "Trainee. I'm only a trainee, excuse me, my lady. But he's a full-blooded Rat, and no mistake."

Yates scrambled away from the counter and us, so fast that he fetched up against the ovens. He yelped and jerked away, rubbing first one arm, then the other. He threw himself toward his friends. They left through the side door, glaring back at Sabine.

"Please, you don't know what you've done."

Gemma was still on the floor. "They'll pay you back one night, Beka. Yates, his friends—they be hard coves."

Sabine leaned on her elbows. "I told you we should have killed him." I saw that her brown eyes were just— interested, as if she talked about cropping her hair. "Have you got apple-raisin patties, mistress?"

"Still warm, my lady," Gemma told her.

Sabine laid out her handkerchief. "I'll take four, if you please."

As Gemma opened an oven and laid four patties on the lady knight's handkerchief, she told me, "I'll keep tellin' him you're with the Dogs now, Beka, but you want to watch for him. And I'll tell Ma. He listens to Ma." She curtsied. "Two coppers, my lady."

Lady Sabine gave her three. "An unusual sort of baker's assistant they're hiring in Corus nowadays," she remarked. "Very tidy work on the wrist grabs, Cooper. Nice, using the counter to anchor yourself and compensate for your weight difference."

I looked down, not knowing what to say. The feeling of doing Dog work had left me in a rush, and I was shy again.

"I was impressed in that hole on Rovers Street, too. I just think you'll regret only holding this Yates fellow instead of breaking a joint or three," she added. "It rarely pays to be easy on that sort." She pointed a finger at Gemma. "You, mistress, should throw yourself on the mercy of the Goddess's temple. No woman needs to let a man knock her about as you have done. They will protect you, hide you, even, if need be." She waited, watching Gemma.

"You don't understand, my lady," Gemma said at last. "I have no choice."

Sabine rolled her eyes. "So they all say." She scooped up her handkerchief and its contents, then took a patty out and bit into it. "Gods, this is good!" she said, her mouth full. She handed me one, and when her mouth was empty, told me, "Mattes was right about this place. So maybe I'll be back." She gave me the tiniest of smiles. "And maybe I'll follow Master Lout to his lair. Dispose of him without *your* disapproving eyes looking on, Cooper. In the interest of the public good, of course."

She left before I thought to curtsy.

"Lady knights." Gemma shook her head.

I looked at her. "What?"

"They think the river will part for them." Gemma was rubbing her arms as she looked at the floor. I think she'd forgotten I was there. "She doesn't know, the men always get their way in the end. That's why I never married. I see what my sisters get every day."

I sighed. I wanted to go home and cuddle my cat. Today suddenly felt longer than all last week. "Would you tell Mistress Noll I said hello?" I asked.

Gemma looked at me, then turned and opened the oven. "If Yates doesn't do it first, of course. Good day to you, Beka."

I shouldered my pack and left that odd little shop, eating the patty. It was *very* good. As I finished it, my mind kept circling back to Yates. Does it prosper Mistress Noll to hire the likes of Yates and take delivery from men who look like veterans of the cages?

Wednesday, April 8, 246

I was putting the cloth on the floor this morning when I thought, What if the others tire of breakfast? They keep later nights even than I do. What if the fun of eating pasties with Puppy Dogs and the odd older Dog like Phelan is not as good as an hour or two more of sleep? Then Kora, Aniki, Ersken, and Phelan came all at once, and I knew I was a fool. We had barely filled the cups when Verene and Rosto walked through the door, Verene with a basket of extras from her mother's workplace and Rosto with pickled eggs.

"I missed breakfast these last two days," Rosto said, once we were settled. "It's a nice start to things. Quiet-like."

Everyone nodded, mouths full. Even I had to agree. I felt easier here, with half of our number on the other side of the law, than I'd felt at Provost's House.

"Did they admire your bruises?" Verene asked me. "Did they want all the details of the fight? Because you ne'er told us. You were too giddy with the healin'."

"You had a lady knight," Aniki said, feeding sausage to Pounce. "Lady Sabine. A bunch of the bully boys who came by Dawull's court last night and the night before looked like they'd been mule-kicked. They said her and a bunch of her friends who just came back from the east bailed out you and your Dogs."

I snorted and almost choked. "It was just my lady

261

on her own, and my Dogs, and me. They wished it had taken more than the four of us," I replied. As Aniki lifted Pounce in the air, my own curst honesty made me add, "Actually, mostly it was her and Tunstall and Goodwin. I did a bit, but they did the true damage."

"Don't go all modest," Ersken said as Aniki kissed my poor cat's head. "By rights all of you should have been killed. My Dogs say someone ought to do the city a favor and burn the Barrel's Bottom down, there's so many fights there. The Night Watch calls it 'the Barrel of Blood.'"

"My Dogs say your Dogs allus do stupid things like that, to make the rest of us look bad," Verene said. I glared at her. She held up both of her hands. "I'm just tellin' you what they said."

Phelan slung an arm around Verene's shoulders and kissed her temple. "Your Dogs are worthless scuts, sweeting. Don't listen when they talk scummer like that. Study the good pairs, like Beka's Dogs."

Verene batted her eyes at Phelan. "That bein' you and your partner?"

Phelan laughed. "We aren't even nearly so good."

"Why try, when it's such an uphill battle?" Rosto asked, and yawned. "When you get in trouble some-place like the Barrel's Bottom, and other Dogs take for-ever to come to lend a hand?"

I nudged him with my foot. "Why take the trouble to serve any of the Rogue's chiefs when they won't fight to move up at the Court?" I asked him. "Because you're a rusher. Because we're Dogs."

"You speak of bein' a Dog like it's somethin' that's in the blood," Verene said with a laugh. "I just didn't want t' fish!"

"It's in Beka's blood," Ersken said. "And I have to tell you, I get to meet more interesting people this way."

"And Beka will never change her mind?" Rosto asked, trying to hold my eyes with his dark ones. "Never, ever?"

I looked back, even though his way of looking at me makes my skin prickle all over. I've had a sweetheart or two, but none of them gave me the tingles like Rosto. He's bad for you, I keep telling myself. Bad, bad, bad.

From somewhere I sucked the words out of my gut to tell him, "The only ones who fitly punished a cove who treated all my family like garbage was the Dogs, Rosto the Piper. Did you know folk have gone to the Rogue for justice when their children were kidnapped, and he's done nothing?"

"Nor did the Dogs," Phelan said. "I'd've heard if we sought kidnappers in the Lower City."

I looked at Phelan. We're going to," I promised him. "That's what makes us different. We're outnumbered, and not all of us care. But eventually some of us will do what's right."

Aniki smirked. "That's sweet, Beka."

Rosto nodded. "I'll believe it when I see it."

Verene yawned. "Too serious. Let's feed the nasty birds afore they come in and swipe our food." She pointed to the windowsill. Pigeons were lined up there, waiting.

I looked at Ersken and Kora. There was no reading Kora's eyes as she studied me, and Ersken was tearing up a roll to feed the pigeons. I shrugged and stood. The others would learn or not. I already know the Dogs will take care of the Shadow Snake, sooner or later. It was the same way with the Bold Brass gang eight years ago. The Dogs just need a bit of help sometimes.

Pounce trotted over to my side. *They'll see,* he told me. *They don't know how mule-headed you are.*

It's not just me, I replied silently, sprinkling corn. There are Dogs who only need an extra bit of help to get started. A little more information in their hands, and they'll be after the Shadow Snake like lice on hens. *And* the one who killed those diggers. If I can get that information, so much the better.

I faced them. "I've heard sommat—mentioned it to Ersken, but you all need to know. It's important." I said it fast. They were friends, but they might decide I was cracked when I finished talking about this. "Rolond Lofts, Crookshank's great-grandson, that was kidnapped and killed? He was taken by someone calling himself the Shadow Snake."

Phelan snorted.

I glared at him. "I've seen proof, all right? And

there's more. Folk in the Lower City have lost children to the Snake for years—and sometimes got them back. Near three dozen families, mayhap more. The Snake takes the little one and leaves orders to pay up sommat of value or the child dies. They get a week. Them as pays gets their little one back. Them as don't . . . Either they see the body, or they never see the little one again. Ever. Up till now it was the poor folk, them who couldn't bribe the Dogs or the Rogue. But Crookshank—the Snake found out Crookshank has something that would make the Snake really, really rich." The fire opals, I thought. It can only be the fire opals. If the Snake gets fistfuls of fire opals now, before they're common on the market, he'll never have to kidnap poor children again. But Crookshank refused to pay, and Rolond's dead. The Snake is still about. What if he goes for Tansy?

"Will you ask about? Find out who fell victim to this piece of pig scummer? Mayhap someone knows sommat, or saw someone. Even if we only know who lost a child, or what the Snake wanted—any knowledge is better than none. I can pass it on to my Dogs." I swallowed and said something I'd hoped I'd never have to say. "Or to my Lord Provost. Either way, if we hobble the Shadow Snake, whether we're Dogs or crooked, folk will think well of us for it."

There was a very bad moment when I thought they might laugh. When they'd call me troublemaker. When they'd say who did I think I was, me being just a Puppy.

Kora looked fierce as she turned to Rosto. "I'll do it. I'll do whatever it takes."

Rosto leaned over and stroked her cheek. "You know we'd help just for your sake, love."

Aniki nodded. "We have our reasons. Beyond ambition, that is. We'll keep our ears open."

Phelan rubbed his temples. "Pox, Beka, I just thought it was wild stories. You have proof?"

I nodded. "My Dogs have proof."

Phelan looked down, grim-faced. "I'll remember where I heard those tales. I'm sorry. I thought . . . Never mind."

Ersken nodded to me. "You already told me about the Snake. Of course I'll listen and ask."

Verene's eyes blazed. "When we catch this Snake, I'll make me a belt of his hide. Child killers—it's sad the Black God shows mercy. They deserve none."

My chest felt warm, warm like those times that Pounce comforted me.

I like having friends.

After my watch.

When we mustered for watch this evening, I presented my new gear to my Dogs for inspection. "Very nice," Tunstall said as he eyed the arm guards I had found in the Provost's House gear room. They fit from my wrist to my shoulder and had tongues that sat over my palm. Some of the metal ribs that fit in sleeves in the padded leather were thin knives. They might come in handy. Better still, a slash like I'd taken in the fight with the river drovers would glance off those guards, cutting only the leather, not my flesh. I'd found a leather sap, too. The pack was my third piece from Provost's House.

"There's another piece of gear you need, particularly for the Cesspool," Tunstall said as Goodwin checked my sap. He reached in his pack and fished out a metal gorget like him and Goodwin wore. "There's a cloth pad on the inside, see, to keep it from chafing. You'll need to wash that now and then. Try it on."

Goodwin and the Dogs watched as I tied the curved metal piece around my neck. It was meant to stop a throat cut. I looked from Tunstall to Goodwin. "I can't—"

"I said I'd get one," Tunstall said. "You need it."

I opened my mouth to argue again.

"Shut it," Goodwin ordered. I did. "You're our Puppy. That means your neck is our responsibility. Besides, it's used. Don't go getting sentimental."

"Are you going to admire the jewelry, or are you ready to catch some Rats?" Ahuda yelled. We lined up for muster, even Pounce. He had decided he was part of the Evening Watch.

We were on our way to the Nightmarket when Goodwin said, "Rosto the Piper killed a cove last night in Prettybone. It was a stupid thing. Looby said Rosto had no right, taking work from Ulsa when there were blades right here in Corus who could do it. Rosto tried to get out of it, my Birdie told me. He asked Ulsa to rule on it, but Ulsa said it had nothing to do with her."

"Woman's responsible for more bloodletting than all Scanra," grumbled Tunstall. "She could have put a stop to it."

"So Ulsa dodged it. Then the cracknob drew his blade. My Birdie says he never even saw Rosto draw his." Goodwin looked up at Tunstall as our partner began to sniff the air. "Why do you even bother to pretend you don't want to go straight for the raisin patties? Let's just visit her booth."

I thought of Rosto, flirting over breakfast after killing a man. Even for a rusher, he was a cold one. I am used to thinking of my Cesspool years as hard. Now I begin to wonder what his were like, that even a fresh murder would leave no clear mark on him.

On the way to Mistress Noll's, I asked Goodwin, "But he was storying, wasn't he? Your Birdie? Or someone blocked his view. Saying he never saw Rosto draw his blade is just storying. No one's so fast for real."

Goodwin glanced back at me. "You live in the same house as Rosto, Cooper. You let us know."

"Or we'll find out ourselves," Tunstall said. "He's not going to stay in the shadows long, not that one."

Mistress Noll was at her stall, kneading bread. She

has strong arms. I could see the muscles stand out as she mauled it. "There's my three favorite Dogs," she said as Tunstall laid down his handkerchief. "And a lively week you had of it, by what I hear. That Ashmiller mot, the one as struck you, Mistress Clary. What a dreadful thing, to attack your own man and children!"

"Yet it happens all the time, Mistress Deirdry," Goodwin said. She leaned on one elbow at the counter, turned so she might watch the passersby. "You know it far better than I. There are all manner of sad tales hereabouts."

Tunstall laid down some coppers. "I'm paying this time, Mistress Deirdry. I won't hear 'no' if it comes from your mouth."

Mistress Noll smiled at him. "Then I mustn't say it, must I?" She was just frying the patties, as if she knew we were on our way. "I owe young Beka an apology, or rather, my son Yates does."

Tunstall raised his brows at me. "Cooper?"

I glanced at him, then returned to my own watch of Spicers' Row. "I saw him and Mistress Gemma when I stopped by Mistress Noll's Daymarket shop yesterday, Guardsman," I replied, being formal before the outsider. "We had a talk." It was a Dog's way of saying I'd had to get stern, but not rough. "My lady Sabine can vouch for me."

Both Tunstall and Goodwin looked at Mistress

Noll. "Yates should apologize to Cooper?" Tunstall asked, his voice gentle.

"I need strong men to haul the flour and suchlike about. Their manners, *his* manners, are not what a mother could like," Mistress Noll said, meeting his eyes. "There's not many places as will hire him and his friends."

"With reason," Goodwin said. Her eyes were cold.

"But coves must work or they're idle, and they're back doing the things that bring them before the Magistrates." Mistress Noll's soft face turned hard, as hard as the face of any Cesspool mot who lived to be her age. "I'd as soon not die with my son in the quarries." She gave me the eye. "I apologize for him, Beka. He was rude to you."

"Cooper?" Tunstall asked me again.

Pounce meowed, as if he ordered me to say sommat. "Better if he gave his sorries to Mistress Gemma. It was her he knocked down." I wanted the subject to change away from me, so I told Mistress Noll, "Lady Sabine enjoyed your patties very much."

"It's the spices," Mistress Noll said. "Most think the fruits is enough, but they lose taste so close to summer. I thank you for your care for Gemma, Beka. I'll have a word with my son." She set out a thin cloth and put turnovers on it, then bundled them up and gave them to me. "For breakfast. No charge."

I hesitated all the same, until Goodwin muttered in

my ear, "You're so rich you can pass up free food?" Pounce hooked my boot and made a loud noise that sounded like agreement. I mumbled my thanks and settled the turnovers in my pack.

Goodwin waited for Mistress Noll to serve a gaggle of merchant lads and their sweethearts. Then she leaned on the counter and said, "Who's been calling themselves the Shadow Snake, mistress? Who's been stealing children and giving them back, some dead, some alive?"

Mistress Noll snorted. "Mistress Clary, the Snake's a tale! I told my little ones the Snake would get them if they didn't eat their kidney stew and do their chores!"

"But someone's been dressing in the tale. You know it and we know it," Goodwin said. "Preying on the Lower City like a taxman wearing bearskin. He steals their children and gives them back when they've surrendered what's valuable. And if they don't, he leaves the children dead."

Mistress Noll fluttered around the stall, poking up the fire, checking dough she'd set over a small oven to rise. She sold buns to an off-duty armsman and his doxie and a loaf of bread to a weary-looking cove with ink stains on his fingers. At last she said, "Nobody cares about missing children hereabouts. Their parents can always make more." She said it with an angry twist to her mouth, as if she quoted somebody.

"We're asking," Goodwin said. "Do you know

aught? Who's been seen where the children vanish, or where they've been found? Mistress, you're in the Nightmarket and the Daymarket."

"What I know is that no one knows," Mistress Noll replied, her voice very soft. "No one knows, no one sees, no one hears. Maybe a monster from tales *does* do this, Mistress Clary."

Goodwin straightened and gave the counter a rap with her fingers. "I don't believe in monsters, not in the Lower City. If there is one, Mistress Deirdry, someone made him. But I'm more likely to believe it's a man, or a gang. I want whoever it is. I want him to dance on Execution Hill for the folk he's terrorized."

Tunstall tied up his handkerchief after setting a patty aside. "We've let him run wild in the Lower City. It's a disgrace to our name. We mean to clean it up."

"Welladay," a man said nearby, "lookit who's come out of Crookshank's burrow. I'd thought mayhap she was dead along with her son."

I'd almost forgot the Nightmarket, so hard was I listening to my Dogs and Mistress Noll. Now I looked around. Here came Tansy all in black, with a black cap covered with a veil for her gold curls. She had a basket over her arm.

A maid walked beside her, one I hadn't seen before. She was odd-looking, forty or so, hair combed back in a sleek black and gray braid, black eyes, short nose, mouth wide with frown lines that drew the corners down. She'd plucked her brows clean off and drawn perfect black arches in their place. She had a black teardrop tattooed on her chin and two more at the corners of her eyes. She looked like she could tangle with Goodwin and fight for every inch she was forced to give up.

Her underdress was a finer cotton than I'd look to see on a maid, though her overdress was plain enough. She wore jet earrings and a necklace with a tiger-eye pendant. The metal of the necklace could have been brass, but it looked gold to me.

"Beka!" Tansy cried. "Look at us, out and about!" She smiled at me, the corners of her mouth trembling. She looked at Goodwin and far up at Tunstall.

"Cooper?" Goodwin asked. "You need to do a mannerly thing here."

"Oh." I opened my mouth, but Tansy interrupted.

"If we wait for Beka to introduce us, it will be dawn. She's shyer than moonflowers. You must be Guardswoman Goodwin and Guardsman Tunstall. I'm Tansy Lofts—Beka's been my friend since we were . . ." Her smile failed, then she forced it back onto her mouth. "Since we were small. My husband is Herun Lofts." She extended her hand. They must have taught her that in Crookshank's house, because she never knew about it in Mutt Piddle Lane.

Tunstall took her hand and kissed it. "Our sympathies, Mistress Lofts," he said, his voice kind. "We are doing all we can to find and hobble the Rat who took your child from you."

Tansy gave his hand a squeeze. "I've heard you two are the best in all Corus," she said. "I know you will do all you can." Not realizing that she'd just set up the hackles on both my Dogs, implying they might fail, Tansy cried, "Pounce, you wicked creature! No greeting for me?"

Pounce said several things to her, all sounding happy, then leaped into her basket. Tansy laughed and braced herself against his weight.

"Mistress, we don't want this dirty animal's hair in the food we buy," the maid said. Her voice was smooth and cold. "He's been on the streets—"

"Nonsense," Tansy informed her. "If you're going to fuss, go back to the house. I said I didn't want my own maid, let alone you." Her eyes were too bright; her lips trembled a little. She was on the edge of her temper. Did this mot see that and hear the grief talking? Tansy rubbed Pounce's head. "I can take Pounce as my companion, can't I, boy? You must be bored if Beka is working." She turned to the counter and saw Mistress Noll looking at her. "Grannylady, why is it every time I see you, you're frowning at me?"

Mistress Noll smiled. "You're mistaken, Mistress Lofts. My heart goes out to you in your loss. I too have babes who died, mine when they were newborn.

I know what you feel, losing your Rolond."

Tansy looked away, her eyes overfull. Goodwin wandered across the row to talk with a vendor. Tunstall sniffed a citron bun as he looked down the way. Where Spicers' Row crossed with the fruit sellers', Ulsa of Prettybone District walked. She was flashy in a red shirt and black breeches, both Carthaki silk. She even carried a curved Carthaki-style sword. Rumor said she could use it. Three of her handsome guards walked behind her. One of her women guards was on her far side, but the guard on her left, closest to us, was Rosto. He was all in black and more graceful even than Pounce. Tunstall watched them.

"I am sorry that you lost any children, Grannylady," Tansy whispered. "Whatever their age. I—I said something bad to you about that once. I think the Goddess punished me for it, taking my son."

"Child, that's water sunk in the ground," Mistress Noll said. My memory is bothering me about that now. What did Tansy say to Mistress Noll that has Tansy thinking the Goddess has punished her?

"You must give over your sorrow now for the child on the way," Mistress Noll said to Tansy. "And you must eat. I have some fine rastons here, fresh from the oven." She offered a big loaf for Tansy's inspection.

I heard the familiar creaking of pigeon wings overhead. Splendid, I thought. They find me, and now they think Mistress Noll is offering a meal.

"I think we'd best go about our watch," Goodwin said, returning. "Cooper, say good night to Mistress Lofts and Mistress Noll—"

The dead clamored in my ears as the pigeons descended into the torchlit row. Customers and vendors moved away as the birds flapped between the torches. The ghosts cried out, dozens of them telling me their complaints.

"Maiden's mercy, what are they doing?" Tansy whispered.

Mistress Noll picked up a frying spoon. She poked the awning of her booth, cursing the birds that had landed there. "Send them away, Beka!" she ordered.

"I didn't call them!" I said. Tunstall set a copper on the counter, breaking up a bun. He held out his hand, crumbs falling from his palm.

"Oh, you would," Goodwin complained as five pigeons descended to sit on his arm and fingers.

"Mama?" The young white bird with black-dripped feathers flew in circles around Tansy's head, then tried to land. She shrieked and threw up her arms, knocking it away. The ghost cried, "Mama, take me home! Mama, I'm frightened!"

I froze. In four years I had never seen a ghost seize its messenger bird before.

"Mama, Mama, I'm lost! Someone took me. He said Grandpapa doesn't love me!" The pigeon who carried Rolond's spirit tangled his claws in Tansy's curls. Her maid unsheathed her belt knife.

"No, you looby!" I shoved the mot out of the way. "Tansy, hold still!"

"Beka, get it off, get it off!" Tansy shrieked.

I couldn't blame her. The bird was in a panic now, whirling as it tried to escape, smacking Tansy with its wings. Pigeon slaps hurt. And this one was mad not just with panic, but with the ghost that rode it, who was so certain Tansy could hear him.

"Mama, take me home, please! I'll be good!" Rolond screamed as the pigeon dodged my hands.

I stumbled against Tansy. We both fell against Mistress Noll's booth.

"The man said there was a parrot, but he lied—"

Tansy let out a shriek that made my ear stop working. "Rolond! Rolond, Goddess preserve me, sweeting, where are you?"

Dear Goddess. She heard him. She was pressed against me, and she could hear her dead son's ghost.

"Mama, I'm sorry I was bad!" Rolond was weeping when I got my hands on the pigeon. It was a young bird, not even feathered all the way up to the plate that formed around its nose holes. "Mama, the cove put me in a bad place, and then it was dark. I don't like it in the dark!"

Tansy hit me. She punched my face and my shoulders. "Where is he, Beka! Take me to him, pox rot your womb! I want my child! He's alive! You know where my babe is!"

Now the pigeon, still tangled in her hair, flew at me, hitting me, too. "Don't you make my mama cry!" Rolond yelled. "You're bad! Mama said the folk in black help and you don't, so you're bad!"

Tunstall pulled Tansy off of me. I shifted to untangle the bird's feet. Tansy wrenched around to attack Tunstall. Once I had the pigeon free and his wings pinned, I looked up at my partner. He made Tansy face me, though he kept her in his grip. She kept struggling. "Let me go!" Tansy cried. "I want my son!"

"Stop it, Tansy," I said coldly. "Stop it right now. You act like a Mutt Piddle trull."

That caught her attention. She quieted, her eyes streaming tears, her chest heaving.

"Look at me," I said quietly. I held her eyes with mine until I was certain I had her attention. Then I showed her the young bird in my hands. Somehow he'd kept clean. His white feathers shone in the torchlight. His black ones really did look like ink. "They carry unhappy spirits. Understand? This poor creature carries Rolond until Rolond decides to go to the Peaceful Realms. But Rolond doesn't know what's happened, Tansy." My mouth was dry. I licked my lips and told my oldest friend, "You have to tell him he's dead."

I cradled the pigeon against my chest so I could keep his wings pinned with one hand. Then I grabbed her with the other. "Tell him. Elsewise he'll wander in that dark he keeps talking about."

"Tell a pigeon he's dead?" Tansy asked.

Someone nearby tittered.

"Mama, why would you tell a bird it's dead?" Rolond asked her. "Birds don't have ghosts, do they? Are there birds in the Black God's land?"

Tansy sobbed. Her knees gave way. I hauled her up. I knew that if I let go, she couldn't hear him anymore or he hear her. "Tansy, do it!"

"Lambkin—sweetheart, of course the Black God has birds," Tansy whispered, straightening. "Beautiful ones. But you won't see them if you stay where it's dark. You have to go to the Peaceful Realms."

"But I don't want to go, Mama," Rolond complained. "I want to come home with you."

"Oh, Rolond, you can't." Tansy reached out her free hand. It shook as she stroked the pigeon I held. "Rolond, you died. The man—the man killed you. That's why you're lost."

"No," he whispered. "No. I'm just in a dark place. When they stole me, I was in a dark place." His voice broke. "There was cloth on my head, and then the girl who was with me took it off. And then the man came back and put it on again. He carried me away."

"And he killed you," I said, since Tansy couldn't. "There's no hood now, Rolond. You need to say goodbye to your mama and go see the Black God."

"I'll come to you," Tansy whispered. "One day, in the Peaceful Realms, I'll come to you there."

His voice was fading. He believed her. "Promise, Mama?"

"Promise, my baby. I love you."

But he was gone.

All around us the market was silent. Tansy made no sound. I think we all forgot where we were until the city's clocks began to chime seven. That broke the spell on the crowd that had gathered. Tunstall helped Tansy to her feet.

"You need to get Mistress Lofts home," Goodwin told the maid. "Now." The maid glared at her. Goodwin stopped and looked the mot over, memorizing every inch of her. "What's your name, wench?"

The maid bridled. "Vrinday Kayu."

"Kayu. Copper Isles name, Carthaki tattoos. I don't like you. I'm going to remember your face. All three of us are." Goodwin's jerk of the head took in Tunstall and me. "You'd best keep your fingers clean when you venture out of Crookshank's house. Now be on about your work."

I thought for a moment Kayu might hiss and scratch Goodwin. I saw shimmering around her hands. Then she put an arm around Tansy and led her back to Crookshank's house. She didn't glance at us again, but from the too-careful way she handled my friend, I'd say she knew we were watching.

"*Maid,* my left nostril," Tunstall murmured. "Mage. You saw that bit of magic?"

"Later." Goodwin said it very quiet-like. She looked around at me. "Can you loose your little pigeon friend now, or will he attack Master Pounce?" She glared at my cat, who sat at her feet. "And where were you when the bird was going mad on that poor girl's head?" she asked Pounce.

Pounce stared up at her, then said, *"Manh!"*

Whatever that meant.

I already looked a cracknob and a half to the crowd that had seen our performance. It couldn't matter what I said or did anymore. I lifted up my head and called, "Slapper! You need to teach this one how to keep control!" I held up the young pigeon in my hand. I didn't even know if it would work. I'd never gotten the birds to take orders, but no ghost had ever grabbed hold of his bird, either.

I hadn't noticed the pigeons overhead had been silent for some time. I did now, because I could hear only one bird flapping toward us. Slapper landed on the dirt of the row. He began the growling coo that was the pigeon anger noise.

"None of that," I said. "He's just a youngling. It's not his fault."

Tunstall crouched before Slapper. "Who's this

one?" he asked. "Slapper, you called him?" He was breaking up another bun. He put the pieces down in front of the pigeon.

"They should be smaller," I said. I couldn't help correcting him, even if he was my training Dog. I worried about the silly feathered nuisances, and so few folk seemed to care about them. "If pieces are big—if they can't break them up, the loobies try to swallow them whole. Often they can get stuck in the pigeon's throat."

"Mithros's teeth," Goodwin muttered.

Tunstall crumbled the roll into pigeon-sized bites. Slapper was already shaking a big one, breaking off a smaller bite for himself. Tunstall hurried to crumble the rest. Gently I placed Inky down in front of Slapper. The young bird went after the bread, eagerly pecking. Slapper instantly smacked him with a wing, then began to limp and dance around him, talking in pigeon.

"Slapper, eh?" Tunstall asked again as he straightened. He was grinning. "He looks cracked, with those yellow eyes."

"Unless you're going to put some coppers in a hat, our play is over," Goodwin told the crowd. "Move along. There's naught to gawp at."

"The pigeons could fight," someone called. "My money's on the black one."

Other birds came down to eat. The crowd was still arguing if, as young as Inky was, he couldn't take crippled old Slapper when the birds finished the last crumbs and flew off into the dark. Then the people really did move on.

"Let's go," Tunstall said. "We'll talk about pigeons and ghosts over supper. Can folk always hear them when you touch them, Cooper?"

We said goodbye to Mistress Noll and walked on down the row. "No, sir," I replied to Tunstall. "No, because my brothers and sisters would lean against me when I fed 'em, and they never heard nothing. Maybe it's the ghost wanting to be heard so bad, or it being a ghost related by blood. . . ."

"We really do need to pay mind to our work," Goodwin said. She sounded apologetic, which was a strange thing in itself. "Much as I want to hear this, attention unpaid—"

"—is a grave that's made." I knew the saying. "Sorry, Goodwin."

"No," Tunstall said. "We should have gotten you to tell us more about the pigeons afore now."

Goodwin halted to stare at a sutler who lingered over a table of spices. The mot glanced at us and moved on. Goodwin spoke as we kept walking. "And the dust spinner thing. Though truthfully, Cooper, that one makes my skin prickle. At least pigeons are birds. They're part of creation. Stands to reason they'd be the servants of the gods. But spinners are just sticks and dust and air."

Tunstall reached out to grab a gixie's wrist. She was

moving into the row, having spotted a fine lady on a man's arm coming her way. Behind them was a foist about my age. The little gixie was the decoy, the doll she held her lure. The game was played when she dropped the doll right before the lady and her cove. The child would scramble to get the toy. Whilst they were distracted, the girl's partner would foist at least the lady's coin, if not the man's, too.

My own eye was caught by a man asking a vendor to change three silver nobles for coppers. Something about it struck me odd. It was too early in the night for the gambling to have started. That was when coves dressed like this one was might need coppers or have silver to change. He'd bought sticks of cinnamon from the vendor for his trouble, but from the vendor's scowl, he'd not purchased enough. Or mayhap it was the sweat on the cove's brow when he put his silver coins on the counter.

I took out my baton and went to stand next to him. "Greetings to you, Master Spicer," I told the spice seller as he placed copper after copper on the counter. I picked up the silver noble. "Good evening, Master—"

He didn't answer but turned to run just as I saw the King's profile pointed to the left, not to the right. The cove might have escaped had I not already set my baton right behind his knee. He stumbled, enough for Goodwin to cut in and twist his arm behind him. I took out my dagger and drew it across the face of the coin.

The thin silver curled up to show lead beneath. I held it up for Goodwin's inspection.

She thrust the captive against the plank counter. "Cooper, empty his purse. You coves are lower than maggots, you know that?" she asked him. "Enough of these false coins get out there and instead of regular folk paying a few coppers for a meal, we must pay a handful of silvers, and whole families get sold as slaves so one or two might eat."

The spice vendor spat on the ground. "I hope they sell yours to south Carthak," he said to the cove with real hate. "Leave 'em with the snakes an' the fevers an' the great farms where they work to death." He swept his coppers away.

Tunstall searched the Rat whilst Goodwin tied his hands. "Let's hope you have the names of whoever gave you these, my friend," he advised in his pleasant way. "Elsewise you have a nasty death on Execution Hill to look forward to."

The Nightmarket kept us busy until suppertime. At the Mantel and Pullet, Tunstall ordered a bountiful meal to repay us for all that work. I thought I might drool when the smells met my nose: spiced pork pie with anise, herbs in beef broth, a raston, and a Tyran custard. To make my happiness complete, the barmaid came over with our jacks, ale for the Dogs and barley water for me.

We ate in silence while the house roared with talk

around us. Then, as I was beginning to think I would not die of starvation, Goodwin put her hand on my wrist and bore it down to the table. I met her eyes and swallowed my mouthful.

"Explain the comedy with the pigeon and Mistress Tansy now. I think I've been patient. Mistress Noll said it, that first night, it was magic in your father's line. Well and good. You have it. You speak to dust spinners, too. I don't understand that, but I'm prepared to exist with it. We live in a world of magics, after all. But that at Mistress Deirdry's stall—those things don't happen, Cooper." She speared a bit of pork with her knife and put it in her mouth.

I took my chunk of fire opal from my pocket and turned it in my fingers. I didn't look at it, but just feeling its roughness against my skin helped me to order my thoughts. "Truth to tell, I was as scared as Tansy."

Tunstall grunted. "You hid it well. Good for you."

I heard a thud under the table. He yelped. She had kicked him. "You spoil her," she said.

I waited until they were watching me. Then I went on, "It never happened before. Not to me. But . . . see, I don't think most folk should know pigeons are the Black God's messengers, or that they carry the ghosts of them that's uneasy and dead. They wouldn't leave the poor birds alone. But I've known that Rolond Lofts was still about, riding a Lower City bird, since the day after I started my training with you. I just couldn't find out which bird at first. He was still with a big flock."

"Why not ask your friend Slapper?" Tunstall asked. He grinned at Goodwin. "I like Slapper. Now there's a pigeon a Dog can relate to."

She kicked him again.

He glared at her. "Are you and your man fighting? Is that your problem?"

"No, you great lummox. I want to hear Cooper," she said, her voice flat. "Go on, girl."

"Slapper and I don't talk," I explained. I was trying not to smile. "At least, we never did before tonight. He's popular with the ghosts, but see, the ghosts don't control the birds, and the birds don't control the ghosts. They just . . . fly around."

Goodwin scowled. "That's not very efficient, you ask me."

"They're dead. I don't think time means the same. Only tonight, tonight I think Rolond wanted his mama so bad, he—broke through, somehow, and made his pigeon go to her. The bird was young. And . . . I'd like to see the Shadow Snake drawn and quartered." There were drops falling on my plate. I was crying, curse it. "He was only three." They knew I didn't mean the Shadow Snake. I wiped my eyes on my sleeve. "I talked to the birds whilst I was home yesterday." I wasn't going to speak of what had happened tonight if it made me act like a looby. "They understood me then, too. I talked with the ghosts who were killed, the ones

murdered all together that the spinners told me about."
I glanced at them through my bangs. Tunstall was
steadily eating. I don't think an earthquake would stop
Tunstall working his way through a plate of food. He
was on his third helping of the pie. Goodwin was drinking her ale and watching me. "There are nine of them.
They were hired to dig a well and taken there blind-
folded. Whoever had them there kept them captive in
some building. They just dug in the pink city rock and
found the gems. They didn't know the rightful name for
fire opals. That's what they told me yesterday."

For a long while, seemingly forever when there was
sweat crawling down my sides, my Dogs said nothing.
I thought they would decide to lock me up with the
truly mad, them as scream and talk nonsense with
themselves. Then Goodwin looked at Tunstall.

"They were digging for Crookshank. He's the one
with the fire opals."

Tunstall ran his fingers through his hair. "If Crookshank meant to kill them all along, he wouldn't let anyone that could be connected to him do the hiring.
He's too canny a bird. Whoever hired them, could be
it's someone we haven't connected with Crookshank's
businesses."

Goodwin looked at me. "They never left that
building?"

She asked it like my ghosts were real human

Birdies, singing the songs Dogs liked to hear. "They said they never did. I think they're buried there."

Goodwin wrinkled her nose. "Nasty smell for whoever might want to dig on that spot again. So he's done at that location—"

"Crookshank won't stop at one building. Not when the pink rock passes all under the Lower City." Tunstall signaled the barmaid to refill our jacks.

Goodwin grinned. My skin began to prickle with excitement. She said, "He'll be hiring more workers. Maybe his folk will tell the new diggers not to say they've got work, but these days? With jobs trickling out of Corus like water from a busted bucket?"

"They'll talk." Tunstall nodded. "Someone will tell a sweetheart, a rival, the one they owe money to."

"He won't hire a lot of diggers," I said. "He won't want folk noticing. And they dig in cellars. Not so much room in those."

"But he'll be hiring," Goodwin explained. "Too many other businesses hereabouts have been letting folk go. It's a ripple, Cooper. You learn to feel for ripples." She climbed onto her bench. Taking her whistle, she blew a sharp blast on it. Heads turned everywhere inside the room. "Harken, you Dogs!" she cried, her voice cutting through the last noise as the room went quiet. "Me'n Tunstall and Cooper have a scent. We'd like you to get it in your noses. Someone hired nine

289

diggers, telling each one they were being hired to dig a well. Each one alone, not all nine, understand? Hired for a one-digger job, but it was nine all told. They're all missing, probably dead. Now the Rats that did it either hired more in the last week or they're hiring right now. A sniff, the tiniest sniff, and you bring it to one of us. Whatever's in it at the end, you'll share. If there's naught in it, we'll remember what we owe."

Tunstall didn't stand on the bench, but he did rise. "Some Rat went and doused nine folk. Now he means to do it twice, under our very sniffers. We can't allow such goings-on, not on our watch."

Them that were Dogs answered him with growls. I could see Ersken and Verene. I think their eyes were as wide as mine. I'd heard of a Growl, when Dogs took up a challenge. It meant ill for the Rats that made them voice it. But it was one thing to hear of it, another to sit in the Mantel and Pullet and hear that rumbling snarl come from dozens of throats. The army folk and off-duty Palace Guards shifted where they sat. The maids and the barkeep had retreated to the kitchen when Goodwin stood on the bench. Seemingly they knew what was coming.

I had what I wanted for the nine dead whose cries the spinners had first picked up. The Dogs would seek them. I'd never even thought that it might be easier to find whoever it was that hired them. But Goodwin was right. These days plenty of folk were out of work. No matter how they were sworn to say nothing of someone looking to hire, word would leak out. Soon enough, a Dog would hear.

Goodwin stood down, but she did not sit. Instead she checked her belt, making sure her weapons and purse were placed as she needed them. It was time to go back to the street. Tunstall emptied his tankard and counted out the coins for our barmaid. When he finished, he looked at Goodwin. I was already up, still trembling from the Growl. I wanted to find a Rat and shake him till he was senseless.

"Well?" Tunstall asked. "Have you a plan? Because I do."

She actually raised her hand and beckoned to him with those two fingers.

"Let's visit Dawull," Tunstall said, and put a toothpick in his mouth. "Let's ask him if he's been dancing for Crookshank. Maybe Dawull's folk don't know Crookshank is killing folk just for digging for him."

"You're a bad lad," Goodwin said, her eyes alight. "Let's go see Dawull."

Dawull held court at the Fog Lantern, near Kingsbridge. It was actually in Flash kennel's territory, since Jane Street's ended at Justice Way. The rules were, Jane Street Dogs could visit district chiefs without asking leave of other kennels, since we had the Court of the

Rogue in our territory. How well that worked usually depended on the Dogs involved. In this case, Flash kennel didn't care what we did.

Tunstall and Goodwin saluted Dawull's sentries on the approach to the Fog Lantern. The rushers looked like they'd swallowed sommat nasty, but none would say anything to my Dogs' faces. In the shadows I saw runners head off down the alleys to warn Dawull. Maybe they went to tell Kayfer and other folk as well. I wished my Dogs had brought some of the packmates who'd been at the Mantel and Pullet. What if Goodwin and Tunstall had given in to the kind of carelessness that got us in trouble at the Barrel's Bottom? I'd hoped to lose the last bruise on my face before I got new ones.

We were almost there when someone gave a two-fingered whistle that almost blew apart the fog that was coming up off the Olorun. One of Dawull's lookouts grabbed his club. Another one, standing in a second-floor window across the rutted street, waved him off.

Three people came toward us from the Kingsbridge end of Rovers Street, two men and a woman. Lady Sabine wore a long tunic in the men's fashion, her sword and dagger sheaths and belt well polished, and slippers on her feet. Her cloak was fastened over one shoulder, leaving her sword arm bare. She'd bound her hair up in a net with small pearls stitched on it. She looked . . . nice. Ladylike. She even wore rings on two fingers of each hand, though none of them were big.

The men who walked with her were knights. They plainly expected everyone to know that, though they wore no armor. They wore long tunics and cloaks like Lady Sabine. There was more gold and gems on their sheaths and belts, but they had weathered faces, and the weapons' hilts were plain. They moved like fighters. They also had that air most nobles have, the one Lady Sabine doesn't. It's the air that says normal folk must drop what they do and wait to see if they have to attend to the nobles.

Lady Sabine walked forward a few steps. "You three—four, excuse me, Master Pounce—blend in so well," she said as my cat patted her shoe.

I squinted through the fog. I hadn't even known Pounce had arrived until that moment.

"I find you in the most dreadful places. Didn't you have enough of Rovers Street last week?" the lady asked.

"It's not given to us to choose where we must walk, milady," Goodwin told her.

"Oh, aye, it is," grumbled the lookout closest to us.

"Silence, lout," commanded one of the knights, who'd come nearer. "You were not addressed."

Sabine rolled her eyes.

"We're on Dog business, Lady" Tunstall explained. He reached out, casual-like, and cuffed the lookout on the ear. "We're paying a visit to Dawull."

"Chief of Waterfront," Goodwin explained. "It's one of the Rogue's districts. We mean to rattle his trap."

"That sounds amusing," Lady Sabine remarked. "Lads, I have an idea. Let's go watch my Dog friends annoy this criminal. We don't really want to go to my Lord of Naxen's party. You know it will be boring to madness. All kinds of noble maidens will simper at you, and their mothers will scowl at me."

Goodwin looked at Tunstall, who shrugged. The two men talked it out in whispers. Finally we walked on, with the two noblemen beside Tunstall and Lady Sabine with Goodwin, Pounce, and me.

"We had an invitation to supper at my Lady of Hollyrose's in Highfields," she explained to my Dogs. "She's elderly, so it ended not too long ago. We decided to walk to my Lord of Naxen's party. The three of us served out in the hill country this last year, so we're used to more exercise than we've been getting of late."

"But at least *we* had a choice about being in the hills, Sabine," joked the redheaded knight. "We could have gone home as we liked. You had to wait until His Majesty pardoned you."

That made Goodwin look at her as we halted in front of the Fog Lantern. "You needed a pardon to come home?" she asked.

"We had a misunderstanding," the lady said, her deep voice quiet. "It's over and done with." She walked through the open door of the tavern. "I wonder if the ale's any good."

Her knight friends followed.

Tunstall waited until they were well inside before he whispered, "Those two had better not be interested in her." He walked in, leaving Goodwin, Pounce, and me to follow.

"The big looby," I heard Goodwin mutter. "Never get involved with the nobility. Everyone knows that. *Everyone.*"

I remembered the rumble in his voice when he'd said that about the knights being interested in her. "I think he forgot."

Into the common room we went, following the nobles. Dawull and his favorites held the far corner. Dawull's rushers and their mots, and his thieves, robbers, and lickboots sat everywhere else, along with Players and gamesters hoping to win some coin from the regular customers. Dogs and children played on the floor whilst maids tried to serve everyone.

At just this moment, though, all was silent. Lady Sabine and her two friends surveyed the room. They looked as out of place as I would have looked at their supper in Highfields. I had a mad wish to giggle and bit my lip.

The blond knight looked at three river dodgers who held the nearest table. He didn't even bother to speak. He simply snapped his fingers at them and jerked his thumb. Surely, I thought, they'll throw the table at him.

But meek as priests' finches, they went to another table. That same knight beckoned to a serving maid as the two noblemen seated themselves. She thrust the neck of her dress lower, when it already did little enough to cover her peaches, and came to see what they would have. When Lady Sabine took her seat with them, the wench actually glared at my lady.

Dawull saw us on the stair and got to his feet with a grin. "Heads high, my pets!" he bellowed. "I smell"— he swung that great red head around, sniffing loudly— "dank fur. Piddle. Scummer. Dogs."

Some laughed. I saw movement in a hall to one side that I'd wager led to the privy, since Aniki came out adjusting her belt. She noticed us and waved. I only nodded, since waving back was not something dignified and Dog-like. Pounce didn't worry himself with such things. He bounded across the floor, jumping onto a four-legged cur's back and up into Aniki's arms. She smiled and gave him a good scratch, but her wary eyes were on the three of us as we walked toward Dawull.

His rushers had their swords half drawn when we stopped ten feet from him. Goodwin put her hands on her hips. Tunstall scratched the back of his neck, as if he did nothing in particular. I clasped my hands before me and set my feet in the rest position. I wished I had my baton out, but drawing it now would put Dawull's back up. I stayed alert for movement on my sides. I was very glad Lady Sabine had decided to come with us rather than go to a stupid party. I couldn't be sure if her friends would help us, but I knew she would. And she was behind me. I need not fear with Lady Sabine present.

"We're looking for Crookshank," Goodwin said. "Tell him to stand forth."

For a moment all was still. Then the laughter began. My Dogs' shoulders didn't even twitch, so I held steady and kept my face still.

When the laughter had quieted some, Dawull bellowed, "Crookshank! I think they stopped watering the ale at the Mantel and Pullet, woman! We have no scales tucked under the tables, have we, friends?"

"No," came the replies. The comic Players, or those who pretended to be, made a game of looking under tables, benches, and the mots' skirts. More than a few earned cuffs and boxed ears from the mots who objected.

Goodwin waited for quiet to return. Then she said, "But we were certain we'd find him with you, Dawull. You have become his back scratcher. Clever trick, to act like you hustled the old man out of the Court. You saved your friend before Kayfer decided to carve him. Too bad riches alone can't buy you the Rogue's crown."

"Is this a jest?" roared Dawull.

"Do I smile?" Goodwin asked, quick as a snake. "How does Crookshank buy you, Dawull? Where does he get coin enough to buy a chief of the Rogue?"

One cove seated near Dawull lunged to his feet and cleared his sword from his sheath. "Mangy bitch," he said. "You'll eat your lies."

I heard another sword clear its sheath. This blade was in Aniki's hand, resting there like a natural part of her arm. She could have drawn it to back up Dawull's man, to help us, or to be ready for a fight.

"Hold!" yelled Dawull, to them and to the others who were getting to their feet, weapons in hand. "Hold, curse you, or you'll tangle with me."

"But sayin' you was bought, Dawull, sayin' you was in the service of that bloodsucker," complained his guard. His sword hung from his hand, useless. "Dog or no, she's got to be taught!"

"What do I care what some fleabit gutter crawler says?" Dawull asked. "Unless you believe her?" He glared at his man.

The killer shrank under Dawull's glare. If he had an imagination, he was imagining his bones were cracking. "No, no. That's why I was going to—"

"Kill a Dog and a thousand Dogs have their teeth in your neck, ducknob! And you'd have to kill all three, besides them loaners back there." He pointed to Lady Sabine and her two friends. "That's why you need me to run this lot." He glared now at all of his cronies. "I'm the only one of you with this." He tapped himself on the head with a finger the thickness of my baton.

"A head?" I heard Tunstall murmur for Goodwin and me alone. Goodwin shifted slightly on her legs. I knew she wanted to kick him to silence him. Some folk show that they laugh in the oddest ways.

"Now sheathe that bread knife of your'n," Dawull ordered his man, not knowing Tunstall had even squeaked. "You too, girl. Good that you're eager, but whatever they do in Scanra, we don't go dousing Dogs just because they've no manners."

It was only after the man put away his sword that I heard the music of Aniki's blade sliding back into its sheath.

"Crookshank was a mad old man that night. Kayfer remembered it when he cooled off—that's why I got Crookshank out of there. We need the bloodsucker and them like him. But me being bought?" Dawull laughed, though not well. "You Dogs shouldn't drink hotblood wine during your watch. It makes you think crazy things. There isn't a cove or mot in Corus as could buy me, unless it was old Roger himself with the crown's jewels."

I heard the scrape of wood as the knights started to rise.

Dawull bowed toward them. "Gods save His Royal Majesty and his lovely Queen. I meant no disrespect," he told them, oil nearabout dripping from his lips. I glanced back. Slowly—very slowly—the two men sat, their hands on their sword hilts. Knights could be touchy about respecting the King. Still, Lady Sabine had her head propped on her hand. If she'd made a move to get up, she had settled again quickly.

Goodwin looked around the room. "Just remember, when it's Crookshank you're taking orders from, we warned you." She turned to Tunstall and me. "Let's sit for a time." As we wandered back to the knights' table, she muttered, "That's why he has a head. Lout."

Lady Sabine grinned as we came near. "I thought we might have to fight our way out again. Have a seat. These two don't mind. They diced with the soldiers under their command for the last year. Those people barely bathed."

"But it's different in Corus," protested the blond one, though he waved Goodwin onto the bench next to him. He was already giving Pounce a scratch, so I decided he couldn't be too bad, for a knight. "Our families are sticklers."

"Never mind your families," Sabine told them. "I want to know who Crookshank is."

"Who cares about a cityman?" the redheaded knight asked. "He's not a real problem, is he? Not like the hill raiders."

Tunstall raised an eyebrow. "Anyone I might know?"

The redheaded knight leaned forward. "We had this one clan—"

The blond knight got to his feet. "Excuse me. I

didn't come home to talk about the hills. A green-eyed wench over there wants to fall in love with me."

"For now," Sabine murmured as he crossed the room. The wench who'd gotten his attention was one of the higher-priced doxies there, wearing a dress and earrings that did not come from Cheappretty Row.

Pounce grumbled and walked over to me. "I hope he's got coin in his purse," Goodwin told Sabine. "Elsewise he'll turn up missing his gems and gold."

"Don't worry about him," Sabine told her as Aniki slid into the seat the knight had left. "None of the hill doxies could pluck him, and they use clubs. Besides, Joreth is all kinds of fat in the purse, and he loves to pay double when he's happy." She turned. "Are you sure it's wise to sit here?" she asked Aniki, who had come over to us.

"I can always tell him I was sounding you out for possible robbing later," Aniki said with her usual cheerful grin. "Besides, he knows me'n Beka live in the same lodging house. Or he will later, because I'll tell him. Or did I tell him last night?" She laughed. "I'm Aniki Forfrysning." She smiled at Goodwin. "Hullo, Guardswoman." She leaned down and kissed Pounce on the head. He glared up at her and said, *Stop that!* in cat. Aniki glanced at Tunstall, but he and the redheaded knight were deep in talk concerning hill people they both knew.

"Actually, I'm glad you came over," Sabine told

Aniki. "I wanted a look at that blade of yours, if you don't mind. It sounds like an Anjel sword."

Aniki nodded. Standing, she removed her sheathed blade from her belt and laid it before Lady Sabine. "One of Master Watson's own forging," she said with pride. "I won't tell you who I had to kill to be able to afford this."

I *think* she was joking.

When Pounce, Goodwin, Tunstall, and I left, Aniki and Lady Sabine were still talking swords. Moreover, Tunstall had promised to return for drinking and more conversation about what was going on in the eastern hills of Tortall.

"Is that why you're going back?" Goodwin asked. "Just catching up on the other barbarians that survived their yearly bath? I'm not going with you, Mattes. And I won't like it if one of Dawull's idiots decides to kill a Dog anyway, even an off-watch Dog."

We walked out into mist so thick we could barely see. Pounce grumbled that he hated this kind of weather.

"I'll be with two knights, Clary," Tunstall said. "And I'll take a sword from the armory after we muster off watch."

It did seem that Tunstall with a sword was more comforting to Goodwin than Tunstall on the street without her. "Just don't get hurt," she warned him as we walked along. "Me and Cooper aren't going to shake the trees for whoever's hiring diggers all by ourselves."

You're not, Pounce said. *You'll have me.* He looked at me, his strange purple eyes gleaming. *Of course, they don't know that. And don't you tell them.*

I wouldn't dream of it, I said as we wandered down the street to the kennel.

Thursday, April 9, 246

Before training, afternoon.

When I opened the door this morning, before I even had my hair braided, Kora stood there with a jar of pears pickled with currants and almonds. Her long eyes were flashing with anger. I could swear I saw blue-green sparks stuck in her lashes.

"A lily pendant on a gold chain," she told me. "Enamel on gold. Maybe so big." She held a thumb up, bending the first joint. "There was a mot at the Glassman Square fountain who was trying to get bacon grease from her man's shirt. We got to talking of the Shadow Snake. She said her neighbor's girl was taken. The lass's father gave up the necklace he bought his wife to the Shadow Snake."

I took the jar. "And the little girl?"

Kora picked up my cat and cuddled him as if she needed to touch something soft. "The Snake gave her back. She wet the pallet she slept on after, though. And it wasn't two moons later, my Birdie told me, before the whole family packed their things and moved from Corus altogether. They said they were going to Barzun, where the only snakes could be killed with a spade." I think I heard her sniff. "He did that to a little girl for a *necklace*."

"But that's why no one's cared about this Snake,

304

love." Rosto leaned against my door frame. He could be so quiet on my creaky stairs.

I nodded. "Because he goes after folk whose lives are so small no one else thinks they have aught of value," I said. Like herb women with lung rot and five little ones who live on Mutt Piddle Lane. Mama's last man had been kin to the Shadow Snake, thinking no one would take vengeance for her. And just as he did, the Shadow Snake would learn how wrong he was.

"I like Lady Sabine, Beka," Aniki said, coming over from her rooms with a cheese and bread halves from yesterday's breakfast. "You should have come back to the tavern after your shift last night. She and Tunstall were doing sword dances like they have in the eastern hills. It was fun."

I shivered. The thought of Tunstall throwing his long legs about in any kind of dance is fearsome. Still, it makes me wonder if Goodwin shouldn't maybe get used to the idea of him and Lady Sabine being friendly, or more than friendly. Tavern dancing usually leads to dancing at home, Mama always said.

I opened the shutters. The pigeons fluttered down, just a handful so early—Slapper, White Spice, Pinky, Mumper, Ashes. None of them said more that was new as I gave them the last of my cracked corn and some bread. They mourned the loved ones who thought they had been left behind. They whispered of the pink city rock. They fought each other over space on my ledge and strutted, cooing as if they had naught in their minds but eggs and feathers.

Of my other, human friends, Verene and Phelan arrived holding hands and carrying hot fritters. Ersken brought half a ham and a cheese tart. We'd invited some of our fellow Puppies, but none of them lived as close as Verene or Ersken nor wanted to roll out of bed so early.

Rosto not only brought more twilsey and raspberry jam, but he gave me a good-sized bag of cracked corn for the silly birds. If he'd given me aught for myself, I could have said no, but corn for the idiot pigeons I'd never turn down.

He didn't try to take advantage, either. In fact, he was the first to go, saying he'd errands to run. The others, too, scattered early. Kora was the last to stand. She lingered, helping me to finish the straightening up.

"Would you remember the mot who told you about that pendant?" I asked her. "Might she be at the fountain again soon?"

Kora gave me her tricky, sidelong smile. "I can do better. I can take you to her home."

"How do you know where she lives? Did you follow her?"

Kora picked up Pounce and laid him across the back of her shoulders. "I put a spot on her, that I might find her again at need." She raised a fingertip. A circle of green-blue light appeared there. It vanished. "I can always find my spots again."

I hardly knew what to say, but I knew I should tell her *something*. Finally I said, "That is a good idea."

Kora scratched Pounce's chin, not looking at me. "A child killer got my older sister. Not a cold Rat like the Snake, who kills for gain. A mad one. But I hate all child killers, whatever their reasons." She took a breath. "You'll need to dress like a gixie. In plain breeches you give off a whiff of Dog."

I put my hand on her arm for a moment. Quietly I told her, "I have two sisters. Whenever I pass the Goddess's shrines, I thank the Lady they live safe in Provost's House."

Kora nodded.

I went to my clothespress and took out a gown.

Kora's glowing spot led us into the streets beyond Glassman Square. The mot she'd spoken to yesterday had a small house of her own, on an alley lined with them. I heard children in the back and the thump of a butter churn. A woman spun flax on the stone path to the side yard. A big, short-haired dog slept on the doorstep. When we walked through the gate, the dog rose and growled, hackles rising. I reached for a baton I did not carry. Kora's magic glowed around her fingers.

Pounce walked forward and meowed forcefully. The dog looked at him and whuffed. Pounce called him what sounded to me like a name. The dog's tail began to wag. Mayhap Pounce just had to prove he was a Lower City cat. I was not sure.

The mot halted her spinning. "My Brute hates cats." She watched Pounce and the dog, a strange expression in her eyes. She then inspected Kora and me. To Kora she said, "I know you. You are the laundress and herb girl. You gave me the salve that healed those burns of mine." She pursed her lips. "And you asked me about stolen children."

"I did," Kora said. "This is my friend Beka. She, too, is interested in stolen children."

"She is a Dog," said the woman. "Dress or no, she stands like a Dog."

"Work on that, perhaps," Kora murmured to me.

"Beka?" the woman asked suddenly. "Cooper? As works with Tunstall and Goodwin? The terrier Puppy, that chased Orva Ashmiller to Northgate?"

I looked at the four-legged dog. I did not want to talk about Mistress Ashmiller. "Is he friendly, your Brute?" I stepped forward, my palm held up. Kora took a breath, but seemingly Pounce had opened the way for us. Brute came up, his tail wagging slowly. He smelled my hand, then let me scratch his ears. "You're a fine boy," I told him.

"I have children of my own," the woman whispered, to me or to Kora, I wasn't certain. "They could be taken from me."

I scratched Brute on the rump. "There are plenty of folk with children in the Lower City, mistress." I kept my voice low. "Many of them already lost children to the Snake who took your neighbors' girl. Too many of those did not see their children come home alive again. When the Snake frightens more of you into silence, you make it possible for him to do it again. And again." I met her eyes with mine this time. "Right now all anyone can see is that you have friends to visit, the laundress from the square and one other. They must be friends, because this fine, handsome guard of your house is wagging his tail. What they think elsewise depends on you."

The woman ladled water onto her flax to moisten it, taking time to think. At last she said, "Come around here. There is a bench." It was placed so she could talk with us as she spun. Once we were settled, she began to work again, though her thread was uneven. She was frightened. I understood that.

Brute followed us. I scratched his ears and rump. Kora talked about people from the fountain square until the mot was calmer. When Kora nudged me lightly, I leaned forward over Brute's heavy shoulders.

"Has anyone you can name given you cause to fear since your neighbors' child was taken?" I asked, keeping my voice soft. Only two of the children I'd heard outside had come to peer at us through the house's open door. They ran away the moment I looked at them. Their mother had trained them to be wary of strangers. I suspected the wall out back was high and mayhap covered with thorny vines.

The woman shook her head. "Brute was a year old then. He guards us well."

I nodded. "Mistress, you told my friend about a necklace."

She halted her spinning. In the distance, we all heard thunder's distant boom. We looked up. There was a thin arm of black clouds reaching over the wall. Mayhap there would be a good spring rain later.

"We were all jealous of it, we mots," she whispered. "Such a pretty thing. Her man had a second job for weeks to pay for it. She thought he was helping a friend to build his house for naught. He give it to her for her birthday, the same day as they'd been married five year. Enamel work and gold. She wore it everywhere. 'Fine work is meant to be seen,' she told us, which scorched our feathers, didn't it? Then the Shadow Snake took her little girl and demanded the necklace."

So quiet were we that I could hear Brute's tail stir the dust as he leaned against my knees. Behind the house I heard the children squabble.

Gently I moved Brute and went to stand next to the mot. "Mistress, what did the pendant look like?" I asked her. "So pretty a thing, you must remember. Can you draw it for me?" I picked up a stick and handed it to her.

"I'm no hand at picturing," she whispered, but she took the stick. She didn't need to be the greatest hand at drawing. The design was simple, the kind of thing that stayed before the eye in a person's mind. Curved lines turned up, like cupped hands. I would remember it if I saw it again.

I thought of something. We'd been taught what questions to put when a crime had been done recently. No Dogs had asked about this crime. No one had reported the child's kidnapping to Jane Street. Still, why not ask? "Did you see anyone, the days before the child was taken, or the days before she was returned? Anyone as didn't live here? Folk delivering aught, lazing about? Folk talking with the children?"

"It was forever ago," she whispered. "No. I am a liar. It were two year, three months, eighteen days. I was so afeared. I've never been not afeared ever since, but I've no coin to go to Barzun, nor family to help me get a new start there."

"You remember it to the day," I said. "You remember the necklace. And this is the Lower City. We always watch down here. Especially folk with comely children." The two little ones who'd come to peer at us had been golden-haired and blue-eyed, slavers' meat.

"Why ask?" she whined. "What difference does it make? The family is gone. The Shadow Snake chews on Crookshank now, gods' blight to them both."

"You might have seen the Snake or the Snake's

rushers," I said. Ahuda had taught us that cityfolk always squirmed like fishes on hooks. Patience got us farther than a box on the ear with them that weren't lifetime Rats. "Because this is how Dogs do it, mistress. We ask who was here. Who was strange? Who asked about the little one or her family? The Snake didn't just walk into that house. The Snake knew where the child slept. He knew when that household went to bed. He had to, if he was to take her with the family sleeping. He had to know if there was someone like this fine Brute in the house, or even my Pounce. Cats have inconvenient tails for the stepping. Who did you see?"

She gave me three names at the last. I set them in my memory. When we said our farewells, the sky was darker, Brute had gone to sleep across the doorstep, and the mot was trembling. I fear we ruined her spinning, but I had three names for it.

We'd gone halfway down the block before Kora got my attention. "What now?"

I stopped and took a deep breath. I was trembling. I looked at her. "I think I need a map."

She went on to run her errands, and I ran mine before the rain began. My lord had shown me a trick he used when some complicated Rat hunt took place in any part of the realm. I would follow his lead and use a map. I had some already. My lord had noticed my love of his and given me a packet of them for my fifteenth birthday. They were a costly gift, showing different parts of the realm, various cities, and, best of all, the different sections of Corus. I had one map alone of the Lower City, as complete as any in the palace.

I went to the Daymarket and haggled mightily for pins and sealing wax. Then I trotted home and took out my map of the Lower City. Carefully I nailed it to the wall. I marked the head of one pin with a ball of blue sealing wax and thrust it into the spot where Crookshank's house would be, on Stuvek Street. That was Rolond's marker—blue would be the color for the dead children. Next I marked another pin in red for the gixie who'd been returned to her family. I set it on the alley that Kora and I had just visited.

When I have more pins, more real news, I will bring it to my Dogs. If I find anything new on Rolond, I will take it to Jewel, since he and his partner, Yoav, are supposed to be searching for Rolond's killer. But this is for me, to help me to remember.

Very well. And to paint a better picture of the Snake. I have heard of no one doing such a picture, and I believe one is needed. Mayhap I am only a Puppy, but I have seen how well this works for my lord. If I can show my Dogs a picture of what the Shadow Snake has done, mayhap they will not mind that the picture has come from a Puppy.

Please, Goddess and Mithros.

Please.

At night's end.

Tonight was the night of the Happy Bag. After muster we went up to the Court of the Rogue again. I could not relax and look about me there as I did last time. I could not amuse myself thinking of the mots who sighed over how handsome Kayfer was in his younger days. All I could think on was the mothers and fathers who came here, hoping that he would find their little ones or give them justice for the Shadow Snake. How he and his chiefs had seen how poor they were and sent them away.

Rosto should have let Crookshank stab the Rogue. Except then Rosto would not be standing with Ulsa now, coming to power here. Aniki would not have her place among the rushers who waited at Dawull's back.

After we handed the Happy Bags over to the horsemen for transport back to the kennel, Tunstall, Goodwin, and I headed on up into the Cesspool.

"Findlay Close?" Tunstall asked Goodwin. To me he said, "Crookshank owns every house there."

Goodwin nodded. "Worth a look," she said.

On the street that lay between Stormwing and Mulberry, Tunstall took out the small, magical pearl light he'd used on the fire opals. Keeping it mostly covered from the view of the families that lived thereabouts, we looked around the outsides of the rough houses. In spots the pink city rock broke through the surface, gray in the lamp glow. Folk used it here as foundation stone, doorsteps, and parts of the walls. It gave no hint of the treasures to be found in it somewhere below, not here on the street.

We saw no heaps of dirt or rock dumped outside those houses to show digging went on inside. Some of them were collapsing. Their doors and shutters were nailed shut to keep the little ones or mumpers from getting in. Folk could be digging inside those and we'd have no way of telling. We didn't get to talk to the handful of folk we saw. They fled the sight of us.

On we moved to Mulberry Street and straight into a bare-knuckles fight. We even got to watch some of it. The first match was between two coves I knew from my runner days. I would have bet on Drew if I hadn't been watching my coppers. I would have won money, too. Then I saw the pickpocket. I grabbed him by the collar before he saw me. I heard curses. Goodwin and Tunstall each had their own little quick fingers.

That's when the fight turned into a brawl. The moment a mot saw we had pickpockets in hand, she spotted a fourth. Seemingly a gang of them has been working on Mulberry Street of late. They've been finding dice games, cockfights, and fistfights. They strike all four at once and escape before anyone guesses they've been picked.

The crowd turned on the pickpockets, which left us with no choice. We were forced to let the light fingers go whilst we held off near thirty vexed mots and coves. I closed up with Goodwin and Tunstall, blowing my whistle as ordered. Two more pairs of Dogs got there to help us break up the crowd. We never even got to see the last two fights.

I'm impressed by that pickpocket gang, though. Someone there has wits.

We had some robberies, some tavern fights, a cove smacking his wife. Then a lucky chance. Stout Robin, wanted by the Magistrates for three killings in Port Legann, was drinking in the Gray Goose. A cattle drover who was drinking there recognized him and went for the first Dogs he could find—us. That's a ten-silver-noble reward to the cattle drover, paid when we brought Stout Robin in. Tunstall showed the drover another way out of the kennel, so with luck he'll reach his lodging with the coin still in his pockets. Ahuda says it's another ten silver nobles to us when we're paid, and Goodwin says two of those are mine, because Stout Robin was a handful in the hobbling.

Not a bad night for the Cesspool, not at all.

Friday, April 10, 246

At day's end.

After so good a night in the Cesspool, I opened my shutters to a spring storm. I woke also to the sneezes and a cough. All I wanted was for the pigeons to talk to me before I crawled back into my bed. Surely they would tell me where their ghosts' bodies were buried. Or give me their living names, at least.

They came to tell me again only what they'd said before. Each time I sneezed or coughed, the loobies would flap off all at once. Then they would return until the next time.

I hate pigeons.

All nine of the diggers came for a time. For all they said, I told Pounce they could have just sent one. And they left feathers on my floor.

Rosto wouldn't even come in my rooms, not that I opened the door wide enough. Aniki wrote down names and the locations of two visits by the Shadow Snake and returned later with a crock of hot soup. She is a good friend.

Kora brought potions for me, which have made me feel better, or at least they make me spit disgusting slime. Ersken fetched tea. Verene sang songs to me whilst they, Aniki, and Kora had breakfast on the landing outside the door.

How did I do without friends?

Pounce curled up with me as I slept the morning away and part of the afternoon. I cannot tell if it was the soup, the tea, or the potions, but I was well enough for duty.

Nightmarket work was exhausting.

Kora was home when I came home. She had more potions.

I am going to bed. Curse all colds. Curse spring. Curse rain. No, no curses on rain or spring, only colds.

Good night.

Saturday, April 11, 246

I hate pigeons with nothing new.

I hate the Cesspool.

I hate festering, ranky, puling, gob-clogging, sarden colds.

I hate dragging my sorry sniffling hacking bum through duty.

I love my warm soft cat.

I have good friends who bring me things.

I love my bed.

Sunday, April 12, 246

In the morning.
Kora:
one gixie—Dragon Mews—December 5, 245—price 8
silver nobles inheritance
not paid—found dead in mother's garden

one lad—Festivity Lane—August 31, 244—price sandal-
wood box with mother-of-pearl inlay
not paid—found dead in own bed
brother taken two nights later
price paid—brother found alive on doorstep morning
after payment

one gixie—Mulberry Street—February 13, 246—price
20 silver nobles in savings
paid—child found in shrine where payment was left
two days before

Aniki:
one lad—Rovers Street—May 8, 245—price 3 Yamani
silver coins
not paid—found dead on doorstep
sister taken one week later
not paid—sister never found

Pox and murrain on the Shadow Snake. Mithros burn his eyes in his sockets, Goddess wither his eggs and the eggs of all his children, or her children.

At night's end.
As healers go, it is a good thing Kora has other talents. I still blow fearsome amounts of slime from my nose and throat. Goodwin tells me it is also a good thing we are not required to watch a Rat in silence, for she fears my breathing can be heard at the palace. She has given me a potion from a mage friend of her own, which she says will help. I pray it will, for we are in the Magistrate's Court tomorrow. If I must snuffle and whuffle through the day's worth of cases, I fear I shall put my head through the floor.

At least I know I will not be called upon to speak before Sir Tullus. There was no Rat we hobbled this week who was in my sight alone for so much as a sneeze. I can hide behind my Dogs.

We have had no word on the diggers, not even a whisper. Or that is, we have whispers of all manner of folk who are missing. Tunstall and Goodwin have a list of names other Dogs brought to them after they checked to see if the missing folk are truly missing. It is a long list. The time to check each name is scarce. Dogs are rarely allowed to do anything that is not part of regular patrols, because there are so few of us to keep the peace. Chasing missing coves and mots just because they are missing isn't a good enough reason to take time from stopping folk from breaking each other's heads or robbing each other blind.

Worse, the spring storms continue. It means no fleets are coming to port, which means no work. If Crookshank has hired anyone to dig his fire opals in secret, they won't speak of it. They know them as are desperate for any kind of work at all could well beat them up to take their place on the digging crew.

Crookshank, or whoever hires the diggers for Crookshank, will count on that. They'll hire a new crew of diggers and make them swear to hold their tongues.

And then they'll kill them to keep them quiet, like the last nine.

Being sick makes me gloomsome. I'm taking Goodwin's potion and going to bed.

Tuesday, April 14, 246

At nine in the morning.

I can't bring myself to go back to Provost's House this week, for all that I bear no bruises. I even feel better, after Goodwin's potion. But I can't face my sisters and brothers again after that farewell last week. They seemed shamed. I will let the memory fade for them.

Besides, Granny Fern says we never spend enough time at her place. I can have a nice visit with her. At breakfast Kora said she would be finished with her washing by noon, if I cared to talk to some of the Shadow Snake folk she had met.

So Granny's it is.

At day's end.

Granny was glad to see me this morning, and glad, too, for the coppers I gave her to help with housekeeping expenses. "The birds follow you as much as ever," she said as we hung out her wash. "Do they help in your work?"

Mayhap it was because Granny taught me how to hear the pigeons and the dust spinners. I told her about the diggers and Rolond. I had the sense to keep my voice low, and to have her swear by the Crone never to tell a soul what I had said. It was Dog business. But I can trust Granny. I told her all I'd heard before I was a trainee, all the bits and pieces I would pass on to my lord or the kennels.

I just feel I must be extra careful to *act* like a real Dog now that I *am* almost one.

Granny was bad troubled about the Snake and the diggers. "What have you done about this?" she asked.

I told her. She was pleased to hear that Goodwin and Tunstall are seeking the diggers. She liked the tale of my map and told me three Snake cases she knew of herself.

She did not like it that I had not told my Dogs about the map. "You say they know better. Either they know better about *everything* you do, or they do not," she told me. And she cuffed me on the side of my head for my trouble.

She's right, you know, Pounce said. He lay in the sun, glaring at Granny's tomcat.

Sometimes I wish my granny Fern was not so tough a mot. But I knew she was right. Just because I feared they would mock my idea for the map—and that when I'd only done as my lord did—was no excuse not to tell them. So I will tell them tomorrow.

Kora returned an hour after I got home from Granny's. She roused Aniki, who had gone back to bed for a nap. The three of us went out into the city, to the house of someone Granny had named.

The lad's da had woke one autumn night last year to find him gone, a snake drawn in ashes in his crib. His ma worked all night in a tavern down by North Gate.

A customer had gifted her just two weeks before with a pair of garnet earrings.

"We had to get a priest to read us the note," she said as her man watched us. By rights he should have been on the docks, loading and unloading barges from Port Caynn. The only trouble was, with the storms, he had no work just now. He could only whittle and pray and stay away from drinking and gambling dens. "It said I was to leave the earrings in a pouch at the shrine of the Carthaki Graveyard Hag, at the burying ground on Stormwing, a week from the day," she told us. "If we did as we was bid, we'd have our lad back with no harm done."

Her lad did not come out from behind his da the whole time we were there. When I smiled at him, he began to suck his thumb. I felt like I'd turned into one of them giant spiders with human heads Mama always said would eat us if we wasn't good.

Next we went to a woman who told Aniki the Shadow Snake had taken her little girl. She was shifty-eyed. Two nights ago I'd seen Goodwin talk with a cove who'd acted much like this. I looked at Kora and Aniki. Something in the way they stood told me they smelled bad meat in the pot, too.

I tried to think what Goodwin might say. "So it was nighttime?" I asked the mot.

She nodded.

"Before the midnight bell, would you say, or

after?" I stood as Goodwin did, arms crossed, weight on one hip. I kept my eyes steady on the mot's face.

"A-after, I think."

"And she was a pretty gixie, was she? Like you?"

"Oh, well enough. Folk gave me compliments. I was a pretty little thing at her age."

"Before the midnight bell, you said?" I looked around the little room. "Did you go out, at all?"

"I might have done." The mot was looking down now. "You know, to talk with friends."

"So they were outside, your friends. With their little ones?"

"The older ones were up."

"There was some light in the sky, then." I could see a little sweat on her face now. There was no sign anywhere of a child's toys or bed, though the gixie was gone just recent. A near-new coverlet lay on the bed, and the mot wore a necklace with earrings that matched. "Around twilight, not later. She might have wandered off."

"No, I took her—"

The mot covered her mouth with her hands.

I finished what she'd been about to say, because now I was certain. "You took her and you sold her. The Snake didn't make the profit, mistress. You did."

She slapped me.

I slapped her back.

Aniki said, "Don't hit her again, Beka. Let me do it next time."

"Get out of my house!" the mot screamed. "Get out, you dirty trulls!"

Kora leaned toward her. "*We* didn't sell our child, mistress. And if I hear you have another, my eye will be on you."

Aniki smiled at her. "So will mine."

I just spat at her feet.

We talked with five other folk who'd said they'd been bit by the Snake. One cove threw us out of his house when Kora mentioned the slave market. He was red with shame. The rest did see that snake figure writ in ashes on a sheet, on a pillow, on their floors. Three whose children were taken in the last fifteen months had all paid up. They knew the Snake meant what he said. They'd heard about the others.

We had supper together at a cheap eating house. For once I had a tankard of ale to wash the taste of the work from my mouth.

"You'll catch 'im, Beka," Aniki told me. "We'll help you."

"That was a pleasure, watching you break that mot down," Kora said.

I shook my head. "I was just being Goodwin."

"If you're going to be someone else, you should be the best," Aniki said. "I'm going to be Lady Sabine."

"Is any of you goin' t' be generous?" Mother Cantwell had found us. She shook her begging bowl under our noses. "I have somethin' for the Puppy here if she'd like to share her crumbs."

In the end I bought her two meat pasties. She gave me six more pins for the map.

I was so maddened once I added Mother Cantwell's Snake attacks to my map that I did not wish to write tonight up at all. This journal keeping is harder than I expected. Mastering my thoughts demands time. There is always mending or cleaning to be done. I feel like my walls grow mold with all the pigeon scummer that collects around my window. And the mice will move in if I do not sweep up all the corn and bread crumbs and breakfast leavings every day.

Pounce will not lower himself to catch mice. He calls them "little brothers" and says he will not take other creatures' lives when he is so well fed. I threaten to starve him. I tell him this is why his mother cat threw him from her litter when he was but a kitten, because she knew he was unnatural.

All he has to do is walk forward with his whiskers pointed to me and jump on my shoulders and purr like thunder in my ear. I forgive him and find a treat for him.

Enough. I came home to put Mother Cantwell's six on my map, though I broke one of the pins when I struck it too hard out of fury. Two children returned to their families alive. One was in her teens, the oldest so far, but her mama had a gold brooch and no other children to take. The gixie had been hooded the whole time and never saw the Snake or his helpers.

"So it's that he takes the easiest, or the most lovable, or one so young the slave sellers won't buy 'em so the family wants to keep them for a time at least." I said it to Pounce and to the pigeons and their moaning ghosts on my sill, since no one else was about. Despite the dark I had my shutters open to air the smell of strong soap from my rooms. "Mayhap the Snake prefers children because he knows folk are likely to still care about their little ones. Even if they just mean to sell them later, they'll care about any coin they might bring in."

Sensible, Pounce said. *Not at all pleasant, but most sensible.*

"I don't think the Snake can even spell the word 'pleasant,'" I said.

Two children were returned alive, then, because their families believed the Snake's notes. Three children of Mother's reported six were found dead. As near as I could tell, they were taken in that first year when no one believed the Snake was real. And one child was still missing.

I drew up a list of what I had on a precious sheet of paper. I can't show my journal to Tunstall and Goodwin tomorrow. They will want a written account of the names of them that was taken, the prices asked and paid for them, the home they came from, and where the child was found, if ever. I've added green wax to the pins that mark what turned out to be false reports. I made certain I wrote them down, too.

Once that was done, I settled to sewing. Aniki and Kora aren't very good at it. I'm not Diona or Lorine, but no girl raised by my lady Teodorie is bad with a needle. To thank my new friends for helping me when I was sick, I've taken over their mending. I'd begun work on my third of Aniki's shirts—does she gnaw the shoulder seams with her teeth?—when Ersken and Verene ran up my stairs.

"Dormice have a better time than you!" I heard Verene cry from below. "It's our lone day f'r fun, you're not sick, and the fan makers are havin' a dance! They love it when Dogs come!"

Ersken banged on my door. "Let's go, Beka," he called. "All the off-duty Puppies from our class will be there. You can hide behind us and still get a look at the new summer fans."

I hadn't seen most of our class since the day we ended training. We'd all promised to stay friends and talk often, but I'll wager that they're near as tired as we are when their watches are done. I wanted to see them and hear what their first two weeks were like.

Besides, maybe they'd heard of the Snake.

"Let me put on a dress," I yelled.

When I got to my feet, Pounce curled up on the mending and went to sleep.

Wednesday, April 15, 246

At day's end.

When I told my Dogs about Snake seeking, after muster, and showed them my list, they demanded to see the map on my wall. Goodwin stared at it for the longest time, while Tunstall read the list. I had made some changes to it after breakfast this morning. Phelan gave me three more additions, Rosto two. It's getting so my belly knots with each new pin.

I opened my shutters to let in as much of what remained of the sun as possible, as well as lit my lamps. Of course the pigeons came to see if I had aught for them. I swear they keep a watch on my place. I laid out bread for them but kept an eye on my Dogs.

"What's this scratched out?" Tunstall asked, pointing to the list.

"Kora found out last night the lad was taken, but it was his father's people," I said. "He and his papa are with the Bazhir. Seemingly they want none of their blood raised outside their tents. So I crossed him off."

"Ah." Tunstall passed the paper to Goodwin.

She asked, "What are these red spirals on the map?"

"Dust spinners," I said. My hands were damp with sweat. "I thought I should mark them down."

Goodwin stood aside to let Tunstall look closer at the map. She read my list. Behind me a pigeon cried of her wedding day being near. She didn't see how she could have gone walking home one night and never got there. My guess was that whoever killed her caught her from behind.

Go away, I thought to her as I watched my Dogs. I can only think of one or two things at a time. Crookshank's people are out there to hire more diggers, if they're not hired already. That's one thing. The Shadow Snake is two.

When I dreamed of being a Dog, I never believed this would be my fate. I never believed there might just be too many hurt by bad folk for me to seek.

"One at a time, Beka," my lord told me once. "We hobble them one at a time, like all mortals do."

"My lord does it this way for cases that reach across the realm," Tunstall said, poking the map with his thumb. "We've seen these maps in his study, right, Clary? And we told Ahuda we could use maps like this. We're all taught the memory tricks, to keep news straight in our own minds." He was thinking aloud. "But for something as twisty as the Snake case, going back three years with no one keeping track . . . This could show a pattern. Mayhap use pins to mark where the payment is left. He likes shrines. Plenty of folk coming in and out, priests serving from the temples, not living there. He knows the shrines well, the Snake."

I can get white wax to mark the shrines. I never realized the places where the Snake collected the payment might be important. I've just been looking at who gets taken and where they're taken from.

"Cooper, did you ever think this might offend us?" Goodwin asked. "That we'd think you are trying to teach us our jobs?"

My tripes turned to water. It was one of those gooseflesh moments. I'd feared only that they might laugh at my map. I never meant to anger them!

I stammered a lot of things. I think I mentioned seeing maps at my lord's house. Mayhap I said my friends go everywhere. I'm sure I said I never meant it to look like I thought I knew better than the likes of Goodwin and Tunstall.

Goodwin sighed. "Cooper, you're eager, and you're quick-witted. You did this because my lord does it. We've been in his house, so we know that. And it's as well for you that you told us about this. But it's one thing to know aught in your head, and another to know it from the street. There's Dogs with clouds for brains that can sniff out a robber because they learned to on the street. And they're the ones as will bite your arm off if you go poking around—as they would see it—behind their backs."

"But it's a fine idea," Tunstall said. "And you do have Birdies, feathered and human. Most Puppies don't. Most Puppies don't live with three young folk on the rise in the Court of the Rogue, either."

"Do us paper sketches of the map," Goodwin said. "With the markings." She gave me a silver noble. "That should pay for paper for a while. Let me know when you run out. Report to us each day. For your day off we'll give you our maps so you can mark them current. And remember, you're a Puppy. Gather word only. All information comes to us."

I was so relieved I could but nod. The hardest part of Dog work for me—apart from not getting my head kicked in—is knowing how folk will bounce. I wish I could see or hear what people think. Mayhap then I'd never step wrong. This time I'd got lucky, thank the Goddess. Next time, maybe not.

"Now, these dust spinners of yours. Tunstall saw you talk to one," Goodwin said. "I want to see it, too. Is there anything that prevents you from taking us to one now?"

Of course there wasn't. I rushed to close the shutters and to collect some of the street dirt I brought to my spinners as presents.

"But we're on Nightmarket, Clary," Tunstall said.

"Nightmarket can wait for an hour," she told him.

I blessed Granny Fern. I'd stepped on the edge of thin ice. Gods alone knew how deep I might've sunk if I'd put off telling my Dogs what I was doing for much longer. It really would have looked like I meant to go behind their backs if I'd done so in a couple of weeks or a month.

Off we went to visit Hasfush. Without the burden of nine dead people screaming within him, he had shrunk to just five feet tall. As the sun faded, there was barely enough light to show him up. My Dogs didn't see him until I pointed out the small, upside-down cone of stirred air that was his foot at the corner of Stormwing and Charry Orchard.

I stepped inside his circle and released the gift of dirt I'd brought for him. Instantly Hasfush filled my ears with several days' worth of gabble. I apologized in whispers for not coming around sooner. It's hard to explain work to a creature that just exists without needing coin to live on or aught to do with himself.

When he'd forgiven me, he let go of all he'd picked up. I heard songs, fights, whingeing, laughter, baby wails and giggles, whispers. Somehow bird and dog noises and the clop of horses' hooves never stick to spinners. Nature's sounds just fall away from their winds. I hear every bit of human cackle, though. I sorted it as I always had, ignoring what was too blurred or nonsensical to work through. There was nothing about the Shadow Snake there, nothing. And nothing about fresh diggers hired for wells in the Lower City.

There was something of importance, though. I walked out of Hasfush to say, "A dancer was murdered just a bit ago on Emerald Street, over in Flash District. Him as did it still has got her blood on him and her bells in his pocket. From what he told his friends in the Daymarket, he's coming this way. He's bound for the Court of the Rogue."

Tunstall and Goodwin hesitated, looking at each other.

Pounce, on patrol with us as ever, scolded, *You either believe her or you don't. Decide!*

I don't know if they understood him. But Tunstall put his whistle to his lips. He blew the call for two more pairs of Dogs and one of the four-legged kind. Phelan and his partner were the soonest to arrive, with their scent hound Achoo. They'd named her for her habit of sneezing when she got a scent. Achoo was a pert, medium height mongrel with tight-curled fur, amber in color. It was said that button-eyed Achoo's nose was so keen she could track a mouse in a flooded sewer.

Achoo backed up when she saw Pounce. My cat just blinked at her, waiting. Bit by bit Achoo crept up until they touched noses. Then she sneezed, twice. Her tail began to wag. Pounce jumped back when his new friend tried to wash him.

"I've never seen the like," Phelan's partner muttered. "She ran from the last five cats she met. Since that ragged-ear tom clawed her on the nose . . ."

Phelan shrugged. "Pounce isn't every other cat," he said, hands dug in his breeches pockets.

"We're not even sure he's a cat," Tunstall muttered to Goodwin. "I say he's a god, shape-changed."

Pounce meowed, *Do I look as stupid as a god to you?*

Tunstall turned his head to give Pounce an owl-like

blink. For a moment I feared Tunstall had understood my dreadful cat.

"This is sweet, but Springbrook and Evermore had best arrive soon," Goodwin said, her voice cold. "If they're canoodling on watch again, Ahuda's going to hear about it. They should have come before Achoo, shouldn't they, girl? Since you and your handlers came from farther off?"

Achoo, knowing Goodwin liked her, wagged her tail and barked.

The two remaining Dogs arrived at the trot, looking winded. "Delivering Rats to the collector," Evermore said, panting. Springbrook shared her flask with him. "Sorry." He gulped from the flask, spilling water over his chin.

"Come on, Achoo," Phelan said. He let out the lead so the scent dog could put her nose to the ground. "What have you got? She'll scent the worst thing," he said, looking at me. "If your Birdie was right and someone tracked blood through here, she'll—ah!"

Achoo sneezed over and over, then growled. She had something she didn't like. Off she went, straight into an alley. She took us up through the very gates of the Court of the Rogue. Goodwin and Tunstall didn't hesitate, even though the tradition was that Dogs shouldn't hobble Rats inside the Court. They just followed Achoo and Phelan through the gate. The rest of us went in after them, our batons ready.

The guards stood aside. They would not interfere with Dogs on a hunt, even here. They would not risk blood with us.

We followed Achoo straight into Kayfer's throne room. There he sat with his chiefs and his foot kissers. A cove knelt before Kayfer, sobbing. Achoo raced straight up to him and barked furiously.

Tunstall hauled the weeping cove to his feet. We all could see the blood on his tunic. "I didn't mean to kill Esseny," the killer cried, his nose running. "I didn't mean it!"

"Esseny the Lily?" Goodwin asked. "That's who you murdered?"

"You know her, then. You know how beautiful she is." The cove fumbled at Goodwin's shoulders. "But she didn't love me anymore," he said. "She told me she would love me forever, but—she didn't."

"She was fifteen, you scummer," Goodwin told him, grabbing one of his wrists. She twisted it up behind him, using the leverage to force him to his knees. "Forever is eight months long when you're fifteen."

Tunstall looked at Kayfer on his barrel and crate throne. "Will you interfere?" he asked the Rogue. The other four Dogs and I formed a half circle facing the court, our batons at the ready. Goodwin had the killer in one hand, her baton in the other. "Is this mumper worth a fight?"

With my back to the throne, I couldn't see the

Rogue. I heard the chill in his voice when he spoke at last. "He's not one of my sworn people. An eighth off this week's Happy Bag and I'll even have my rushers help you cart him out."

The killer wailed.

"We'll cart him," I heard Tunstall reply. "You've got your eighth off, but we'll do the calculations. Your people can watch."

I heard steps and the spitting that meant they'd struck the bargain. Then there were more steps and the scraping sound of boots on the floor. While I listened to that, I kept my eyes on Dawull's table.

Dawull spun a dagger on his fingertip. He didn't seem to care that the Rogue had just turned a cove over to the Dogs. I saw other folk of the Rogue stir, but no one would speak against Kayfer, not for someone who didn't belong to the Court.

Just so had Kayfer ignored the pleas of the folk who'd lost children to the Shadow Snake when they came to him for help. Aniki glanced at me. Then she turned to whisper to the cove who'd drawn his sword on us at the Fog Lantern the week before. That fellow sat with his fists clenched on the table, a look of plain disgust on his face. Because we were there? Or because Kayfer had surrendered a man who'd asked his help and Dawull had said nothing?

I spat on the floor on the way out. It didn't take the bad taste from my mouth. I'm glad we took the murdering scut without a fight, but did Kayfer care about nothing but coin? The Rogue is supposed to look after the folk of his Court at the very least.

You're counting the price of a free meal, I keep telling myself. Be sensible!

Off we all went, back to the Lower City. The other Dogs took our killer in to a collection cage, and we went on to the Nightmarket.

Now that I am home, I have swollen feet and a sore back from chasing after minnows and forcing them to hand over their thievings. Tomorrow I must start work on copies of the maps for Goodwin and Tunstall.

Friday, April 17, 246

Maps are harder than they look. I wasted three pieces of paper before I figured out I should try first on a slate. That is what I have done yesterday and today, apart from my watches. My fingers cramp when I so much as grasp a pen.

Sunday, April 19, 246

After my watch.

Now I have the trick of drawing so I can get the whole map in the right amount of space. It took a *lot* of chalk and erasing. I am still working on the maps. It is why I have not written in my journal. I believe tomorrow I can risk working on paper again. I have spent more coin on colored inks.

This afternoon a mot came into the kennel as we arrived for training. I lagged behind because I'd seen her yesterday morning. She'd talked to Kora on Glassman Square over the laundry tubs. I might never have noticed them, except I passed them on my way to visit my Cesspool dust spinners. She and Kora had been sitting there, heads together like sisters.

Mayhap I was jealous. Me and Kora have been going out a lot of late, talking to folk that have been bit by the Shadow Snake. So I remembered this mot. Her walking into the kennel, her eyes glassy, was a shock.

She went straight up to the Day Watch Sergeant's desk. "I done it," she said, her voice loud. "I had a man in my eye, a new fellow, fine and handsome, only he never wanted no children, and I had me a little lad. I tried to get my man to move in, sent the lad out to play when he'd visit me, but he wouldn't allow for it. Said he wasn't meant to live with little ones. So one night I took the blanket and I put it over my boy's face until he stopped breathin'. Then I snuck 'im to the river in a basket and slid 'im in for the god Olorun to take to the sea for the Wave Walker's mercy. I told the neighbors the Shadow Snake had 'im. I wept and wept and wept because I knowed I done a terrible thing, but my man is livin' with me now."

There was no sound in the kennel, not a one. Everyone there looked at her. She stood, swaying. Suddenly she stumbled against the Sergeant's desk. A Dog standing nearby grabbed her by the arm.

She began to scream. "What've I done, what've I done?" she cried. "It's a lie, all lies! I was magicked! I was magicked for the lie!"

Fulk came out of his room when she began to scream. He walked over to her, a crystal held in his fingers, and held it before her eyes. "Did you kill your child?" he asked. The crystal gleamed.

"No!" she screamed.

The crystal shone out red.

"Liar," Fulk said. He smiled. "You did kill him. Were you magicked to tell us this?"

"Yes, yes!" She tried to yank free of the Dog who still held on to her. "I was magicked to lie."

The crystal shone out green. "You were magicked to tell the truth," Fulk said. "Who cast the spell?"

The mot stared at him, her eyes huge. She opened her mouth several times. At last she said, "I do not remember."

The crystal shone out green. "Pity," Fulk said. "Magicking someone to speak against her will is as great a crime as that of murder. The mage would have died beside you, had you been able to remember his name." He shrugged and walked back into his room. The mot began to scream again until the Dog who held her slapped her silent.

When I came in from duty tonight, I rapped on Kora's door. As it happened, she was home.

I told her about the mot and her confession as she made us tea. "I'd hate to think you had cast truth spells or compelling spells," I said. "Any Dog who knew you did such things would have to bring you in."

Kora gave me a cup of mint tea with the sweetest of smiles. "I would never work such naughty magic," she said, giving Pounce a scratch. "Not even on a mot who killed her child to please a man."

"That's the trouble with you northerners," I said. I couldn't even pretend to be angry. With a choice between Kora and that foul woman, I knew who was the Rat. "At least Corus Rogues fake proper regret."

"I'll try harder," Kora said as she picked up her cup. "Truly, I will."

Monday, April 20, 246

Night time.

I hate missing breakfast. It isn't even that I want the food, because I always bring sommat to eat at home the night before the Magistrate's Court. I just miss the gathering of our flock or covey or whatever we are. I miss having the surprise of whoever new comes that day, be it from the Rogue's side or from the Dogs' side. I miss Aniki telling jokes. Mayhap, too, I miss the chance that I'll hear the right name that will connect me to the Shadow Snake. Yesterday Phelan brought Achoo to play with Pounce. That was a morning's worth of laugh in itself, with Achoo bouncing around the room, flirting with my cat, and Pounce jumping over Achoo just to make the dog addled. It distracted me from my gloom over no word on the diggers.

But there's no breakfast gathering on court days. The others are still abed when I leave for a day on my bum. I did have the finished maps, which I gave to my Dogs as soon as I got there, as well as copies of the lists of the Snake's crimes and victims through yesterday. Tunstall and Goodwin looked them over through the morning and told me at last I'd done well.

"You should've seen her workin' on 'em all week," Verene whispered to Tunstall. She was too far off for me to kick her. "She wasn't satisfied till they was just so. She's picky, Beka is."

Tunstall smiled back at her. "She also has good friends."

Verene actually blushed. I didn't know she could do that.

Today again I had no need to talk. We had hobbled killers, robbers, brawlers, illegal slave sellers, thieves, and burglars aplenty all week, but Tunstall and Goodwin had been in view the whole time.

When Sir Tullus took a break from his chair about noon, I got up and looked at the crowd behind the bars. Tansy and Annis were there. I asked my Dogs for permission to have a quick word with them.

"Don't you look all official, on the Dogs' side!" Tansy teased when I came to them. "Do you report to the Lord High Magistrate today?"

I shivered. "What brings you here?" I asked her.

"Day Watch caught some rushers who robbed one of Father's shops," Annis said. She nodded to the other side of the room. Crookshank stood there, burly rushers at his back, talking with the Provost's Advocate. "He's here for justice. We're here to get out of the house. It still reeks of smoke, for all the airing we've done."

I looked back over my shoulder. Sir Tullus had yet to return. "Tansy, if ever you're up and about come eight of the morning and you'd like a change, some of us gather for breakfast at Mistress Trout's lodgings on Nipcopper Close," I told her. "You're welcome there any day but Monday. It's me, some of my Puppy and Dog friends, and others we know."

"Father Ammon keeps me on a tight leash," Tansy said. She smoothed a hand over the bulge of her belly. "I'm carrying another Lofts, after all. And he sends me out with that mage, Vrinday Kayu. You saw her, pretending to be my maid."

"Hush," Annis whispered. "This crowd has ears." She put her arm around Tansy's shoulders. Tansy looks too thin for a mot that's carrying a babe under her heart. "It would do you good to get out with some young folk, not that I'm promising." She nodded to me. "You're a good soul, Beka."

"What of the birds?" Tansy asked. "Do you still hear the ghosts of little ones in the birds?"

Sir Tullus was returning. "You know I do," I said. "Some go on to the Peaceful Realms, but the others are taken unawares." I started to go.

"Beka!" Tansy grabbed my arm through the bars. "Herun gave me another," she whispered so even Annis couldn't hear. "Do something with it—give it to a temple or something." She shoved a lump into my hand and freed me.

I rushed back to my bench. At least I'd finally made my invite to Tansy.

Settled next to Tunstall, I looked around for Crookshank. He stood where I'd seen him last, lean face pressed to the bars. He watched the Provost's

Advocate walk back to his desk. What kind of "justice" had he bought for the poor scuts as had tried to rob someone who worked for him?

I put my hand between my knees and opened it. She'd given me a knotted handkerchief. Carefully I untied the knot and peeked inside. An orange fire opal bedded in pink stone blazed there, glinting with lilac, green, and red lights. This one was clear all the way through at the center.

Pox take the mot! I thought. Doesn't she understand how noisy these curst rocks are? I can't sell it. The whole town will know I have one. Folk will think I stole it, or I know where there's more.

And curse Herun for not telling her what it is he's giving her.

"Pretty," Tunstall whispered in my ear. "What will you do with it?"

I tied it back up in the handkerchief and gave it to him. That's what a Senior Dog is for, right? To make the choices I'm too green to make?

Let it be his headache.

He showed it to Goodwin at the end of the day. Goodwin only sighed. "Doesn't the girl understand the value of the things?"

"Herun told her they'd make their fortune," I said. "She believes Rolond's life was worth more. She thinks they're connected, and she's right, after all."

"Too bad Crookshank didn't care they were connected," Tunstall muttered. He looked up and his face lit. Lady Sabine lingered by the gate to the court. Goodwin rolled her eyes.

I left to meet Kora and Aniki at the Nightmarket. We bought ribbons so I could trim a bodice for Aniki, then had a cheap supper on the riverfront. A nasty storm sent us home early, but it was still fun.

If only I could get better news of the Shadow Snake or of where the diggers were buried, I would be well pleased with my life. Twice this week Goodwin, Tunstall, and me checked Crookshank's houses in the Cesspool but found no sign of mining. And we have names of missing folk but no way to tell if they are alive or dead, in a pit under one of Crookshank's places, downstream in the river, buried somewhere else by someone else, or living happily in another town entirely.

I'm surprised more Dogs don't crack down the middle.

Tuesday, April 21, 246

Five of the afternoon.
Granny Fern gave me four more names.

FOUR.

Six silver nobles. A gold ring left by a cousin. A charm
guaranteed to cause a wife to birth sons. Three magical
curses done up as pendants and ready for use. That is
the value the Snake places on the little ones.

Two children came home alive. Two came home dead.

Affter midnight.
Rosto, Aniki, and Kora awaited me wehn I came home
and took me to teh Fog Lanterun. I fere I broke my rule
and dranke more wine thann I shuld.

Wednesday, April 22, 246

Noon.

This morning when I let the pigeons in, I found two I had not seen before. One of them, mixed brown, white, and gray, lunged for the bread I'd put out, whilst the other, blue-gray and white, slapped him, knocking him from the sill. As he began to eat, the brown, white, and gray bird flew in to land on top of him.

"Slap me, will you!" his ghost cried. "When 'twas your idea to jump Rosto in the first place!"

The blue-gray and white bird spun on the sill, trying to get the other off him. "*My* idea?" his ghost said. "*Ulsa's* idea!"

"Right." The brown, white, and gray bird jumped to the sill and smacked the other with a wing. "'Here, brother,' says you, 'we can make us a bit of coin. Teach that upstart Scanran pretty boy a lesson.'"

"Who do you think gave me the coin, cracknob?" the blue-gray pigeon asked.

"And Rosto killed us! Did you think he might be quicker than us, you sarden looby?" his brother's ghost asked.

I smacked them both off my sill. Did Rosto know Ulsa had paid to have him attacked?

When he came to breakfast, he sported a long scar down one cheek.

"Don't look at *me*," Kora said when she saw me

351

notice the cut. "He went to somebody who's better at healing than I am. Two brothers jumped him last night in Prettybone. Rosto won, of course." She nudged him with her foot as we sat around our cloth. Outside, the rain poured down. None of us can wait for real spring to come so we might eat outside.

I watched Rosto through my bangs as I sewed. Should I tell him about Ulsa? Chances are, he's already guessed or even knows Ulsa was behind the attack, I figured. By passing on this news, I'd be putting my Puppy paw in a foggy area. What is good Dog work? What is helping a Rat?

Yet if I do give a useful tidbit to Rosto, he'll owe me, I thought. If my instinct is right and Rosto is going to rise in the Court of the Rogue, that would be worth something.

I finished the seam I stitched, anchored the thread, and cut it off. "What do you think, Pounce?" I asked it as if I wanted Pounce's opinion of my sewing, though I meant, What should I say to Rosto?

Pounce knocked my spool over and rolled it to Rosto, who smiled and threw it lightly back to me. I caught the spool and put it away before my cat could try anything else inventive. I still decided to buy Pounce fish for supper for answering my question.

"Only you'd ask a cat what he thinks of sewin'," Verene said.

"I think it's the first time I've ever seen Pounce act

like a cat," Ersken told us as Rosto lifted Pounce into the crook of his arm and scratched my animal's chin.

"If he *is* a cat," Kora said. "Did you know mages have named certain constellations 'wanderers,' because they appear and disappear for decades at a time? One of those is the Cat. At present, the Cat is missing from the night sky."

"Star pictures go missin' all the time, season by season," Verene said, and laughed.

"You're telling us a tale, Kora!" Phelan said.

Kora had a lady's shrug, one that made her dress ripple. She would never argue. And she had not said the constellations named by the mages vanished for seasons. She had said they vanished for decades.

I looked at my cat. He'd rolled over on his back and was batting at Rosto's fingers.

Folk began to leave soon after. Ersken offered to help Kora take her washing to her favored place. Verene and Phelan went next, hands linked. Aniki took her mended shirts to her room and closed the door.

"Rosto?" I called before he reached the stair.

There was a loud thud from Aniki's room. She had begun her sword exercises. Rosto turned back to face me, his face hard.

"Look, Beka, I don't want a lecture. For one thing, you're too young to be lecturing me. For another, it was a clean fight, understand?" He was angry, but not at me. At the men who'd attacked him, I guessed. "I've witnesses who saw the whole thing," he went on, "two of them the Dogs that did up the report. They're going to tell the Magistrate I was challenged by these spintries and I defended myself."

With the noise that came from Aniki's room as she stamped and yelled her way through her practice, I knew no one else could hear me. "Ulsa paid them to do it," I told him when he took a breath.

For a moment he said nothing. Finally he asked, "How did you come by that bit of news?"

I jammed my hands into my pockets. "Birdies told me." My hands were sweaty fists. He couldn't see that, with my big loose shirt and breeches to cover them. I didn't want him knowing that I was nervous to talk so bold as I looked into his black eyes.

"But your information is sure?"

I thought of the two dead brothers, smacking each other on my windowsill. "It doesn't get any surer."

Rosto grimaced. "Ulsa. Normally I wouldn't be so trusting, you understand, but added to other things that have come to my ears, well . . . You are so positive about your source. I don't suppose you'd give up the name for a gold noble?" He made one appear in his fingers. It wasn't magic, but a quick-hands trick I'd seen him show Verene.

I think I surprised him when I grinned. That's when he blinked. "Ask me naught, I'll cheat you not," I said, and grabbed my door. "If you'll excuse me, I'm off to visit some friends." With that I closed it in his face. I couldn't be certain, but I believe he was smiling. And I was off to feed my other pigeons, in case they had anything new for me.

I was leaving the house for my watch when I heard a loud whistle. Rosto loped up to me like a Scanran greyhound.

"I'll walk with you," he said. "Training, right? You let that stumpy little Ahuda kick the feathers out of you, and then you go on watch. I'm amazed any of you live out the night."

Pounce chattered at him as we turned onto Jane Street. "Shows what you know," I replied. "It's because of Ahuda we're alive."

"Ow. Lovey's got a bite." He was holding a red gillyflower behind his back. He offered it to me with a bow.

I faced him. "I'm not your 'lovey.' I'm not your doxie. You're six years older than me, Rosto. There's mots your age more than willing to be your flirts! And you've Aniki and Kora besides. You've white hair, you great looby!" I turned and walked off, keeping my head down so he wouldn't see my grin. I knew what he would say.

"I'm blond!" he shouted. "My hair isn't white, it's blond! Corn silk! Sun-colored! Gold! That Ahuda's knocked you on the head too many times!"

Rosto is vain. If he starts that nonsense with me

again, I know a way to distract him now. I've no patience for that kind of flirting game. For one thing, Kora and Aniki are my friends.

Mayhap they're used to sharing a man, but I'm not. And he's a rusher. I'll never go with a rusher. Not even one so handsome as Rosto. As well end up like Mama that day when I was eight, both eyes blacked and mouth bleeding.

"I was trying to thank you!" Rosto yelled.

Pounce, trotting beside me, said, *"Mah, mah, mah."* To me it sounded like he said, Bad, bad, bad, in the most approving way.

"Thanks," I told my cat. "We'll teach him not to treat me like one of his gixie toys."

After watch.

We heard more tonight at the Mantel and Pullet. Ulsa denied any plotting against Rosto, who was popular for all he was new. Since the word had somehow leaked out all over the city, she knew she had to do something. She had to make it right with Rosto and with the rest of her people, who'd worry which one of them she might want to have doused next. She made Rosto one of her gang chiefs. In Prettybone the Happy Bags were filled by small thievings, doxies and spintries who hired out to the nobles, and most of all by gambling. Ulsa gave Rosto the command of a gang that controlled a fat chunk of gambling to show him she would never pay anyone off to kill him.

"Will it work, Cooper?" one of Verene's Dogs, Otelia, asked me. "Will that satisfy him? Verene says you know him best. He lives in the same lodging house as you."

I shook my head. I didn't like so many Dogs looking at me as they did when they heard that. I didn't like them thinking I might be sliding to the crooked side of the fence.

"She can't stop folk from living where they like." I also wished Ersken didn't feel he had to stand up for me. I had to find the courage to do it for myself. How could I manage if Ersken didn't even wait for me to try?

"Otelia wasn't saying that," Tunstall said. "Were you?" He looked at her.

She swallowed hard. "Never, Tunstall. But she runs into him, doesn't she?"

"Me too," said Verene from her seat next to Otelia. "So does Ersken. But Beka does know 'im and his mots best."

"Rosto will do what pleases him," I said loudly to our table.

"If you're so curious, put yourselves in the way of meeting him," Goodwin told the rest who were listening. "Rely on your own gut. That's the best way to be sure." When Otelia, Verene, and their male partner,

Rollo, left, Goodwin muttered, "Bugnob. Otelia wants a Puppy to do a Dog's work."

When I came home, a cracked pottery vase with a bunch of red gillyflowers in it sat in front of my door. In spite of myself, I smiled. Rosto, seemingly, doesn't hold a grudge. And the flowers give a nice, spicy scent to my room.

Thursday, April 23, 246

We had just handed off the Rogue's Happy Bag tonight when we got word of a brawl at the Doxie's Skirt. We hobbled ten loobies and my nose was broken. It was healed at the kennel. I'm in no mood to write of my day—I'm going to bed.

Saturday, April 25, 246

Day.
No more word on the Shadow Snake since the 21st. Kora and I have talked with seven families. I have talked with three. All are true victims of the Snake.

After watch.
No more word on diggers. If anyone is hiring them, they are keeping it quiet. Last night Tunstall said over supper, "Sad thing for us, we got us some smart Rats. Stupid ones would have talked. They'd let word get out that they wanted diggers. Mayhap Crookshank has hired a crew already and he's got them locked away, mining his fire opals under guard. And mayhap Crookshank knows we're watching. If he checked his desk, he knows someone took those Shadow Snake notes. So he's bound to be extra careful. But he'll slip. Or them that does his dirty work will slip. We'll have him then."

I have to believe Tunstall. He's been doing this for years. He knows best.

I just fear that each morning I'll open my shutters and there will be new pigeons there with new ghosts, whispering about the pink city rock.

Tuesday, April 28, 246

Nothing. Nothing.

NOTHING!!!!!

Pox and murrain on the Snake, on Crookshank, on this curst city that keeps its secrets so close! Not another word will I write until I have SOMETHING!

Wednesday, April 29, 246

Dawn.

The funniest thing happened last night, though I was too sour to write it then. I came home from Granny's early and knocked on Kora's door to see if she was about and wanted to put together some kind of supper. She answered it in only her shift, though the day was cool and rainy. Moreover, I saw Ersken pulling on his breeches behind her.

"Come back in a little bit," she said with a bashful smile. "We'll be able to come up with a decent supper between the three of us. Aniki's got something doing with Dawull and his people, so she's not home."

I looked past her at Ersken and wiggled my eyebrows. He blushed! Kora, seeing what I did, laughed and gave me a shove.

"Rosto?" I asked softly. I didn't want Ersken ending up on the wrong end of Rosto the Piper's blades.

"I'm my own mot and can say who shares my bed," Kora told me. "Rosto knows." She smiled. "We're still friends, just not bed friends. I've someone cuddlier now."

That was more than I needed to know, in truth. I backed up and let Kora shut the door.

Noon.

When we had breakfast this morning, Rosto presented

Ersken with a sausage and bowed. I got the giggles whilst Verene stared at me.

"Would you like one?" Rosto asked me, holding up the sausage. I could only shake my head no whilst Ersken blushed.

It was nice to have aught to giggle about after having no news from Granny at all yesterday.

I am glad for Ersken and Kora both, particularly if Rosto's nose isn't out of joint. I don't know if it will last, but Kora will treat Ersken well. And I think if she ends it, she will be kind.

I feel a bit lonely, seeing them together, but not so lonely as to tell Rosto I'll be his second mot. Aniki seems happy to have him to herself, and I'm not so lonely as to start canoodling with a rusher.

Thursday, April 30, 246
Beltane

I must write about today, because so much has happened. I think the only way I can write it is to write of my watch, and do so as I lived it, without knowing how it will end. Elsewise, I'll be unable to put it down sensibly, and there are things I want to remember.

We were out in force tonight. For Beltane, with the bonfires at sunset, a third of the Day and Night Watches are added to the Evening Watch. That's when the most folk are out and about. Everyone who celebrates the day wants a chance to leap over the embers in hopes of a fruitful harvest of some kind. After the embers comes the fire, as the saying goes, whether folk are a pair before they came to the bonfire or just for the night. Even if people don't want more children, they hope fertility will mean coin in their pockets and good fortune in the coming year.

With so many couples occupied and so many priests and priestesses to bless the goings-on, the robbers, foists, and cutpurses were also out. Beltane is a thieves' holiday.

I was happy to be on duty with my Dogs. Canoodling is one of those things that's more fun in the doing. I've done it once and kissed a bit, but never in public. Bagging Rats for Beltane was more to my taste. Besides, I've no one I wish to canoodle with.

Goodwin, Tunstall, Pounce, and me were on
Koskynen Street when we heard noise in an alley leading off to Pottage Lane. The flicker of light told us whoever was in there had a torch. Tunstall put out a hand
to warn us to wait. Pounce ran forward to the alley's
opening. He howled as if he was in battle with other
cats and dashed back.

"On'y cats fightin'," someone in the alley muttered. "Git 'er earrings!" Thanks to Pounce, we knew
we had found robbers.

Goodwin nodded. We all took our batons in one
hand and our saps in the other. I was nervous. I hate it
when I can't see what we're getting into. I quickly
checked my gorget to make sure it was firmly tied. The
thing bothered me, but suddenly I was glad for it.

Goodwin whispered, "Cooper, stay back unless it
looks like one of us is about to get killed." She strode
forward as if she owned that alley. "In the King's
name!" she cried.

Tunstall was at weapon's length to her side. I
moved off to her right so no one could dodge around
her. I hated keeping back, but I knew my orders.

There were four rushers. I knew them all from the
Court of the Rogue. They were Kayfer's men. They had
planted a torch in the ground, the better to see what
they did. A man dressed as richly as a noble lay on the
ground, a big purple knot on the side of his head. They
had stripped him of his weapons, his belt, even his

boots. One of them held a well-dressed lady from behind, one hand over her mouth, another around her
waist. Two more Rats were stripping off her rings,
bracelets, and necklace. The fourth was cutting away
the embroidered strips on her dress.

The fourth Rat was the first to drop what he did
and unsheathe his sword. He was too slow to turn as
Goodwin darted by him. She struck the back of his
neck with her sap. He folded like wet cloth onto the
muddy ground. The next Rat dropped the lady's left
arm and drew his sword. Goodwin raised her baton to
block him.

The one who had been stripping the lady's remaining arm of jewelry dropped it, leaving both her arms
free. Now he drew his blade, dodging Tunstall as Tunstall struck with his baton. Tunstall turned as the Rat
went into open ground to fight, keeping his baton between him and the sword.

The lady, her hands now loose, sank her nails into
the hand over her mouth. The Rat who still held her
grabbed one of her arms, but he couldn't hold both and
grip her waist. He lifted her off the ground, his mistake.
Now she could kick back at him with both feet, and she
did. A pity she wasn't wearing clogs or pattens. She
might have hurt him bad if she'd worn those instead of
her pretty leather slippers.

The one Goodwin had struck down tried to stand.
He fell sideways against her, knocking her aside. She

stumbled and dropped to one knee, getting her baton up as she braced for a hit from the attacker. He saw his chance and lunged at her, blade raised.

I know it was cracknobbed, but I wasn't close enough to use my baton, and I could see her baton was at the wrong angle. He'd have her.

I threw my sap at his head. He was moving, and I'm not that good at throwing small things. Of course I missed. He did swerve to dodge my sap. He looked about him. Tunstall folded his man over his baton and struck him on the head with his sap.

The Rat hanging on to the lady must not have been a thinker. He'd not yet seen it was time to kill her or dump her and run. He was still trying to get control of her. She finally got her teeth into the hand over her mouth. He grunted with pain and tried to shake her teeth loose, but she would not let go.

Goodwin put her whistle to her mouth and blew the call for help from Dogs.

The man I'd distracted with my sap saw he and his Rats were beaten. He cursed and ran.

"Puppy," Goodwin said. She was getting to her feet to take the Rat who still clutched the lady, unless it was the lady clutching *him* with her teeth.

Goodwin didn't have to say "fetch." I grabbed my sap and took off after the fleeing Rat. I think I'd been hoping for a chance like this since I'd fetched Orva Ashmiller. For all the annoyance she'd given me, there was something clean in chasing a Rat. I'd naught else to think on, no birds or spinners to work out, no people to try to understand, no officials to talk to. It was just me, the Rat, and the alleys of the Lower City.

He tried to ditch me. He wasn't as good at it as Orva, and he didn't have hotblood wine to keep him going. He didn't know the back ways so well, for all he belonged to the Court of the Rogue.

One of Kayfer's lapdogs, I thought as I gained on him block by block. Not used to any real need to run or hide. Just serve the Rogue and be safe. Well, here's safe for you, my buck, I told myself as I chased him straight into Whippoorwill Mews. Now you're in a corner.

That's when it occurred to us both that he had a sword and I a baton.

I grabbed my whistle and blew the call for help. I got it out once. Then he was on me, his sword coming down like a scythe. I gripped my baton at each end and swung it up to block. The sword bit into the wood, struck the lead core, and got stuck. The rusher cursed and kicked at me. I turned, taking his kick on my hip as I twisted my baton. I hoped to yank the sword from his grip but he pulled it free.

He cut sidelong at me. Still holding my baton at each end, I blocked him a second time. He yanked the blade back, taking a chip out of my wood. I scooped my own kick forward and up, between his legs, and slammed a metal codpiece with my foot. Had it been solid metal, not pieces, I might've hurt myself. Instead it gave way under my kick. The rusher groaned, his eyes rolling up in his head.

I hadn't seen him draw a dagger with his free hand. It slid just past my right side, slicing my loose tunic and shirt.

I leaped back. We'd both made mistakes. I hadn't minded what he was doing with his left hand. He'd not guarded himself against my feet, thinking me a green Pup. Now we'd both learned sommat. He thrust his dagger back into its sheath and kept his sword on guard before him, steadied with both hands. I went from side to side, looking for an opening.

"Don't be a looby," I told him, panting. "Give up now or when the other Dogs come, it's up to you. You're cornered here."

You're really cornered, I heard Pounce say.

"Lay down your sword, in the King's name," Tunstall ordered. He'd come up close behind me. "You are under arrest."

The rusher spat on the ground. Then he placed his long blade gently on a dry patch of stone. "Wasn't about to surrender to no pimple-faced puttock," he said. He spat again, aiming for my boots.

"The dagger, too," I said. I didn't want to pick up the sword until I was sure he'd no more blades.

"You heard her." Goodwin had come along with Tunstall. "Stop wasting time. Your friends will go to the cages without you. You don't want to miss that."

"We'll be out before dawn," he told us. "Th' Rogue'll see to 't."

My tripes clenched. I knew he spoke the truth. "Dagger," I said, my hand sweaty on my baton's grip. "Don't make me kick you twice."

Tunstall and Goodwin moved to stand on either side of me, their batons in their hands. I heard other Dogs behind us. They'd been called by my whistle.

"Where'd she kick you?" Tunstall asked him, as if to pass the time.

The rusher cursed me. Then he fumbled for his dagger and lurched forward to put it by the sword.

"I'll wager I know," Goodwin said. The torchlight gleamed on her teeth as she grinned. "Thought our little terrier was wore out from the chase, did you? I guess she taught you. Cooper, get his weapons."

I picked them up, handing them hilt first to Goodwin. Tunstall grabbed the rusher and shoved him against a nearby house, bringing out a thong to bind the rusher's hands. I stepped in to search the man. I found boot knives and a knife for the back of his neck. I moved off with a nod to show I'd found the last of his arms.

"Not so fast." Goodwin came close. She spoke quiet, so the two Dogs who watched us couldn't hear. "These liars' fanfares do more than protect a man's treasure in a fight." She reached around the rusher and grabbed his metal codpiece.

"Oh, sweet one," the cove said with a moan, "my lovey, my—"

"Shut up." Goodwin yanked the codpiece hard. Buttons popped as it came off. The rusher choked on a yell, his eyes rolling. "What kind of scut chafes a Dog who holds his treasures? See, Cooper?" She held it up and slid a coil of wire out of an inner pocket of the piece. Rawhide loops were secured to its ends.

I drooped. I know I drooped. I'd been thinking so well of myself till that moment.

"You missed one, Cooper," Tunstall said, his voice soft. "But you didn't let him kill you with that knife, eh?" He shoved the rusher to the Dogs who waited behind us. "Will you take this one along to the collectors? Don't feel you have to be tender with him."

"Cut-coin looby, not having a solid metal scoop like the knights wear," Goodwin remarked, watching the cove waddle off with the Dogs. "Cheap and very stupid—though you don't see the strangling cord in the cod trick that often. Maybe his mother taught it to him. Cooper, everyone makes mistakes. You just try not to die from them. Let's see your baton."

I handed it over, feeling a touch better. I reminded myself to tell Verene and Ersken about the strangling cord. Our teachers hadn't mentioned that one. Mayhap it wasn't that popular. They'd mentioned rushers keeping wire and rope cords in a dozen other odd places.

Pounce wound between my feet. *I brought*

Goodwin and Tunstall, he told me. *I knew you'd catch
that idiot.*

Goodwin returned my baton to me. "Not bad for
a sword fight. Get the chunk he took out of it fixed before training tomorrow. Come on, Cooper. The night
isn't over yet." Goodwin steered me out of the mews.
Tunstall kept step with us.

"That's low," he said as we set off toward our assigned part of town again. "Setting on a couple at
Beltane." He must have known what I was about to ask,
because he said, "The young lord's got a dented head.
There was a healer coming when we left to catch up
with you. Maybe he'll be an idiot, maybe not, but that's
up to the healers his da can afford. The lady's shaken,
but she's not hurt. And your clever cat brought us
straight to you." He leaned down and picked up
Pounce. "Otherwise some other Dogs might have been
the ones to teach you about the strangling cord."

"The lordling's an idiot already," Goodwin said.
She still had her baton out. Now she set it to spinning,
casual-like. "Coming into the Lower City with all that
flash. Her too. Is it real, do you suppose?"

Tunstall scratched Pounce's ears. "As real as it gets.
You know how it is with these moneyed types, Clary.
They think the Common instead of Palace Hill is excit-
ing. Wicked, even."

"*Dangerous,* even," Goodwin replied, her voice
mocking. They continued to talk like that, back and

forth, gentle-like. That lasted until we ran into the brawl outside the Merry Mead.

The evening continued busy, with no time for supper. Our assigned patrol took us up to the Common. That was luck for hungry Dogs. Each Beltane, Mistress Noll set up a little tent there to sell ready-baked treats. Goodwin sent me over with our coin.

The only maggot in the pasty was Yates. He waited on folk alongside his mother. When I stepped up to the counter, he gave me the ugly eye but dared to say not a word about our last meeting in the Daymarket. I filled my handkerchief and thanked Mistress Noll as I handed over our coin. When I went to give our quick meal to my Dogs, I saw they had found Yates's two friends, the ones I'd seen that afternoon at the Daymarket. Tunstall had placed one of them against a tree. Goodwin used her baton to keep the other at a respectful distance. Seemingly they'd been making deliveries to Mistress Noll's tent here, too.

"I just don't see you scuts helping an old lady from the goodness of your heart, Gunnar," Tunstall was telling his Rat. Tunstall's baton tip was pressed under Gunnar's chin, where it made a deep dimple. "You're rough work. You've always been rough work. So if I hear of you harming a hair on Deirdry Noll's nob, I'll break yours, understand?"

"You got it wrong, Dog." Gunnar was the blond cove I'd seen at Yates's counter in the Daymarket.

"Yates'd kill us for it, wouldn't he?" He looked at the other cove who'd carried flour that day.

"Cut us twelve ways from midnight," the other Rat told us. "We'd never cross 'im. Never."

"Good," Tunstall said, and lowered his baton. After a moment, so did Goodwin. The two Rats didn't waste time in getting clear of us.

I offered my Dogs their pasties.

"Funny," Tunstall said, taking one. "I never found Yates Noll so fearsome."

"No more I," replied Goodwin. "And if we'd time to dig deeper, we might, but we need to get down to the Nightmarket. Things are cooling down here."

It was true. The priests were letting the fires go out. More and more folk were rising from the grass. They would be bound for the taverns and the market to buy trinkets and memories of the night.

By the time our watch was done, my knees felt like jelly, I was so weary. My baton seemed to be triple its weight. My arm throbbed. Pounce, who'd left us after the tavern fight, appeared out of nowhere. He near-about tripped me as we entered the courtyard of the kennel. I was too tired even to scold.

"Where have you been?" Goodwin asked Pounce. Even spent, she still noticed a black cat in the shadows. "Wooing yet another lady cat for Beltane? Blessing the world with your kittens?"

We walked into the kennel to find that things were

not right. Ahuda sat at her tall desk, her head in her hands. Most of our watch had come in already. Some of the mots were weeping. Coves looked at the floor or leaned their foreheads against the wall so none could see their faces. Others sat in small knots on the benches, talking softly. Phelan got up from one such group and walked into the chapel, to my confusion. Did he forget we weren't mustered out yet?

No one who was not a Dog was in sight. No Rats, no visitors for the Rats. No onlookers, no beggars. Of my fellow Puppies, Hilyard leaned with his face to the wall. Another sat on the floor, her head bowed on her knees. The rest huddled near the healers' room on two benches. Ersken had an arm around two girls. He looked at me with eyes that were red and puffy.

Verene's Dog Otelia stood by the healers' door. There was blood dotting her cheek. Her tunic sleeve was ripped. Her arms hung down limp before her. I saw no sign of her baton and remember being as shocked as if she was naked.

Inside the healers' open door, two people lay on the beds. Their faces—their whole bodies—were covered by sheets. I saw bloodstains there, too.

Otelia looked up and saw us. "They blindsided us, Clary," she said. "Verene got in the way of the biggest one. Rollo thought— Mattes, you know he always thought he was quicker than he was. Poor Verene never had a chance. Rollo died coming here." Otelia slid to the floor, tears rolling down her face.

My hands went numb, then my arms, and my belly, and the rest of me. I didn't believe I heard aright. Then I looked at Ersken. I knew I'd heard proper enough. Otelia had told us Verene was dead. Verene, and Verene's male Dog, Rollo, were both dead. On Beltane.

I looked up at Tunstall. "We had breakfast this morning." I told Goodwin, "Just this morning."

Pounce stood on his hind feet and put his forepaws on my thigh. Obedient, I picked him up. He stood in the circle of my arms and purred in my ear, as if trying to make this easier, as he did the day Mama died. My friend Verene lay in that room with an old cloth over her. I'd split the last piece of cheese with her just today.

And Rollo. He was a veteran. He'd lived on the streets for seven years. He was just as dead.

I carried Pounce over to the benches and sat with the other Puppies. The girl between Ersken and me left the shelter of his arm so I could slide in next to him. I kept one arm around my cat and put the other around my friend.

I hope I have written the worst of this. It is strange to say, when I fought the writing lessons so hard, but it soothes me some, to put this on paper. It makes me weep, too, but it means I won't make less of this night in my mind now. If it fades in my memory, I can see it afresh on this paper. I can value my friend's death and not let it vanish from my remembering.

Friday, May 1, 246

After the buryings.

Ersken didn't want to face his family last night, so I told him he could stay at my place. Kora wasn't in—she'd gone to Prettybone, for fun, she'd told us over breakfast yesterday. We all knew it was to watch Rosto's back. She still hadn't returned when we arrived. I made up a pallet for Ersken in my room. It took me forever to get to sleep, even after writing in my journal. I don't know about him. I kept thinking, It could have been me. That night at the Barrel's Bottom, it could have been me brought back to lie in the healers' room under a bloody sheet. It could have been me tonight if I hadn't gotten my baton up between that rusher's sword and my skin. It could be me any night of the week.

I don't remember when I slept. I remember my dreams. They were all of pigeons and their ghosts.

Ersken and me woke empty-eyed. We cleaned up in silence. What would we do with ourselves on such a day? Then Kora knocked on the door. So she had to be told, then Aniki and Rosto.

The five of us were feeding bread to my pigeons when Phelan walked in. He looked like he hadn't slept. He hadn't shaved. Nor did he seem like he knew where he was.

We mots fussed over him. It helped us as much as Phelan. I made him drink some raspberry twilsey to clear his head. Aniki ordered him to eat two chicken-raisin turnovers when he said he couldn't remember his last meal. Kora opened a tiny vial under his nose. He sniffed, shuddered, and came around a bit. Ersken inspected Phelan's dagger and sharpened it before he slid it gently into its sheath. Pounce ran the pigeons out of the room, then leaned against Phelan as he ate.

Rosto said nothing, only looked on. At last Phelan got to his feet. "I'm sorry—I can't stay. I don't know what to do now, but I can't seem to keep still."

Rosto stirred. "Come on, lad," he told Phelan. "Let's go for a walk."

"Don't you think he's done enough walking?" Ersken wanted to know. "He's got the shakes."

I thought Rosto would be impatient, but he was only cool. "It's not sitting that will cure his shakes. Come on, Phelan. We'll go look at trees or sommat."

The rest of us cleaned up the breakfast leavings, then went to the Jane Street baths. We had to look proper for the funerals that afternoon.

Rollo was buried at noon. My lord came there to speak. He did that for every Dog who was buried. Other Dogs had a word for Rollo, too. My lord told me once that folk got friendlier with a Dog for each year that Dog lived in the King's service. It stood to reason that a six-year Dog had plenty of folk to talk about their memories and how much he'd be missed.

After Rollo's burying came Verene's. Making the

arrangements last night, we Evening Watch Puppies had voted for Ersken to do our talking at her burial after my lord and her family spoke. They drew off, leaving us time alone with her plain coffin.

"We'll miss you at Beka's breakfast," Ersken said to it. "Well, not just you. Your coin, too. I guess we'll have less sausages, or eggs." Aniki, Kora, and I giggled. We couldn't help it. Even some of the others, who knew of our mornings, smiled. "But it's not just the coin, really, Verene," Ersken went on. "It's the bad jokes, and your telling us about your night's patrol. It's training with you. It's the times you helped us with the memorizing studies. You were always good with the ones that needed such help. And we remember your singing. We think you should sing for the Black God, who makes a peaceful place for us all to come to. Everyone in the Peaceful Realms is safe from Rats. I know the kind God of Death has to treasure the ones like you, Verene, that fell while making the mortal realm a safer place."

He bowed his head. A tear dripped from his cheek to the ground.

I went over to wrap my arm around Ersken's shoulders. I pressed my face to his. "Good Dog," I said softly.

"Don't say that!" someone whispered.

"'Good Dog'? Cut your tongue! Bein' a good Dog's what got Verene killed!" The jackass bray came from Hilyard. I'd scarce been able to look at him. He came to our graveyard in a cityman's tunic and leggings.

He pointed at Ersken with a shaking hand. "Good Dog,
yes, to say nice things about dying in this stupid work!
Good cur! Good—"

I couldn't bear it. I grabbed Hilyard's ears, forcing
him to meet my eyes. He scrabbled at my wrists with
his nails. I wouldn't let go. I wouldn't let him look away.
I held him with my eyes.

"Enough, scummernob," I said, quiet. Aniki told
me later my eyes and my voice were as cold as smoking
ice. I know I felt numb. "Think shame to you, disrespectin' Verene so. Comin' here dressed common when
she died in uniform. Think shame to you, disrespectin'
the words of Ersken's heart, and my Lord Provost's
presence. Now shut your sarden gob, or get out." I let
him go with a shove. He staggered away from me.

I walked back to my friends before I could give way
to anger and kick his bum clean out the gate. Mother's
mercy on me, for a moment I'd wanted to kill him.

"I'm out!" he yelled at more of a distance. I turned.
He was walking backward, toward the gate. Whatever
madness seized him, he'd forgot my lord Gershom
stood right there. "You ought to get out, too, the rest
of you, if you're not as cracked as she is. Look around—
those're the graves of Puppies. Look who's standing
with you. Not real folk—Rats." Rosto, Aniki, and Kora
looked at us and shrugged. Hilyard kept on shouting.
"Dogs' friends aren't cityfolk, they're Rats. Rats are the
only ones who understand the way Dogs talk! *Ulp!*"

My lord had grabbed Hilyard from behind. "I'm glad you're leavin'," he said in his slow way. "If there's one thing Dogs must know, it's how to act when we lose one of our own. Gods forgive you for speakin' so before Verene's blood family. It's plain to me you never would have been one of us." He turned. The group of Dogs—my two and Ahuda among them—opened up. My lord tossed Hilyard hard and far, out of our burying ground.

Dusting his hands, my lord nodded to the training Dogs, them who had been our teachers. The parent Dogs always sing to show the Dogs' road to the Peaceful Realms to a Puppy who didn't survive.

As Mother Dog, Ahuda sang the first line of the song. She had a warm voice, sweet. I never thought mean little Ahuda had such beauty in her. As she gave voice to the rising first line of "The Puppy's Lullaby," my knees felt weak. The other female Dogs chimed in at the second line, the male ones at the third. I realized that the regular trainers would have sung this song many times. Two of every ten Puppies die. The work is that cruel. How can they bear it? I can hardly stand it, and this was my *first* Puppy burial. Trainers must teach for a year, doing their best to make certain their Puppies stay alive. How can they bear singing them into the Black God's care like this?

As they began the second verse, pigeons flew down to light on the graves. Only two of them settled on

Verene's. One had a dark pink ruff—the kind that shone in the sun—dark pink bands on its wings, and a pale pink body. Its head was a pinkish gray. The other pigeon was mostly blue with a mottling of white on its wings and gleaming purple feathers on its neck. I knew both, or their twins. They tended to be the sort of birds who carried spirits only for a short time.

"Farewell," I heard Verene whisper. "Until we meet in the Peaceful Realms, farewell."

"Gods all bless," said Rollo's ghost.

Pounce walked over to those two pigeons. The trainers kept on singing, but all eyes were on my cat. He sat before the birds like a king, his paws placed neatly before him.

They bowed. Later, folk said that pigeons bow all the time. A moment after these two did it, the other pigeons bowed, too, their beaks almost touching the ground. Then the whole flock took off, heading up into the sunlight. We watched until we couldn't see them anymore. By then the song was done.

The Dogs filed out of the graveyard. We Puppies said our last goodbyes, then followed our Dogs. It was time for the Evening Watch.

Ersken put his arm around my neck and kissed my cheek. "I like being called 'good Dog,'" he whispered.

After the end of my watch.

When we mustered for Evening Watch, Ahuda told the

rest of it. The five Rats that had killed Rollo and Verene and roughed up Otelia were a mixed bag, a pair of Barzun sailors and three of Flash District's rushers.

"Flash District's chief can't disown them fast enough," Ahuda said. Her face was like stone. "He says they were up to something with no orders from him. Night Watch caught them in Unicorn District, trying to sneak up over Palace Ridge. They were still full to their eyeballs of hotblood wine. They've been handed over to the Palace Guard until their trial. There will be no . . . accidents." Some of the Dogs growled. "I mean what I say. They'll pay for what they did, under the law."

Tunstall stopped her before she could send us onto the streets. Once he'd whispered to her, Ahuda called up another Dog pair and announced a change in patrols. Goodwin, Tunstall and me were supposed to be on Nightmarket duty tonight. Instead Tunstall got us switched off with a Cesspool pair, one that didn't have a Puppy. He and Goodwin knew I couldn't face the cheer of the open market or even the noise around Rovers Street. The Cesspool was better. Nastier. There was more to distract me. More that wouldn't give the lie to the numb, dark feelings that had settled in my heart.

First we went to get the week's Happy Bag from the Rogue, since we'd had Beltane duty the night before. Strange it was, all those Court rushers and their like telling us how sorry they were about Verene and Rollo.

Even the chief of Flash District came over to say how bad he felt that three of his own people had killed Dogs.

My lord Gershom and Lady Sabine found us eating at the Mantel and Pullet. "We were havin' supper at Naxen's Fancy when a Magistrate's runner brought this to my attention," my lord said, putting a paper in front of Goodwin. He beckoned to Nyler Jewel and Yoav, who ate at the next table. We all had a look.

The paper was an official announcement of a slave sale on Skip Lane, complete with seals. My lord pointed to the seals. "The year reads one forty six, not two forty six," he said. "The wax is solid red. The Ministry of Slave Sales uses ebony shavings in their wax to mark genuine seals. The ribbon's cotton, not silk, and the king on this seal is named Roger the Third."

Goodwin sighed. "And scribes at the Ministry put an extra curl on their capital *S*'s, to make it easier to spot forgeries."

I looked. The *S*'s on this document were plain.

We got up from our table without another word. Together with my lord's personal bodyguards, we headed for Skip Lane. The "auction house" was an abandoned stable there, set up to look like a proper slave market. I watched from outside the open front doors as the others entered. Lady Sabine had begged my lord like a little one wanting a treat, so he let her greet the auctioneers. I watched her sweep up to the sellers' table and place the announcement before them.

She pointed to the seal. Then she drew her sword.

The sellers were loobies. The ones in back of the sellers' table tried to hustle the slaves, all gixies, out the back. The ones at the table grabbed their coin.

Lady Sabine dashed for the door at the rear. The mob of buyers clogged a side door. My lord, his bodyguards, Jewel, and Yoav blocked that door and two more. Goodwin and Tunstall took charge of the sellers with the money.

I ran around to the back, my usual post. I'd seen an old cove in the rear gather up a ledger and a box the moment he saw Lady Sabine. He'd gone out the door even before the others had thought to escape, but he wasn't exactly quick on his feet. When I grabbed him, he offered me ten gold nobles to let him go.

It was more than I'd make in my Puppy year and my first year as a Dog. I took it. Then I set aside his money chest and account books to hobble him, tying the rawhide with a care to his old limbs. No rule said I had to do as he'd paid me to, and I hadn't liked that line of scared gixies, waiting to be sold to a room of greedy-eyed buyers. Still, it wouldn't be wise to take a bribe and not give value for it too often.

"Better luck next time," I said. "If you get one." We waited there, him cursing me dreadfully, to see if anyone might join us.

We took a bag of five Rats at the auction. Once our Rats were on their way to the collection cages and I'd signed book and money box in for evidence and the Happy Bag, we continued on our rounds. Lady Sabine wandered off. My lord came with us, talking to Goodwin and Tunstall. I remember guessing how many weeks he would spend in a guest room for this. When a Dog was killed, he made it a point to walk a while with each team on that Dog's watch. Each day he spent out with the Dogs was another week that my lady's bedchamber was locked to him. She was terrified that one day he would not come home from such walks.

I said naught to him, nor he to me. When he left, he fell back for a moment and clasped my shoulder. The warmth of his big hand came through my numbness for a moment. Then he was off to let another Dog team know they weren't just servants to him.

"He makes me proud to be a Dog," Goodwin said. Then she turned to me. "Did the bookkeeper try to bribe you? Cough up."

I paid over her and Tunstall's half of my bribe. That's when they told me about the Happy Bag tax, one-third of my bribes if they were over a silver noble. Since that went for Dogs' medicines, healers, and burials, I didn't complain. Tunstall made the change for me. Goodwin ordered me to get a belt with inner compartments to hold big coins like gold pieces.

"Not that you see takings like that more than once a year," Tunstall said. "But it's good to be prepared."

Saturday, May 2, 246

After my watch.

This morning I was feeding pigeons, trying to listen to their ghosts, when I heard a knock on my door. I let Aniki, Kora, and Ersken in. It wasn't our usual happy group, to say the least.

Pounce made them welcome as they set out the cloth and our meal. I kept feeding birds. It was just the ones who carried the diggers' ghosts, as if I needed to feel more downhearted. They repeated their complaints to me. However many times I tell them I'm still looking for their graves and even their names, they never seem to hear. They want to be found right off, as if I'm a god who can see who they are, who their families are, and where their poor bodies have been hid.

I wish that the dead were more patient, but them that are waiting for justice aren't. Verene's murderers were taken up right off. I figure that was why she and Rollo only stayed long enough to say goodbye at the burying, because the one big debt the living owed to them was paid. The diggers are still waiting, just like the Shadow Snake's victims. Mayhap I wouldn't feel so helpless about their whingeing if I knew we were getting somewhere.

I was breaking some final chunks of bread when Kora asked, "May I help feed them?"

"I don't usually feed them from my hand," I said.

She was holding her fingers out to the birds. Shy ones like Mumper and Inky scuttled away. White Spice and Ashes tried to bite her fingertips, thinking they might be food. "Here." I put the bread into her cupped palm. "Just know that they learn fast. Feed them from your hand once or twice and they'll come straight to you after that. Do it often enough and they'll climb on you." Pinky tried to land on my chest, slapped my face with her wings, and took off. I sighed. "And they'll leave scummer on you and their feathers in your room." Slapper dropped to my shoulder. He wedged his clubfoot in the hollow between my shirt collar and neck, grabbed my ear, and tugged. "Curst things think they own you!" I pulled Slapper's beak off my ear. He pecked my fingers until I gave him a bit of bread.

"But they're so beautiful," Kora said. White Spice and Ashes pecked at the bread in her hand. "Some of them, anyway."

I put bread before Mumper and Inky. "Some are native to the Lower City. Others, well, folk breed pigeons in colors for racing and for messengers. Some of those birds escape. They bring in the pinks and the coppers and the whites." I swore at Slapper, who'd bit my ear again.

"You're an ingrate," Rosto said behind me. He pulled Slapper off of my shoulder and my ear. Slapper voiced his pigeon war cry, a furious *"Croo!"* I turned. Rosto had the bird in the right hold, wings pressed flat to his sides. "You're a warrior, aren't you, for all you're bent out of true," Rosto was telling my cracked pigeon. "Stop attacking the one person who treats you well."

I looked beyond Rosto. Phelan had come. He and Ersken sat cross-legged on the cloth with Aniki, eating breakfast. They looked as weary and beaten as I felt. Pounce was leaning against Phelan's side.

Phelan looked at Kora, Rosto, and me as we finally sat and took up our own food.

"You need to rest," Kora told Phelan. "Come to my rooms after breakfast and I'll give you a tea that's good for sleep."

Phelan nodded. I don't know if he was agreeing or if he did so just because something told him that was what he was supposed to do.

The rest of our meal passed in silence. We were closing up jars and packing odds and ends away when Phelan cleared his throat. "Ersken, Beka, I quit the Dogs last night."

We both looked at him. I couldn't say as I was surprised. If I read Ersken's face aright, he was no more startled than me.

"Don't hate me," Phelan said. "If you don't want me here come morning, I'll understand." Phelan's eyes filled up but didn't spill over. "It's not the dying. Well, it is. But that Rollo was stupid and Otelia was drunk."

"Drunk?" Ersken whispered. "On duty?"

My belly felt like it opened up into a huge pit.

"You think it never happens?" Phelan asked. "Mostly they put the drunks on Night or Day Watch, but Otelia doesn't drink regular. But why'd they give a Puppy to those two?" He hung his head.

"Transfer to another district," Ersken said.

Phelan was shaking his head. "I'm through. It's everything. All Ahuda ever did was her work. They took her off patrol for just that, put her to marking the roll and training Puppies. And they send Puppies out to die in the Lower City. The Provost's Guard is cracked. Don't tell me different, Beka. I'm going to do sommat sane with my life."

Phelan stood and walked out of my room before I could have said a word, could I have thought of aught. Truth to tell, I couldn't. I felt I should argue. But hearing that Verene was given to a fool and a drunk had left me flat. I was ready to die in a fight. Goodwin and Tunstall would never use me as stupidly as Rollo and Otelia used Verene. But the thought that I might die for a stupid reason, that *Verene* died for so stupid a reason, preyed on my mind.

Phelan wasn't the only one to quit. Hilyard was missing at training, of course. Good riddance. One of the other cove Pups left, though, and two of the mots. For one bad night, we'd lost nearly half of the Lower City trainees. Only one, the Crone be praised, was the Black God's prize. It was a hard blow for those of us who remained.

Tuesday, May 5, 246

Around four in the afternoon.

I have had no heart for writing in this journal this week. The weather has been as cold and gloomsome as my spirit. I write today only because I must correct Goodwin's and Tunstall's maps and lists. All told we now have verified twenty-three suspected Shadow Snake kidnappings. In company with Kora, Aniki, Mother Cantwell, and Ersken, I have spoken to nineteen folk who lost children or were close to them as had children taken by the Snake. I have fifteen yet to check.

Granny had but one new name to give me today. Mother Cantwell had two. The names are drying up. I should be glad, but without more knowledge, I fear the Snake will escape us. I stare at the map when I come home at night, thinking, He will get away with it. He will get away with it all.

The poxy weather is no friend to any of us. Because of the storms, the trading fleets still have not come. There are no cargoes arriving from Port Caynn, which is to say, no one is getting hired to work the riverfront or the markets. Them that have jobs are keeping them, for fear they won't get another, however bad their masters are.

If anyone is hiring diggers and telling them to keep their gobs shut, they are doing so. They will not risk losing work when no one else is finding any.

I know Crookshank's people are looking to hire, or they have done so. Crookshank is greedy. He wants fire opals. He thinks only the Shadow Snake knows he has them, and no one believes in the Shadow Snake. He won't be able to keep himself from getting more out of the ground, wherever he gets them from.

I must mark up the maps and add to the lists.

Thursday, May 7, 246

Noon.

Today I woke to pigeons everywhere in my room.

I yelled as Slapper hopped on my head to peck me like the demented cuddy that he is. "Pounce! I told you, never open the shutters!"

"All I wanted was some work," a mot's ghost said. "It were strange, that they didn't want me t' say a word, but they was hiring." That was a cove, not much older than me from the sound of his voice.

"I did all they said. Still, they poisoned me in me sleep," another cove complained.

"We dug wi' picks till we bled," a ghost near my head told me. "Fillin' buckets full o' rocks with glass in 'em—"

"I tol' you, 'twasn't glass," a new ghost interrupted. He had some kind of Carthaki accent. "It's fire opal. It's worth plenty of coin. I used to dig it back in the mines of Carthak. Gods' fire, it's called."

"If you're so clever, scut, why'd they kill *you?*" a hard-voiced mot asked. "They buried you deep as us, once we couldn't get no more rock out wi'out diggin' into the cellar wall an' maybe collapsin' the house."

I sat up careful-like. Seventeen pigeons had raided my room. Nine were from the first group of murdered diggers. Eight of them were new. "Pox-rotted pus-leaking mumper bags," I whispered as I got out of bed.

Crookshank's folk did it. They'd hired fresh diggers right under our noses. They'd killed them there, too.

I got dressed and grabbed my pack. Then I went out. I left my part of everyone's breakfast at Aniki's door. I needed to get to the Cesspool dust spinners while their gleanings from last night were fresh.

Pounce and I headed for Hasfush at the trot. For the first day since her murder, my grief for Verene was pushed back, eaten up by anger.

How did Crookshank do it? I wonder if Tansy knows. Impossible. She'd never have slept knowing nine people died to put pretty clothes on her back, let alone seventeen. It's one thing to know your grandfather-in-law got rich from cheating thieves. It's another to know—to let yourself know—he makes money on killing. And any killing he'd done before this was spoke of in whispers or laid at the Rogue's door.

Hasfush is scarce to be seen in the first light of most mornings. Today, his foot was a soft whisper in the grit of the street. I knew just looking at him that he'd not heard so much as a scream. Still, I stepped inside his breezy circle to listen. I strained to hear any voices he'd caught up, but all I heard was whispers.

What did you expect? I asked myself. This lot said they'd been poisoned. I waited longer, grinding my teeth. But I heard naught that sounded like the voices of them hired to dig under a house.

At last I walked off. I made it a block down the

street when I heard Pounce meow loudly. I looked back. He stood by Hasfush, violet eyes furious, his tail whacking in anger. He was vexed with me.

I knew why, too. I thought, Shame to you, Rebakah Cooper. Just because Hasfush don't have what you want, that's no reason to treat an old friend rude.

I'd given him nothing. No more had I taken away the burden of all the chatter he'd picked up since my last visit.

I turned around and went back. Pounce looked up at me. *About time,* he said.

"Don't rub it in," I told him.

From my pack I got a pouch filled with dirt I'd gathered on Palace Way. I stepped back into Hasfush. First I apologized for leaving him as I had. Then I poured out the grit.

His sides squeezed me, like my ribs squeezed when I took a deep breath. Hasfush was pleased. When he settled lower to the ground, I opened myself to voices caught in his breezes. Gossip, quarrels, flirtations, it all poured into my ears as he let it go.

Now a set of whispers caught my attention. "That's the second crew. How long d'you think they'll keep us guards alive?"

"'s long as we do th' work 'n' keep our gobs shut. Don' be a fool, Jens. We're mage-marked. Drink up. Hotblood wine makes it easier to stand what we do. And we're paid well enough."

I held still until I heard nothing in Hasfush but the brush of wind and street grit on stone. Once I'd paid my debt properly, I stepped out of his circle. Thinking, I started brushing dust and trash off of me.

"Jens. We have a name, Pounce," I said. My hands shook. "Finally I've got a name. And I wouldn't've had it if you'd not called me back to be polite."

He leaped to my shoulder to purr in my ear. *You learn slowly, but you do learn.*

I had to fight myself not to run to Tunstall's and Goodwin's places with my news. Instead I visited all of my Lower City spinners in the hope I might get more. I did get a hint of an illegal slave sale and a kidnap plan. Those I could pass on to Ahuda.

Then I turned my attention to the pigeons. I bought bread and fed them in the fountain squares to glean what I might. At Glassman Square a mumper staggered by, soused. He asked me for coin, but I shook my head. I was busy. One bird's ghost was telling me about her son. One day he'd said he couldn't afford a ma that wasn't able to work and drowned her in a washbasin.

The mumper stomped through my flock just when the ghost was going to tell me her killer's name. "Hey! Puttock!" the cove yelled. "Wha's yer matter—y'love them lousy birds more'n yer own kind?"

It was too much, knowing there were seven more digger ghosts today. He'd scared the bird and lost me the name of yet another murderer, to boot. So though it shames me to write it, I will be truthful. I lost my temper. I grabbed his ears and stared him full in the face. "Get out before I give you the nap tap." I hardly knew my own voice. "You're a shame to the woman who bore you. All her blood and pain, for what?" I let him go. "Find sommat of use to do with the life you have."

He fell back two steps and made the sign against evil. "Ye've ghost eyes!"

"You're drunk afore noon," a woman shouted. "Begone, afore we stone you. You've earned it, spilling yer piss when folk never bothered you."

Others who stood about the square joined her shouts. Some even threw rocks from the street at the mumper. Seemingly I wasn't the only one he'd insulted. He stumbled away, chased by their jeers.

I made myself look at them. "Thanks," I said.

"He's a mule's bum," said the mot who'd first called out. "You was just feedin' birds. It's a treat, seein' you bend down like you listen to 'em talk. The cat there lookin' like he listens, too."

"Y' talked to th' tosspot like you's a Dog," a gixie said, wringing out something gray.

"Ain't y' seen 'er with Tunstall an' Goodwin? Evenin' Watch, she is. Cooper, right?" the first woman asked. "Doin' good work for only a Puppy."

That was enough attention for me. I thanked them again and left. I still had enough time to give Jens's name to Mother Cantwell and my other Birdies. There could be a hundred coves with that name in the city, but how many take Crookshank's coin?

After watch's end.
As soon as we finished muster tonight, I told my Dogs what I'd learned about Jens.

"Tricky," Tunstall said as we walked to the Court of the Rogue. "He's got that mage mark on his hand. When we do find him, I don't know if Fulk is up to countering a death spell."

"And mayhap it begins to work when we hobble him, even before he starts to talk," said Goodwin. "We need to know where to lay hands on this Jens first. Then we'd best give Berryman that walk-along we've promised. *If* he can put a freeze on one of those mage marks, anyway."

"He should," Tunstall said. "He's a gem mage, isn't he? How many smugglers, thieves, and counterfeiters are marked to die before they sing the names of the ones who hired them? Berryman can do it." He looked at me. "Do you know, Cooper, those spinner and pigeon informants of yours have their uses. Did you get anything else from them today?"

I told them the other bits I'd already given Ahuda, keeping watch on the streets and buildings in case someone felt brave enough to throw something at the Dogs passing below. Pounce trotted ahead of us, on the lookout for mice. It was a normal enough evening. The only oddity came when Goodwin spotted Yates Noll and his two friends down one of the twisty lanes off Stormwing Street. We stopped to watch. When they caught sight of us, they scurried out of view.

"There's sommat I don't understand," I said. "What's in that greasenob Yates to make those two rough lads talk fearful about him? He's no prize bull."

"Good question, Cooper," Goodwin said without turning around. "I was wondering about that myself."

"They're hiding something," said Tunstall. "I'll put some seed before my Birdies. Maybe they've a song about Yates to sing."

The gates of the Court were open wide. The guards were new since the night Crookshank had hidden a blade from the old ones. These muttered but let us by as Goodwin idly flipped her baton up into her grip on its thong and down again. Through the halls we passed, my fifth such walk now.

Kayfer was on his throne. He'd foreigners with him, two Yamanis with their hair in topknots. With them stood the Carthaki who'd had Kayfer's ear my first night at the Court. They all looked like dangerous folk. The talk at the Mantel and Pullet was that the Carthaki was a gem seller. Were the Yamanis the same, come to wait for Crookshank's rumored auction in August? I could feel my rough fire opal pressing against my thigh.

The first thing I saw when I looked away from Kayfer was Ulsa, seated at her table. As ever, she was dressed to startle. Tonight she wore a silk shirt that clung to what she had and silk breeches. Her personal guard sat at her table with her, mots and coves. Rosto guarded her back.

So did Phelan. He stood beside Rosto, wearing a tunic and breeches and carrying a sword. He'd gone to serve the enemy. That's why Rosto had spoken to him.

When Phelan saw I was staring at him, he looked away. Well he should.

Kora caught my eye and shrugged. She sat on the floor where we'd talked that first night, laying out fortune cards. Already she had three coves waiting for her to tell them their futures. A fourth sat cross-legged beside her, watching as she put the cards down. She winked at me and murmured to her audience.

I continued to eye the room. I was telling myself that Phelan's life was his own. If *my* lover got killed through the stupidity of his training Dogs, would I do as he did?

No. I would never do that. But he is angry with the Dogs. Rosto wants someone he can trust in Ulsa's gang with him. Now he's got Phelan. They say the line between rushers and Dogs is a thin one. For Phelan, it was thin enough to step over.

I looked for Aniki. She stood at Dawull's back,

hand on her sword hilt. With her stood the fellow who'd drawn blade on us when we'd visited Dawull's court. Seemingly they had moved up in Dawull's regard, from extra swords to personal guard. I wondered how they'd managed it, but I wasn't going to ask Aniki. I'd a feeling I wouldn't like a truthful answer. Nor would I care for it if Aniki lied to me. Usually such promotions meant blood.

Kayfer kept us waiting, as ever. Mayhap I wouldn't have minded if it had come from a Rogue I respected. Coming from a daisy-livered slack-kneed spintry like him, it was hard to take. Whilst my Dogs talked to the Rogue's chiefs, I crouched on my hunkerbones and looked at Kora's cards, trying to see how fortune-telling worked. Pounce patted at a card with a smith's anvil painted on it.

"Don't look at 'em, Cooper," protested the cove she read for. "You'll curdle my future. The purple-eyed cat's bad enough."

"Beka doesn't curdle anything," Kora told him, her voice stern. "Eyes like hers, they see clearest of all."

"I don't want that," he said. "No more would any cove wi' sense. We— Tricksters all, what have you wrought?"

I wondered what cracknob would call on trickster gods during a fortune reading until I realized he meant it for what was happening at the door. Goodwin and

Tunstall moved together fast, like they hadn't been half a room apart. By the time they reached me, I was up with my baton out and ready.

Crookshank strode toward Kayfer Deerborn's throne, his eyes bulging. His hair looked like he'd torn at it with both hands. His velvet coat, trimmed in ermine, was half on, half off.

Beside him walked Fulk, who never should have been there. The Evening Watch mage wore a chain with a gem that sparked in the torchlight. Its blue and orange fires rivaled the fever in his eyes. Somehow the greasy cuddy had gotten a fire opal.

Behind Crookshank and Fulk came mots and coves armed with crossbows, staves, and swords. These were hard customers. Some I knew from the Mantel and Pullet and the streets, all soldiers and members of the Palace Guard. With the rest of their group having the same look, I guessed they were more of the same, off-duty fighters Crookshank had hired. I did a fast count. He'd brought near forty folk with him. What were they doing? They had no business in the Court of the Rogue!

"Now it comes out!" Crookshank screamed, walking up to Kayfer. "Now the whole kingdom will know you for the Shadow Snake! Where is my grandson? Where is Herun?"

I couldn't breathe. Herun? The Snake had Tansy's

husband now? I'd feared for Tansy, mayhap her babe when it was born—not her man!

Kayfer stood. "You cracknob old skinflint, what are you doing here with this army?"

The archers spread along the wall and across the door, their crossbows ready. There would be more at the gate, I guessed. They'd have been needed to hold the guards.

Now the raiders armed with swords and staves walked through the room. They thrust the mots and coves of the Court against the wall. More raiders stripped the rogues of their weapons.

"Don't lie, Kayfer!" Crookshank yelled. "You're the Shadow Snake! You took Herun to get my treasure! You won't have it, you scummer-lapping maggot! I'll see you in the cages! You'll die on Executioner's Hill if you don't give back my boy!"

As easy as if she folded sheets, Kora picked up her cards. "Another time, friend," she told her customer.

"I could see it wasn't goin' well anyway." He got up and offered Kora a hand to help her to her feet. She took it and rose. They both moved to the wall as a soldier we all knew came toward us to disarm the Rogue's folk nearby.

As the soldier passed us, Tunstall murmured, "What are you doing?"

"Gettin' paid very well," the soldier replied. His

lips barely moved. "Crookshank said he'd give two gold each t' tweak the Rogue's nose."

Goodwin whistled. I felt sick. He was paying eighty gold just to them in this room. That didn't count the other fighters he had outside. And I'd wager half a year's earnings he'd gotten Fulk for a fire opal or two.

I looked at Kayfer. Crookshank was there, trading hot whispers with him. He clutched the Rogue with a claw of a hand.

Kayfer shook him off. "You're raving!" he cried. "I'm no child's tale—there's no Shadow Snake! And you're cracked straight down the middle, to bring out-siders here!"

"You kidnapped a young man of standing," Fulk told Kayfer. "On Master Ammon Lofts' behalf, as con-cerned people of the city, these men and women and I will search for him." Fulk smirked. "I'm sure we'll find something for our trouble."

The soldier turned Kora and the thief to the wall. As he searched them, he said to Tunstall, "Get out."

Goodwin and Tunstall nodded. We made for the door. The raiders were happy to let us leave. "More for us," one of them said as we passed them.

Once in the hall outside, Goodwin asked Tunstall, "Now what?"

"Get work as Players?" Tunstall said. He dodged Goodwin's kick. "What can we do? Crookshank's set the Court of the Rogue on its head. We warn the others, we collect the Bag another day, and we have extra time to see if we can find where Crookshank does his digging."

Goodwin shook her head. "Bets on how long Fulk lives after this night?"

"No bets," Tunstall said. "He's a mage. He'll use the opal Crookshank gave him to take the next ship out of Port Caynn. Kayfer's not Rogue enough even to douse Fulk, though I'd pay to watch."

Goodwin looked at me. I shrugged. "I hate Fulk. I hope he dies. But I won't bet on a mage," I said.

"So let's finish our watch," Goodwin said. "I hope we get to collect that Bag soon, or it'll be a lean week for the Dogs with families."

We headed for the meeting place to give the Happy Bags to the Dogs who take them to the kennel. We could tell they'd had no whiff of Crookshank's raid. They sat around a fire, not expecting us for a time.

"Wake up," Tunstall said. "You won't believe what's happened."

They listened to him, jaws agape. I couldn't blame them. I'd never heard of such a thing happening at the Court. I wondered how many of those off-duty fighters would live to spend their gold and how many of them we'd be scraping from the gutters.

"So there's no Bag tonight, but news to spread," Goodwin said when Tunstall was done. "Two more things. We know the Shadow Snake's real. It's not

Kayfer. If Crookshank's not having waking dreams, the Snake's got Herun. He's a nice lad and doesn't deserve to die. And we're looking for Jens. He's a rusher hired by Crookshank or one of Crookshank's folk. If you find Jens, don't let him know you're seeking. Don't hobble him. He's got a mage mark on him that'll kill him the moment he's caught. Just tell us what he looks like and where he may be found."

"Warn all our Dogs," Tunstall said. "It's going to be a strange night."

"Them soldiers shoulda took sick as soon as they found out where they were goin'," grumbled one of the Dogs. "I woulda done."

"Get moving," Goodwin said. "Spread the news."

"You know how these skewed nights work—the world goes mad, or it goes quiet," Tunstall said. "Our lads and lasses need to be awake for both."

The others took to their horses. We put out their fire. After that, we followed our regular patrol route. Walking along, I found my brain was abuzz. The Snake had taken Herun Lofts. "I was wondering . . . ," I mumbled to the road.

"Speak up, Cooper," Goodwin said.

"Crookshank's rushers were with his boughten search party," I said. "So who's at Crookshank's? If the Snake took Herun, mayhap he left some trace of his coming and going at the house."

For a moment they were quiet. Then Goodwin told

Tunstall, "All right. I was against having a Puppy. I thought she'd be a lot of work and a lot of trouble. But I have to say, you were right." She looked back at me. "Let's have a toddle over to Crookshank's house, on advice from the sharpest Puppy in the whole litter."

It felt good to hear that from her.

Crookshank's house looked deserted. The front door torches were out. The mourning wreath for Rolond hung off one of its nails, some of its ribbons torn from their anchors. Pounce trotted around the side of the house. We took the same path, bound for the kitchen door. The side gate was unlocked and open, which was not right. Anyone might come in as we did.

The kitchen door was open, too. All three of us took out our batons. Inside, the room was dark, the inner door shut. Tunstall went through first, noiseless for all his size. He held the door open and motioned us through.

Two maids, the cook, and a manservant were bound on the kitchen floor. Goodwin motioned for me to cut the cook's gag. "Soft," I whispered in her ear.

"He's got Mistress Annis and Mistress Tansy in the master's rooms," the cook told me. "He come in wi' a knife to Tansy's throat and had me bind the others, then had her bind me. Then he had her call Mistress Annis. He was talkin' about treasure."

Goodwin knelt beside us. "Just one man?"

The cook said, "Aye."

We left the servants there and trotted up the back stair, trying to keep our steps light. It still smelled of smoke from the old fire the night of our last visit. As we reached the rear landing, Goodwin whispered in my ear, "Servants' door."

I remembered it. Crookshank's rooms had another entry. We'd seen it last time. I watched her and Tunstall run behind Pounce to the main door to Crookshank's chamber. Pounce beat them inside. I raced across the servants' landing to the second door and had my hand on the latch when I heard Pounce roar.

At least, I think it was Pounce. It was the most fearful thing I'd ever heard, a roar that echoed through the house. It was the sound of a far bigger creature, one that was mayhap related to a cat. The hairs stood on the back of my neck.

A man shouted in surprise.

A moment later he yanked the servants' door open. I slammed him in the belly with my baton. He stumbled back into Tunstall's grip.

Tunstall wrapped one arm around the Rat's neck and used the other to twist the man's arm up behind his back. Swinging the Rat around, Tunstall rammed him headfirst into the bedpost, then dropped him face-first onto the floor. It was done and Tunstall was kneeling beside the Rat before I'd closed the servants' door.

"Well done, Cooper," Goodwin said from the other side of the bedroom.

Tunstall twisted the Rat half to the side to take his dagger and look at his face. He smiled. "Clary, here we were saying we were getting lonesome for the old faces, and the gods took pity on us."

Goodwin spotted Tansy and Annis, tied up and left by the hearth. She jerked her head toward them in a silent order for me to free them, then knelt beside Tunstall and the Rat. "Gunnar Espeksra, you revolting piece of bug dung. I thought you and Yates Noll were joined at the hip."

I glanced at our prize.

"Your friends aren't getting any more comfortable whilst you stare, Cooper," said Tunstall. "Is he more handsome than Ersken Westover or Rosto the Piper?"

"There's pigs on butchers' meat hooks that's more handsome," I said. "I think he was with Yates when we saw him earlier tonight."

"What treasure were you looking for, Gunnar?" Tunstall wanted to know. "Only a looby would think Crookshank kept it here, where anyone might walk in and lift it."

"Pox on yer privates if ye think I've a word for ye," Gunnar said. "An' Yates has naught t' do wif it." He looked away as he said it, lying through his teeth.

"Maybe Mistress Annis and Mistress Tansy know something," Goodwin said.

I cut Tansy's gag first. She was weeping. "What do I care about what he wants? Herun's been kidnapped by the Shadow Snake! You're not searching for him!"

I cut the rest of her bonds. "Are you sure it's the Shadow Snake?" I asked. "Not your grandfather-in-law thinking that's who's done it now, after the Snake taking Rolond? Because so far as we know, the Snake only takes little ones." I cut off Annis's gag.

"We saw the note, before Father stuffed it in his tunic," said Annis. Her eyes were puffed from weeping, but she wasn't in Tansy's state, for all Herun was her son. "It's the same as the ones that came for Rolond. The very same. Herun took receipts to the Goldsmith's Bank, and he never returned. Father came home to dress for a merchants' supper, and the note was on his bed. Then . . . We were beside ourselves, after Father ran screaming from the house. Tansy went to search without telling anyone. I'd only just noticed she was gone when she came back with *him*." She could only jerk her chin at Gunnar. I was still hacking at her ropes.

"Stupid doxies," he said. "All ye had to do was say where he keeps them sparklin' stones and I'da been gone!"

Tunstall thumped Gunnar's head on the floor. "How do you know about sparkling stones, a gutter crawler like you?" he asked.

Gunnar didn't say, though Tunstall bounced his head several times more.

"Save it," Goodwin said. "Let the questioners get it out of Gunnar. We already know he'll lead us to Yates Noll." She put the hobbles on our Rat.

"Bad idea," Gunnar told us. "Ye don't want to go crossin' Yates, not ever."

Tunstall flicked Gunnar's head with his finger, using his thumb to give the small blow force. "Nobody asked the opinions of a fawning scut like you, Gunnar," he said. He sounded outright friendly. "Either tell us what we're asking for or swallow your tongue. We've no real druthers about which." He got up.

"Mayhap it's no accident he's here tonight," I said. "Mayhap he knew the household would be in an uproar or even out searching the streets."

"Hmm." Goodwin had finished the hobbles. Now she sat on the backs of Gunnar's knees. "And mayhap you and Yates and your other Rat friend took Herun yourselves. There's a good trick. You lure the old man out, not to mention his household, so you can rob the place. Or did you just hear of the kidnapping, and come to help yourself?"

Annis and Tansy watched, their faces hard. There's scant mercy in Lower City folk. I would have been startled if they had told my Dogs to stop hurting Gunnar when he'd kept his knife to Tansy's throat for so long. I could see a red, swollen ridge where he'd cut her and the line of dried blood he'd left.

"I'm on my own," Gunnar cried. "And that's my last word! Torture me all you want!"

"Not us," Tunstall said. "We'd stain our uniforms.

The cage Dogs, though—they get leather aprons, special issue. It cuts down on their laundering expenses."

Most street Dogs don't care for torture. The cage Dogs go in for that. That was partly how they made their extras. We have the Happy Bags to share. Cage dogs get paid direct, by families and patrons of the Rats, and by the crown for what they can get from Rats in pain.

Knowing the cage Dogs waited didn't loosen Gunnar's tongue. He kept silent after that. We took down details of what he'd done as we untied the servants, then found the cage cart and dropped him off.

Then we went back to the Cesspool and our regular patrol. By then word of Crookshank's raid on the Court of the Rogue had reached the kennel. All around us, runners slipped by with a wink or a wave. They were lads or gixies like I was once, picked because they had sense and they knew the Lower City. It was their job to get the news to the Dogs on watch without being caught by Rats or cracknob cityfolk.

By the time we took supper, the Cesspool was still. The rushers, doxies, spintries, and drunks had all gone to ground. Everyone wanted to see what the Rogue would command once the invaders had left his Court. There were no cockfights or dogfights, no corner dice games, and scarce tavern business. I'd never seen it so unnatural.

We poked around three of Crookshank's buildings

for signs of cellar digging or the smells of rotting dead, without luck. We'd thought to look at one more, since most folk were off the streets. A pack of pit dogs growling behind the place discouraged us. Perched atop the rear wall to look at them, I could see their chains did not look securely fastened to stakes in the ground. We'd have to return with sleep dust for these four-legged brothers. Pounce, sitting on the wall beside me, did not care to get involved this time. We gave up and headed off down Charry Orchard.

"Crookshank's search must still go on," Goodwin said when we saw the Red Feather gang wasn't holding their nightly dice game at their usual corner. "That's why we've seen no one from the Court."

Tunstall listened to a far-off watchman call the quarter hour. "I'd like a word with Mistress Noll. See if she knows where we might find her boy Yates."

"You think he'll make a run out of Corus?" Goodwin asked, thinking out loud. "To his brother in Port Caynn, or the one in Blue Harbor?"

Tunstall was shaking his head. "Not those two. They want to look respectable. Both of them would send Yates home in a sack."

"So busy working, building it all up, she never noticed what a Rat her littlest lad turned out to be," Goodwin muttered. "There's a mother's lot for you."

Pounce jumped up on my shoulder as we entered the Nightmarket.

"Deirdry Noll's got five good children, Clary," Tunstall said. "Every barrel has one rotten one. Yates is hers."

Mistress Noll had plenty of customers. Gemma was there to help. We hung back, watching as Gemma served while Mistress Noll cooked. The old mot worked fast, but then she'd been doing this longer than I'd been alive. She was a baker's daughter who'd married another baker. Watching her, I wondered if she dreamed of flour.

The custom thinned out. My Dogs stepped up to the counter. Gemma said, "Ma."

Mistress Noll turned. "My favorite pair." She reached for the patties without thinking, then stopped herself. "But somehow I think it's not for our wares." She wiped her face and neck of sweat with a cloth she kept over one shoulder, then leaned on the counter. Now she looked as hard as her arms. "What may I do for you, Guardsman?"

Tunstall asked her about Yates's whereabouts. She denied knowledge. My attention was on her necklaces, disordered when she wiped her neck. Among her beads and brass chains was a thin chain that looked like real gold, with a lily pendant made of green and white enamel.

What is it about that necklace that seems familiar? I've never seen it before, I am certain.

"I told Yates Gunnar Espeksra is worm scummer."

Mistress Noll's voice was sharp. "Why do you bother my boy, with Herun Lofts missing and poor Tansy mad with fear? Such a sweet child. She's had a lifetime of trouble in two scant months."

"Your boy's friend put a knife to sweet Tansy's throat this evening," Goodwin said. "We think he may have told Yates what he was looking for. Surely that's harmless enough."

"Nothing's harmless when you hand a cove to the cage Dogs," Mistress Noll said.

"We don't mean to hobble Yates," Goodwin told her. "Unless he's done aught to be hobbled for?"

"I've not seen him in five days," Mistress Noll said, her voice iron hard. "Nor would I tell you if I had. No mother would."

I looked around. My tripes itched me like fire. I know that feeling from sifting pigeon and spinner gleanings. Something that matters had crossed my attention just recently—two somethings. If I let go, try *not* to think about them, sometimes they become clear.

Tunstall sighed. "Mother, I know you're not thinking kindly of us, but we're only doing our work," he said, keeping his voice low. "And here's some advice you'll thank me for. Close early. You and Gemma go home with the crowd. Better still, find a strong fellow to take you home. There may be trouble with the Rogue."

She looked us over. "Is there, now?"

"Some off-duty soldiers raided the Court tonight," Goodwin said. "They were hunting for Herun Lofts. They're still searching the place."

I saw Gemma make the sign against evil on her chest. I could hardly blame her.

"Searching the Court. Kayfer's own palace," Mistress Noll repeated, as if she couldn't be sure of her own hearing. She wrapped her fingers around her Goddess charm. "Has the world run mad?" She looked at Gemma. "Start packing. No. I'll pack up. Find the lads. They'll be at the Sticky Fingers. Run!"

Gemma ran.

Mistress Noll began to place food on the counter. It was a signal to shoppers that a vendor was about to close and had reduced prices. "Two patties or a turnover each to the three of you for the warning, no cost," she said briskly, her hands swift at their work. "With what cause was this search made?"

"The Rogue will be upset, Mother," Tunstall told Mistress Noll. "That's enough of an explanation for now. Tell Yates we want a word, if you see him."

"I'll tell him," the old woman said. "The gods' blessings to you for the warning. I pray this passes soon, and you find poor Herun Lofts."

It depends on whether Crookshank pays those stones to the Shadow Snake, I thought as I followed my Dogs out of the Nightmarket. He won't find his grandson at the Court of the Rogue. Kayfer Deerborn is no more the Snake than I am the Queen. The Snake kept his sights low. . . .

The Snake kept his sights low until Crookshank found a fortune in the Lower City, I realized. I halted.

"Cooper, wake up," Goodwin said. "Now's not the time to be napping. Remember your friend Verene."

"I was thinking," I said.

"Then share your thoughts," Tunstall told me.

"Until now the Shadow Snake kept to the shadows," I said. They moved closer to me. Pounce settled on my feet. I kept thinking out loud. "Then Crookshank found fire opals. Mostly he kept it a secret, and that's where he let the Snake in. Because the Snake lives on secrets. He feeds on them. That's how he's made his little thievings over the years and gotten away with it. Everyone fears to tell, so only a few know. Them as tell the Dogs, or the Rogue, are brushed aside. So Crookshank never heard the Snake was there. He didn't believe in the Snake. He can't hurt the Snake."

Tunstall rubbed his beard. "So when Crookshank gets hurt by a kidnapper, he goes to the home of the kidnappers, the Court of the Rogue. He knows Kayfer has heard of his sudden good fortune. He thinks it's the king of kidnappers who's taken his great-grandson, and now his grandson. And that he's just *signed* the name of a children's bogey."

"Crookshank never gives way to greedy business partners." That was Goodwin's voice in the dark. "He's famous for it. He didn't pay the Snake for Rolond. He thinks that now the Snake knows he won't pay what he asked, the Snake will demand a lower price for Herun. Crookshank doesn't understand that the Snake is mad—that the Snake will keep killing until he gets what he wants."

"We could tell him," I suggested. "Show him the map, explain the Snake never backs down."

"Do you believe he'll listen?" Tunstall asked me.

I had to tell the truth. "I just suggested it because anyone who isn't cracked would believe us."

"Crookshank is more than cracked," Goodwin said. "He's smashed all to pieces."

"He's got to pay this time," Tunstall said. "He's running out of heirs. Herun's all that's left, unless Tansy has a boy. So let's pray the old man comes to his senses."

"And Kayfer doesn't cut his throat," Goodwin added. "No, Kayfer won't do that. He does too much business with Crookshank. But gods help those folk who are searching the Court."

As we walked on, Pounce jumped up to my shoulders and rode. "He's hiring a third crew, or he's hired them," I said to my Dogs.

"The one good thing about a shake-up like tonight, Cooper," Tunstall said. "Plenty of people are going to be upset. Upset people are talkative people."

"And maybe we'll get lucky, and there'll be a

change in the Court of the Rogue," Goodwin said. "There are always opportunities in times like this, for everyone. Your friends Rosto and Aniki could find themselves on the rise. And we could hobble Crook-shank and the Snake."

I would like that. It's hard to feel sorry for a cove who orders the murder of folk in lots of nine and eight. And the Shadow Snake never should have stepped out of scary stories to become real.

Friday, May 8, 246

Midafternoon.

This morning Pounce woke me. He was washing my fingers, then nuzzling between them. I clung to something. He meant to have it. He'd get his teeth on it and pull until his teeth slipped. Feeling muzzy, I brought my hand to my face and opened it. I held my fire opal. I'd stared at it until I fell asleep. Seemingly I'd hung on to it all night.

In my dreams, I had played by Mistress Noll's house with my childhood friends. Mistress Noll chased Tansy with a broom as Tansy mocked her. It had happened often when I lived in Mutt Piddle Lane.

"Rocks aren't food, you coal-colored mumper," I told my cat, looking at the stone. A ray of sun poked through the shutters and touched it. The glassy bits shone cherry, green, and yellow.

Now Pounce rubbed against my face, purring like thunder and getting hair in my nostrils and on my lips. When he leaned on my nose, I pulled him down, hugging his silly person in both arms.

You are not respectful! he complained.

"If you want that, get yourself a noble," I said. He smelled like clean cat, just a little musky and sweet. "Someone who'll give you a collar with gems and let you ride on her horse, above all us gutter runners." I kissed his head. "But you have me and a job with the Provost's Dogs. So very sad."

The shutter gave a thump that brought me bolt upright.

Pounce said, *They want in.*

"They can't come in," I said, putting him down. "I can't face them." I went to the crack. "I can't handle seventeen ghosts!" I said. "Today will be bad enough without me thinking I could've saved eight more of you!" I put the stone on the inside ledge and skinned out of my nightshirt. "Don't you go a-lettin' them in, Pounce!" I warned him. "They'll catch me outside anyway!"

I dressed and braided my hair. I was just finishing when Aniki and Kora rapped on my door.

Aniki smiled. "It's too warm to stay up here. Let's sit in the sun!"

The pigeons will love that, I thought, but after so much rain, I was sick of eating on my floor, too. As I packed up my share of our settings, I asked her and Kora, "Did anyone find Herun?"

Kora shook her head. "Crookshank's raiders found plenty of the Rogue's other little treasures, but no Herun. Is he as handsome as they say?"

"He's married to my friend," I said, frowning at her. "He's well enough in looks. Not that clever."

Aniki swooped on Pounce and swung him into the

air. "Who needs handsome idiots when we can have kitties!" she cried, spinning around with him. Pounce glared at me as if to say, *Stop her!*

I shrugged at him. Figuring I'd buy the birds off with food, I grabbed my bag of pigeon feed, then swiped a fresh cherry from Kora's basket. Aniki freed Pounce and collected a pot she had left by her door. My belly growled. I'd had only stale biscuits when I came home last night. Aniki had Tyran custard in that pot.

I stared at her. "Tyran custard's costly."

"It's not so costly. And I think we deserve a treat, with all that's gone on." She lifted the pot to her nose and inhaled. "Of a certainty we deserve a treat. Pox take Crookshank and Deerborn, that's what I say."

"As Mithros wills," I whispered.

"As Mithros wills," they repeated.

We had almost reached the ground floor when Ersken came to the front door. "Where were you?" he asked Kora. "I went to the Mermaid like you asked yesterday morning. You never came. I waited until they closed. Then I went to the Court of the Rogue. They wouldn't let me in. I even checked the kennel in case they'd caged you." I heard him gulp. "I would have bought you out of the cages," he said. "Then I thought maybe you'd gone off with Rosto . . . and then I came here. I brought a ham." He held up a small string bag.

Kora ran to him and flung her arms around his neck. "My dearest! I had no supper at all. Fulk and another mage boxed us Rogue mages in a spell-proof room. I thought Kayfer at least would put out word. . . . They kept us until dawn!" She kissed him. "You sweet, adorable laddie, searching all night!" Then she kissed him again for a goodly time. I grabbed the ham, as it seemed they would be occupied for a while.

In the patch of rear yard by the garden, Aniki set her pot on the bench and scooped Pounce up. "I like bad lads with black hearts," she proclaimed. Pounce struggled madly.

This is undignified! he said. *I am not a toy!*

I watched the pigeons that settled on the wall around the yard. All seventeen carried the ghosts of the murdered diggers. None of them flew to us as we set out breakfast, not even when I put down food for them. When other pigeons approached, the diggers' ghosts uttered a storm of the hard coos that were their angry cries. The other birds flew off, frightened.

Aniki looked at the pigeons. "What's the matter with them?"

"I wouldn't let them in this morning," I told her as I sliced the ham. "Eight more diggers are dead. That's why I wasn't about yesterday—I was trying to learn more about it."

"But I didn't hear a word of hiring!" Aniki stared at me, holding a spoon over the jam jar. "None of us did! Someone would have told me—Fiddlelad, or Reed Katie, or Lady Mae, or Bold Brian." Those were her best friends among Dawull's rushers.

"Whoever hires them for Crookshank does it without word leaking out." I cut ham into slivers and looked for Pounce, but he was gone. Silly cat, I thought. He'd never fled Aniki's or Kora's play before, just sat where they couldn't reach him. I poked the ham and said, "Gods curse Crookshank. I'd say it serves him right to lose Herun, except Tansy is cracking with grief. And Herun's a decent cove. At least he'll be home safe and sound before much longer. We know the Snake delivers once he's paid."

"You think he'll get paid?" Aniki asked.

A chill crept up my back. "Crookshank knows what happens if he don't. The Snake killed Rolond. He must pay." I wasn't believing it, even though I said it.

"Crookshank's had seventeen people killed to keep the secret already, remember?" Aniki's blue eyes were steady. "Seventeen you know of. And the stories I hear of the man? Goddess's tears, Beka, even for the Lower City he's a monster."

Kora and Ersken wandered up hand in hand. They sat and leaned against each other with idiotic smiles. "Let's eat," Kora said.

"With the Lower City run mad, it's good this is the same." Rosto had come. He still wore last night's clothes. Phelan walked behind him, carrying a basket of hot breads. Kora and Aniki made room for Rosto, though I think Kora did it as much to snuggle against

Ersken. Phelan waited until I nodded to him, then sat next to me. What was I going to do, tell him no, after so many mornings over this same cloth? So he's a rusher now, when he was a Dog. I don't have so many friends that I can afford to turn my back on any of them.

I offered the bottle of twilsey to Rosto. "Here, old man."

"I'm not old," he said instantly, though he wasn't as vigorous about it as usual. "And I've mint tea, thanks, you pert gixie. Chilled, no less."

"You're only coming in just now?" Aniki asked them, one eyebrow raised. "I hope you two spent the night in good company."

"Ulsa wanted guards in the taverns," Phelan said. "I'm the new lad, so I got to stay with her." He yawned.

"I was in the cages," Rosto said, grabbing a turnover. "A cove tried to punch me." Aniki raised both eyebrows at him. "I suggested that the Rogue's lost all respect in this city, for Crookshank's raid to happen," Rosto explained. "He punched me, and I punched back. Sadly, some Dogs were eating supper where he landed. They took offense." He brushed at his sleeves. "I thought about telling them I was friends with our Beka, but then I remembered she'd as soon tell them to lock me away until the Stormwings return."

"Pretty bold, to talk that way about the Rogue," said Ersken with a glance at me. I wasn't going to say it. I was comfortable with Rosto, but not that

425

comfortable. "He'll be angry when he hears."

"Someone's got to say sommat." Rosto answered Ersken, but he watched me. I have no idea why. "Someone's got to tell folk that Kayfer Deerborn is a joke and his chiefs are a joke for letting him rule. I don't care if old Crookshank's as mad as a midden hen. He'd never have raided the Court if Kayfer was feared as a Rogue ought to be feared. Am I right or no?"

None of us answered. He was dead right.

"Now Kayfer's giving orders to have all the raiders killed," Phelan said with disgust. He passed me a hot sausage roll. "Not Crookshank, mind. Just the poor cuddies as did his work. Gods help anyone who gets in the way."

Ersken shook his head. "That'll make our jobs so much more interesting."

"Just remember to duck," Kora said. "And I'm making safety charms for you and Beka alike."

We both stared at her.

Kora turned red. "I'm bad at healing, but I do know my way around a basic safety charm!"

"Kora?" Three young men stood in the gate to the yard. One was the flirty cove who'd had Kora reading his fortune last night. "We heard you had breakfast with friends here sometimes." He held up a string bag. "We brought strawberries and cherries." He looked at Rosto. "Just friends, like."

"Kora?" Rosto asked, watching the newcomers.

He wanted her to say if they were all right or not.

"They're good lads," she murmured. "Beka? Ersken?"

"Your word is good enough for me," Ersken told her with a smile. He squeezed her hand. I shrugged.

The cove whose fortune-telling got interrupted looked down. "Is it movin' day?" he asked.

For a moment we were confused. Then we saw what was coming into the yard.

"Mithros, Ruler of All," Ersken whispered.

Pounce trotted past the newcomers, carrying a black kitten with a white bib and mittens in his mouth. The small creature hung in Pounce's grip, ears flat, hindquarters and tail curled up. It seemed as dejected as a body could be at my cat's handling.

The young rushers followed Pounce and took seats, watching him with awe. My cat dropped his captive in Aniki's lap. He then lectured her in meows, saying, *I cannot let you maul me about. Do it to him.*

"Look at this!" Aniki said. She lifted the kitten and checked between his legs. "Oh, poor little man! I suppose Pounce carried you off from a happy home!" She looked him over. "Though your fur is tatty, and you're thin. Is he a street kitten?" she asked Pounce.

Pounce nodded. Aniki gulped, then cuddled the kitten.

Kora grabbed Pounce. "Why her?" she asked, holding Pounce up. "I'm a mage. By rights I should have a cat. You like Aniki more than you like me!"

Pounce wrestled himself free and raced away. Kora watched him go. "Beka, you have a very strange cat, there."

"So I've been told," I said.

"He has purple eyes," one of the new coves said. He looked a bit spooked. "Purple eyes. Is he magic?"

"Aren't all cats?" Ersken asked.

As Rosto talked with our guests, Aniki offered her little man some ham. He shrank from it, then sniffed. She shook the piece. He licked it, then bit. With Aniki offering him meat a piece at a time, he settled down to a meal. We began to eat ours.

Once he was done, the kitten wandered over to eye a bug near Rosto's knee. Rosto offered his fingers for the creature to sniff. The kitten blinked, then swiped at him with his claws. "Ow!"

"That's my laddybuck!" Aniki said. She laughed. "There's his name, Laddybuck. You're a ladies' man, aren't you?" She snatched Laddybuck up before Rosto could take vengeance on the kitten. Though Rosto was sucking blood off the tiny scratch, I didn't believe he would hurt the creature. He seemed to reserve that sort of thing for human beings.

"He's mincemeat if he draws my blood again," Rosto threatened. "I've had a long night. Those cages of yours aren't very safe," he told Ersken and me. "One poor mumper got doused in there. Throat cut."

My gut went tight. "Did they give a name?"

"Gunnar," Kora's former customer said. "My ma's cousin—they brung the word around dawn."

"Our sorrow for your sorrows," Ersken said. He was that sort.

The cove shook his head. "No sorrow. He was a stupid scut, no more brains than you can blow out your nose. Allus sayin' his friend Yates would make 'im a big man in the city." He laughed.

"Pox and murrain," I whispered. No one could question Gunnar now. How had this happened?

Ersken said, "I think Pounce is in a giving mood today."

Here came my cat with a second kitten. This one was a light and dark brown ball with thin black stripes and spots. Pounce dropped it in front of Kora.

All of us were silent. Kora slowly reached down and picked up the ball of fuzz. After a moment of her stroking, it unrolled. It had four paws, two ears, and very green eyes.

Ersken quickly chopped some ham. Kora put the cat down in front of the meat, whispering to it. The ball wobbled and fell on its bottom, then attacked the food. Within moments it had eaten three times what Laddy-buck had. Kora's polite check under its tail told us that this, too, was a boy. Once he was done, her kitten, his belly now much bigger, hooked his way onto her lap and stared about him with those startling eyes. When

Kora petted him again, he produced a very big purr.

That made me smile, at least. We finished our breakfast as the two kittens napped.

I excused myself after a time and went back to my rooms. I could not get my dreams out of my head. Not them, not the sight of the lily pendant against Mistress Noll's sweaty throat. I wanted another look at the map.

It was hot and close under the roof. I had a choice. I could light my lamps and suffocate, or I could open my shutters. In the end it was no choice. I couldn't help but feel I owed the diggers' ghosts and their birds an apology for my rudeness. I opened my shutters wide. Since I faced the morning sun, I had more than enough light by which to see the map and all its markings. When the birds came, at first I didn't even notice. I was too busy studying that map with a new eye. I'd finally remembered why Mistress Noll's necklace seemed familiar.

Back when, a neighbor to one of the Snake's victims had drawn his prize for me: a lily pendant. She'd described it, enamel on gold, but it was her rough sketch in the dirt of her yard that'd stuck in my nob. Graceful that pendant was, the kind of thing any mot would like to have, even me. Even Mistress Noll.

I think Yates Noll gave the lily pendant to his mother. I looked at the map afresh because I was thinking Yates Noll is connected to the Shadow Snake somehow. He works for him or *is* him. If Yates *is* the Snake, it would explain why his friends are afeared of him. Could it be, as Mistress Noll's business grew from Mutt Piddle Lane to the Daymarket, Yates was able to spread out and hunt? On his errands for her, working in her stalls, he'd hear who had aught worth taking. From being in the cages and the court and Outwalls Prison he'd know other hard coves, including some as wouldn't balk at kidnapping a little one for coppers.

"Beka? Are you well?"

I'd left my door open for the air. Kora had come in. She wore a cloth sling fashioned from a scarf around her chest. Her kitten peered out of it, his green eyes fixed on the pigeons on my sill.

"Remember the mot who told us of the lily pendant?" I asked her.

I saw a muscle jump in Kora's cheek. "I remember them all," she said, coming over to me.

"I think I saw the pendant last night, on Mistress Noll's neck. You've met her son Yates?" Kora shook her head. "He's a hard cove. Not clever enough for the Rogue's Court, I'd thought," I said. "But mayhap he's learned sommat in his life, enough to pick off the minnows. Enough mayhap to come by a pretty now and then to give his mama for all the times she's paid his fees and given him work."

"So why stare at the map?" Kora asked. Her kitten was struggling to climb out of the sling.

"I'm trying to see if there's a pattern," I said. "If

the folk whose children were stole lived near Mistress Noll's home or near her shops. He lives and works with her, see. She moved from Mutt Piddle Lane two years back, and she sold goods there, on the Common, in the Nightmarket, and in the Daymarket."

"So he's been everywhere for her," Kora said, putting her kitten on the floor.

"Everywhere," I said, feeling downhearted. "Him, his friends, anyone who came to her and gossiped with her or Gemma. I could as well be singing to the moon for all the good *this* does."

"We'll go out and talk to some more folk," Kora told me. "Today might be the day you learn the golden bit of news, Beka. So put on your dress and we'll go. We've those five folk we wanted to try out toward Charry Orchard, remember."

I remembered her kissing Ersken downstairs. "I, um, thought you and Ersken . . . ," I began, and stopped myself. I didn't want to come right out and say I thought they were going to go straight to her room and stay there till it was time for Ersken to leave for training, but that's what I thought.

Kora had that wicked smile on her face. "There is time for that. He knows how important this is to us both. And I've promised him a treat for later."

I was grateful to her. So many good mots lose sight of the other things in life when they get caught up with a new cove. I think I startled us both when I hugged her as once I'd hugged my sisters and kissed her cheek. "Thank you," I said. "I'm feeling that useless about the Snake."

Kora stared at me. "But you have that map, and the Birdies. You're putting it all together, Beka!" She kissed my cheek. "You really are a terrier."

Far in the distance, thunder rolled. The kitten mewed. We looked and saw him under the window, staring at the pigeons. They stared back at him. I heard the ghost on one of the new birds say, "She looked like a queen in silk."

"A queen in that bad place," a new cove's ghost said.

"She give a flask t' them guards," a mot's ghost whined. "He put it in soup. I saw 'im."

"The soup were good that night." That ghost's voice was cracked and rasping, like he'd breathed smoke, mayhap, or had the lung rot. "It were the best we had."

"It were th' last we had!" one of the new mots' ghosts snapped. "Poisoned, it were! An' that mot brung it in her flask!"

"Black tears on her face." The raspy-voiced cove sounded weary. "She had black tears on her face."

My heart banged against my ribs. Crookshank's houseguest, Vrinday Kayu, the mage who'd acted as Tansy's maid in the Nightmarket—she had tattoos of black teardrops on her face.

I could be wrong. Others used black drop tattoos, often to show they had taken a life. But I would tell my Dogs of this tonight. I would bet a month's wage that Kayu was the poisoner.

The kitten leaped. The pigeons took off. I looked at the small fuzzball and sighed. He was too tiny even to jump as high as my windowsill. Still, the birds had fled and were not returning.

Before I go to bed.

We came back from our talks about two, as a true summer storm crashed overhead. In the oven of my rooms I changed into my Dog's gear. At least it would be cooler by the time I came off watch. Meanwhile, I had time yet before training. I wanted to see how Tansy did.

Outside, lightning flashed, Mithros wielding his sword against the monsters of Chaos. Thunder roared as they screamed their pain over their wounds. Rain came down in buckets, racketing on my wide straw hat. Pounce kept to the side of the buildings, staying dry under the eaves. The streets were empty. Everyone was taking shelter until the downpour slacked.

I went to the kitchen entrance at Crookshank's, not wishing to be turned away at the front door. The maid gawped for a moment, then turned and said, "Mistress Annis, it's Beka Cooper!" She nearabout dragged me into the house by the arm. "We never had a chance to thank yez fer savin' us last night, me'n Zada'n Cook'n Otto—"

"Enough." Annis herself was in the kitchen, which smoothed my way. "We're all in debt to Beka and her partners." She tried to smile, but her mouth was shaky.

"Mistress Annis, I hope the Goddess brings Herun home safe," I told her. "And soon." By the light of day I could see the old smoke streaks on the ceiling, leading from the front of the house.

"My thanks, Beka," Annis said. "D'you want to see Tansy? I'll need to sneak you up the back stair. Father Ammon isna . . . well." I think she meant he was cracked, plain and true.

"He seemed upset at the Court of the Rogue last night," I told her, as meek as a priest's mouse. Behind me I heard the cook choke.

"This way," Annis said. She led to the servants' stair and up. "Will you tell Goodwin and Tunstall I'm grateful for what they done, and you, yester e'en? I'm not even askin' how the three of you came to be here."

I was glad her back was to me, since I think I flinched. I'd wondered if anyone in this house had noticed and questioned what had brought us there so conveniently. To distract her I said, "A Birdie tells me Gunnar Espeksra is dead."

She looked at me. I'd shocked her. The confusion was plain on her face in the lamplight. "Dead? Was he in a fight?"

"No, mistress," I said. "He was killed in the cages."

She walked onto the third floor landing and waited for me. "In the cages? Goddess's tears. Oh—oh, you think I paid to have it done." Annis shook her head. "Beka, I was too milled about to buy the murder of anybody." Her lips trembled. "I just want my boy home and safe."

"The Goddess willing, Mistress Annis," I said. The dreadful idea that Crookshank won't pay for Herun clung to my mind. I was curst if I'd say it to her, though.

Mistress Annis led me to Tansy's room and opened the door. "Tansy, Beka's here, to see how you do." She let me go in, then closed the door, leaving Tansy and me to ourselves.

Tansy stood by the window. The shutters were wide, giving her a view of the garden and the rain. Three pigeons pecked at corn on the broad sill. I heard the ghosts whisper, but softly: old ghosts, almost faded clean away.

"Ever since that night," Tansy said, "it don't seem right to watch them without so much as a greeting and a bit of food. They might carry some other child."

I put my hat on the floor to drip and came over to listen to the ghosts. "No. This one?" I pointed to one that was mostly gray. "This mumper here carries a mot as was killed by her man for cheating on him." The black pigeon had but one toe to each foot.

"Poor thing," said Tansy, tears filling her eyes.

"Beka, how can you bear it?" Tansy asked. "Knowing their stories?"

"I've been hearing them awhile," I said. "I'm accustomed."

Tansy laughed a little. "So matter of fact. You've always been that way."

"You need me to balance you," I reminded her. "If you break your heart over each one of them, you'll go all cracknobbed."

Tansy smiled. "Never mind me, Beka. I cry over wilted flowers, more than I ever did when we was small. My son is dead, Herun's gone. Father Ammon thinks the Rogue took him, you know. I believe I will turn into tears. I thought I would be safe." She rubbed her arms. "I told myself there'd be no danger when I was free of Mutt Piddle Lane."

Only Tansy would think sommat so silly. Even as little gixies we'd heard of robberies and murders in districts as fine as Highfields and Unicorn, let alone here. "There's danger everywhere," I replied. I wished I knew what I could do for her. Telling her Gunnar was dead wouldn't help. It would only let her know the Dogs couldn't keep their captives safe.

"I'm just not good company now, Beka," whispered Tansy.

I hugged her. "I only came to see how you did after last night. I no more expected to see you dancing than I expected to fly." Another pigeon came in, one with no rider. "Don't work yourself up over this one, girl. He carries no ghost at all." I was always glad when that happened. I thought the birds deserved rest. Unless they didn't see it as rest, as I did on my day off, but boredom, with naught to occupy them. "Don't forget the little one that's coming," I told her. "I pray the gods for Herun's safe return."

I let myself out. I did it on the quiet, not wanting to break the silence in that tomb of a house.

Crookshank and the woman he spoke to in the hall did not hear me. I stopped cold when I saw them. She was Vrinday Kayu, the Carthaki who was with Tansy the night she talked to Rolond's ghost. Then, she'd dressed like a maidservant. Now she wore a yellow cotton tunic over white cotton, the cloth finer than Annis's or Tansy's dresses. Kayu's head veil was silk. She wore perfume that smelled of something foreign, like temple incense. Her eyes, when they flicked to me, were lined in black paint.

And there were those black teardrops tattooed at the outside corner of each eye, and one at the center of her chin. I was sure of it. Kayu had brought the poison for the diggers.

Cold sweat covered my skin. I wanted to put the hobbles on her then and there. Writing this, my hand shakes. She is a murderer. Only I cannot prove it. I have but the word of ghosts. A mage might get the truth, if she did not spell herself to die first. A mage might get the truth from Crookshank. But he has noble friends who will not let us arrest him without good cause.

She is a poisoner. I will see her in a cage. I will see her on Execution Hill if I can.

Crookshank turned. "You—Dog." His voice was hoarse. I suppose it was from all the screaming he did at the Court of the Rogue. "What are you doing in my house?"

I tucked my hat under my arm and stood with my feet braced. "I'm Tansy's friend."

"My granddaughter-in-law doesn't have Dogs for friends." He waved off Kayu. She scuttled down the stairs.

Crookshank advanced on me. He still had not shaved, though he had changed his clothes from last night. "What good are you, eh?" He trembled from head to toe. "The Rogue steals Herun from under your stupid noses! When I am forced to bribe amateurs to seek him out, the Rogue laughs up his sleeve and smuggles him away. Again, under your very noses! What good are you cuddies? Why are we taxed to pay for you? Why are we taxed again for your poxy Happy Bags?"

Heat built up behind my eyes. How dare this murdering old scut speak so of Dogs? Of them that chase the Rats from his storerooms so he can get fat on his gains? Though he is skeleton thin now. When I chanced a look at his face, I saw the skin hanging in folds on the sides—he used to have more flesh under it.

His voice got soft. "Unless you are working for Kayfer. I could afford you, I suppose. What is the gold I've paid already compared to the fortune I will have? You Dogs are always sniffing after coin. It need not even be much. I could have you for coppers."

Our trainers taught us to hit Rats only when there is aught to be gained from it. Over and over they had said it, shouted it, yelled it. That order was the one thing that kept me from slapping Crookshank. I clenched my hand on my hat so tight I crushed the straw brim.

"Are you in this with Kayfer?" Crookshank reached for me. "Where is Herun? I will pay you well. More gold than you could dream of. I will buy you a new life in, in Tusaine, or Maren, or Barzun."

I have a temper. It is not my friends' temper, exploding in flames. Mine is ice that numbs me all over. I know it is bad when I cannot feel my face. I am told my eyes look like death at such times. Crookshank gulped.

"I wouldn't take every fire opal you've ripped from the earth of this city, you bloody handed scut," I told him. He flinched when I said "fire opal." He thought a nothing like me would never know his precious secret. "Any gift from your hand is bought with death. I will see you tried for your crimes."

He blinked fast, his mouth a-tremble. Then he said, "I will have you killed."

That did it. He threatened me, with no regard for my uniform. I told him, "Then me and the seventeen diggers you've slaughtered will haunt you. You'll see us in every bit of shiny wood and glass, every puddle, every mirror, understand? They're here, followin' me about the city. I'll make curst sure we follow you. And when you dance at the rope's end, we'll be waitin' at the gates of the Peaceful Realms. There'll be no peace for a murderin' pig like you." I shoved him. "Kill me. You'll never sleep a night through again!"

He went to backhand me across the face. I grabbed his wrist and twisted. I might have broken it, but a door behind us opened.

"Grandfather?" I heard Tansy ask.

I dropped Crookshank's arm.

"Go to your room!" Crookshank ordered.

"You're fighting with Beka."

"Go to your room!"

"Shall I tell her?" I asked, keeping my voice low. I tried to talk educated again, though I was still in a fury. "About you rippin'—ripping seventeen people from their loved ones to make your fat purse fatter?"

He slapped me. I didn't try to stop him this time. I wasn't sure I would not break his arm. I had to be better than him.

"No! She's my friend!" Tansy ran up to us.

I smiled at him. From the way he looked at me, I'd not made him feel better. I didn't mean him to. "I let you have that blow. I won't give you another," I said.

Crookshank cursed me and strode down the hall.

I looked at Tansy. "I'm off. I'll see you another time." I knew she was scared, but I had no time to ease her mind. I needed to catch up with the old bastard. I had one more thing to say, for Tansy's sake and Herun's. I caught up to him on the stairs near the second floor.

"Crookshank."

He glared up at me. "You take the servants' stair, and you never call me by that name!"

I will never take the servants' stair in that house again. "I could hobble you now for striking me. You know it, and I know it, you worthless pustule. I'll let it go. Others will put you in the cages for bigger things."

"You doxie." He put his hand on his belt knife.

He'd let me get too close. I gripped him so he could not draw the knife. "Stop it, afore I use my baton to make you listen," I said. How did he get so rich if he was so stupid? "For Tansy's sake, hear me. For your grandchild's sake. Your greed killed Rolond. It'll kill Herun if you don't mind me."

His eyes bulged. "I'll see you raped and your body left in a midden, your throat cut in two."

I struggled to move my mouth. I'd gone numb with rage again. Never have I been spoken to in so filthy a way. The worst of Mama's men had just knocked me aside. I'll never forget his words, never, but I could not let him stop me from speaking. I had to remember Tansy, Tansy and her unborn child.

"Pay the poxy ransom. Kayfer isn't the Shadow Snake. There's a real Shadow Snake. He's been working the Lower City for three years. He killed Rolond because you were too sarden mean to pay. He'll kill Herun. He's mad. You can't play with madmen."

Crookshank fought my grip on his hand. "The Shadow Snake is a children's tale. Kayfer uses him to frighten jinglenobs like you."

"He's real. Ask anyone in the street."

Crookshank didn't mean to pay. He thought Kayfer would make a deal before he'd risk a second raid like last night's. Herun had six days to live if the Snake followed his schedule. If his grandfather thought he could bluff a second time.

I saw naught but hate in Crookshank's eyes. I could've argued more, but what could I say? I let him go. He ran down the stairs and into a ground floor room.

I cursed him softly and left the house. Mayhap he would think better of what I had said once he'd cooled down. I prayed he would, for Tansy's sake.

I began to shake as my cold temper thawed. I'd come close to punching the second most powerful cove in the Lower City. I'd have to tell my Dogs. Please,

Goddess, may they understand. Besides praying for Tansy and Herun, I need to pray Crookshank won't take his revenge on Goodwin and Tunstall as well as on me.

Goodwin snagged my arm as soon as my training class arrived for muster. She towed me over to a corner. "I've word from the pigeons, the new ones," I told her in a whisper as we walked. "The poison they had came from the mage that was pretending to be Tansy Lofts' maid, Vrinday Kayu. They didn't know her name, but they knew the teardrop tattoos."

Goodwin nodded. "Now here's a tidbit for you. A cage Dog was killed before dawn this morning, in front of his house," she told me as we crossed the floor. "Knifed in the kidneys. We think he's the one who killed Gunnar Espeksra in his cage last night." She gave me a quick look. "You already heard about Gunnar, didn't you? I should have guessed. So not only did we lose our Rat, we lost the cur Dog that killed him. And nobody knows who paid him to do it."

I thought curses to myself as we joined a knot of Dogs waiting for us in the corner. Tunstall was there, along with Jewel, Yoav, Otterkin, and a fistful of the best Dogs of the Evening Watch.

"Right," Otterkin said. "That Jens you're looking for, the one you think guards the opal diggers? A cove of that name hires on at the slave markets oftentimes.

He gets work through Inman Poundridge. And we all know Poundridge will work for them as work for Crookshank, on the side, like."

"We caged one of Poundridge's helpers five months back," Jewel said. "Dream rose smuggling. We could never pin it to Poundridge, never mind Crookshank himself."

"How many folk does Poundridge hire out of the slave markets?" one of the others asked.

"'Bout fifteen regular," Jewel replied. "They've been scarce in sight of late."

"It's stupid to have only three guards on eight or nine diggers all the time," Tunstall said quietly. "You'd need folk you trust. Folk you used before. And you'd use them in shifts."

"There's that mage mark, the one they put on the guards," Goodwin pointed out. "They'd have showed the guards it works. They'd have killed someone in front of them."

"Kayu. The mage in Crookshank's house," I said, not thinking. They all stared at me.

One of the Dogs said, "Puppies don't yap 'less they're smacked."

"No, let Cooper talk." That was Jewel, not one of my Dogs, though they nodded. "Cooper's one smart Puppy."

"Go on, Cooper," Goodwin said, giving me a sharp elbow. "Finish what you started."

I put my hand in my pocket and held my fire opal chunk as I made myself look at these veteran Dogs. "It's that woman my Dogs think is a mage, Vrinday Kayu. I was at Crookshank's today. Tansy Lofts, his granddaughter-in-law—she's my friend. I saw her, Kayu, talking with Crookshank. They saw me, too. Anyway, I think her room is on the same floor as Tansy's. She's not in the attics like a maid. And she doesn't dress like one."

Goodwin said, smooth as glass, "One of Cooper's Birdies told her Kayu maybe did for these diggers. Eight more are dead, right, Cooper?"

I nodded.

None of them said a word at first. I began to feel like a great ducknob. I could hear them shift on their feet. Finally Goodwin spoke. "If we put in for permissions to sit on the mage, on Poundridge, and on Jens when he checks in with Poundridge, would you folk be good for it?"

Yoav looked discomfited. "Mages . . . and one Crookshank hires? I like my skin stuck to my flesh, where it's supposed to be."

Jewel jabbed her with an elbow. Was that where Goodwin learned it? Jewel was her senior partner when she'd been a Puppy. "Shut up, Yoav." He looked at us. "What about Fulk?"

"He'll run straight to Crookshank," Tunstall said, his voice firm. "If he's alive, after helping with that raid on the Court of the Rogue last night. Remember our Birdie, the gem mage Berryman?"

One of them whistled. "He's a serious mage, for all he's a looby."

"Berryman will help if it gets ugly," Tunstall said. "If we just watch Kayu, how will she even know we're there? We keep this to Evening Watch—we can't trust Day Watch or Night Watch. We Dog Kayu. If she makes a foul move, we get Berryman. But we keep an eye on her, on Poundridge, then on Jens. We know the mage marks kill them if they talk. Maybe even if they're hobbled. So we can't touch any of our Rats until we know where they go and we're ready to cage the whole foul nest."

Jewel nodded. "We're in. Ain't we, Yoav?"

Yoav grumbled. "'Specially you keep me away from that mage. I'm in."

The others voted to do it. I think Tunstall and Goodwin knew they would when they gathered them together. These were hard Dogs, them that took Lower City duty serious. I was honored to be asked to stand with them.

I followed Goodwin and Tunstall over to the Sergeant's desk. "Ahuda, we need papers," Goodwin whispered. All eyes were on us.

Ahuda scowled at her. "How many of you?"

"Nine. Two Rats to watch right off, so two sets of papers," Goodwin said.

"Four pairs off patrol?" Ahuda demanded. "For how long?"

Goodwin just looked at her.

Ahuda cursed. "You couldn't have picked a less crazy time? Don't answer that. Muster up!" she yelled. "And clear the room! Dogs only!"

All our onlookers left, with plenty of whining. We Dogs fell into our ranks.

When the doors were closed and bolted and even the cage Dogs had gone, the room got quiet. "We're in the cracked season, children," Ahuda told us. "Master Fulk has been naughty. He's being sought by the royal mages. Stay clear of him. If he has sense, he's on a ship for Carthak right now."

She took a deep breath. "Kayfer Deerborn has sworn a complaint against Master Ammon Lofts. He says Master Lofts *invaded* the Court of the Rogue. Apparently it's a meeting hall for craftsmen as live between Festive and Riverfront nowadays, which came as a great surprise to me—" She didn't even try to speak over the bellow of laughter from the Dogs. She simply waited it out. She looked at a paper on her desk. "Master Crookshank invaded the craftsmen's meeting hall with a gang of toughs recruited from off-duty soldiers." She tapped the paper. "That's what it says. They wrecked the hall, including Kayfer's personal quarters, stealing various items and destroying furniture. It was all in the name of finding Master Herun Lofts, who has been missing since last night. Day Watch is investigating that, by the by. Crookshank says a note came to the Lofts house from someone claiming to be the Shadow Snake, demanding ransom for Herun. The ransom is to be delivered a week from the day Herun was taken. Crookshank says Kayfer had the lad stolen. Not unreasonable. That's why Crookshank and some, *he* says, 'friends' exercised 'cityman's privilege' to search the Court of the Rogue."

"Cove wants to die," someone called.

"Plenty of people will." My lord Gershom walked out of the Watch Commander's office, the Watch Commander at his back. My lord went over to stand beside Ahuda's desk. "Three of the off-duty soldiers that Crookshank hired were found in the river this mornin'. They had rawhide strings with a gold noble on them tied around their necks—Kayfer's way of sayin' this is what takin' Crookshank's gold gets you. Get out on the streets, all of you. Show your faces to the city. Put a stop to this. If the Rogue wants to kill anyone, let him kill Crookshank, and good riddance. But both of these men had best learn it's not their city, but ours."

We answered him with growls.

He nodded to us and left the kennel. The Watch Commander disappeared into his office again.

"You heard my lord," Ahuda said. "In the meantime, Birch and Vinehall, here is Kayfer Deerborn's complaint against Crookshank. You two take four of the cage Dogs and execute it on him." She held up a parchment laden with seals. Grinning, Birch went to get it from her, Vinehall to call four cage Dogs. Crookshank would be out of the cages soon after he'd been tucked into one, but it was still worth it to tweak his tail.

"Enough lollygagging," Ahuda snapped. "Dismissed." Goodwin went to the Sergeant's desk as those of us who wanted to keep watch on Kayu and Jens waited. Ahuda sighed. "Were you listening? My lord wants you on the street, not working some special rig."

"We've got something, Ahuda," Goodwin said. "Seventeen dead, and more to come. Our information's good. We've been chasing our tails. Now we have two scents, but they're tricky. One hops between jobs, the other's a mage. Don't make me call in your debts to me, gixie."

"You heard my lord," Ahuda told her and us, her eyes glittering. "And you have debts to me, too, Clary. Seventeen dead? Why haven't I heard about this?"

"Because only the dead are talking, Ahuda," Tunstall told her. "You know Cooper can hear them." Ahuda glanced at me. I stiffened. How many people knew? And why didn't I know they knew?

"I can't turn eight—nine—Dogs loose from patrol when times are like this," Ahuda said. "You three, and you three alone. If you want to start tonight, go—I'll have the papers for you at muster tomorrow."

"Just one pair and a Puppy?" I couldn't tell who of us said it.

"Ahuda—" Jewel began.

"That's my last word."

They could tell she meant it. We all turned away. The others went outside. When we left the kennel, they were waiting.

"We talked," Jewel said. "Who are you three watching?"

Goodwin and Tunstall traded looks. "Poundridge," Goodwin said. "He's got Jens reporting to him. Jens will take us back to the diggers. Right now, they're looking to hire more. Once they have new folk, the mage will visit *them,* not the other way around."

Jewel nodded. "We agree. We're all going to work it out, try to keep a watch on Crookshank's and on that mage. Unofficial-like." He winked at us. "Better than nothing."

Goodwin walked on out into the street. I think Ahuda telling her only the three of us could go had hit her hard. Tunstall clapped Jewel and a couple of the others on the shoulder in thanks. I followed him on the way after Goodwin. It made sense. Jens was a guard. Sooner or later he'd go to his master, Poundridge, for his pay. We could follow him back to those he watched over.

Off we went to the Market of Sorrows. On the way Tunstall told me about Poundridge. From four until midnight, give or take, he supervised guards from a booth set between the pens and the market stage. From there he greeted folk who came to see the slaves waiting to be sold and bossed the guards. That made it easy for them that worked for him in other parts of the city to report to him for their pay or to get more work. And it made him easy for us to watch. An alley down and across the street gave us a place where we could see him do business without him seeing us.

We'd been there long enough for me to get bored when Goodwin asked, "Cooper, what happened when you visited your friend Tansy? You looked skittish, talking about it."

"Not skittish. Angry. For you," Tunstall said.

I told them, keeping my voice low. When I was done, Pounce laid a dead mouse on my boot for some reason. "No, thank you," I said. "You can keep it."

"I'm not sure you should have let on you knew about the opals. Not when he's trying to keep them secret from the world," Goodwin whispered.

"I lost my head," I said. In the cool summer night, with my temper in my grip, I felt shamed. "I'm afeared he won't pay up and the Snake will kill Herun."

"Even Crookshank's not that mad," Goodwin replied, but she didn't sound like she believed it.

"Madder than a snakebit bull," Tunstall said. Then he gave the softest of whistles. "Who have we here?"

A party of eight nobles had come on horseback,

with servants to help them. They drew up before Poundridge's booth. Most of the nobles dismounted.

A woman said loudly, "Are you *joking*? Is this the 'diversion' you spoke of?" We all knew that lady's deep voice well.

Someone laughed. A man said, "My dear Sabine, you aren't a dreary reformist, demanding that we do away with slavery, are you? If it was good enough for our grandfathers—"

"I'm not your dear anything, you louse! Slavery breeds vice—gods curse it, why do I even talk to you!" A horse turned out of the crowd. Lady Sabine looked very different in a dress. She didn't look like the friend who'd fought and eaten with us wearing breeches. She looked like a great lady.

"Stop gawping, Cooper," Goodwin said. "She's the nobility. They're bad for you."

"I know I overreach myself," Tunstall said. He scratched Pounce, seemingly not vexed a bit. "Pretending it's Cooper you give advice to doesn't fool Cooper and it doesn't fool me. I wish Sabine wasn't noble."

Goodwin rubbed her neck. "So do I, Mattes. But she is."

Thinking to stop a budding quarrel, I said quickly, "Mistress Noll wears a necklace the Shadow Snake took for ransom. The lily pendant. I think maybe Yates is the Snake."

They didn't answer for a time. Tunstall finally said,

"A crew of diggers weighs more than one kidnap victim, Cooper. We'll have Ahuda put Yates Noll on the watch list, but we need to keep on the diggers before Crookshank hires—and douses—more of them. You know he will as well as we do."

Tunstall's reasonable voice was like a hammer in the shadows. I knew he was right, but I had the taste of the Shadow Snake like blood in my mouth.

And yet there were the ghosts, seventeen of them. How many more would come in the morning? Would it be poison again, or swords like the first time?

It was a long, wearisome watch. The nobles left. Mumpers swarmed around their horses, whining for coins and grabbing at their stirrups. At one noble's order, a servant threw a handful of coppers into the street. The mumpers scrambled for them as the nobles rode off. My heart burned to see mumpers treated like pigs in the street, but I had to say it was a good way to clear the road.

Suppertime came. Goodwin and I left through the alley's back exit to fetch some food. While we waited for the eating house to pack what we'd bought, Goodwin showed me the marks Tunstall would place on buildings. That way, if Poundridge left his booth, Tunstall could follow him, and we'd follow Tunstall. So far, though, all Poundridge had done was take a nap and entertain a doxie.

Tunstall was still there when we returned. Some

merchants came to look at slaves next. It was common entertainment for them that had coin to bribe the guards. More mumpers flocked in to wheedle this lot. Instead of giving a servant coins to throw, these folk either rode straight at the beggars or kicked them out of the way. Three ladies gave coins to the younger mumpers and got scolded by their men for softheartedness.

That was the excitement for the rest of the watch. Pounce gave up and left. He still hadn't come back when we went to the kennel to muster out.

I feel as useless as I have ever done.

Saturday, May 9, 246

Writ at three in the afternoon, in the kitchen garden. More younger folk of the Court of the Rogue came to have a word with Rosto over breakfast. By "younger" I mean mots and coves from our age into their early thirties. Most brought food. Pounce, Laddybuck, and the kitten that Kora has named Fuzzball ate well. The pigeons did, too, though the seventeen ghost diggers are standoffish around others. Slapper perched on my head and pecked at me until he fell off. Then he left me alone. The thieves who saw it left me be, too. Mayhap they thought me cracked for talking to a pigeon like he knew what I said.

Ersken and I drew back from Rosto's guests. Them as waited for a word with him could talk with Aniki or Kora if they wished. They were here on Rogue business, even if it wasn't Kayfer's. Ersken finally whispered he'd see me in training and took off. Kora noticed and made sure to kiss him goodbye. Rosto waved to him. I was grateful for that. These folk would notice that Rosto was friendly to Ersken, and they would be friendly to him in their turn.

I waited till Aniki was free, then asked her, "You'll clean up? I've things to do."

She grinned. "Go seek your Snake, Beka," she said. "I'll handle this. And when you're ready to kill the

Snake? I'll help cut off its head." She patted her dagger hilt.

I raised my brows at her. "I won't kill it unless I must," I told her. "The Snake'll stand his trial."

Aniki's friend Reed Katie heard me. "What if he's got a patron?" she asked in her sweet voice. "So many of them as gets away with everythin' do. What if the Snake's got a patron as buys 'im out of the Magistrate's Court, Beka?"

"Then I'll Dog him, and I'll catch him, and I'll cage him again," I said. "And again, and again, and again, until his patron tires of him and the Snake tires of me."

"Or until he kills you," someone else said.

"Nobody's killing Beka," Rosto told them, his eyes turned to black stone.

"Nobody," Phelan said with a nod.

"Nobody," Aniki and Kora added.

"If you folk don't mind, I can protect myself." I tried to say it loud. I felt a blush creep over my cheeks. "I've no mind to be doused by any Rat nor any Snake."

"It's true." Bold Brian toasted me with a flask of barley water. "You really are a terrier, ain't you, Cooper? Get your teeth in and never let go."

I can't say I ran, because I didn't. I did shake my head and walk out of the yard fast. Didn't these loobies know they might be the next Rats I got my teeth into? Were I in their shoes, I might admire the Dog with my prison shackles in her teeth a bit less.

"Psst! Beka!" My landlady hung from her front window, waving to me with both arms. She gestured madly for me to come into the house. I went, my heart thumping. Had Pounce's mysterious ways in and out admitted less-welcome guests, like four-legged rats? Did she object to our crooked tenants? Did she want me to move so she might have room for another rogue? I'd thought she'd rented to me for the safety of having a Dog in her house, but there was safety in having rogues and mages, too.

She grabbed my hands when I came to her door in the inner hall. "A Birdie told me ye're talkin' with them as ran afoul of the Shadow Snake." She pulled me into her rooms. "Ye've been seekin' all over the Lower City. Kora, Aniki, even Rosto—they've been askin' questions for ye." She didn't look angered or fearful. Curious, more like.

"Someone's got to put a stop to it, mistress," I said. "My Dogs, Goodwin and Tunstall, are on it."

She gave me a sly look. "They're fine Dogs, but the one I *know* that's seekin' is you. And the mot as asked to talk with ye learned you was doin' it, Beka. I never even heard the Snake got her little one, never! She told us all it was slave stealers that sold 'im to the Yamanis, swore it was. O' course we believed her."

I rubbed the back of my neck. "Mistress, if we might get past the riddles?"

"My brother-in-law's sister, Amaya Painter," my landlady told me. "She's a mage. Three years gone her little boy, done vanished. Now she heard of ye askin' about the Shadow Snake. She asked if ye'd come see her." The address she gave was up by Patten District. "Not that she allus lived there. She bought that place not long after the boy was took," my landlady said. "She used to live just two blocks up this lane. Done well, she has. Mayhap the gods made it up to her for losin' her only child."

If her little one was took that long ago, she'd be one of the first Snake victims. She'd be worth seeing. I went up to my rooms to change into a dress. To my startlement, Ersken sat on the landing by my door.

He gave me his shyest smile. "Tell me you're going to talk to people who've seen the Snake, and I can come with you," he said. "I remembered on my way home that if I show my face, my sisters will make me run errands with them. It wouldn't be so bad, but of late they've arranged it so we 'accidentally' run into their friends who aren't spoken for."

I grinned as I took out my key. "You could tell them you *are* spoke for," I said.

"And I'd have to explain about Kora. Then they'll wail and tell Mama and Papa—Beka, I'd sooner walk the Cesspool naked. In the dark. Just let me come, so I can tell them I was off seeking, will you?"

Of course I said yes. Ersken and Aniki had both

459

gone to speak with the Snake witnesses on days when Kora couldn't. Mots in general liked Ersken. Today he'd be more useful still. I didn't like to have Kora along when I talked to other mages. There was no telling how mages would get on with one another. They were like cats that way.

When Ersken, Pounce, and I saw Mistress Painter's house in Patten District, I thought my landlady had a point about the gods making it up to the mage for her child being took. The house was half stone, half timber. Magical signs were writ about the windows and set in the flagstone path.

"The Snake must've been mad, to go after a real mage," Ersken said as I rapped on the door.

"You'd think so," I said. My cat sniffed at a symbol painted on the doorstep. "Pounce, leave that be."

The door opened as sparks and a puff of nasty smoke shot from the symbol.

Pounce looked at the woman who'd opened the door and yowled. *Awful work.*

The woman looked at him, her face thoughtful. Finally she inspected Ersken, then me. "Do you know who this creature is?"

"I'd prefer not to think on it much," I said. "It complicates things. Mistress Painter? You asked for me. I'm Beka Cooper."

Mistress Painter turned her eyes to Ersken, narrowing them.   .

"This is Ersken Westover. He's been plenty of help to me in this," I said.

She stood aside, holding the door open for us. "Come inside. Wipe your feet."

Ersken wiped his boots eagerly. "Do *you* know what the cat is?"

Mistress Painter looked at me, then at Pounce. "Only that he dwells in the Divine Realms," she told Ersken. "They glow, to them with the power to see it. But he could be anything from there. What he does here . . ."

She seemed to want an answer. "He eats a fair amount of fish," I told her. "And he gives kittens to his friends. Mistress Painter, our day is short, what with training and the Rogue being in a bad mood and all. I thought you wanted speech with me for the sake of the child you lost?"

That seemed to wake her up. She remembered we had not come to buy charms from her. She dropped into a chair. She could afford a sitting room decorated with statues, herb wreaths, and hangings. There was a corner shrine to the god Apetekus, Guardian of Slaves. The braided flower garlands were dried up, the candles unlit. If she had given offerings to the god, it was some time ago.

"My friend's grumpy," Ersken said to Mistress Painter, his eyes kind. "Her Dogs are on another case just as frustrating as this. And the Rogue's angry with

Crookshank. You'll have heard about the murdered guards and soldiers." He talked to her as he would to someone official, someone who read the daily reports and knew the city news. She softened, listening to him. It's his boy's face and them blue eyes. He gives off respect like a pretty smell, too. "Beka lives in the Lower City, so it upsets her more than most. That's why she couldn't let the Shadow Snake stories alone."

Mistress Painter looked at me. "I heard. What makes you think you can catch him?"

"Because my Dogs are Tunstall and Goodwin, and I report all I do to them." It was my turn to build on what Ersken had started with her. "I'm doing the questioning for now. I tell them all I've gathered. When they know who we're after, we'll hobble him and his fellow Rats. And Tansy Lofts is my friend. I knew her boy, Rolond." I held up a hand. I didn't want to hear what she was about to say about Crookshank. "I don't care about her grandfather-in-law," I said. "Tansy didn't ask to have Rolond killed no more than you asked to have your lad took."

The mage reached into her tunic for a leather packet. She drew signs on it with her finger, releasing spells, I supposed.

Pounce sneezed. Mistress Painter glared as if he'd made a scornful remark. "They're good enough for the Lower City, Master Immortal or whatever you are."

"My sweetheart says he's mayhap a constellation," Ersken said, being helpful.

Mistress Painter started to make a magical sign on her chest, then stopped. "Interesting," she said. Then she coughed and opened the packet. With fingers that shook, she took out a sheet of parchment and gave it over to me.

By now I know one of the Snake's notes as well as I know my own name. There were differences in this one. There was a clumsy head on the snake. The curves were more round, not so long. The writing was shaky, as if him that did it was scared.

"When was this?" I asked Mistress Painter.

"Firefall," she said. It was the mage name for the first of February, a powerful night for certain kinds of spells. I had a feeling Mistress Painter hadn't the power even to draw the circles that began such spells. "Firefall, 243."

I looked at Ersken. He blinked. It was the earliest Snake stealing we'd heard of. Could it be the first?

"You lived here?" I asked, though I knew she hadn't.

Mistress Painter shook her head. "Westberk Street, just off Stuvek," she said. "A smaller house." Her lips quivered. "Happier . . . Calum was the most independent wee lad. He'd be out of our loft before my spells let me know, out the door before the bells could ring. He near drove my man and me crazy." Remembering, she lost the polished talk she'd picked up here in Patten District. "Vonti, my husband, he doted on Calum. Always said we should have more little ones, when I could hardly keep an eye on the baby and sell my potions and charms. Vonti said he made enough for us. When Calum got taken, Vonti was in the streets for hours, calling and calling. He'd be in the taverns, the markets, bringing back word of this spell and that I could try." She looked down. Tears dropped in her lap.

"But you got the note," I said when the tears had stopped. I looked at it and read what the Snake asked for. "You had a— What's this it says? A ruby pen-du-lum?" It was a word I had read before but never had to say aloud, the name for some mage tool that hung from a chain.

The mot wiped her eyes without looking up. "I thought it was a joke." She said it like we'd accused her of something. "The Shadow Snake? I'd told Calum t' mind hisself or the Snake would have him! Eat his beets and stay in the fence or the Snake would come! It was a joke, I was sure of it, a cruel joke. The whole neighborhood knew I'd a ruby pendulum. I'd bragged of it like a fool, bragged of its powers."

"You didn't pay the Snake," Ersken said to her gently. "Any woman would think the same."

"And your man?" I asked. I gave no sympathy.

Ersken would do that for us both. I'd learn sommat in the way she acted when I broke through her gratitude to him. I saw something of importance now in the way she drew back from me. "You didn't tell him." I told her, I didn't ask her.

"I said, I thought it was a cruel joke." She looked away from me again. "That anyone might send a note like that was hard. I never even showed it to Vonti. Before, that note would have torn his heart. After—after Calum didn't come home, it tore mine." She glared at me. "I cursed them that took my child."

"Did it work?" I asked, not letting her glare frighten me. For one thing, Pounce sat on my feet. It was good to have Pounce nearby when I vexed a mage. For another, she had not found her little boy, for all the spells she had tried.

"I need sommat of the one I cursed, and I had naught," she told me. "Naught but this note, and it's useless. I'd already tried spells on it. Spells to find Calum, to find his kidnappers, to find even where he'd been. Clever bastards took the charms I'd put on Calum to bring me to him, and pitched them in a fountain. Without them, my skills were no good." Her head hung loose, like her neck couldn't hold it up. "I'm fair enough with healing, desire. Things of the body. Folk think I can see a bit, but it's all in knowing the neighborhood and the ways of them that live here. I made them think I was better than I am."

I looked at Apetekus's shrine. "You never got him back?"

Mistress Painter sighed. "Never. I lied. I told folk he'd been taken by slavers, and they sold him to the Yamani Islands. He was a page in the emperor's palace, wearing silk all day. I told them—I told Vonti—I could see him, every day. I lied so well that Vonti left to go there. To buy our son back. That was two years gone, and he's not returned. His ship went down with all hands off the coast of Scanra."

"Our sorrow for yours," Ersken whispered. "If only you'd gone to the Dogs, Mistress Painter. If you'd taken his sheets and blankets, the scent hounds might have picked something up."

She stared at him. "Are you cracked? What had his bedding to do with it?"

"They took him from bed, right?" Ersken asked it slow, as if he let the words drip through her brain. "Like the others."

"Calum was took in the Nightmarket," Mistress Painter said. From her look, she thought we were mad. "Vonti was done with his work for the week, so we thought we'd have a sweet, wander about, see the sights. I'd a little extra from delivering a babe, so we bought cinnamon for our porridge and honey fritters for that night. We were talkin', and . . . and . . ." She fell silent, her eyes on her lap. She'd spoken of it so many times she could no longer cry.

My ears buzzed. "You couldn't see him. You called for him and he didn't call back," I said. Mistress Painter nodded. I went on, "You were in Spicers' Row. And everyone from the neighborhood knew you worked magic with a genuine ruby pendulum."

"I wore it for a necklace," the woman mumbled. "I was proud and foolish, and my child paid. I know he is dead, and my husband is dead. Nowadays I do well and I have the ruby to warm my dead heart."

"Other people didn't show off what was precious to them," Ersken said, his eyes on me. "The Snake preyed on them, even so." He could tell by the way I rubbed my nose that I was thinking. "If the Snake heard of it—Beka's found that the Snake learns about people's treasures—it wouldn't matter if you wore it or no. You could have buried it in your garden with no one to see, and the Snake would still have picked you. The Snake's a greedy pot of puke, Mistress."

The first Snake stealing was a child right out of Spicers' Row, I thought. Ersken talked on with Mistress Painter. He promised her we'd give the note back when we were done. He told her we'd send word if we found anything out.

I was thinking, The Snake saw that pendant and wanted it. He grabbed Calum then and there. Of all the folk on Spicers' Row then and now, the one who keeps coming under our noses is Yates Noll.

"How did he get so clever after years of small

messes?" I asked Pounce as we left the house.

"Who?" Ersken asked.

I looked at him. What should I do? "I think I'm supposed to tell Goodwin and Tunstall first," I said at last. "It's an idea confirmed, but they may still think it's Puppy piddle."

Ersken halted me in the middle of the street, out in the glaring sun. "Be very careful, Beka," he said, his eyes sober. "If the Snake, or the Snake's gang, starts to think you might know enough to have a real name? They might try dousing you and anyone else you've told. Nobody wants the death that waits for a child killer on Execution Hill."

Sweat was rolling down my back. The day had come on scorching. "We can't go worrying about what Rats will do to us, Ersken," I told him. "It just gets in the way of bagging them."

He smiled at me slowly, the corners of his eyes crinkling up. "As you say, Guardswoman Terrier."

"Stop that," I ordered, feeling very, very odd—not over the smile, though when Ersken smiled at someone, he put all his heart into it. "Don't go calling me 'Terrier.' Names like that belong to them as do big deeds. I've done none." I walked off, as much to get into the shade as to get away from the idea of having a nickname before I was even a Dog.

Ersken trotted to catch up with me. The sweat was

soaking his brown curls, but elsewise he didn't seem to mind the heat. He clapped me on my shoulder as we turned onto Stormwing Street. "You'll do big deeds, though, Beka. Everyone knows it. Even your Dogs. The only one who doubts it is you."

"Are you forgetting 'Fishpuppy'?" I asked him. "How 'bout the fact I still can't give the Magistrate a report without my tongue going in knots? Or—"

Sommat soft and wet plopped against my back. I smelled it as I turned—pure scummer. Ersken scrabbled in his pocket for a handkerchief to wipe it off before it dripped over more of the back of my dress. I passed him mine as I looked for them as threw it.

They stood at a corner, Orva and Jack Ashmiller's three children. The middle one, a girl if my memory served, was the one whose hands were brown with muck. The older one was a girl, too. She kept the littlest close to her by a cord tied to her wrist and his. That one was plainly a boy. He wore no napkin, only a shirt.

I walked up to them, furious. I hate scummer on me, always have. I hate the stink of it and the feel that I might as well be back on Mutt Piddle Lane. I was so angry I tripped over their begging bowl. Three whole coppers fell out.

That stopped me. I bent and gathered the coins, tossing them up and down in my hand. They stared at me, not moving. They feared I would take the money.

"Does your da know you're begging?" I asked the oldest one.

"Who cares if he does?" the middle one said. "He done left us, and the landlord kicked us out. And it's your fault!" she yelled, her face gone crimson. "You great sarden puttock! You rutting pig! You took our ma, and then Da hunted and hunted for work and he couldn't get none!" She would have thrown herself at me, but Ersken got behind her to grab her by the back of her tunic. She fought, trying to get to me, not even thinking to turn on him.

"Excuse me," he said at last. "It's too hot for this." He gathered her up with an arm about her waist. Then he carried her on his shoulder to a horse trough across the street as she screeched. He dumped her in with a great splash. That silenced her.

I looked at the oldest girl. "Did your da say he had work when he left?"

She'd reeled the boy tight up against her side and clutched him close. He was squirming. "What?"

I repeated my question. "Ersken won't hurt your sister," I added. "And at least now she don't have scummer on her hands. Did your da say he had work? It's important."

"Don't talk to her!" screamed her sister as the passersby laughed or bustled on their way. "She's a dirty, evil, gods-curst—" Ersken hung her upside down, using one hand to modestly keep her skirt around her knees as he held her calves to his chest with the other. She could breathe—just. She could not swear at me or at him.

The older girl just looked at me. She wouldn't open her gob even if Ersken beat her sister's head against the street. I fished in my belt purse for a coin and flinched when I brought it out. It was a silver noble. I started to put it back, then saw the lad's eyes on me. He sucked on his fist. My brothers had done that when they was hungry. I put the coin in the begging bowl.

The older girl scooped all the coins from the bowl before I might change my mind. "He said they was digging, but it was secret," she said. "They wasn't to tell a soul, a'cos there was only a few jobs, and folk would mob 'em, work bein' hard to find."

I whistled. It was a good story and partway true.

"He said he only told me a'cos I had to know he wasn't leavin' us for always. He'd come home soon with the rent money and more. I was t' keep the door bolted and pretend we wasn't there, and make the food last. But he was gone three days, and the landlord busted the door and kicked us out." She was crying. "He give us the bowl and said if we got enough, he'd let us back in. An' he laughed."

The little boy reached out with a shriek of glee. Pounce trotted up to us with a stick loaded with chunks of grilled meat. It was horse well seasoned with garlic, from the smell. The older girl took it from my thieving cat with a hand that shook.

Ersken put her sister down. As she ran to us, he said, "There's an idea. I'll be right back." By the time the three of them had jammed the meat into their mouths, he returned with more, and three turnovers. They ate those, too, in silence.

I couldn't leave them there. Slavers might bag them, or worse than slavers. They could disappear.

I had some extra coin, thanks to the slaver bookkeeper's bribe. Now I know why the Goddess sent such a windfall my way. It wasn't to save against hard times, as I'd hoped. But how long will it last? How much do napkins cost? There is my landlady to be thought on. I can bully her for a little while, as long as these three keep quiet.

How much will it cost to feed them?

It can't be helped, I thought. I hobbled Jack Ashmiller's wife. I won't tell him I lost his children, too.

I got them past my landlady by telling her that Mistress Painter gave me good information. After that, she was so flattered that she didn't argue over me bringing three mumpers into the house, at least not right off. Ersken helped me to haul buckets of water upstairs so they could wash.

"You'll stay here for now," I told them as we rearranged things. "I'll find your da."

"Why believe you?" the middle girl asked.

Her sister smacked her head. "Because we're here an' off the street. She didn't take us to the slavers or the foundling hospital, so shut yer gob." She looked at me. "Don't make a liar of me, you Puppies." She looked at Ersken. "I'll curse you with my every breath."

Though they weren't allowed to watch Poundridge, the Dogs that first volunteered came to listen when my Dogs and I traded news before muster. I guessed they'd want to know, so I told everyone about the Ashmiller family's fate. For a moment no one made a sound. Then I heard some of the best swearing of my life. Seemingly all of them believed as I did. Jack Ashmiller was hired by one of Crookshank's folk. Now his days were numbered.

"No use beggin' Ahuda or the Commander for more of us to watch Crookshank's folk," Jewel said, squeezing his hands into fists. "Eight of them Crookshank used to raid the Court of the Rogue was killed last night, four of 'em right in their barracks. And that's not countin' the usual murderin' and thievin' in the Lower City. We're keepin' eyes and ears open. Near as we could tell, Kayu's stickin' close to Crookshank. Mayhap he thinks folk might want him dead." He looked up at Ahuda, who glared at us. She knew we needed more watchers. "Eyes and ears open, mitts tied, and the Lower City like an upturned hive." He walked to his place like an old man.

After muster, Goodwin stopped Tunstall, Pounce, and me as we walked into the outside courtyard. "We need to talk to your houseguests," Goodwin said. "A proper talk. You're learning, Beka, and I've heard naught but good of Ersken, but mayhap we can winkle a bit of gold out of them you didn't know they had."

I knew she was right, but my pride twitched. I'd thought we'd done a fine job talking to children who'd as soon curse my name as breathe. They'd come home with me, hadn't they?

"Good idea." Tunstall thrust his slab of a hand out to Goodwin. "Pony up, Clary." She glared at him. "Cooper's housing them on Puppy wages. How long can she do it? We'll tell Ahuda they're witnesses, and reclaim what all three of us pay out from the jewel box fund. Some of it, anyway."

A fist under my breastbone relaxed. I could get back a bit of what I'd spent? That would help. I stopped counting and recounting my store of coins.

Goodwin cursed under her breath as she opened her purse.

Tunstall said, "Don't even think it, Clary. I know every copper you have on you. That thing is just to madden thieves."

Goodwin actually snarled. She thrust a hand inside her tunic, yanking out a second purse. "Lout!"

"Coin cutter," he said.

But that settled the argument. With Pounce following, we went off to the Nightmarket. Tunstall didn't spend only Goodwin's money. He dug out five silver coins of his own. We bought used clothes, with me guessing at the right sizes, sandals, food that would keep, and a hot meal. We went to my lodgings with full packs and baskets.

A surprise waited for me on the landing by my room and Aniki's. Tansy sat there, dressed for the world I lived in. A fat pack and a leather bag were by her side.

She looked at the three of us, her lower lip quivering, and moved her bags. Goodwin and Tunstall walked around her. Pounce rubbed against one of her hands and washed it with his tongue.

I stood there. Which god did I vex so badly today?

"I've nowhere else to go," Tansy said. "My family turned me out when I married Crookshank's grandson. And Beka—Grandfather said he'll make me lose the babe so the Rogue can't use my newborn child against him. I think he's gone mad."

"He's always been mad," Tunstall said, comforter that he was. "He's just gibbering with it now. Cooper, will you let Mistress Lofts in?"

I began to see why Goodwin kicked him so much. *He* was not going to house five people in rooms that were comfortable for one.

I unlocked my door. The three Ashmillers were in a corner, huddled like they expected a beating. The shutters were open. Pigeons were everywhere.

The little ones had found my bread scraps.

My head began to ache. I never told them they shouldn't open the shutters.

Slapper flew to me and tried to perch on my head. Of course he slid off. I looked at the Ashmillers. "My Dogs want a word," I said. "I forgot to warn you about the birds." I looked behind me. Tansy was still huddled on the stair. Did she think I would kick her down them? "My friend Tansy will be staying with us. She'll have the bed. And you'll be kind to her."

Tunstall and Goodwin unloaded the packs as I talked. I don't know if it was my speaking or the smell of hot food that made the Ashmillers nod. When Goodwin set out pasties and a pot of hot noodles on my table, they edged toward it. I got down my dishes and cutlery for them. Tunstall made them smile a hair when he perched on a stool too small by far. Goodwin shooed the birds off, though they went only so far as the windowsill and the edges of the roof. I could hear them and their ghosts over the late day breeze.

Tansy brought her things in. She had a string bag of food that she served out. She'd remembered my love for fruited honey cake. I watched as it vanished between the young ones and Tunstall. As Tansy moved about the table, getting a napkin onto the boy, brushing the younger girl's hair and braiding it, my Dogs asked their questions.

I felt a looby when Tunstall and Goodwin sought

information I had not. Had the children followed their papa on his search for work? They went with him sometimes, the oldest girl said. The places she named we had checked several times. She told Goodwin that in the last two weeks, her papa had gone elsewhere, alone. He'd found places where not so many others were there for the same jobs he was.

The job he'd got at last was night work. He'd left for it and hadn't come home in the morning. Three days later, the landlord had come. He had kept all but what was in the small bundles he'd let the children pack. He'd watched them put those together. He didn't want them taking aught of value before he kicked them out.

The older girl, who did most of the talking, fell silent. Goodwin drummed her fingers on the table. That's when the younger girl jerked her chin at me and said, "She only took us in from a bad conscience. Because it's her fault we've no ma and no da."

Tansy tugged the little demon's braid. "You hush," she scolded softly. "It's rude to bad-talk them as offers you a roof, whyever they offer it." The polished speech she'd learned at Crookshank's vanished when she talked with the Ashmillers. They, in turn, softened around a young mother from Mutt Piddle Lane.

"Your ma was a problem," Tunstall told her. The words were hard, but his voice was kind. "You're old enough to know that. Shall I find a mirror to show you the scar on your face? We can guess who put it there,

477

and you know. You can see the ones on your hands yourself." The girl looked down. "If not for Cooper here, we wouldn't even have a place to start seeking your da."

I could feel myself turn red. I hate it when people talk about me whilst I'm in the room.

Goodwin stood. "We're off. If you young ones think of anything that your father let slip about where he was going, about who hired him, tell Cooper. You want him found, we're the ones to do it. Don't mess about." The two girls nodded. The boy was smearing raisins on his face. Tansy began to wipe him clean.

"We'll be about our work, then. Stay inside and lock up," Tunstall said. He even bowed to Tansy. "Gods keep you safe."

"Gods keep you safe," Tansy said. "All of you. And Beka, thank you."

I just waved at her. "Don't bolt the door so I can't get in." I followed my Dogs out of my rooms.

"Well, that was a pot of piddle," Goodwin said as we went downstairs.

"It needn't be," Tunstall said. "Let's go to the house. Mayhap the landlord hasn't sold Jack Ashmiller's goods. We can put Achoo to sniffing from there."

"Achoo will have trouble tracking a wagon," Goodwin argued. "Cooper's pigeons say the diggers are carried to the cellars in a wagon. What's this?"

A clump of folk was coming in the door, joking. I

recognized Aniki and four rushers from Dawull's court. In their turn they saw Dogs and went to draw their swords.

"Hold, right there," Goodwin said, bringing out her baton. "I don't fancy a battle in these surroundings, and I doubt Cooper wants her stairwell chopped up."

"Throttle it, you loobies, it's Goodwin and Tunstall," Aniki ordered. Her blue eyes were worried. "Is everything all right?"

"I've houseguests," I said. "Orva Ashmiller's husband got digging work and vanished. His children were thrown into the street, so I brought them here. And Tansy left her in-laws' house. She's here, too."

Aniki's mouth twitched, I suppose at all my guests. Then she frowned. "Digging—and he vanished?"

"Jack's not dead," I said quickly. "The little ones let the pigeons in and fed them. He's not among them. This crew's still alive."

Aniki was carrying a bag with two wine bottles in it. She held it out to one of her friends. "Find another place to grumble, lads." She looked up at us. "Tell me where to look or who to watch. Beka said all but you three are on street duty, trying to keep the Rogue from killing any more of the ones who helped on the raid. Here I am, fancy free. Put me to use."

"What about Dawull?" Tunstall asked.

"I quit Dawull." Aniki gave Tunstall her relaxed grin, the one that said she hadn't a care in the world.

"He ordered a clutch of us to go kill the Rogue tonight." The coves with her were nodding. "I told him, in Scanra, when a chief wants to become Rogue, he challenges the Rogue, straight and honest. He told me to do as I was ordered. I told him to stuff his lousy orders. My friends did likewise. We were going to come here and drink ourselves silly." She looked at the others. "Sorry. I can't do that if more Lower City folk are going to die to make Crookshank richer."

"How do you know they're dyin' an' it's Crookshank as profits?" one of them asked. "Folk vanish all the time hereabouts."

"If Goodwin and Tunstall believe it, I believe it," said one of the others. "That's why you was lookin' for Crookshank at Dawull's tavern, innit? Crookshank buys Dawull off with stones these poor beggars bought with their blood."

"We can't say Dawull knows Crookshank kills the diggers," Tunstall said gravely. "Mayhap he thinks Crookshank just bought him to make certain Kayfer behaves."

"Dawull knows there's blood in it," replied that cove. "No one pays out the fortune Dawull's been braggin' of without blood. Dawull's gettin' rich whilst cuddies like us is dyin'." He shoved his bottles at another cove. "I'm with Aniki. Show me who to watch."

In the end, only the bottles went to Aniki's room. We had five new watchers to put on the lookout for

Jens, none of them Dogs. After talking it out with Goodwin, Tunstall gave them the description we had, then their assignments. They knew Crookshank's people, just as they knew the various exits to the Market of Sorrows. It was the sort of thing any self-respecting thief or rusher had to know, once he or she made it into a chief's court. Off they went. Aniki winked at me as she left.

"They'll never believe this back at the kennel," Goodwin muttered as we walked to our watch post at the slave market. "Pigeons, dust spinners—and now rogues. Cooper, since you became our Puppy, my Dog work has turned upside down."

"There's something more I need to tell you," I said. I thought my gut would explode if I waited any longer. "Mayhap me'n Ersken talked to the first mother bit by the Shadow Snake." I told them about Mistress Painter. "I think it's Yates Noll," I said as we came up on the market. A cloud of slave stink washed over us. "The Painters had just bought from Mistress Noll. Working for her, Yates and Gunnar and their friend go all over the Lower—"

Goodwin put a hand on my arm. "Eight or nine lives for one, Cooper," she said gently. "Even with your crooked friends to help, we can't get distracted from the diggers right now. First we nail Crookshank and his murderers to gravestones and give the Ashmiller children back their father. Then we go after the Snake."

"But Herun," I said. I knew she was right, but I had to remind her all the same. "He dies in five days if Crookshank don't pay up, and he won't."

"Jack Ashmiller and whoever's with him against one, Cooper," Tunstall said. As we neared the alley that was our watch post for Poundridge, he drew his baton. "Now, what mischief is this?"

Someone crouched in our spot, then rose tall in the shadows.

"You've been boring me to tears over our suppers, Mattes," Lady Sabine said. She wore dark leather sewn with black metal rings. Her breeches were dark, her boots unshined. She spoke just loud enough for us to hear. "Muttering about catching a drop in a net with just three Dogs and one cat to watch the whole Market of Sorrows. The only way I can get you to pay attention to me is to lend a hand."

Goodwin looked at Tunstall. "'Our suppers'?" she asked in a forbidding tone.

"Relax, Guardswoman. It's just suppers—so far." The lady looked from Goodwin to Tunstall. "Are you actually going to refuse my aid?"

"We're going to sit on the Spidren Walk entrance, Cooper and I," Goodwin told them. "That one's been itching me, and now I can scratch it. Since you and my lady are so friendly, Mattes, you can tell her about our crooked helpers." She marched back down the street.

Pounce meowed a greeting to Lady Sabine and trotted after Goodwin.

"It's all right, Cooper," Tunstall said when I hesitated. "Clary's just cross that I never asked her permission to go a-courting."

As I hurried after Goodwin, I heard my lady say, "You'd better not be planning to court me for anything serious, my lad. I like my single state."

And I heard Tunstall's low chuckle.

Thunder rolled far off. A fine rain that was hardly more than a fog began to fall. It would soak us to the skin in a hurry.

Goodwin and I walked into the alleys behind the Market of Sorrows. We passed the watch posts of Aniki and her friends, pretending to ignore them. Finally we reached the small gate on Spidren Way, the entrance closest to Rovers Street. It's not the most used gate, which was why my Dogs had sent our helpers to other places. It was the only one we'd had no one for, until now.

One of the buildings across the alley was set back from its neighbor. It gave us a sheltered spot where we could watch the gate without being picked up by the light from the covered lanterns around it. Our view wasn't as good as at Tunstall's watch spot, but we could hear every squeak the gate made.

We settled with Pounce between us. I listened

to the rain, the laughter of the slave guards, and the passing of folk in and out. Finally I had to ask.

"Are you that angered at him? At them?"

"Hmm?" I'd startled her. "Mattes? Oh, he's a fool. Getting mixed up with a noble. It never comes to any good, not with so much distance between them—a lady and a hillman, Crone witness it!" I heard her but doubted anyone passing a foot away would notice. "Still, Lady Sabine . . . She's not like most of them. She's more my lord Gershom's sort. Useful." She was silent for a time. Then she said, "Cooper, we do care about Herun Lofts. Tansy is a fine mot—no one should lose a child and a husband in the same year. And we want the Shadow Snake. If we allow ourselves, we Dogs, we would go raving over all the crimes that go unpunished whilst we can only follow one. It's maddening to have but two Dogs where we need twelve or more. It's so maddening we've jumped to add rogues and a lady knight to our roster, gods bless them."

I smiled in the dark. I couldn't have put it better.

"But this is the Dog's life, Cooper. We seek and we hobble and we cage. Sometimes we can only do it a little at a time." I nearly missed what she said next— "And sometimes we lose more than we catch, curse it."

We waited in silence again, watching folk as came and went through the gate in the rain. It fell harder. Soon enough we were soaked even with our shelter.

We'd been there two hours and my belly was grumbling when a short, plump mot walked up to the gate. She had three tough-looking coves with her. One of them held a Yamani parasol over her to keep her dry. Goodwin stiffened.

"Uta Norwood," she whispered as the guards let the four of them enter. "She keeps Crookshank's books. What business has she got here, do you suppose?"

"The old scale was in no mood to buy slaves," I said. "If they need someone for the house, wouldn't the cook or the footman do the buying during the day?"

"I'd like to get my hobbles on Norwood as bad as Crookshank," Goodwin said. "The two of them have beggared more families . . ." We heard steps in the alley as the gate closed behind Norwood. Goodwin was up with her baton out. It was just Aniki. From somewhere my friend had gotten a round, pointed straw hat like the farmers wore. It shed the rain like a little roof.

"Hope you don't mind the company," she said cheerfully. "They're moving child slaves in through our gate. I can't abide the sight. There was three of us watching that one already, and the other two are used to slaves." She sank to her heels.

"Are there so few child slaves in Scanra?" Goodwin asked.

"Few slaves at all. We can't feed 'em. We can barely feed ourselves—that's why Rosto said we should give Tortall a try." Aniki bounced on her heels, hugging her knees. "If I live to be old, not that I'm counting on it, I'll never get used to child slaves and child-sized shackles. Cooper hates it, too." They both looked back at me.

"I didn't say anything," I said. On watch here, I couldn't get away from the business. Before my lord had taken us in, any one of my family could have ended up inside these stinking walls. So could the Ashmillers. And look at all the trouble the slave sellers make for my Dogs and me, sneaking about, trying to dodge taxes on their trade. They're more trouble than they're worth.

Aniki went on, "Listen, Goodwin, I know if we talk loose about this, if Crookshank panics, we might get killed the diggers Crookshank has right now. But if these diggers turn up riding pigeons, too, we need to shout the news from the rooftops. Let folk know the work comes with strings attached."

"There will still be folk stupid enough, or desperate enough, to hire on and tell no one," Goodwin warned her.

"But not as many," I said.

"Not as many." Goodwin nodded. "You're right, Aniki. You're wasted as a rusher, girl. Come be a Dog."

Aniki's teeth flashed in a grin. "For the splendid wage and respect that you Dogs get? I think not, Guardswoman Goodwin. I want to rise higher."

"To the Rogue's dais," Goodwin said.

"Only if there's a proper Rogue to stand beside," Aniki told her. "Here comes someone."

Norwood and her guard were leaving the market. Goodwin looked at Aniki. "Can you manage the streets on your own?"

Aniki smiled and patted her sword hilt. "As well as anyone who serves the Crooked God," she said, mentioning the thieves' god, who went without a proper name.

"Then Dog Norwood until you're weary or attacked. Report to Cooper," Goodwin ordered. "Go!"

Aniki left our nook like a shadow. I could never work it out how a good-sized mot like her could go unnoticed when she wished.

I couldn't help what I said then. "You never let *me* watch alone."

"You're *my* responsibility, and you're not a swordswoman," Goodwin said. "And I'm teaching you things I'd not want her to know, not so long as she's crooked." Goodwin shook her head. "What a waste!"

Pounce had found himself a dry spot and been forgot by us. Now he "*manh*ed" his agreement, making Goodwin and me jump.

We ate bread and cheese in the cold rain. Finally it was time to go back to the kennel for muster. Then Goodwin, Tunstall, and my lady half dragged me to the Mantel and Pullet for hot food, mulled wine, and soup to thaw me out. I didn't object to the wine, I was that miserable. Afterward Pounce and I slapped home through the mud.

I left my clothes hanging over the banisters, my boots and armor on the landing, and entered my rooms in breastband and loincloth. Tansy slept on the pallet, her arm around the little boy, the younger girl beside her. The older girl watched me unblinking from her bedroll as I did up all the bolts on my door.

No one stirred whilst I put on a nightgown and took my underclothes off, then undid my hair. Pounce, the cuddy, shook himself off on me. Then he climbed onto the older girl's blankets. Growling to myself, I went to bed and right to sleep.

It was another dream. I had little Nilo in a sling on my back. Will was tied to my wrist by a cord. My other friends were skipping rope. I watched. I wanted to play, but I wasn't yet to the point of untying Will to join in. I already knew that if I did set him loose, he'd be off after any passing horse in a lightning flash.

"Come back, you little trollop!"

We all turned. Here came Tansy, curls bouncing. She held her skirt up to make a basket for a bunch of small, fresh-baked cakes. Mistress Noll chased her with a broom raised high.

I sat up, my heart beating. Why was I scared? Tansy escaped that day. We'd stopped Mistress Noll without meaning to, scrambling for the cakes that fell from Tansy's skirt. We took the broom blows meant for Tansy. I got two extra when I put myself between the angered Mistress Noll and my brothers. It was a small thing on Mutt Piddle Lane, naught to wake up over.

Tansy was awake, too. I heard her by the shuttered window and smelled the rose-scented soap she used. She sniffed, then blew her nose.

"Tansy?" I whispered. "You're crying?"

"I cry over everything, Beka, remember?" She sat on the bed and felt around until she grabbed my hand. "Promise me you'll do all you can to find Herun."

"I can't do much," I said, keeping quiet. "I'm bound to my Dogs and the digger search."

"Just promise to try. That's enough for me. I can care for these little ones if I know you're seeking my man." Her grip tightened.

"Tansy . . ."

"Everyone knows you're looking hard, Beka. No one else is even looking, let alone hard. You think I wouldn't hear it? How you had folk out asking? No one expects you to do anything—you, a Puppy! And yet you went seeking. Talking to them the Dogs and the Rogue turned away, you and your friends. You'll find Herun."

I heard one of the children stir. "Papa," she whispered in her sleep. It was the older girl.

"Promise me," Tansy whispered.

"Go back to bed," I told her. "Before they wake." I lay there, listening as her wakeful breaths turned to sleeping ones. Then I got up to write in this journal on the landing of my stairs. Writing helps me think things through. Writing down the dream just now made me see what about it sat so ill.

Mistress Noll told my Dogs and me that Tansy was sweet. She spoke highly of her, said she always liked her. Mayhap she wished only to speak well of a grieving mother. The truth of it was, Mistress Noll hated Tansy back on Mutt Piddle Lane. I could not count the times she tried to beat Tansy black and blue. Tansy always stole her best baking, the kind that customers ordered special. The kind that cost Mistress Noll her own money to do a second time.

It could be a polite lie, but why, then, had Mistress Noll lied so hard? To protect Yates? Mayhap he saw a way to get revenge for his mother and to make one last, big haul. Mayhap his mother knows it.

Sunday, May 10, 246

Writ about ten in the morning, on the stairs.

I woke to the little boy's wail. It was near dawn. He was screeching, his face scarlet. Tansy and his older sister bent over him. Tansy changed his napkin as his sister wriggled a toy before his nose. The middle girl curled in a corner, her hands over her ears. Pounce was nowhere to be seen.

The floor shook as someone stomped up the stairs. "Beka!" Rosto yelled outside. "Beka, what've you got in there, a sarden nursery?"

The oldest girl dipped her finger in the honey jar as I pulled on my breeches. Whilst I undid the bolts, she stuck her dripping finger in her brother's mouth. He quieted at once.

I yanked my door open. "Rosto, you savage, we're shutting him up," I said. Rosto wore only breeches, showing off his lean chest. "What're you whining for? It's almost time to get up anyway."

But now the younger girl began to cry. She shrieked that she wanted to go home. Rosto stalked into my room and picked her up. "If you could go home, you wouldn't be here, would you?" he asked, giving her a shake. "Shut your gob. It's too early for such noise."

She went silent and stared at him as she hung in his hands. I glared at her. She never shut up for me, though to be sure, I wasn't the sight that a half-naked Rosto was. No, she was too young to appreciate him. It wasn't that.

Tansy propped her fists on her hips. "Well, aren't you the man, bullyin' a child as was beggin' on the streets yesterday." She cuffed Rosto on the head. "Put her down, you scut."

Slowly Rosto set the girl down. He ran his eyes over Tansy, who wore naught but a thin nightgown. "Aren't you pretty, even with a pert tongue in your head and a little one in your belly. Who's your friend, Beka?"

"Married, and none of your business," Tansy snapped. "Out! Out!"

I looked at Rosto. "You heard her." I towed him outside. "She's Herun Lofts' wife Tansy, a friend of mine," I said. "The little ones are Jack Ashmiller's. I hobbled his wife, Orva. Now he's vanished—got hired for a job and hasn't been home since."

Rosto was always fast to catch on. He raised his fair eyebrows. "And your ghosts? The diggers?"

"No new ones yet. We're on watch. But, Rosto, I need a favor." I swallowed. Asking favors of rushers was a chancy business. If I wasn't desperate (if Herun's life wasn't shorter by another day) I never would have done it. "And don't ask me for murder to pay you back."

If I'd ever needed to be sure that my dealings with him in future would be serious matters, I knew it now.

The irritation left his face and sober attention filled it. He crossed his arms over his chest. "What's the favor, then? Short of murder as repayment?"

"I need to find Yates Noll, fast," I said. "My Dogs are wrapped up on the streets. Me and Goodwin and Tunstall are sitting on our best bet to find the diggers. You're in a better way to find him than us right now." I smiled at him. I did have a possible bribe to offer. "If we find Herun Lofts, I bet he'll be grateful. And it's his family that has the fire opals."

"True enough," Rosto said. He yawned and smoothed back his hair. "All right. I—"

Feet slammed up the stairs. It was Aniki. She looked like she hadn't slept a wink. She thrust a bag of hot turnovers at Rosto. To me she said, "I got friendly with one of Norwood's rushers after she turned in for the night. That basket she had on her arm? She was dropping off Crookshank's pay bags. The folk Pound-ridge has to pay start to come around at the beginning of his shift. This afternoon." Aniki stood there for a moment, panting. She seemed more awake than I'd ever seen her. "Well?" she asked.

"Thanks," I said. "I'll see what Goodwin makes of it. Wake Ersken." I dashed into my room. If Aniki was right, Jens and the other rushers who guarded the diggers would come for their pay—come, mayhap, and be gone by the time we mustered tonight. I wanted to give Goodwin plenty of warning. If she and Tunstall had any miracles in their pockets, miracles that would get more than the three of us to raid the diggers' prison and free them tonight, they'd need as much time as I could give them to put their miracles together.

I scrambled into my clothes and barely blessed my teeth with a cleaning. I handed the turnovers to Tansy and the children, grabbed my pack, and raced downstairs with Pounce at my heels.

The floor outside Kora's door was scorched. Rosto leaned on the frame. He stepped aside to let me in. Aniki was slumped in a chair with a grin. "Lucky our Aniki knows what happens when you wake Kora from a sound sleep," Rosto said, pointing at the charred wood. "She stood out of the way. Kora is good at fire spells."

"Thanks," I told Aniki.

She waved off my gratitude. "It's fun. Kora needed a new door anyway. The old one was coming apart."

Ersken was trying to dress under the bedclothes. Kora's kitten, Fuzzball, pounced on him as he moved under the covers, which slowed him down some. Kora had pulled her sheets over her head.

Rosto finally took pity on Ersken and picked up Fuzzball. "Come here, ferocious hunter," he said. "Leave the lad some dignity."

Ersken popped out of cover to glare at Rosto. "I can see these two tormenting Kora, but why wake me?" he asked. "Breakfast isn't for another hour."

"I need you to fetch Tunstall," I said. "Tell him that Jens gets paid at four. Aniki followed their paymaster last night and found it out. Let Tunstall know I've gone to Goodwin's with the same news."

Ersken repeated what I'd said and finished dressing. "D'you think this is it, Beka?" he asked. "You'll be able to follow Jens to Ashmiller and the other diggers?"

"Please, Mithros and the Goddess." I made sure my clothes were tucked in. "I'm off."

Rosto put a hand on my arm as I passed him. "I'll find Yates," he said. "Things will change in the Lower City, Beka Cooper. Between us five and our friends"— he looked at the girls and Ersken—"leeches like Crookshank and the Snake will get burned."

I met his black eyes. I believe him. If he succeeds, the thieves will be harder to catch—but the common folk will have someone to turn to. That *has* to be better.

I didn't run to Goodwin's. I did make good time, cutting through the alleys. Even main streets like Palace Way and Eversoul Road in Flash District weren't too crowded so early in the day. It was quiet yet, quiet enough that I heard the clap of wings overhead. Most of the city's birds were just beginning their songs. I finally stopped and looked up.

They stopped, too, roosting on whatever perch was nearest: Slapper, Ashes, White Spice, Pinky. Seventeen in all. I saw no other pigeons anywhere, just these. Just the ones who carried the ghosts of them Crookshank had murdered to keep the secret of the fire opals. They knew something was going on.

The sight of her house on Dun Lane drew me up short. I did not expect Clary Goodwin to live in a pretty stone place with a well-thatched roof and orderly garden. Chickens already pecked through the rows of vegetables, seeking insects. Sleepy goats eyed me over a wood fence to the back. The charms over the door and the welcome wreath were fresh made. When did Goodwin find time to do it? I felt slovenly, knowing there was mending undone in my basket at home.

I rapped hard on her door, then harder.

"Enough!" someone finally cried hoarsely. "Will you rouse the district? If this is not dire . . ." Goodwin yanked the door open. Her hair was tousled. She clutched a long robe about herself.

Goodwin took my attention from her feet by saying, "Cooper. And Master Pounce. I should have known *you'd* be close behind. Get in here—it's chilly out." She closed the door behind us.

There was but one story to the cottage and half of a loft overhead. A man stuck his head over its edge. His hair was gray on the sides and brown for the rest. He looked like the cheerful, steady-working coves from the country farms. I'd heard it somewhere that Goodwin's husband was a master carpenter, as easygoing as she was not. "Clary?"

"Duty, love," she called, poking up the hearth fire. "Go back to bed."

"So that's Cooper." He could ignore her and live. I was impressed, and unnerved that he knew who I was. "And that's the god cat? I've never seen a god before." He winked at me and vanished back into the loft. "I'll dress meself and cook up breakfast."

Goodwin stumbled to a table and ladled water into a basin. She splashed it on her face. "Report, Cooper."

I told her what Aniki had told me, then waited for her to speak. There was a towel folded over the back of a chair near her. She ignored it. She just stood there and stared into the distance, her face dripping. At last I summoned my courage and handed her the towel. She rubbed her face, but not like she knew that's what she was doing.

"Four this afternoon," she said at last, thinking aloud. "I've got to shake that paper out of Ahuda, convince her we're going to move tonight." She rubbed her mouth. "Tunstall and I can do it. My lord will give permission if we can Dog this Rat to his burrow soon. Ahuda will be fine if my lord approves. Thank the gods Poundridge goes on duty same time as we do. Cooper, you think your friend Kora might help?"

"I'm certain of it," I said.

"Get her, too. I want her in this. We'll have Berryman, but two mages are better. And I trust her price will be right?"

I thought of the Ashmiller children screaming and thumping over Kora's head. "I think I can bargain with her," I said.

"Good. Do you know where Nyler Jewel lives?"

I'd carried plenty of messages to him from Lord Gershom. "Yes, Goodwin."

"Fetch him here. Ahuda?" I nodded. "Tell her my man's cooking. And then your friend Kora. Go. We'll have breakfast when you return."

I looked at her. "You should be Watch Sergeant," I said. Mayhap it was seeing her bare feet that emboldened me, I don't know. "After Ahuda, anyway."

"Scat, Cooper," Goodwin ordered. Pounce and I scatted.

Outside, Pounce halted me with a pat on the ankle. He told me, *I will bring Kora. You get the others.*

"Is this it?" I asked him, wanting it to be true. "Do we have them?"

Scat, Pounce told me. He raced down Eversoul Road.

Cats must always be cats, even when they are gods, or constellations.

I got Ahuda first. She was up and dressed. I feared she'd bite my head off when I asked her to Goodwin's for breakfast or, almost as bad, question me. She only grimaced. "I knew it would come to this. All right. I'm on my way."

I didn't wait for her to think better of it. I ran to Nyler Jewel's house. As ever, I had to wade through the grandchildren that lived on the first two floors. Sometimes I wondered how he slept. Then I had to do it again, because Mistress Jewel told me he was in the garden, weeding.

On the way to Goodwin's he made me tell him all that took place the night before. Then he asked sharp questions about Aniki, Kora, and Rosto. I was relieved to see Goodwin's house. Being questioned by Jewel was like being questioned by my lord, Ahuda, Goodwin, and Tunstall at the same time. No detail was too small to slide past the old Dog, including the fact that Rosto flirted with me all the time.

I checked around once before we went into Goodwin's. Slapper and the other sixteen birds were still with me. They'd followed me to Ahuda's, to Jewel's, and back here.

Tunstall was not there, but Lady Sabine was. She was sharpening her sword with a little stone whilst she talked with Goodwin's man. Kora and Aniki were there, Aniki dozing in a corner.

There was food on the table—fresh-cooked bacon, eggs, cheese, fresh milk, strawberries, day-old raisin buns. Everyone else looked like they had made a good meal. Goodwin pointed Jewel and me to the plates.

"Your Cooper told me what you've learned," Jewel said. "Where's Tunstall and Ahuda?"

"Up at my lord's, asking permission for a Rat catching," Goodwin said. "If we get it, you and I need to work out who we want and where the crew must wait. It all depends on us Dogging Jens back to where the diggers work. Tunstall's going to get the gem mage Berryman to help. He owes us some debts and we want to cash them in. We need to be sure we can handle Crookshank's mage, Vrinday Kayu. We think she's put a death mark on the guards. Those guards have to live long enough to talk, to give evidence on Crookshank and his people." Goodwin looked at Kora. "We're hoping you'll be able to help Berryman."

Kora gave her sly smile. "Will he want my help? To him I'm naught but a Scanran hedgewitch."

"He'll need convincing, then," Lady Sabine murmured, inspecting the edge of her sword for nicks.

Kora nibbled a fingernail. Then she nodded. "I can do that."

Goodwin sat on a stool. "Starting at four, we watch the Market of Sorrows for the guards to pick up their pay. We'll know them by the death marks. Figure we'll need Dogs to follow them to the burrow. And then we call the rest of the crew to move in."

Jewel rubbed his unshaved chin. I could hear the scrape of his whiskers. "Sounds good. You think my lord will approve it?" he asked.

"Ahuda did when we told her," Goodwin said.

"Then let's send these young folk home for some

rest. Are you in this, my lady?" he asked.

"Wouldn't miss a moment," replied Lady Sabine. She thrust her sword into its sheath. "Besides, Mattes might get his head creased if I don't watch it for him." She grinned at Goodwin, who actually smiled back.

"We'll muster where?" Jewel asked Goodwin.

"There's a stable with a loft on Spidren Way," Goodwin said. "I'll get the key and lock up the owner for the time being so he doesn't blab. Three o'clock."

I didn't think I could rest in my crowded rooms, but I knew I was being dismissed. I decided it was time to go make some offerings to the gods. Just in case.

Sometime after dawn on Monday.

The stable loft was hot and stuffy by the time we reached it at mid-afternoon. Berryman kept sneezing. At least he no longer whined once Goodwin offered to give him a nap tap. Kora was posted with Tunstall and Lady Sabine on the other side of the market, holding a spell in her hand that would let her talk to Berryman. Jewel and the other Dogs who would follow the guards once they'd been paid took the places of Aniki's friends from last night. We couldn't be sure the diggers' guards would come to the Spidren Way gate to be paid, so Goodwin arranged for all the gates to be watched. Aniki was with us. She lounged next to the window with Goodwin.

My lord Gershom had given permission for

everything. He took but ten guards off Evening Watch, but Ahuda handpicked another ten from the Evening Watches in Flash and Patten districts, solid Dogs who could be trusted. Six of my lord's personal bodyguards joined them and the Dogs who handled the cage wagons. All of them waited at the kennel, ready to move as soon as they got word from us. We just had to follow the mots and coves who took their pay with death-marked hands. Berryman would make certain we could see that. We'd have to follow a number of them, not knowing which of them were on guard duty with the diggers and which were finished with their work for the day.

When Goodwin got us into the loft that had been locked in last night's rain, my gut cramped. I didn't want to be kept to that hot box. I felt like the terrier they'd named me, quivering from head to toe. I was tired of waiting. I wanted to chase some Rat back to the hole where they'd hidden Jack Ashmiller and the others.

Crookshank's folk were the worst kinds of law-breakers. They preyed on those whose only value in coin lay in their ability to work. That was wrong. They took the best part of a mot or cove, the one thing someone from the Cesspool could be proud of, and they used it to lure that person to an unmourned death.

"Hello," Goodwin said. "Cooper. Who's this? Aniki, you know him?"

I came to the window. Aniki shook her head, but I

recognized the cove. "He's one of Crookshank's rushers. I've seen him about the house months past, when
I've visited Tansy," I said. "He hasn't been with Crookshank at the Court of the Rogue, though." I looked
harder. "Goodwin, his boots."

There was pinkish mud on the heels of his boots,
like he'd mayhap been around pink rock dust.

"Aniki, get Otterkin and her partner," Goodwin
said. "I want 'em here to follow when this cove comes
out."

Aniki was gone in a heartbeat.

"Good catch on the mud, Cooper," Goodwin said.

"You noticed it, too," I replied.

From the corner of my eye I saw her thin smile.
"I'd mope if you were better than me so soon. Berryman, did he have the death mark?"

"I didn't have enough warning," the mage said,
and sniffed. "I wasn't ready."

"Dogs have to be ready," Goodwin said. "I thought
you were all eager for true Dog work."

"Why can't I be on watch with Tunstall?" Berryman asked.

"Because we tossed a coin and I lost. Are you ready
to check or not?"

"I'm ready," Berryman mumbled. Worked up as I
was, I tried not to laugh. Tunstall was better than
Goodwin at making the gem mage feel important.

Slapper fluttered onto the sill of the stable loft.

"Crone shield us, what's he doing here?" Goodwin asked me.

Behind him I saw the pigeons with the other diggers' ghosts settle on the roof of the Market of Sorrows. They stared at us, yellow, blue, gray, and dark eyes steady. Knowing, like.

"He thinks we've got something," I said as I lifted Slapper off the sill. He pecked at my hands. I flinched. Berryman came closer to sneeze and stare. "All the diggers' birds do. They've followed me since dawn. The others are on the roof across the alley." I reached in our sack of food for a roll. I crumbled it in my hand so he might peck at that instead of me.

"There go Otterkin and her partner—good, they've turned the corner," Goodwin said with satisfaction. "Grouse though I may about Otterkin's mage work, she knows her street craft. And here comes our Rat. Berryman?"

Berryman stuck his head between mine and Goodwin's. His lips moved. On the back of the Rat's hand a sign writ in yellow fire blazed. Yet he didn't so much as twitch.

"That's your death mark," Berryman said. He drew back. Sweat rolled down his cheek. "A good one. I— I think I could counter it, but . . . perhaps not." He swallowed. "I will be glad for Mistress Kora's help after all."

"Very well, then. Just make sure you keep a couple

of these guards alive. We need them to bear witness against them that hire and pay them," Goodwin said. "But they don't all have to live."

Slapper fluttered up to my shoulder. He could set there, stump tucked into the hollow of my collarbone, but he wasn't steady. If he slipped, he'd grab my skin and hold on with his beak and the claws of his good foot. Carefully I lifted the bird down and cradled him in my arm, stroking his feathers. "Soon," I whispered. "Please, Crone and Black God. You and the others will be avenged soon."

Pounce jumped to the sill. Leaning in toward me, he touched his nose to Slapper's beak.

"Settle, all of you," Goodwin said. "Too much movement up here and we'll be catching someone's eye. If those slave market guards were mine, I'd kick their bums between their ears for working behind the gates instead of in front."

"Shadier behind the gates?" Berryman suggested. He sneezed into a handkerchief.

"They're supposed to care about folk watching the market, not their own comfort," Goodwin told him. "But what do you expect of guards who work the slave business? Lazy scuts, or they'd get real jobs— Here we go. I know this one. She's been on Crookshank's payroll for years. Must've done something to vex him bad to get this job. If she has it. Berryman?"

He muttered. We saw the yellow flash even as the

hard-looking mot passed through the market gate.

"How can they not see that?" Goodwin asked.

I missed the answer. I went to look at the foot of the loft stairs. Aniki was below. She hadn't chosen to make the climb when she returned. I glanced back at Goodwin, who told me, "Jewel and Yoav."

I passed their names to Aniki. She went off to let them know we had someone for them to follow.

The third death-marked Rat went to Tunstall, my lady, and Kora. The fourth was Goodwin's, Berryman's, Aniki's, and mine. We went out, scattered. Berryman seemed to be a merchant looking to buy property. Aniki was herself, a rusher on an errand or looking for work. Goodwin and me were in uniform. Goodwin had taken the Puppy trim off my clothes in the loft.

"A Dog alone with a Puppy is unusual; two Dogs, even two females, isn't," she said when I gasped. "You can sew it back on tonight."

As we moved on up into the Cesspool, I could see Berryman was ill at ease. He stood out, too. Finally he raised a hand. I saw a glint of yellow. Then he seemed to be gone. I say "he seemed," because he did not think to avoid the wet edges of the deeper ruts. We could see his footprints. Aniki grinned, following the prints with her eyes. At last she moved ahead of Berryman and our Rat to buy ale from one vendor and a turnover from another. She drank and ate, ambling just ahead of the Rat, keeping him in the corner of her eye. Then she slowed enough to let him move ahead again.

Pounce had it easier than any of us. No one noticed a black cat in the street. He stopped here and there to sniff aught of interest. Wherever our Rat stopped, Pounce was there, close enough to see up the Rat's nose. I was so proud. Now there was a proper god, making himself useful!

Since my thought might be deemed blasphemy, I said silent prayers to the Goddess and to Mithros. I begged forgiveness and asked them not to misunderstand. Since I wasn't blasted where I stood, I guess they forgave me, or they hadn't heard my blasphemy.

Our Rat never guessed he was followed. Without a look behind he went to Mulberry Street, where he turned southwest. He walked but a scant two blocks down before he stopped and looked about.

We did not halt nor flinch. That would have given us away. There were plenty of folk about at this hour. Dogs patrolled out here often enough. Aniki stopped by a knife grinder's cart and gave over her dagger for sharpening. Berryman's footprints appeared in the mud a yard from our Rat. Lucky for us the mage had stopped sneezing once we were out of the loft.

The guard walked up to a ramshackle house three stories high and banged twice on the door, then five times. It opened. He walked inside. Pounce trotted over and leaped atop a crate that sat beside the door. He curled up there in the sun.

A moment later the footprints crossed the street to us. I heard Berryman say, "There are watch spells on the place. I can handle them."

Trees lined the other side of the street, on the edge of some empty land. "Cooper, into that tree," Goodwin said. She meant a great old oak whose heavy branches would give me an easy climb, one that stood right across from the house. "I'll be up behind you. Berryman, let the others know where we are. Carefully. They can find me here. And then I hope you can keep that no-seeing on you for a time." We waited until a hay wagon passed between us and the house, then climbed into the oak.

Aniki left the knife grinder with a coin and found a comfortable spot under our tree. She pretended to sleep. Pigeons came down from the sky. Some perched along the roofs to either side of the house we watched. Slapper, White Spice, Mumper, and Ashes settled around me. None of them made a sound.

Crookshank must have chosen this house because a vein of the pink rock that carried opals in it came up in its cellar. Did he know how easy it would be for us to spy on it? No one built anything on the southwest side of Mulberry Street. Two hundred years ago, they say, metal human-bird monsters called Stormwings and giant human-headed spiders known as spidrens fought a great battle here. The land was cursed. Brave souls hunted rabbits in the tall grasses, but mostly the place was left to weeds and trees. We could hide a hundred Dogs to watch this house and Crookshank's guards would never know.

Nevertheless, we were lucky no guards were posted outside. Of course, if they'd been, the local folk would have noticed and talked.

We'd not been there long before Tunstall, Lady Sabine, and Kora came in the wake of their Rat. The Rat entered the house. Our friends found places to watch the house and settled to wait.

Two hard coves and a mot soon went in. I knew two of them: the ones Jewel, Otterkin, and their partners had been set to follow. Berryman whispered up to Goodwin that these Dogs had come and were hidden away nearby.

Those Rats and diggers have a nasty place to work, I thought. All the windows were shuttered, despite the heat. I saw another house closed up the same way, two buildings down, and another just behind this one, on a thin alley to its right. Families had lived in these places once. Where did they go? Did Crookshank toss them out or kill them?

Carefully I moved down a few branches and whispered to Goodwin about the shuttered houses. When she nodded, I went back to my post.

Seven rushers left the place as we watched. Was that all of them? We had no idea how many were used with the diggers. The guards looked weary, coves at the end of a day's work. Berryman worked his spell from wherever he stood, showing us the death mark on their hands.

Tunstall waited until the clocks struck six before he came over to our hiding place from his. The sun had gone behind the wall for the Lower City, making it easy for him to keep to the shadows.

Leaning against the tree, he murmured up to Goodwin, "I think the rabbits are in the burrow for the night, Clary."

"I think you're right," she said. "Berryman? Tell Ahuda where we are. It's time to move."

The mage had a fresh spell to link him to our raiding party. He used it now. Kora seemed to appear next to Aniki. I'd have thought her part of the tall grasses. Certainly I'd never seen *her* footprints in mud. "It's about time," she murmured to Aniki. "I've been playing good little washerwoman for weeks. I'm ready for some fun."

Aniki, still seated between two knotted roots, grinned up at her. "Rosto is going to cry when he finds out he missed this."

Tunstall moved over to a screen of tall grass. That was when I saw Lady Sabine was also there, stretched out on her belly, counting over a set of worry beads in her long fingers. She had unsheathed her sword and placed it on the grass beside her, ready for use in case someone surprised her.

I'd thought to be hungry and stiff. I'd even thought to be bored, though the stream of Cesspool folk, carts, and messengers on horseback was interesting. As I sat on my thick branch, carefully brushing away ants and easing out cramps a bit at a time, more pigeons began to come. They roosted in the trees all around me. They made no sound the others could hear. But me—their ghosts had plenty to say to me.

"Ma, he offered cakes an' threw a bag over my head."

"Papa, I'm hungry an' she said ye have t' pay 'em t' let me come home!"

"A monster grabbt me clean outen me bed!"

It went on and on, the cries of little ones taken in the dark. The pigeons on the roofs across the street dove at the newcomers, trying to drive them off. They'd get caught in the twigs and nearly break their silly necks before they got themselves right again. White Spice, Mumper, Ashes, and Slapper flapped their wings to distract me until Goodwin hissed, "Do they want folk to notice us?"

They stopped flapping. The children's ghosts talked on.

I glared at Slapper as tears sneaked from my eyes. You sarden bastard, I thought at him. You and your flock kept them from me, didn't you? You was so bound that I would free you first—war among ghosts! I'm caught in a war of ghosts, may the Crone witness it!

Then I saw movement down the street by torch-light. I heard rustles in the grass behind me. Tunstall returned from his hiding place beside my lady. The shadows had grown so long I could no longer see her.

"Ahuda's here," Tunstall said. "Berryman, Kora, get ready." Berryman appeared right next to Tunstall. He was sweating, but he wore a big grin. Tunstall clasped his shoulder, then called softly, "Clary? Cooper? Time to go to work."

We climbed down from the oak. I held on to the tree when I got down, my muscles stiff and sore. That was when riders came trotting up Mulberry. They drew up before the house—three nasty-looking rushers and Vrinday Kayu. I saw them clear because one had a torch. He set it in a stand by the house, then held Kayu's horse as she slid off.

Goodwin whispered, "Berryman! Kora! It's the mage—don't let her go inside!"

The street echoed with a roar I'd heard once in Crookshank's, the sound of a cat like a god. The horses reared, fighting the reins. In the torchlight I saw Pounce leap onto Kayu's back, his claws shining in the dark.

Blue-green and yellow fire shot across the street from our mages. Both colors dropped over her like fishing nets, passing through my cat like he wasn't there.

"I thought I'd have to fight only the woman's spells, not the woman herself," Berryman complained.

Kayu tried to throw Pounce off her. She was screeching. Magic rose from her in a reddish mist. It flowed across the street toward Kora and Berryman, following the lines of their own spells.

Tunstall, Goodwin, and I charged across the road, batons in hand. Lady Sabine and Aniki were right behind us, swords out. I heard Ahuda blow the signal for the attack. I looked over my shoulder and saw her burst from the tall grass, Dogs at her back. One of them carried a hammer that looked near as big as I was.

Kayu's two mounted rushers jumped to the ground and closed in to protect her. The horses yanked free and ran, knocking down the one who had carried the torch. He lay where he fell, his skull broken.

One rusher came at Tunstall, sword raised high. The cove didn't even see Goodwin lunge in under his strike. She struck him full in the belly with her baton. He doubled over, retching. She knocked him out. "Idiot," she said.

The third rusher tried to run. One of the Dogs who'd come up from the tall grass took him.

The Dog who carried the big hammer gave it to Tunstall. Roaring like a bear, Tunstall smashed the door with it. He was the first one through the opening, Goodwin and me behind him, Lady Sabine and Aniki on our heels.

There was lamplight within the house. From the back and sides I heard the smash of wood. The other

Dogs were breaking in. Guards attacked us from ground floor rooms, swords raised. Goodwin and me ducked low as my lady and Aniki caught the swords on their own blades. I clubbed my attacker hard across the shins on a swing to the side. He—I think it was a he—cried out, knees buckling.

I don't know what happened to him, or what Goodwin and our swordswomen did to get the upstairs guards out of the way. Things went so fast after Pounce's huge roar, I only remember them in flashes. With Kayu down, my only thought was that the cellar guards might already be killing the diggers.

Down the front hall there was an open door lit by two lamps. I could feel a damp draft coming from it—cellar air. I ran down the hall, through that door, and down the stairs. Tunstall was ahead of me.

The guards below were attacking the diggers, just as I feared. The diggers fought back with picks. Two people lay bleeding on the floor already. I struck at the guards. I tried to bring my prey down but not kill them. I wanted their masters.

The mage marks glowed on the guards' hands, flickering, then fading completely. Berryman and Kora had bound up Kayu's magic or killed her. The guards would not die, not from mage marks, at least. They'd live to tell who hired them.

I kicked a guard's feet from under him and knocked him to the floor, then stood with a foot on his shoulder. A digger came at us, pick raised. His eyes were locked on my prisoner. I raised my baton, keeping it between us as the digger moved around me. He was determined to bash my Rat's head in.

"In the King's name!" I cried. "This man is arrested and will stand trial!"

The digger paused. He was shaking.

"In the King's name," I repeated. "Kill him and I'll hobble you for murder."

He stood there for longer than I liked. Finally he lowered his pick. I looked around me. The cellar was bigger than I'd expected, and deeper. Just as well, because there were ten Dogs here as well as the captives and the guards. Some Dogs gently took picks from the diggers' hands. Goodwin and two others hobbled the guards who were alive.

Everyone was staring, whatever their hands did. Those who'd worked here had put water in shallow bowls cut in the rock walls. In them were pieces of raw fire opal. In the cellar torchlight they shone with spangles and veils of red, blue, purple, gold, and emerald fire. Deep green, crimson, orange, and amber pockets glinted like dragons' eyes from two walls of pink stone that had been dug out twelve feet below the eight-foot-deep cellar.

Opals vanished that night. I know they did. The bowls were empty when the house was cleared out and placed under guard by the army. I blame no one, Dogs or diggers, nor even Aniki or Kora, if they helped themselves. I don't know that I could have stopped myself if I'd not had something bigger on my mind. I'm not sure if Goodwin or Tunstall got any. The ones we'd had before, the finished ones, had all gone into the Happy Bag. I know, because I was there when we logged them in. If they took some this night, they didn't talk about it.

As I hobbled my guard and dragged him to his feet, the digger actually helped me. "They were going to kill us," he said. "I heard two of them talkin' when I carried stones upstairs. That's why they made us swear to tell no one we'd been hired. My children would have been left to starve—" He dropped the Rat's arm, letting the man sway against me. "My little ones!"

"They're safe, Master Ashmiller," I told him. It had taken me a moment to recognize him. He was caked in dirt and thinner by far than he'd been when I'd last seen him. "Safe and sleeping on my floor." I shoved the Rat toward the corner of the cellar where the rest of the surviving guards were kept.

"Cooper," Master Ashmiller said. "The determined one."

"No more determined than your younger daughter," I called over my shoulder.

We cleaned up as fast as we could. The cage wagons rolled out with full loads. Ahuda wanted to get paper issued against Crookshank, his paymistress

Norwood, and the hiring man Poundridge, then have them arrested before they could flee the city. The diggers, including Jack, had to see healers and tell the kennel's clerks what had happened to them. I told Jack I would take him to his children when I came back to the kennel to muster out.

Berryman and Kora got rides on the seat of the cage wagon that held the bound and magicked Kayu. She would go to the mages' prison. Our two mages would have to undo their spells once they got there, to let the King's mages apply their own.

Aniki and Lady Sabine vanished. I think they feared they would have to give reports to the kennel clerks.

Soldiers came down from the Northgate barracks. A crowd was gathering, drawn by the shouts and the fighting. The soldiers would keep them out of the house until the Magistrate's Court decided what to do about the vein of gems under it.

The rest of us gathered outside. With the diggers and their guards on the way to the kennel, we could take a breath. Our Dogs leaned or sat. I wondered if the excitement had rushed from their veins as it had from mine, leaving them feeling old. We would have to go back to Jane Street. We had reports to give. For those of us still on Evening Watch, it was too early to muster off. Kayfer's folk were still in the streets, looking to take vengeance on Crookshank's raiders.

One wagon had not left. It held shovels and twenty

sheets of canvas. I was hoping I wouldn't have to deal with that wagon, but my hope was cracknobbed. Out of the dark came pigeons. They flew down to the ground in front of me, all seventeen of them.

"They know something, don't they, Cooper?" Tunstall asked me as Pounce wound among the birds. "Can they show us?"

"Show us what?" one of the tired Dogs asked.

I pointed to the shuttered house down the alley. "That place and another two doors down on Mulberry," I said. "I'll bet it's them two."

"Shovels," Tunstall ordered. "Spare handkerchiefs." He gave me a shovel and showed me how to tie a pair of handkerchiefs together to make a mask over my nose and mouth. Goodwin took another shovel, Jewel a third, Otterkin a fourth. Tunstall kept a fifth for himself. All tied on masks.

We walked down the alley behind a group of Dogs who kept the crowd back. I was glad to have a mask to hide behind. My tripes were a solid knot. I would have given a year's pay not to enter that lonely looking building. It was a ramshackle place, peeling and cracked, the roof collapsed inward on one side. Only the shutters and the door looked solid.

Someone handed along the hammer from the first house. Tunstall put his shovel aside and smashed the door out of its frame. The others passed lamps to the rest of us. Goodwin led the way inside.

Down the stairs we went, into the cellar, while my heart drummed in my chest. The area under the place was a big hollow, though not as big as in the last house. Pink rock showed on two sides, and the floor had been dug down fifteen feet. Half of the cellar was under a huge mound of dirt.

I gagged. The smell was dreadful, like a Cesspool butcher's dump in the summer heat.

"Breathe through your mouth, Cooper," Jewel said. He sounded kind, his voice muffled by the handkerchief. "It's not so bad that way."

It was still vile.

"Quickest done, quickest over," Tunstall said. Carefully he set his shovel to the mound of dirt and started to dig. We all began to help.

We worked gently, fearing what we might hit. I'd just felt the tip of my shovel touch sommat when we heard wings in that hot space. Eight pigeons had followed us down.

They lined up on a shelf, their eyes glittering. I wasn't sure, color being so strange, but I think Ashes, Pinky, and Spangles sat there, waiting on us.

We found eight dead there. Nine in the other closed-up house. The pigeons had gone all that day in the hope that we would get to those sad bodies and set their ghosts free. It was why they had driven off all the other ghosts. Being left there, unmarked and unmourned, had driven them mad. Once we brought their poor bodies into the open, the birds flew out into the night and were gone.

We needed morgue carts for the dead and more soldiers to guard the houses. The crowd was growing. It was too quiet for a Cesspool gathering. I didn't have to be a longtime Dog to know that. I was a Lower City girl. The best crowds are the ones that laugh and make jokes. Silent ones mean trouble.

Dogs are taught to break up crowds when we can, but none of us had the strength for it. It made me feel better to see the senior Dogs were as weary as me, reduced to slumped shoulders and blank stares by what we'd found in those cellars.

We should have returned to the kennel for muster, but Jewel led the way to a bathhouse instead. The nobles are starting to split up by sexes, lords bathing separate from ladies, but this was an old-fashioned place. We all soaked in the hottest water we could bear and soaped ourselves over and over to rid our hair and skin of the stink. Even Pounce dove into a tub after one group of us left it, rolling over and over in the water. I took a handful of soap and washed his fur. He'd never taken a proper bath before. I supposed he'd never been in summer graves before, either. The attendants looked like they wanted to object. Someone would have to clean the fur from the tub, after all. Pounce meowed at them. I was not to know what he said. Whatever it was, they closed their gobs and kept them closed.

When I was done, Goodwin held a clean uniform out to me. It was long in the arm and leg and there was no Puppy trim, but it was good enough. The veteran Dogs tipped the attendants well. It was enough to turn their fearful looks over the muck we'd carried in with us into small smiles. They even thanked us for our custom, though they did not invite us to return.

Seemingly word had gone out as to our whereabouts. Ersken, Berryman, Kora, Lady Sabine, Aniki, and Jack Ashmiller all waited outside the bathhouse for us. Ersken bore a message from Sergeant Ahuda. He delivered it wide-eyed. "The Sergeant says come in early in the afternoon and write up your reports. She had a talk with the Provost's Advocate at the Magistrate's Court. He says you will all present your cases next week, not tomorrow."

My head spun. I'd forgotten I would have to tell Sir Tullus about the robber that I'd run down on Beltane. Now I had a reprieve. I was so grateful it hurt.

Goodwin read Ahuda's note. "She says we're to have supper, on my lord Gershom's orders." She looked at Ersken. "She also mentions Lord Gershom's coin."

"Oh." Ersken grinned and held out a small pouch of coins. "Sorry, Guardswomen, Guardsmen."

Tunstall took the pouch and handed it to Jewel as Senior Corporal Dog. "Come on," Jewel said. "We never pass up a meal. All of us," he added, looking at our friends. "We have all earned a real feed."

Jack hesitated. He wanted his children. I swallowed. I was wobbling with hunger, but if the man needed to see his little ones . . .

"I would be grateful for a meal," Jack said. "A quick one."

In silence we trooped to the Mantel and Pullet. Our evening had left us wordless. Even for veteran Dogs, this was not a normal watch's work. I felt like what we'd done was just too big for talk.

"It's not often we can be proud of a night's striving," Lady Sabine told us when the maids had served our supper and filled our jacks. She had a cup, befitting her place as a guest and a noble. She raised it. "Let us savor it, and pray the Black God's mercy for the souls that were set free."

"Black God's mercy," we all whispered, and drank.

Jack was good about me needing food, but he ate fast all the same. To thank him for his consideration, I ate fast, too. Nobody said aught but good night when we left with Pounce.

"I've been thinkin'," Jack said as we walked home. "When I've built me strength up a bit . . ." He dug his hands in his pockets. I heard something click, like rocks. "I mean to train for a Dog."

I stopped and stared. "You've been in a cellar too long," I said flat out. Pounce leaped to my shoulder and added his noises to mine. "You're a cove with children—"

"I saw tonight the good that Dogs can do for coves with families," he said.

"Think long and hard," I told him. "I buried a friend from training already. And Dogs get precious few nights like this." I saw a lump of dark clothing where Pottage Lane met Jane Street. Surely the Night Watch could have rousted a drunkard in so public a place.

I went over and prodded the lump with my baton. Torchlight from nearby taverns gave me a better look. This was no drunkard. It was someone laid flat, with a black veil cast over his face. I tugged at the veil.

Fulk lay there, eyes wide in death. Around his neck hung a leather cord. On it was a gold coin.

"Guess you didn't escape Kayfer after all, you stupid cuddy," I whispered. I put my whistle to my lips and blew the summons for a murder.

Monday, May 11, 246

Though it is several hours past dawn and the room is hot, I have done no more than dress and move out onto the landing with my journal. To do it, I had to leave my bed without waking Tansy, then dress and cross the floor without waking one of the four Ashmillers. Lucky for me, everyone was worn out from our late night return. I spent the quiet time writing up yesterday, since I can hear no sound from any rooms but my landlady's on the ground floor. Seemingly my other housemates are also tired from yesterday.

I wonder what Rosto was up to, since he did not catch up with us.

The children are stirring. Mayhap I will go to Mistress Noll's and buy a treat to celebrate Jack's

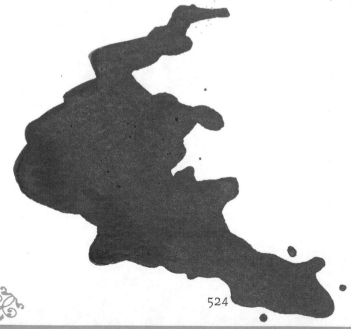

That mess happened because someone whistled so loud from the ground floor that my hand jerked. My pen went clear out of my hand. I ruined a *whole page* in this journal. I went running downstairs. Even seeing the lad's armband with the Provost's badge on it didn't stop me from saying, "Don't you know folk are *sleeping*? And that after a sarden lousy night?"

He shrugged. "I'm told Puppy Cooper lives here."

I tried to stay cross, but I'd been a runner, after all. And a runner wouldn't be after a Puppy unless the matter was important. "That's me."

"Riot duty. They're calling the Fourth Watch and the Evening Watch in for backup duty. Muster at Westberk and Koskynen," the lad said. "They told me you might know where I'd find Puppy Ersken Westover."

Riot duty? Pox and murrain, I thought. "I'll get Ersken," I said, my gut twisting. "What happened?"

The lad grinned at me. He was missing two bottom teeth. "They found four dozen dead folk in one of Crookshank's houses, and the mob wants t' tear 'im apart. So I hear." He dashed off down the street, on his way to rouse some more Dogs.

Upstairs, I heard Jack's little boy start to cry. "Piss," I said. I ran up to Kora's rooms and pounded on the door. The door was new. I remembered why and stood to one side of the frame so as not to get blasted.

"Wha?" I heard Ersken moan inside.

"Riot backup duty!" I called. "Get dressed!"

I went upstairs and put on my uniform, boots, belt, and armor. "There's a riot, if you didn't hear," I told the Ashmillers and Tansy. All of them watched me with scared eyes. "If it comes this far, go to the kennel. They'll protect you. Pounce, stay with them. A riot's no place for a cat, even you." I closed the door behind me and trotted downstairs. Ersken and Kora lingered at her door, kissing.

I grabbed him as I passed. "I'm not having fun, you're not having fun," I told him as I towed him along.

"You sound more like Goodwin every day," he mumbled.

"I begin to see how she got the way she is," I said.

Even as we approached the mustering point, we could hear the distant roar of the riot. Gooseflesh spread over my skin. Anyone of the Lower City knows that sound and fears it. Folk caught up in a riot aren't our cousins and sisters, our brothers and uncles. They are part of a big animal with many arms and claws, armed with stones and sticks.

Armorers handed out rectangular shields. We lined up for ours, then found our Dogs. To my shock, Goodwin grinned when she saw me. "Days like this, you're glad you're a Dog, admit it, Cooper," she said.

Tunstall scratched his head. All of his short hair stood on end. "She acts like this when she's worn to the bone," he told me. "You'll get used to it. No Master Pounce?"

"He's too wise to come out here," Goodwin said, putting her helm on and doing up the strap. "Why should he? He's not paid to get kicked in the head."

The Night Watch Commander was still in charge, since the riot had started on his watch. He passed among us, giving orders. "Keep calm," he told us. "With luck, you won't be needed." Other Dogs were out already, in the thick of it—Night Watch Dogs and Day Watch. Soldiers were in place to the south and west, he told us, squeezing the mob. It was our duty to wait and to be ready, just in case.

After he moved on, I asked Tunstall, "Is it true? The mob wants Crookshank?"

"It's true," he said. "It started brewing when we found those graves."

"They started talking, and then they started drinking," Goodwin said. "It's not like the old scale never made any enemies in the Cesspool. Seventeen dead, finding out eight more were lined up to die next, that Crookshank kicked two dozen families out of those houses so he could dig there—I heard that on the way here this morning—folk got upset."

I felt the fire opal in my breeches pocket. Crookshank would pay a high price for his stones.

Other Dogs came over to talk to mine about what we'd found last night. That was when I had the time to think. If the mob got hold of the old man, I'd not shed a tear. But Herun was still with the Shadow Snake, still alive, with three days yet before the kidnap deadline. If the mob tore Crookshank to pieces, the Snake had no reason to keep Herun breathing.

I fidgeted, sweating under my armor in the thick heat. I listened to the distant roar and watched the mages who were present. They huddled over crystals and mirrors, calling out all manner of reports to the Watch Commanders. It sounded confusing to me. What wasn't confusing was the crowd's noise. It was coming closer. We were but two blocks from Stuvek Street and Crookshank's house.

Madly enough, vendors came by, offering food for sale. Tunstall bought raisin buns and shared them, two for Goodwin and two for me. "You don't know when we'll eat next," he said.

The pigeons arrived, their wings making high-pitched noises in the heavy air. I looked up, thinking they'd come for the food. Instead they flew at me, wings beating at my head. The ghosts of children screamed in my ears, demanding mothers, fathers, sisters, brothers. The birds soared and plunged around me. They dodged as my Dogs and I swung at them, trying to drive the cursed things off. Ersken, his Dogs, Jewel, and Yoav, who stood with us, all tried to help.

"What do they want?" shouted Jewel. I'd never seen the old man so pale before.

"The Shadow Snake!" I shouted. I grabbed one

and held it as it pecked and smacked at my face. "They want me to—us to get the Shadow Snake!"

Suddenly they flew to the rooftops. I stood there gawping, a pigeon in my hands. "Now what?" I asked.

"Beka!" a voice I knew shouted from down the street.

I turned to look. Rosto the Piper walked down Koskynen like he owned it. He'd a long cut over one cheekbone. The blood on it was dry, but the cut wasn't that old—mayhap a few hours.

"Guardsfolk," he said, and smiled. "Lovely day for a riot." They glared at him. "Beka, might I have a word?"

"We're on duty, you know," Tunstall said.

"Three companies of infantry just arrived from Riverfort," Rosto said. "They're moving up Mulberry Street. Phelan sent a message to Kora that two companies of cavalry are crossing Kingsbridge right now from the Highfields barracks. Your rioters are going to get crushed. Cooper?"

I looked at my Dogs. Tunstall shrugged. Goodwin gave me a tiny nod.

Still holding my pigeon, I went to Rosto.

"If you wanted another pet, couldn't you ask that cat to get you a kitten?" he wanted to know. "Since he's distributing them?"

I just stared at him. I'd been having a hard week.

"Oh, I can see you're in a mood. What *you* need is a man."

He seemed more than a bit cracked today. And I couldn't let him talk to me like that. He thought I'd be one of his deadly mots, like Aniki and Kora, though seemingly Kora had changed her man, if not her place with the law.

"How'd you get that?" Even knowing better, I couldn't stop myself from touching his cut.

It's hard to hold an angered pigeon with just one hand. The bird burst out of my grip and smacked us both with its wings. Then it escaped into the sky, its curst ghost laughing.

"You told it to do that," Rosto complained. The pigeon had struck his cut. It opened to bleed afresh.

I gave him my handkerchief. "No, but it was funny. Master the Piper—since you've no last name—I'm on duty. What did you have to say to me?"

Though the cut must have hurt from the pigeon's blow, he'd been smiling. Now the humor left his face. He leaned down and put his lips beside my ear. "Yates Noll," he told me. "One of my people got word to me. He and three hard coves are laired at the Sheepmire. They moved into one of the special sheds two days ago, after dark."

I looked up at Rosto, blinking, my brain scrambling like a rabbit. They had sheds in back of the tavern, I remembered. I'd run past them that night

I'd chased Orva Ashmiller down. Mostly they were said to hold goods that the Rogue considered his. It wasn't healthy to inspect them, and the price for leaving them be was part of the weekly Happy Bag.

"You're trying to get me in bloody with the Rogue," I said in his ear.

Rosto kissed my cheek. "Forget Kayfer," he told me. "Do you want Yates or not?" He trotted past my Dogs with a cheerful wave. "Don't mind me," he shouted. "I'm off to chat with Dawull."

Tunstall and Goodwin came over to me. "He looks like a rat with cheese on his whiskers," Tunstall said. "What wickedness is he up to?"

I told them what he'd said. "Please, can we go?" I asked, though it was begging, more like. "You know what'll happen with soldiers' horses in it. We'll risk our nobs along with the crowd. Herun's only got three more days if Crookshank obeys the note. If he don't or if the mob gets 'im . . . Please, we've got to try!" I had my fire opal tight in my fist. I could feel its edges biting into my glove.

Tunstall rubbed his chin. I heard whiskers rasp on his gloved fingers. "She's got a point, Clary. And just think—the digger case and the Shadow Snake wound up in the same week. That's tidy Dog work for you."

Goodwin gave us both a look that would peel rock. "Now I know why you like having a Puppy so much," she said, disgusted. "It makes you all eager again. Like you were getting bored." She stomped over to the Night Watch Commander.

"She was bored, too. Though I confess, I didn't think Puppies brought such big crimes with them," Tunstall said. "Or found big crimes so quick." He gave me a funny look. I thought there might be shame in it. "Mayhap it's just you see with fresh eyes when you have a Puppy to care for. You see bad business that's been there all along."

I didn't know what to say, so I kept my gob shut. The pigeons wheeled overhead, their wings flapping. Slapper landed near me, stumping his way along as he pecked for crumbs.

From somewhere toward the river we heard the call of trumpets. Toward the palace, we heard trumpets answer. The military was closing in.

Ersken came over to us. "Take me with you," he said. "You're going after Herun Lofts—I want to come, too. I've done as much walking and questioning on this as you three. My Dogs will release me if you say so!"

Tunstall looked down at him. "How'd you know what we were planning?"

Ersken pointed at me. "Look at her eyes! She's got the scent of something. Lately only two things do that to her!"

I could barely stand still. I was just thinking, Dogs be cursed, I'll go on my own and take the conse-quences, when Goodwin returned. "Let's go, you eager young things. I hope Rosto's tip is a good one. The Commander says to take our shields. Roving parties of looters are escaping the Guard nets." She looked at Ersken, then back at his Dogs. They nodded to her. "Come on, Ersken. We may as well have a Puppy parade."

Ersken only grinned at her.

We grabbed our shields, though I would have been happy to leave the curst heavy things behind. Off we went at a trot, Ersken beside me, Tunstall beside Goodwin. We'd just passed Nipcopper Lane when someone said, *"Manh!"*

I looked at Pounce. His purple eyes glinted up at me. He looked very pleased with himself as he ran at my side.

The deeper we went into the Cesspool, the quieter it got. Folk were staying indoors. The sky turned a sickly green-gray as deep black clouds climbed high overhead. I thanked Mithros silently. A thunderstorm would dampen the mob and put out any fires that got started. In the meantime, though, the air was thick and sticky. I felt like I was dragging it into my chest.

We'd reached Crow Street when a clutch of twenty-odd looters charged out to meet us. These were the ones smart enough to go around the places where Dogs and soldiers would place traps. They were using the riot as an excuse to rob.

We raised our shields. Ersken and me moved sideways like we'd been taught, getting in a line at Tunstall's right. We smashed into this small mob hard. Clubs smacked my shield. A mot moved around to my side to hit me with a bucket, of all things. I smacked her raised elbow with my baton. She squealed and dropped the bucket, grabbing the elbow with her other hand.

Pigeons flew down to attack the looters, flying into their faces. The looters cursed and yelped, then called on their gods. Before my shield I felt them give way. All four of us put our shoulders behind our shields, ramming ahead. The looters stumbled. One fell under Tunstall's feet. He kicked the lout in the belly. That left the man too busy puking to leap on our backs as we passed.

Behind us we heard the clatter of horses.

I chanced a look to the rear. Four armored knights and ten mounted soldiers rode toward us. "Break," Goodwin said quietly.

We split in the middle, Ersken and me to one side of the street, Goodwin and Tunstall to the other, letting the horsemen ride through. The pigeons flew up out of the way. As the looters ran from the advancing horsemen, Tunstall beckoned to us. He led us into one of the twisty side streets, away from Koskynen.

We saw some who might have been looters after that, but once they glimpsed us, they ran. Any bigger groups, with numbers to give them courage, were looking for richer pickings on toward the markets.

We heard the first roll of thunder as we passed through the sagging gate at the rear of the Sheepmire. The place looked even more depressing than it did at night, crumbling and nasty.

Tunstall motioned for us to put down our shields. Here they would only get in the way.

We looked around. There was the tavern, half stone and half timber. It had a stable, though I hated to think of horses there. Pigs and chickens did their best in the yard. We saw a chicken coop. The pigeons came to rest on its roof, as silent now as the birds with the diggers' ghosts had been the day before.

Two of the sheds were good only for wood storage. Two more weren't big enough for five men, if Herun was still alive. That left three the size of small cottages. We looked at the first. There was leaf litter at the front and rear doors. Tunstall shook his head. No one had opened those doors in a week at least. Quietly we crossed the yard until we stood between that shed and the one next to it. It looked more promising, it and the one closer to the tavern. These two had clear doorsills.

Tunstall signaled Ersken to check the other shed. As he went running across the open yard I listened at the wall next to me for any leak of sound. I heard men laugh inside just as Ersken shook his head.

Tunstall signaled him back. Goodwin beckoned him around to the rear door. Tunstall and I had the front. Tunstall held out his hand and counted fingers off for me, giving Ersken and Goodwin time to get ready: one, two, three, four, five. Then he hit the door with all of his weight.

Mayhap it had been a strong door. It wasn't up to Tunstall's strength and weight, though. It snapped from its hinges. Three men who were dicing on the floor scrambled to their feet. I lunged at the first with my baton and swung it up under his chin as hard as I could. He dropped and lay still. Behind him, in a corner, I saw a man bound hand and foot and hooded like a hawk. With the cold, clear attention that came to me in a fight, I recognized the embroidery on his tunic. Tansy loved to sew that griffin and flower pattern.

Goodwin and Ersken broke through the rear door. Thunder boomed, shaking the very air. They hit another of the rushers from behind as Tunstall hit him from the front. That one just wilted to the floor. I was on the third rusher. He tried to fend me off with a footstool until I kicked him between his legs. When he doubled over, I struck him down with my baton and tapped his kidneys so he wouldn't rise for a time.

Yates Noll had been sleeping on a cot in the corner. The sister beater and child stealer sported heavy whiskers, and his hair was greasy from lack of washing. As we moved in, he backed into a corner, waving a dagger. He was smiling.

"Drop it," Goodwin ordered. "We arrest you in

the King's name, for murder and kidnapping as the Shadow Snake."

"I must stay shadowed," he said, his eyes a-glitter. "Di'n't your little terrier tell you about me? How I'm a hard cove, a cruel one? All the Lower City fears me now. What good is it if I die screamin' on Execution Hill?"

"You've nowhere to go," Tunstall told him. "It's time to answer to Mithros."

"And I will," he said. He thrust the dagger into his throat under his jaw. He did it before we could move, and no amount of healing could have saved him. He bled to death fast, making a frightful mess. I don't think I will ever forget the look in his eyes.

"Good," Tunstall said at last. "Saves the realm the cost of caging and trying him."

"No, it's the execution that's the expensive part," Goodwin said. "Well, and caging him until then. That gets costly."

Tunstall spat on the dirt floor.

Pounce had run over to Herun. Suddenly the ropes slid off Herun's wrists and ankles as Pounce dragged them away in his teeth. Ersken hesitated, then lifted the hood off Herun's head. "Master Lofts? You're free." Herun just stared at Ersken, dazed. Ersken began to chafe Herun's ankles, working the blood back into them. "It's all right." Ersken's voice was gentle. "You're safe. We'll need a report from you, understand. We still have to try these fellows." Pounce clambered onto Herun's lap and began to knead one of his pale wrists, purring. Herun reached out and petted my cat.

Tunstall was already hobbling one of the downed men. I remembered my duty and hurried to help. Yates dead, Herun free . . . I felt odd. Not quite attached to the world, as if I was a ghost myself. Who would tell Mistress Noll?

"Where's the loot?" Tunstall asked his Rat. "Not here. You weren't dicing for it." We looked at the coppers on the floor.

"Where's the loot Yates got for those kidnapped children?" Goodwin asked as she bound the hands of the second of the three Rats we'd taken. "What did you do with it?"

Ersken hauled the third Rat to his feet. "There wasn't much coin, all told. They could have spent it."

"Yates kept sayin' how we'd never need another job after this," his captive said, his voice bitter. "No more handfuls of coin and bits of jewelry to sell for half the worth—"

"If he'd let us sell," complained Tunstall's captive. "The best stuff just vanished and we'd get paid in coin."

"We'll tell you what you want to know. On'y keep us from the mob," Goodwin's Rat told her.

"We'll think on it," Tunstall said. It took him and

me both to haul his Rat up. He was on the heavy side. "Went out and had a look this morning, did you, lads? Got an eyeful of what a mob might do?"

The Rat shuddered.

Goodwin propped her Rat on the wall and started to collect their packs, stuffing whatever might be of use to the Magistrate into them. Ersken went through Yates's pockets and turned his things over to Goodwin. I hobbled our Rats in a string, like slaves.

Tunstall got a horse and a canvas from the inn's stable, and the innkeeper came out to squall. He'd been too afraid to do so while we were making noise in his shed, but now that it looked like we were real Dogs who were taking his horse, he had plenty to say.

Tunstall ignored him. First he wrapped Yates in the canvas. Then he tied the body to the horse's back. I'd've expected a beast to be unhappy near the stink of so much blood, but not this one. I think he might well have been used for such a purpose before.

When the innkeeper protested one time too many, Tunstall grabbed him by the collar. "Come to the Jane Street kennel to fetch it," he said, friendly for all he half lifted the man in the air. "And thank the gods we will give the horse back. Don't try to tell me you didn't know you were hiding wanted men." He dropped the innkeeper. After that, we heard not one squeak more from the cove.

Once we'd gathered all that might be useful,

Goodwin handed a pack to Ersken and a pack to me. "It's a long walk back to the kennel in the rain," she said. "Let's see how much of it we can manage before the storm breaks."

I wondered if fish in jelly felt as I did on that walk. We'd finished the Shadow Snake. He was dead, the Lower City safe. These Rats were eager to talk, to be spared the cage Dog torturers and the mob. If they had information of value to trade, they might turn their executions to lifetime labor in the quarries or on the roads of the realm.

That was not my affair. I still had a feeling of things left undone.

Someone would have to tell Mistress Noll that her youngest son was dead. That his presents to her were paid for in the blood of children. Did she suspect? She was a wise mot. She had to think the son who'd never done well in the world had come by pretty things like that lily pendant in some crooked way.

Did he give her only the odd present, or did she get more? My mind showed me pictures with each flash of lightning. It wasn't just that pendant, sommat any son might give his mother, loot that wouldn't fetch much coin from a scale. I remembered the lists of the victims and the prices for their return I had kept for weeks. Among the more than twenty payments I knew of, there had been a spell book. Pearl earrings. Other pieces of jewelry our Rats hadn't kept.

The rain came down in a roar before we reached Crow Street. Even with our shields held over us, we could scarcely see where to plant our feet. Then the hail began, fist-sized chunks of it. We had to protect the horse with our shields, the poor beast. There were no rioters now. They'd fled indoors. We did, too, at the first chance, ducking into a collapsing warehouse. We sheltered there until the hail ended, then trudged on. The closer we got to the kennel, the more we noticed the stench of smoke. There had been fires near the Nightmarket as well as in other parts of the Cesspool. Near Crookshank's house.

The line of Dogs with rioters to be caged stretched from the kennel to the Nightmarket. We all moaned even as we fell in behind the last pair and their captives. A packed cage wagon rattled past. That meant the Jane Street cages were full. They were sending the overflow straight to Outwalls Prison. The rain poured down. Just when I thought it was easing, I heard the approach of thunder. A fresh storm was coming in.

My Dogs talked with the others that fell in line behind us with their captives. Ersken went off to find his Dogs and returned with news. One of the fires was lit at Crookshank's house. The old man never got out. Two had been trapped with him, but not Annis. No one knew where she was, but the servants that escaped said she wasn't home, nor was Tansy.

Goodwin looked at Herun. "I'm sorry your grand-father's dead," she told him. "Sorry you had to hear in such a way."

Herun was leaning against the wall of a building under the eaves, out of the rain. He only nodded. He'd said little since we brought him out of the shed.

Goodwin's words made me itch under my skin. "May I go to Mistress Noll?" The words just popped out of my mouth. Tunstall, Goodwin, Ersken, even the captives stared at me. "That innkeeper won't keep his gob shut. Even if he does, his servants won't. She did good things for me when I was little. Wouldn't it be kinder for her to hear it from me?"

Goodwin sighed. Tunstall looked at her. "We don't need Cooper to log the prisoners, Clary. And Mistress Deirdry's fed us often enough. She deserves better than hearing it from the nearest busybody. Someone who'll tell her it was worse than it was."

"Do it quick," Goodwin told me.

I gave my shield to Ersken and took off through the rain, splashing water up above my hips as I trotted. Pounce ran next to me. The mud slid off his glossy fur like it was coated with oil.

As the second downpour eased, the pigeons soared along the streets ahead of us. Why were they still with me? Yates was dead.

Mistress Noll made her new home of the last year or so on Whippoorwill Mews and Pottage Lane. It was far better than the place she'd had on Mutt Piddle Lane. That crowded little house had three ovens and a flock of children living all around waiting to grab whatever she made. This place had ten ovens. Her married daughters lived on either side. They helped her. She had hired workers, too, where once her husband had run her business into the ground. He'd never had a head for money matters.

The servant who answered my knock looked at my uniform and let me in. Other workers were putting away the gate braces and continuing the day's baking. The servant waved me toward the house, not even noticing my cat. I scraped my boots and walked into the kitchen. A maid fetched Gemma for me. Like the man who'd answered the gate, she paid no mind to Pounce.

"She's doing the accounts," Gemma said when I asked for her mother. "This way." As I followed her, she said, "I'm that surprised to see you. I thought certain you'd be with your Dogs. They're saying the mob is setting fires."

"They're out, and the army is in the streets, keeping order," I said, thinking, They've not heard about Yates. Thank the gods Tunstall wrapped him before we took him through the city.

I watched Gemma as she walked through the narrow hall between the kitchen and the main house. She wore her hair up in a cloth, and there were flour smears on her long outer tunic. I wondered if she ever stopped working. Leaving her neck uncovered as she had, she'd also left bare a bruise shaped like a man's fingers.

At least that has ended, I thought. Yates will beat her no more.

Why had Mistress Noll permitted it? I knew she had ruled her man and children with an iron will. She could have stopped Yates from hitting Gemma.

"Why didn't you leave here?" I asked her. "Why stay and let Yates treat you so bad? Couldn't you live with one of your sisters?"

"Ma wanted me here," Gemma said. "In this house, you do as Ma says."

"Always?" I asked, having a very bad thought. No. Not the grannylady. Not the woman who had given me and my family bread when we were hungry.

We walked into a tidy little sitting room, Gemma, Pounce, and me. Mistress Noll was bent over a table, squinting at an account book. "You stupid slut, did I not tell you we needed those custards made as soon as may be?" she asked, without looking up. "Riot or no, the Shoemakers' Guild has their supper tonight—" She finally thought to glance at us. "Beka Cooper. Surely your Dogs have work for you just now. Gemma, be about your business."

"Actually, I have news for you both, Mistress Noll," I said. "My Dogs sent me."

Mistress Noll set down her reed pen and leaned back in her chair. Pounce leaped up on her account book to stare her in the face. "And what news is so important that it brings you to my home in the middle of a riot?"

"The riot is done," I said. "I have news of Yates."

Mistress Noll went very still. "What of my son?"

"He is dead," I told her. I heard Gemma gasp. "Forgive me. We have his partners in the Shadow Snake kidnappings in hobbles. We took them all together. Yates would be alive, but he killed himself."

Mistress Noll's face was as hard as iron. "And he said he was the Shadow Snake?"

"Ma," Gemma whispered.

"Shut your gob," Mistress Noll ordered.

"Yates said it," I replied. "So do his friends, who we took alive." I did not take my eyes from her face as I bluffed, "But we know he's no more the Snake than I am. It was Tansy made me wonder about you, Mistress. Tansy and that lily pendant you wear."

She raised a hand to the necklaces around her throat. The lily one was hidden again, under her clothes. "What has that waterfront trull to say about me?" she asked.

"When my Dogs were there, you talked so well of Tansy," I said. I kept my voice polite. Hearing Yates was dead had cracked sommat in her, for all she talked so hard. She was going to pieces before me. "I remembered how much she cost you, how she'd put you in a rage. You were glad when you somehow got word of the fire opals. It gave you an excuse to hurt her. I think you'd've killed Rolond even if the old man did pay." I saw her hands turn to big-knuckled fists in her lap. All those years of baking—she could strike a fearful blow, even at her age. "Did you mean to even kill *her* in time?"

"You lived on Mutt Piddle Lane, Beka," Mistress Noll said. "We worked like slaves to get out, and that brat took coin from my pocket. Every time she robbed me, I had to replace what goods I'd made. I'd not gain a copper on business that was meant to put me and mine ahead in the world. I was happy to feed you neighborhood children on the overdone stuff and the day's leavings. You made deliveries. You fetched firewood and water. But you'd let her steal from me and then you'd laugh. No sense of gratitude, any of you. Content to wallow in the filth and let others feed you."

"Why the other kidnappings? Those folk were your customers. Your neighbors." I watched her, trying to keep my voice steady.

"Why?" She raised her eyebrows at me. "You ask me that? I'd not stay on Mutt Piddle Lane! There I was, breaking my back over the ovens, getting us a table here and a stall there, and along comes Mistress Painter with a ruby pendulum. A *ruby* pendulum, when all know she'd not enough Gift to whistle up rain in a thunderstorm. Her brat was running about, kicking dust on the front of the stalls for amusement." She bowed her head, raising a hand to her throat. "I lost my temper, as I've lost it now. But you'll not live to tell of it." I heard a snap. She flung something at me, something she'd broken from one of her necklaces. I remembered too late that curse charms were among the things she'd taken.

Pounce, who sat forgotten on her account book, leaped. He caught the thing in his jaws and dropped to the floor. I cried out and jumped at Mistress Noll, smashing her chair against her table. She punched at me with her heavy baker's hands. I seized all of her necklaces and dragged them over her head, scraping her cheeks and nose, pulling off her head cloth, and yanking her hair from its pins as she bruised my ribs and chest. I dropped the necklaces to the side of the chair and planted one hand over her nose, third fingertip on her left eyelid, index fingertip on her right.

"Gemma, help me!" she cried.

"No, Ma," I heard Gemma say. "Not this time."

"Shut your gob," I told Mistress Noll, "or you'll lose an eye for killing my cat. Both eyes if you rush me."

She went still. She could not abide the thought of being maimed. She knew I would do it. I, too, came from Mutt Piddle Lane.

One handed, as we'd practiced it in training, I tied a thong to her right wrist after feeling it for more charms. Swiftly I grabbed her left arm with the hand I'd used to threaten her eyes and bound her wrists together.

"You've no proof," Mistress Noll said, her eyes cold. "You think *she* will be a witness against me?"

"You have all the things you didn't sell," I said. I drew my dagger. From the heap of necklaces I fished out the lily pendant and two others I recognized from the descriptions I'd been given. Her pearl earrings looked familiar for the same reason. To be sure, I took them off her and checked the silver backs. There, in tiny letters, the cove who'd bought them had asked the smith to carve his mot's initials, T. L. "The charms and the books of spells will be in this house. And the mages will have the rest of it out of you and Gemma."

"You can't arrest me," Mistress Noll said. "You're only a Puppy who's got above herself."

"No, I can't arrest you. But I can drag you by the hair if need be," I told her. "And as we go to Jane Street, I'll shout what I'm taking you in for. It's not raining so hard that folk won't hear me. Mayhap you won't make it alive so my Dogs can arrest you proper." My blood pounded in my temples, I was so cold and so angry. I had believed in her kindness until today. She had kidnapped and murdered children and destroyed families for gain and for spite. "Or you and Gemma can walk along with me peaceful-like and get arrested on the quiet. Then you'll answer for it all before a proper court. Before the law." I looked at Gemma. "You knew about this. I'm taking you with us."

Gemma nodded.

I made myself look around for Pounce then. I ground my teeth, trying to ready myself for the sight of him dying or dead. He'd attacked a curse, after all.

Instead I saw him roll something around in his mouth, the better to chew it. Tiny red arms shot out around his teeth, flailing. Then they curled up. Whatever Pounce ate got smaller until he swallowed the remains. Then he began to wash.

"You're alive," I said like a ducknob.

Partway through licking a paw, he stopped and glared at me. *You think me a poor creature if you believe a tiny curse like that would even ruffle my fur.*

Properly scolded, I knelt so Mistress Noll would not kick me and began to hobble her ankles.

When I came back to my Dogs, Ersken, Herun, and Yates's gang, they were a block from the kennel in the line. Tunstall raised his brows when I joined them towing Mistress Noll and Gemma.

"I thought you were breaking sad news, Cooper. This is a strange way to do it."

I explained about my dreams of the old days and knowing the way Mistress Noll ruled her children. And how one idea had led to another.

"We were thinking about how much of the loot she got, once our feet started to hurt," Tunstall said. "Why the Shadow Snake still lived in his mother's house and worked for her hauling bakery goods. We just didn't see

how we could go talk with her dragging these three."
He tugged the rope that tethered Yates's hobbled
friends.

"An old woman did this?" Herun whispered. "An
old woman had my boy murdered, me kidnapped, for
charms and a few coins?"

"For fire opals, lad," Goodwin said. "So she could
stop dealing in charms and coins and never make another pasty."

Suddenly Gemma, at the back of the three men of
Yates's gang, started to laugh. We looked at her and at
her mother. Mistress Noll raised her tied hands to her
mouth. Gemma was laughing, but thin tears trickled
down her mother's cheeks.

The Rat who was tied next to them moved back as
much as he could. "He told them Crookshank's dead,"
Ersken said to us. "Gemma thinks it's funny."

"Never again, she swore," Gemma said, gasping
for air. "All over after this. And it is! Ma's a prophet-
ess, because it *is* all over forever. But it was for naught!"

She began to laugh again. Suddenly Mistress Noll
swung her arms. She smacked her daughter on the side
of the head, knocking Gemma to the ground. Tied to
the string of captives, Gemma almost pulled her mother
down with her before she scrambled to her feet.

"Shut yer useless gob, you sarden addlepate," Mistress Noll ordered Gemma, her voice flat. "You'll get
us torn t' bits. At least your brother was of use."

Gemma stared at her. "And he got us killed, Mother," she said. "When we scream for the executioner's mercy, you'll remember Yates left *us* to face it! And I never did a thing but share your house!"

Tunstall walked over to Gemma and put a hand on Mistress Noll, keeping her away from her daughter. "Agree to give testimony against your mother, and we'll get you mercy. You'll live." He looked at the bruise that was shaping on the side of Gemma's face, then at Mistress Noll. "We'll even tie you at the front of the string right now, close to us."

Gemma nodded. I retied Mistress Noll to the Rat who had told her Crookshank was dead. Ersken brought Gemma up and tied her so that she was the first of our string of captives.

"Guardsfolk," said Herun. He nodded to the Dogs in front of us. They were standing aside. They made their Rats move, too. They'd cleared the path to the kennel.

"What's this?" Goodwin asked, hands crossed over her chest.

"We been listenin'," one of the Dogs in front of us said. He was a big Scanran who worked the Night Watch. "You got the Shadow Snake's gang. Go on."

"I don't want favors," Goodwin said.

Ersken looked down, making a face. If his feet hurt as bad as mine, I know he wanted a favor or two.

"Don't call it a favor, then," the Scanran's partner

said. "If word gets out that's who you've got, we'll have a fresh mob on us. Go."

Other Dogs waved us on.

"Guardswoman, I don't know what has become of my mother," Herun said quietly. "And I don't know where my wife is."

"Tansy is at my place," I told him. "She came to stay with me two nights ago."

Herun smiled at me shyly. "I would like to see her before dawn," he told Goodwin. "And I want to find my mother."

Goodwin looked at him. Then she headed for the kennel, Herun at her heels. Tunstall led our string of captives. Me and Ersken brought up the rear with Pounce, the tip of his tail a jaunty black flag.

As I passed, Dogs clapped me on the shoulder.

There was good news for Herun inside. Mistress Annis was in the healers' room with three of Crookshank's servants. The worst harm they had taken was in breathing a bit of the smoke. For an extra blessing, Tansy had come the moment she heard where she could find her mother-in-law. Once she saw her man, it was all we could do to pry Herun away long enough for him to give a report of his kidnapping. Since I had work yet to do, I sent them all to my lodgings for the night. They could find a place to live in the morning.

"You'll let Cooper get away with just going to

arrest a Rat on her own?" Ahuda asked my Dogs when she looked over our reports.

"I didn't plan to do it when I went there," I said. I shut up the instant Ahuda scowled at me.

"She's a Puppy," Tunstall said. "She hasn't even been in the work for two months. She'll learn."

"If she doesn't die," Goodwin added. "If we don't all three die of sore feet and empty bellies."

"Everyone dies," the Day Watch Sergeant said. He was logging in prisoners, too. "Down here, sooner before later. Take off. If you die tonight, at least you should do it with a full belly."

We looked at Ahuda. She glared at us. "Go away," she ordered. "Cooper, leave the arrests to your Dogs."

Wednesday, May 13, 246

Noon.

I woke in the morning to sunlight and a knock on the door. The shutters were open. Pigeons fluttered there, eating from Tansy's hand. Herun, wearing a wrinkled shirt and breeches, watched her from a corner. There was a light in his face that wasn't anything to do with the morning sun. I saw then that he truly loved her for more than her looks. That was a good thing.

She turned to smile at him, the same light in her eyes. Then she yelped. A pigeon had pecked her for taking away the hand with the food in it.

One of the Lofts servants opened my door. Aniki poked her head inside. The two Ashmiller girls got up to pet Laddybuck, in Aniki's hand. When I sat up on my blankets, Aniki said, "Breakfast?"

We went outside so there'd be room to move. The storm had cooled things off. From somewhere we found enough benches and barrelheads to sit on. We had but odds and ends—stale breads and old turnovers and pasties. Luckily sausages and cheese kept, and there was dried fruit. No one could shop for fresh food during a riot. At least we had plenty. That was as well, because there were plenty of folk to share it with—the Lofts household, the Ashmillers, my housemates, Ersken, Phelan, and me.

When they came down to the yard to eat, Kora let

go of Ersken's hand to hug me fiercely. "Crone's blessings on you, Terrier," she whispered in my ear. "You've caught and killed the Snake."

I hesitated, but truly, on this day I felt too good to lock my heart away. I hugged her back. "*We* did it," I said. "All of us. All of us. The Lower City killed its own Snake."

I heard a mew. I'd nearly mashed Fuzzball in his sling. "He'll never walk anywhere if you go on carrying him," I said. Kora took him out and put him on the ground.

"If she puts him down, he heads straight for the nearest food," Ersken said. "Uh-oh. He thinks Master Pounce will stand for that."

Pounce was eating cheese. He was particularly fond of it, though it did not improve his breath. Fuzzball grabbed a piece. Pounce smacked Fuzzball, sending the little one rolling into Laddybuck. Laddybuck reared back, mewed, and smacked Fuzzball himself.

"Now there's a king," Rosto said of the fierce kitten as he joined us. The Ashmiller girls shrieked with joy. Rosto carried a honeycomb in a bowl as well as half a loaf of bread. He gave it over to them and picked up Laddybuck, looking him in the eyes. "Don't let anyone show you disrespect, my lad, that's right. From furball to rusher." The cut he'd had on his cheek was nearly mended, only a long scar left of it. I frowned. He could have gotten a mage to heal it with no scar at all.

Unless he *wanted* a scar. "Mother's milk, you did it," I said. "You killed him. You're the Rogue."

Rosto cupped Laddybuck in one hand, grabbed me by the back of the neck, and kissed me on the mouth. I should have punched him, but his mouth was sweet and soft. I will punch him next time.

"I promise, I won't let my head get swollen," he said after he let me go. "But things had to change, Beka. You knew it as well as we did." He looked around. "This house makes a good headquarters. We could turn it into a tavern. The Court of the Rogue that we have, that building is all wrong. It gives people notions that they're royalty. They forget they're supposed to look after the Lower City first."

Aniki slapped him on the calf. "Wonderful plans. Now sit down and eat."

Around nine a runner came to tell Ersken and me that all Dogs were off duty for a few days. The King had proclaimed martial law in the city. Soldiers would keep the peace in the streets. Folk could shop, but no crowds of greater than ten would be allowed to form.

Tansy, Herun, Mistress Annis, and the Lofts servants were the first to leave. They had money—Herun is his grandfather's heir. They would stay in one of Crookshank's Patten District houses. I watched them go, feeling relieved. Slapper landed on my shoulder. He had no ghost on him. He didn't, always.

Thursday, May 14, 246

Jack and the children left yesterday. He said he'd come by some money. He didn't say how. I didn't ask, though I fingered my fire opal as they packed their things. The girls never warmed to me, but I did teach their brother the clapping games I'd taught my brothers.

Yesterday afternoon a runner came for me. I was to report to the Magistrate's Court, in uniform, today at nine. I would have to stand before Sir Tullus and tell those parts of the capture that were mine alone. He had chosen to hold what's called an "eclipse session." It is for the trial of Mistress Noll and the Shadow Snake gang. It is feared that if they are tried on our regular Court Day, there might be another riot, soldiers or no. Folk want revenge for three years of fear, and they're angry that the Dogs did not catch her and her gang before this.

I threw up so many times last night that naught was left to come up but water.

I carried Pounce to court. When we approached the gate, he struggled up to my shoulders and scolded me fiercely. *Calm down, will you? It will be over soon and then you can find a rock to hide under.*

The Dogs on the gate eyed us strangely but admitted us. There were no rules against cats, even in an eclipse session.

I felt my stomach heave. Luckily there was naught

557

in it. Anyone who saw me would think I had only belched. Common folk were barred from an eclipse session, but Dogs were not. With the army in the streets, they were off duty. Seemingly, plenty of them were bored.

Surely they have sleep to catch up, washing to do, gardens to mind? I thought, looking at a river of black uniforms. There were so many they flowed into the onlookers' section, behind the bars. In truth, the front benches of the Dogs' section of the court were empty but for three people: Goodwin, Tunstall, and Ersken.

Now I went to take my place with them. Goodwin patted the bench beside her. I sat. Pounce jumped down and went to greet them, like a captain reviewing soldiers.

"Calm down, Cooper," Goodwin told me. "After the last month, I'd think you'd be able to look Sir Tullus in the eye."

Just to try it, I glanced at his desk and flinched. In the places where the soldiers who represented the Crown were accustomed to stand, the court Dogs had placed two chairs with the royal emblem of the crown and sword carved in their backs. People would sit there today. Nobles. Nobles who represented the King.

A hand gloved in kid patted me on the shoulder. "Keep this in your mouth." Lady Sabine offered me a spicy yet pleasant-tasting lozenge. "A friend sends these to me from the Yamani Islands. Tunstall said you get very nervous. Just remember, nine people are alive because you are a Terrier among Dogs." She clapped my shoulder again, smiled to my Dogs and Ersken, then went to the other side of the front half of the courtroom. As a knight, she could command a seat in front of the onlookers' bars.

"I wish people wouldn't call me that," I muttered, though my lady's kindness warmed me as much as the lozenge warmed my mouth.

"You gripped the digger case and the Snake case and wouldn't let them go," Tunstall whispered. "Get used to the name."

"The diggers' guards dealt for mercy on execution and informed on the whole job," Goodwin said. "They were terrified to come to public trial. Kayu had some potion—she killed herself in the mages' prison. Good riddance. Norwood and Poundridge are singing like little birds, trying to buy their way out of the quarries— Up we go. Maiden's tears."

She said that as we stood because Sir Tullus came out with the Lord High Magistrate himself, and my lord Gershom of Haryse. They took those two carved chairs. I sat before I fell.

Though the Lord High Magistrate was present, Sir Tullus ran the trial. It might have been an ordinary court day, except for the handful of Rats, only four Dogs, and two great nobles seated to either side of Sir Tullus. One thing was the same. The morning took forever, because we had to place all of the Shadow Snake matter before the court. My Dogs told some. They showed the maps we had kept and told how I, and my Birdies, found information, and how I brought it to them. They mentioned Ersken helped me, and we both nodded. Rosto, Kora, Aniki, Mistress Painter, and many other folk became "informants of the Lower City," according to custom. They told everything up to Yates's cutting his own throat. Then I had to get up and tell the rest.

I dug my nails into my palms and stood. Pounce leaned against my leg, purring so hard I trembled with it. I swallowed the last bit of lozenge and looked up, fixing my eyes on Sir Tullus's chest.

"My—my lord, I was to tell Mistress Noll Yates was dead," I began. "But I remembered that Mistress Noll tried to, to hit Tansy with her broom." I heard chuckles from the Dogs and gave way. They were listening. I had never seen so many Dogs gathered in one place in my life. They were all listening to me.

"I wish to know how it is that these Guardsfolk came by so much information," said the Lord High Magistrate. Startled, I looked at him. His eyes were pale as mine. If that was how *I* looked at people sometimes, so they felt frozen over, no wonder they didn't like me staring at them. My throat went bone dry. "Goodwin and Tunstall report that this *trainee* Guardswoman, Cooper, enlisted folk of the city to talk to those who had suffered the crimes of this gang. What have you to say for yourself, girl? How did a trainee come to even think a childhood nightmare might be real?"

I looked at the floor. He made it sound like I thought myself better than my Dogs. Like I thought myself better than anyone.

Goodwin rose. "She did this because she has been well taught. We approved her doing so, because we were already hard-pressed, and she had unique connections, my lord," she said. She sounded as calm as if she spoke to him each day over breakfast. "She went over everything with Tunstall and me. And she has magic. My Lord Provost will tell you, trainee Guardswoman Cooper hears the voices of the dead. When she showed us her skill, we understood her information was valuable. It was the proof that we found tricky to get."

"Mages among Dogs have unusual ways to seek, my lord," Tunstall said, getting to his feet. "We have all seen it. May I add, respectfully, that has made this a very good week for us."

The Lord High Magistrate blinked like a lizard. "Very well. Sit, both of you. I will still hear Cooper speak for herself."

Sir Tullus sighed. "Look at the floor, Cooper." To the Lord High Magistrate he said, "She is shy in public speaking, my lord. She will do better if she does not have to look—"

"No."

Lord Gershom's voice brought my head up. I stared at him. He leaned forward in his chair, hands clasped between his knees. We might have been in his sitting room, just us two and Pounce. "Tell me, Beka. Tell me how this all came about. Just look at me, and tell it."

I stumbled a few times. When my lips stuck to my teeth, I accepted a flask of cool tea that Ersken passed to me. Eventually I told my lord all of it, from Rolond's death, to the map, to the lily pendant, to the capture of Yates's gang, to going to see Mistress Noll that last time. I was even able to glance at her toward the end. Mistress Noll stared directly ahead, more like a stone than a woman.

"Very well, Guardswoman Cooper," Sir Tullus said quietly when I had done. "You may be seated."

The rest went as it should. The Shadow Snake gang was sentenced to Execution Hill and smuggled from the court. Gemma was set free, though she was sent from the city for not reporting her mother and brother to the law. The officials left, but for my lord Gershom. He came down to us, smiling. "A very good week," he said, shaking hands with my Dogs and Ersken. "And a new Rogue. There will be changes in the Lower City." He looked at me. "Some people would like you to go to supper." He pointed to the onlookers' bars. I heard him tell my Dogs and Ersken, "You are invited. I believe Tunstall and Goodwin know the place."

I felt odd. My brothers and my sister Lorine stood in the onlookers' section, Nilo jumping up and down like a looby, Will grinning, and Lorine wiping at her eyes with a handkerchief. Diona was not there, but this was miracle enough.

"They miss you," my lord said in my ear. Pounce ran over to them, sliding through the bars to get picked up and petted. "Give them another chance? I would like to see you now and then, too."

I nodded. I didn't want to speak for fear of getting emotional. They were proud of me. I could see it on their faces—they were proud of me.

We walked out, my lord in the lead, with Goodwin and Tunstall, Ersken, Lorine, and me just behind, and Will, Nilo, and Pounce behind us. We passed through that crowd of Dogs and into the outer courtyard. It was packed with folk who'd heard and gathered despite the army in the streets. That's the Lower City for you. Folk can always find ways to break the rules.

As I walked by, they kept reaching out to brush my arm with their fingers. I heard them whispering, "She's a Terrier, that one. A Terrier."

The Provost's Guard

Founded: 127 H.E. by His Royal Majesty King Baird III of Tortall
First Lord Provost: Padraig of haMinch (127–143)

Use of the terms "Dog," "Puppy," "Growl," "seek," "kennel," and related terms in the Guard became popular about fifty years after the founding of the Guard.

Four Watches

Day Watch: nine in the morning until five in the afternoon
Evening Watch: five in the afternoon until one in the morning
Night Watch: one in the morning until nine in the morning
Fourth Watch: covers each of the other three watches on their Court Days and off days

In most districts, the best of the Guards are put on Day and Evening Watch, when there is the most activity on the streets. The slackers are given Night Watch, when the least amount of activity is going on. The only area that is different is the Lower City, where the Day Watch is less active as well. Evening Watch is busy there. So is Night Watch, but while no one will say so, the truth is that the criminals own the streets during Night Watch. The very worst Guards have duty then. They are the ones who just don't care about the work, the ones who are regarded as expendable. Everyone knows it.

DISTRICTS
Corus's Watch Districts, interestingly, often (but not always) correspond to the way the Rogues divide the city for their own organization:
Highfields District
Prettybone District
Unicorn District
Palace District
Flash District
Upmarket District
Patten District
Temple District
The Lower City: Conditions are very different in the Lower City overall. Since it is the poorest area, the bribes are the lowest and so is the prestige. The casualty rate is the highest because it is the most violent part of the city. Most of the Guards assigned there are Guards who are regarded as not being bright or promising enough to make a good impression elsewhere. Even so, the elite Guards of the Lower City are the most respected. They are also the toughest and the smartest.

Chain of Command

Lord Provost: governs the realm's districts
Vice Provost: assists Lord Provost (one per region in Tortall)
Captain (District Commander)

Per District:
Watch Commander
Watch Sergeant
Corporals (varies by district)
Senior Guards (varies by district)
Guards
Trainees

Training

Formal training in 246: One year in school. There is no screening or testing to enter the training program. Trainees are simply required to pass the classes.

All Guards are required to attend combat practice for their first four years of service.

Weapons and Law Enforcement

Primary weapon: Two-foot-long hardwood baton with lead core

Guards don't use swords: A sword is a killing weapon. The majority of reasons a Guard uses a baton don't demand an intent to kill. Wielded properly, the baton can stop most swords. Also, swords require years of training for proper use, they are expensive and require extensive maintenance, and they can break just when they're most needed.

The law and bribery: Law enforcement is a loose affair, something that is still being created. A law-keeping force under the control of the national government is highly unusual. Most law-enforcement groups are formed and run by neighborhood associations, guilds, or individual cities, or they are part of the military. The members of the Provost's Guard, like such groups, have a great deal of discretion in whom they arrest, whether they take bribes, and whether they do the thing they have been bribed to do. Bribery is the standard way to ensure that the underpaid people who protect merchants remember individuals and, at times, overlook their behavior. (Too much of a history of taking bribes and not following through on them does get a Guard killed. It is wise for a Guard to do what he's bribed to do most of the time.)

Guards memorize the laws and rules they are taught in training. They learn the rest of their skills on the streets and from each other. Some Guards are smarter than others. Some Guards are more motivated than others. And they all make up police work as they go.

CAST OF CHARACTERS

ROYALS AND NOBLES

Roger II	King of Tortall, House of Conté; first Queen, Alysy, deceased; second Queen, Jessamine (married one year), has just presented him with a son.
Jessamine	Roger II's second Queen (not named in this book), mother of his heir
Alysy	Roger II's first Queen, deceased
Sabine of Macayhill	lady knight
Joreth	knight, friend of Lady Sabine's
Tullus of King's Reach	knight, Magistrate of Lower City courts

DOGS (THE PROVOST'S GUARD)

Acton of Fenrigh	Watch Commander, Evening Watch, Jane Street, nobleman
Alacia	Puppy, assigned to Unicorn District
Birch	Dog, Vinehall's partner
Cape	Dog, Otterkin's partner
Clara Goodwin	"Clary," Corporal, Evening Watch at Jane Street kennel, seventeen-year veteran, Beka's

	female partner, lower middle class of Corus
Clarke	Puppy on Night Watch, Prettybone District
Ersken Westover	Puppy, Beka's good friend, fourth son of a middle-class family, Jane Street kennel
Evermore	Dog, Evening Watch, Jane Street kennel
Fulk	mage for the Jane Street kennel Evening Watch
Hilyard	Puppy in Beka and Ersken's year, Jane Street kennel
Jakorn	Dog, one of Lord Gershom's private Guards, taught Beka when she was small
Kebibi Ahuda	Sergeant on the Evening Watch at Jane Street kennel, combat training master of Dogs, thinks Beka will do well, very tough
Matthias Tunstall	"Mattes," Senior Dog, Beka's male partner, Jane Street kennel, fifteen-year veteran, eastern hillman
Nyler Jewel	Corporal, Yoav's partner, Evening Watch, Jane Street kennel
Otelia	Verene's training Dog,

	Jane Street kennel
Otterkin	Dog, has magical Gift, Evening Watch, Jane Street kennel, Cape's partner
Phelan	second-year Dog, Evening Watch, Jane Street kennel
Rebakah Cooper	"Beka," Puppy, Evening Watch, Jane Street kennel, training Dogs Goodwin and Tunstall, sixteen years old
Springbrook	Dog, Evening Watch, Jane Street kennel
Verene	Puppy, friend of Beka's, Jane Street kennel
Vinehall	Dog, Birch's partner, Jane Street kennel
Yoav	Dog, Jewel's partner, Evening Watch, Jane Street kennel

CROOKSHANK'S HOUSEHOLD AND ASSOCIATES

Ammon Lofts	"Crookshank," scale, or receiver of stolen goods, landlord, in business with crooks and honest people alike
Annis Lofts	Crookshank's daughter-in-law
Herun Lofts	Crookshank's grandson, Annis's son, and Tansy's husband

Rolond Lofts	Tansy's son, murdered
Tansy Lofts	Crookshank's granddaughter-in-law, Herun's wife, Rolond's mother, friend of Beka's from their Cesspool days
Inman Poundridge	hirer of guards for slave market and Crookshank
Jens	guard of fire opal diggers
Otto	footman at Crookshank's house
Uta Norwood	Crookshank's bookkeeper and paymaster
Vrinday Kayu	Carthaki mage working for Crookshank
Zada	maid in Crookshank's house

COURT OF THE ROGUE AND ASSOCIATES

Kayfer Deerborn	the Rogue, king of the thieves
Dawull	Rogue chief, Waterfront District
Ulsa	Rogue chief, Prettybone District
Aniki Forfrysning	Scanran rusher and swordswoman
Koramin Ingensra	Kora, rogue and mage
Rosto the Piper	Scanran rusher, thief, friend of Aniki and Kora
Bold Brian	Dawull's crew, Aniki's friend

Fiddlelad	rogue, Dawull's crew, Aniki's friend
Lady May	Dawull's crew, Aniki's friend
Reed Katie	Dawull's crew, Aniki's friend

PROVOST'S HOUSE

Gershom of Haryse	Lord Provost under Roger II, husband of Lady Teodorie, took in Beka and the Cooper family when Beka was eight years old, Beka's sponsor
Teodorie of Haryse	lady, Lord Gershom's wife
Jakorn	one of Lord Gershom's personal bodyguards, trained Beka
Myaral Fane	"Mya," cook at Provost's House, Beka's foster aunt
Ulfrec Fane	Mya's husband, head footman at Provost's House

THE COOPER FAMILY

Diona Cooper	Beka's fifteen-year-old sister, studying to be a lady's maid
Fern Cooper	Beka's grandmother, mother of her father, lives in the Lower City
Ilony Cooper	Beka's mother, deceased

Lilac	Beka's cousin
Lorine Cooper	Beka's thirteen-year-old sister, training to be a fine seamstress
Nilo Cooper	Beka's ten-year-old brother, training to be a stableman
Willes Cooper	Beka's twelve-year-old brother, good rider, training to be a messenger

THE COOPERS 200 YEARS LATER

Eleni Cooper	former priestess, single mother of George Cooper
George Cooper	Eleni's only son, six when she writes in her journal in 406 H.E.

OTHER PERSONS AND BEINGS OF INTEREST

Aveefa	dust spinner
Hasfush	dust spinner, found at the corner of Charry Orchard and Stormwing Streets
Shiaa	dust spinner
Deirdry Noll	prosperous baker, former neighbor and friend of Beka's
Gemma Noll	Deirdry's youngest daughter,

	unmarried, helps with baking
Yates Noll	Deirdry's youngest son
Gunnar Espeksra	rusher, or thug, runs with Yates Noll
Jungen Berryman	gem mage, fascinated by Dogs, friend of Goodwin and Tunstall
Jack Ashmiller	Orva's husband, father of three children
Orva Ashmiller	drunkard, hotblood wine addict, Jack's wife, mother of three children
Amaya Painter	mage, mother of a Shadow Snake victim
Calum Painter	five-year-old, kidnapped and killed by the Shadow Snake
Vonti Painter	Amaya's husband, lost at sea
Esseny	murdered dancer
Inknose	street denizen
Mother Cantwell	mumper (beggar) and thief
Paistoi	Carthaki slave merchant
Parkes	surname of a pair of brawling brothers
Wildberry	pretty woman with sisters

GLOSSARY

Barzun: country to the south of Tortall, on the north shore of the Great Inland Sea

Birdie: informant

Black God: the hooded and robed God of Death, recognized as such throughout the Eastern and Southern Lands

Black God's Option: suicide

bugnob: person of little brain

cages: holding cells for kennel prisoners

canoodling: sexual activity

Carthak: ancient and powerful slaveholding empire that includes all of the Southern Lands, a storehouse of learning, sophistication, and culture

Chaos, Realms of: one of the four Realms (Mortal, Divine, Peaceful, Chaos); the one where everything is unending change, destruction, and remaking

cityman: any respectable person who is not noble; knight's usage means peaceable, sheeplike person

Copper Isles: slaveholding nation south and west of Tortall, originally named the Kyprish Isles. The lowlands are hot, wet jungles; the highlands are cold and rocky. Traditionally their tie is to Carthak rather than Tortall.

Corus: capital city of Tortall, on the banks of the River Olorun

cracknob: madman

cuddy: slob
Dog: member of Provost's Guard
douse: murder
doxie: female prostitute
ducknob: person of low intelligence
dust spinner: a being of air and spirit, a continuous whirlwind that gathers breezes, conversations, emotions, and other bits from its surroundings
elsewise: otherwise
filcher: small-time criminal
foist: master pickpocket
Galla: country to the north and east of Tortall, famous for its mountains and forests, with an ancient royal line
gauds: bright, costly things
get in the way of: become; learn
Gift: human, academic magic, the use of which must be taught
gillyflower: carnation
gixie: girl
glims: eyes
gorget: mail plate cover for the neck, like a collar
Happy Bag: the collection of weekly bribes for Provost's office—jewels, coins, art, magical objects—anything of value that can be sold for cash
hedgewitch: worker of small magics, not powerful enough to be called a mage, with little formal education
hobble: tie up or arrest

hobbles: rawhide restraints used on prisoners

hotblood wine: wine spiked with an amphetamine-like substance

Human Era (H.E.): time period that began 246 years prior to the present book, marking the exile of the immortals from the Mortal Realms

hunkerbones: haunches

immortals: creatures that, unless killed, live forever, including Stormwings, giants, spidrens, winged horses

jack: tankard, often leather

jinglenob: empty-headed person

kennel: Provost's guardhouse; police station

Ladymoon: symbol of the Goddess

liar's fanfare: overstuffed codpiece

loaner: mocking term for nobles' sale of heirlooms they buy back when they get more money; also a scornful term for a noble

Lord Provost: nobleman in command of the Provost's Guard throughout the realm; most take a personal interest in the Guard in the capital, Corus, as well as in the running of the Guard throughout the realm.

Maren: one of the Eastern Lands, east of Tusaine and Tyra, rich and powerful land

midden hen: chicken that lives in dung; someone completely crazy

minnow: very small-time criminal, not worth the trouble to arrest

Mithros: the chief god of the Tortallan pantheon, God

of War and the Law; his symbol is the sun.

mot: woman, common-born

mumper: beggar

murrain: plague

nob, noll: head

noble: large coin in copper or silver

Olorun River: river that flows east to west through the heart of Tortall

Outwalls: Outwalls Prison, jail for serving long-term sentences

patten: hard wooden shoe, keeps feet out of the mud

Peaceful Realms: home of the spirits of the dead; where the souls of the living go to heal from the pain of life

Players' jollity: professional performance, play, or musical entertainment

Puppy: trainee, Provost's Guard

puttock: low-level female prostitute

raston: bread loaf stuffed with buttery bread crumbs and light filling

Rat: criminal; prey; captive (to Dogs)

river dodgers: hard men and women who work on and around the river, on boats, in shipping and trade (and smuggling)

rushers: thugs

sap: handheld lead-filled cylinder, six inches long, with a loop for the wrist; a knockout or bone-breaking weapon

sarden: blasted; damned; detestable

scale: fence, or receiver of stolen goods

Scanra: country to the north of Tortall, wild, rocky, and cold, with very little land that can be farmed. Scanrans are masters of the sea and are feared anywhere there is a coastline. They also frequently raid over land.

scummer: animal dung

scut: idiot

seekings: investigations; hunts for criminals or missing persons

Shakith: one of the Carthaki gods of the underworld, she is the blind seer and the goddess who weighs things for their true value; thus, she is the goddess of justice, bankers, jewelers, and traders in gemstones.

sommat: something

spintry: male prostitute

Stormwings: immortal creatures, banished before the Human Era. They had steel birds' wings and claws and half-human heads and chests. They lived on fear and battle-killed dead; *very* nasty personalities.

sutler: thief who takes goods from shops or vendors' stalls

ticklers: fingers

tosspot: drunkard

treats: bribes

trollop: woman who is morally lax, usually sexually

trull: very low-class kind of woman; the dregs

Tusaine: small country tucked between Tortall and Maren

twilsey: drink made of raspberry or cider vinegar and water, most refreshing

Tyra: merchant republic on the Great Inland Sea between Tortall and Maren. Tyra is mostly swamp, and its people rely on trade and banking for income.

Acknowledgments

With thanks to Mallory Loehr, my Random House editrix, who suggested first person and the journal format, and to Bruce Coville, my reading partner in crime, who worked extra hard with me on the dynamics of first-person writing and on Beka's very real voice: if the shape of this book is unique and works, it's due to both of you.

To Lisa Findlay and Sara Alan, who also gave me much-needed editorial advice on a very tough book.

To Christine M. Cowan at Undiscovered Treasures, source of my first fire opal in matrix (and many other glorious stones and crystals).

To the posters of SheroesCentral, who didn't know (as I didn't) that they were teaching me to write journal entries!

To the pigeons of Riverside Park, including Gloucester, Gimpy, Cloak, Hart Crane, Tex, Footloose, Bandit, Pinky— What? You thought I made them up?

To Jack Olsen, a gentleman and a crime writer, with a good word to spare for someone with an unpopular opinion.

TAMORA PIERCE captured the imagination of readers more than twenty years ago with *Alanna: The First Adventure.* As of September 2006, she has written twenty-four books, including three completed quartets—The Song of the Lioness, The Immortals, and Protector of the Small—and two Trickster books set in the fantasy realm of Tortall. She has also written the Circle of Magic and The Circle Opens quartets, as well as a stand-alone Circle title: *The Will of the Empress.* Her books have been translated into eleven different languages, and some are available on audio from Listening Library and Full Cast Audio. Tamora Pierce's fast-paced, suspenseful writing and strong, believable heroines have won her much praise: *Emperor Mage* was a 1996 ALA Best Book for Young Adults, *The Realms of the Gods* was listed as an "outstanding fantasy novel" by *VOYA* in 1996, *Squire* (Protector of the Small #3) was a 2002 ALA Best Book for Young Adults, and *Lady Knight* (Protector of the Small #4) debuted at number one on the *New York Times* bestseller list. *Trickster's Choice* spent a month on the *New York Times* bestseller list and was a 2003 ALA Best Book for Young Adults. The sequel, *Trickster's Queen,* was a *New York Times* bestseller, as was *The Will of the Empress.*

An avid reader herself, Ms. Pierce graduated from the University of Pennsylvania. She has worked at a variety of jobs and has written everything from novels to radio plays. Along with writer Meg Cabot (The Princess

Diaries series), she cofounded SheroesCentral, a discussion board about female heroes; remarkable women in fact, fiction, and history; books; current events; and teen issues. Though she no longer sponsors Sheroes-Central and Sheroes Fans as she did for five years, she is still a devoted member of the sites.

Tammy lives in Syracuse, New York, with her husband, Tim, a writer, Web page designer, and Web administrator. They are currently cowriting a female superhero, White Tiger, for Marvel Comics. They share their home with five cats, two birds, and various freeloading wildlife.

For more information, visit www.tamorapierce.com.

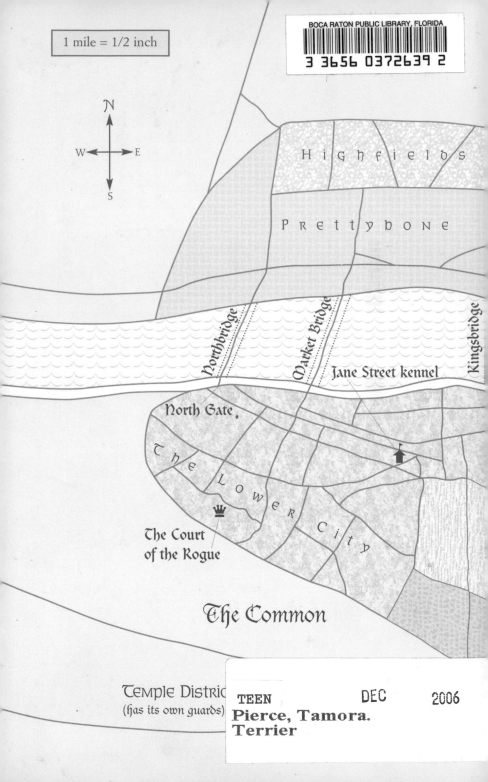

1 mile = 1/2 inch

N
W ←——→ E
S

H i g h f i e l d s

P r e t t y b o n e

Northbridge

Market Bridge

Kingsbridge

Jane Street kennel

North Gate

T h e L o w e r C i t y

The Court
of the Rogue

The Common

Temple District
(has its own guards)